NOT ALONE

The Beginning
The Fighter Series

By Kolleen Bookey

Cover designed by Kolleen Bookey

This book is a work of fiction. Names, characters, places, and incidents either are products of the author's imagination or are used fictitiously. Any resemblance to actual persons, living or dead, events, or locales is entirely coincidental.

Kolleen Bookey
Visit my website at www.kolleenbookeyblog.com

Printed in the United States of America

DEDICATION

This book is dedicated to my Patient and Loving husband John, my cheering section and beautiful daughters, Jolleen and Corri, and my muse Rowdy (RIP), whom you will come to know as Max.

*Not everyone is safe
from the trouble that stirs.
An unseen storm is coming
infecting thousands with insanity.
This turbulence is more powerful than the sea,
sitting silently in the wake of the first apocalypse.
This is where the devil lies in wait.*

The infection has begun.

Millions of people are dead.

There is no metered electricity or water.

Utility facilities are broken.

All food and other production have stopped.

Cities have turned lawless.

To keep your stayer status, you must fight.

Who will survive the apocalypse?

PROLOGUE

JUNE 11, 2014

Two nights before the apocalypse.

Exhaustion caught up with her, and at some point, she fell victim to a deep slumber, allowing the nightmares in. Demons chased her until a noise caused her to wake. Riley Collins slid her hand under the pillow, wrapping her fingers around the pistol. For a moment, she wondered if the sound had come from her dreams. Then through the thumping of heartbeat, she heard the clatter again. The fogginess in her brain began to fade, forming an embraced fear-filled clarity that no one else lived in the house but her.

Just last week, she slapped a well-deserved restraining order on her husband, Mark. The brutality of his attacks had landed him a nice little court order to stay five hundred feet away from her. The order was a definitive resolution for him, but not so much for her. He was a pompous asshole who did pretty much whatever he wanted, ignoring anything that told him otherwise.

The order did force him out of the home, giving her ample space to prepare for an escape. Her co-workers were watching his every move, one benefit of being a cop. She guessed a high maintenance underage young woman, wearing stilettos and a size too small skirt, sat on his lap right now. He was probably sucking expensive liquor off his competitor's secretary's fake boobs right now. Those women, in the past, had kept Mark distracted.

Cunning and just as dangerous, it would be like Mark to send someone else to do his dirty work.

Dirty to the core, she reminded herself.

The protective order meant nothing to her, but to Mark, the order meant war. He hid his dirty little secrets, and he sure as hell would not cave so easily to rules.

NOT ALONE

If he'd broken into their house, she had the right to shoot if she felt threatened. She could only hope. Soundless, she slid her finger to the trigger and listened. Her heart thumped so hard; she felt it beating in her ears.

A warm Northern California breeze stirred outside, causing a branch on the Elm tree to brush against the side of the house. Mark promised to trim the branches a month ago, but the tree remained untouched like most chores.

Promises made, promises broken.

The tapping tempo stopped, quieting the room to near silence. Then another burst of wind, this time stronger causing another thump but much louder. Riley raised her eyes to the night table, searching for her cell phone. The edges caught a glint from the streetlights outside, and blue shadows danced in the summer breeze making creepy shapes projecting and bouncing on the bedroom wall.

She shifted her gaze to the clock, which read after midnight. *Only the wind,* the inner voice inside her, spoke so clear, she thought someone other than herself lay next to her. That space next to her said otherwise. The house breathed again, rattling side panels and making floorboards groan.

Houses settle, boards move. The alarm, triggered by any movement, remained silent.

Her ears hummed with the quietness. *No one could be inside.* She grabbed the pistol in one hand and her cell phone in the other. She tapped the top contact and waited to hear the ring. The busy signal thumped in her ear. Shivering, she slid from the sheets to the floor and redialed. *Busy.* She moved slowly to the door, pressing her pistol forward.

With already shattered nerves, she anticipated the doorknob moving. She felt the slight indent where the trigger guard was millimeters from where her finger lay. There was no room for mistakes or hesitancy.

She waited for the alarm to break the silence.

She sensed something was wrong. She listened, waiting for the floorboard outside her bedroom door to moan underweight. The silence sent chills across her skin.

The soft click of the doorknob sounded. Riley knew she'd locked it. Now she held her breath as someone jiggled the handle. The hairs on her neck lifted. Her index finger no longer lay alongside the gun. Her finger was millimeters away from the trigger. Someone, uninvited, stood beyond the door, someone who knew about the weakness in the flooring.

Riley pushed aside a rise of terror. She had anticipated some scare tactic from her husband.

NOT ALONE

Mark was not the man she thought him to be. He was far worse than her worst nightmare.

A slight tap of metal touching the knob suggested the trespasser was trying to pick the lock, but she had a little surprise hidden on her side of the door. The second lock her co-worker Jackson installed the day Mark left the house.

One-handed and on silent mode, she pressed 911. Holding her breath, she took a step backward just as something or someone crashed into the door. Something big. The first hit didn't break the hinges but splintered wood, and particles fell to the floor. The nearest painting on the wall dropped, busting the frame.

The door exploded open. Wood and metal blasted apart. The knob broke free and rolled to the furthest end of the room. Riley was pushed aside, caught her footing, and darted sideways. She spun around to face her attacker, and as she did, her phone slipped from her hand but not before she heard the 911 operator say, "911, what is your emergency?"

The intruder stepped through, stopping several feet from her. All features blended with the night shadows except for two thin red rings that flickered like fire where his eyes would be.

She stepped backward. The department's training had prepared her, but it hadn't stopped her husband from nearly killing her. With a life insurance policy and the freedom to cheat, he would be a happy man. But tonight wouldn't pay off. Tonight, she was as controlled as one could be as she pressed the trigger. The aroma of gunpowder rose in the air. It was a solid shot. He should have fallen right then, but he didn't. The slip of a chuckle, a step, him coming toward her ripped her from the terrifying dream.

Wet covers tangled around her as she fought to sit upright in the bed, gasping for air. Sweat soaked her tank top, making the material stick to her skin sticky as warm honey. Dry in the throat, she smacked her lips together, trying to slow the beat of her heart by taking control of her breathing. She woke and reached for her pistol but found no gun. The bedroom door she closed and locked every night upon going to bed was open. A clatter of vibration pulled her attention to the floor. Her cell phone lay face-up on the hardwood flooring, the screen on and calling. She shivered.

"Not a dream."

As she sprang from the bed, she scooped up the phone. Eric's name glowed at the top. "Eric. Are you there? Eric," she pressed the phone close to her ear.

"Riley?" his voice touched her but did not calm her.

"Someone was here," she stared at the door, imagining someone on the other side. "Mark must have sent him. He knows too much about the house, me, you. He called you. Moved my gun."

"Get out of there, Riley. Go to Jackson's. Get in the truck and go now."

Holding the phone while she searched for her gun, she felt a cold wash of fear when she saw the Smith and Wesson sitting on the chair, the barrel pointing at the bed. The trespasser had watched her sleep, somebody who had access to the house. Riley shivered. He'd opened the one-sided lock somehow without making a sound.

Impossible!

"I'm going to Jackson's. I'll call you when I get there," she whispered even softer, staring at the door.

"Riley, keep the phone on. Just do what you need to and get out. Keep the phone on."

"I'm okay. I'll get a room for the night. Leaving now." Then she hung up. She needed to give Jackson her service weapon and ID, and he wouldn't be on shift until tomorrow night.

Riley grabbed her gun, checked the chamber, and then dropped the magazine. One bullet remained in the chamber, the magazine empty. The intruder had unloaded her gun. In a hurry, she reached for the prepacked bag she kept under the bed. She slipped on running shoes then grabbed her keys. Locked and loaded with ammo, she ran from the house, not bothering to reset the alarm or closing the door.

1

The next day.
June 12, 2014

Sirens blasted in the air, calamity resembling African termites sending out vibrations in warning to prepare for an attack. Riley's first thought was to go back in and stay with Jackson, but doing so meant delaying what she had procrastinated for too long. It was after midnight as she passed through the gate toward the walkway leading down a row of office buildings, an explosion, heard but not seen, shook the ground under her feet. She stopped mid-stride. The lights overhead flickered and then shut off, leaving her in a position of sightlessness.

"What the...?" she strained to listen.

As far as she could see, no artificial light glowed. The full moon looked fuller than usual and showered a lucent amber glow, lighting a path for her to follow by. The blackened city and the chaos surrounding her sent a clear warning to keep under the moonlight. She trembled as long shadows threatened to reach her.

The wires overhead that typically trapped electricity and phone conversations and usually buzzing like a stampede of honeybees went eerily silent.

An increase in urgency to get on the road raced through her. An act of terrorism would hold her here. A fire, a gas leak, whatever shut down the power to this part of the city caused her to pick up her pace.

She needed to go, now.

The enlarged colored moon created a filtered guiding light. However, dark cumulus clouds were moving fast, threatening to cloak the moon's glow with the coming of a storm. From experience, she knew animals and people reacted to a full moon, and tonight, she chose not to stick around to watch the freak show. She'd overheard a talk show host talking about the coming of this moon.

Let the bodies hit the floor!

The rare full, amber Honey Moon caught the interest of photographers, lookie-loos, and lunatics from all over. Sirens began to hum.

The sound of more sirens signaled in the distance, and the air went static, prickling her senses. The smell of smoke united with the warm air where dark gray thick clouds stretched across both sides of the moon, threatened rain. Why should any part of her plan go smooth, weather and blackouts included?

"Transformer," whispered Riley, pulling out her cell, dialing the office number. "Had to be a transformer."

The message saying, "your call cannot be completed at this time," signaled a warning. Eric's voice screamed in her head, *hurry! Stop messing around before he kills you. Get in your truck and get out!*

Still cradling the phone and gun, she heard muffled voices. Just beyond her truck, a man, woman, and child walked toward a black BMW. Riley slipped to the next breezeway of another office building closing the distance between them. Even at this distance, she recognized Tim Hunt. He had made media headlines all year as he campaigned to run for attorney general.

Where is your security? She thought.

The lack of safety seemed odd this late at night. While Tim fumbled for his keys, his wife pulled in their daughter close to her. Her voice took on an urgent tone.

"Hurry, Tim."

Something was wrong. Very wrong. Riley thought as she watched the family. More sirens blasted through the night, Tim turned startled.

Riley stepped out from under the covering as a group of men slipped from the darkness. The pack walked with intent. She knew bad things were about to happen. A wealthy politician in a desolate parking lot without security was far too risky.

Without forethought, she pulled her nine-millimeter in closer and then noted the forty strapped to her leg underneath her jeans. Protection, not paranoia. After all, her husband had crossed all boundaries of marriage. She slipped between two office buildings.

The atmosphere held a sinister mood as dark as the clouds hung on all sides of the amber moon. Liquid light splashed down, revealing the intentions of the rebel wolves surrounding their prey. Tim Hunt and his family were in grave danger. His daughter, no more than seven years old, pulled on her baby blue sweater, drawing the material close to her lips.

A blanket of sweat covered Riley's skin, not from the humid atmosphere but jarring nerves shaking her from the inside out. The absence of the humming electricity shooting through the power lines hummed a strange silence even under the whining of sirens. She stepped into the parking lot at night, over a thousand times through the years, and constantly vigilant about safety. Tonight was different.

"Shit," she tried the office number getting the same message. 911 was the same. If she turned back now, they might see her. If she went forward, she might die. Tim and his family would die.

Just seconds ago and after midnight, she handed in her badge to Jackson, and he signed her transfer papers with a heavy heart filled with concern. Loaded down with two weapons minus the uniform, Riley prepared to run to Arizona.

Get on the road now. Get out of the city fast.

"There's only one of you and more than ten of them," she whispered, feeling the rush of adrenaline pumping through her body. She tried the phone again. Same! She was far enough from the office that if she turned back, they'd see her.

In the distance, to the right of the full moon, a single distant strand of lightning popped. The weather forecast for the day claimed clear skies. Mother Nature or some other unexpected force threatened to unleash its fury. One hell of a storm brewed above, threatening the city below. Something more than rain gathered overhead. A cataclysmic, catastrophic change promised to rear an ugly head.

"What do you want? I have money," Tim shouted. Twenty-dollar bills fell from his wallet onto the ground. "I have a car." He shoved the keys at one man. You don't understand! Something terrible is happening all over the city."

Something terrible is happening all over the city!

More of the pack stepped out of the alley. Tim, his family, and Riley had nowhere to go. If only Tim had been packing a gun. At a distance, she caught flashes of emergency lights bouncing off buildings.

A short strand of silence fell that lasted an eternity. She heard one pack member say, pointing to Tim, "I'll take the keys, the woman, and the kid. I don't need you."

Riley pressed into the wall melting into the shadows. A soft glow from the moon reflected on Tim's face, doing nothing for the tailored business suit that must have cost thousands of dollars. Tim's wife stood behind him, using his body as a shield to hide behind. They clung near the black Mercedes, hoping for a second to escape. There would be none.

The dim cargo bulb shone a cast of light so dim it reflected the mood making trunk suitcases sitting on the cement appear as an afterthought. The pack did not want the family's belongings or their money. They wanted so much more.

Riley saw the little girl turn in her direction. Riley saw her lips move, but her voice she heard only in her mind. "Help us, Riley?" she whispered.

Riley blinked, trying to clear her mind. Through the shadows, she saw the girl's ashen face. Riley felt her fear. Long locks of twisted hair framed her doll-like face. Interlocked arms around her mother's thighs tightened. Her mother pulled her inward. To die to save her child was instinctive.

"Please, help us." Her words entered Riley's head so crisp it rose the hairs on her neck.

Impossible! But everything about this night seemed just the opposite.

A tall silhouette stepped from the shadows. The man's energy alone forced Riley's attention from the girl to him. Tall and broad, he appeared from out of nowhere. His pack parted as he approached, leaning against the front of the car as a king would his throne. Shadows cloaked his features, and his face was hidden by the hooded jacket, creating obscurities under the amber light. The man, a reaper minus the horse, held the black air surrounding him with Satan's confidence. Beneath the shadow cast on his face, Riley recognized the rim of fire around his eyes from her dream.

I've seen you already tonight, she thought, wondering if maybe she was still dreaming.

The enemy moved toward the family, his gun aimed at Tim's heart. Slowly, Riley reached down and withdrew her forty. She was going to need both weapons. More of the pack gathered as the moon disappeared altogether, and it started to rain.

Dread washed over Riley.

Too many.

With her index fingers still resting on the sides of her guns, she anticipated the situation to get ugly. The family, trying to buy time, faced grave danger.

Something terrible is happening all over the city!

Riley sensed Tim was right. Something more than a down transformer caused a complete blackout. Another explosion, this time much closer, shook the ground under her feet. The screams of unseen faces trickled to where they stood.

"Sweet Jesus, we're being attacked!" she whispered, and he turned. The leader stared at the space in which she took. He'd seen her.

Riley stepped out of the shadows into the darkening light.

"Leave them alone," she yelled.

The pack divided. An expected ring of gunfire scattered all the men but one. A spray of blood exploded outward into the sheets of light. The red liquid sparkled between the falling strands of rain, creating a Christmas light effect. Riley fired. In fear of the outcome, she thought of her brother Eric, who would be expecting her in twelve hours. Angry, she might be late; she sent another bullet into the animal advancing toward her. A bullet sliced the calamity of chaos taking place elsewhere.

NOT ALONE

The bullet connected with her body, and she realized she might never see Eric again. Her flesh burned as she fell backward but not before hitting her third target with a nine-millimeter slug to the forehead. Several of the pack lifted their weapons, but the alpha male barked out orders, commanding his dogs to stand down. The family depended on her for help.

"Get out of here!" Bleeding, she climbed to her feet, her voice strained.

The leader advanced after another bullet blasted her right side.

"Stop!" he shouted, holding his hands out, eyes flickering in anger.

The impact of the hit shoved Riley backward. She buckled over, but not before catching another glimpse of those blue fire-rimmed eyes. She felt the rage inside of her grow. The gang rallied, pacing from side to side in a fevered thirsty state.

Like the wolves that they were, they wanted blood.

Though wounded, Riley had kept hold of her two guns, which she aimed at the pack. Tim's wife, crying, pulled their daughter in close, wrapping her arms around the girl's body, pressing her face into her hair.

Wet strands of hair fell in front of Riley's eyes, making it hard to see. On the ground under her feet, dammed by an overflow of water, her blood pooled. She waited for them to end this attack, but they weren't done yet.

Tim reached Riley and grasped her by the wrist, jerking her to her feet. The pack was going to kill them all, but not without a worthy fight.

"Run!" Riley cried.

Tim hesitated and then leaped toward his wife far too late to save either of them. A pop sounded in the air. Puffs of red liquid exploded from his wife's chest, painting her fancy white coat red. Through the dim light, the woman's face contorted in pain. She held to her daughter until she fell backward. The little girl, covered in her mother's lifeblood, let out a bloodcurdling scream.

Riley squeezed the trigger dropping the woman's executioner in one shot. The bullet cut through bone and flesh, exploding the evil buried inside his heart. The dying was barely down on the ground before another pack member grabbed the girl and started to run.

Riley put her sight on the kidnapper's knee and tapped the trigger, catapulting him and the girl to the ground. The impact of the fall set the girl free. Dropping the empty magazine, Riley reloaded as swift as the day she gained respect from her academy instructors. Locked and loaded, she captured a surge of strength and shoved away from the realization, death was upon her.

Another shot blasted her thigh, causing her to buckle backward. She saw Tim Hunt race after his daughter. The tips of guns shot flame as bullets shredded through the air, catapulting Tim into the air like a ragdoll. The expensive suit ripped as he landed on his side. The impact broke his watch free as dead weight made an impact with the cement. The gold Rolex skipped across the pavement stopping inches from the ringleader's feet. The girl ran toward the streets through the walkways between buildings, alone.

Rain pelted Riley's face as an army of footsteps pushed her way, and for a heartbeat, she wondered where Jackson was. A burst of power poured from her as she rolled over and fired, but the next bullet broke her wrist, causing her to drop the nine.

Numbness washed over her, a sense of failing consciousness. As blood seeped from her wounds, her forty slipped from her other hand. The metal clanged on the cement as she fought and lost.

Promise me you'll leave tonight, her brother said in her mind.

I promise.

Through a heavy downpour, a child's voice broke through the storm, "Riley, get up!"

A crack of thunder roared overhead. The faint outline of the hooded man loomed over her as his boot connected with her ribs. She never felt the breaking of her bones because the world went black. The rain stopped, and the darkness took her.

TWO YEARS LATER
POST-SHIFT
CURRENT DAY–FALL 2016

2

The girl, no more than 12 years old, wrapped her long fingers around the small human bundle, hugging life close to her body for warmth. Sounds of the unknown made her shudder and then stillness. The dirty blanket beneath her hand moved, becoming smooth rhythms of breath. Utah closed her eyes, listening to the sounds of the storm outside. Thunder rolled from the heavens above and finished with a slap of lightning, shaking the walls of the old school so hard; she thought the roof might crumble. Predicting the next round, she estimated the distance by sound and then counting.

Tonight the storm looked for revenge, but she and her baby sister remained safe from its fury. Her thin body shivered, though cold. She forced herself to control it. Not wanting to wake her sister, Utah clamped her fingers around the edge of the blanket and pulled it close to them, her last try to entrap all their warmness into a tiny space.

"Utah, where is your sister?" asked her mother. The words floated through the crevices into the empty gymnasium and then moved near her echoing off the walls. "Utah, go find your sister."

"I have her mama. She's with me," she whispered.

No answer came, only the sound of the rain pouring down on the weathered roof. Blackness should terrify a child, but Utah braved its wicked deception with courage. She had to. The last of their candles flickered out.

The pitch-black room lent no comfort to the girl and her 7-year-old sister. The calamity of light and dark grew into a cruel punishment. Creatures created themselves and played in Utah's mind. The abyss of the gym added to ugly details she could not see but could imagine. She guessed the monsters to be as giant as the ceiling, others to be small and wickedly fast. They crept, crawled, and slithered through the room toward them, intending deception while smart like a fox. Utah caught a wisp of air as they slipped past her. She squeezed her eyes shut, forcing the images from her mind.

"There's nothing there, Utah. See!" Her mother opened the closet door exposing a hole, which held the monsters hostage waiting for the eldest human to disappear. Standing with one hand on her hip, she gave her daughter a reassuring smile. Utah opened her eyes wider, trying to see into the obscurity of the building's walls.

"I can see them. Why can't you?" Utah cried as her mom hugged her and stroked her long hair with gentle fingers.

Living in extreme fright, long before witnessing death, Utah feared the creepy beasts. They revealed themselves at nightfall and only after her mother said goodnight. Neither she nor her sister Megan would survive to see adulthood unless the monster living with them, their stepfather, Steven, left this world. The girls' brutal abuse suffered from their stepfather, on days their mother worked long hours at the hospital, weakened them. He hurt them, belittled them, and grabbed them, striking them if they made too much noise. Steven had even touched Utah in ways that she knew felt wrong, but she kept that secret. Utah's adolescent churned like a raging river, and as many times as she played it out in her mind, the result remained the same.

The day Steven killed their mother, he'd ripped a leg off a kitchen chair and slammed it over their mother's head. His reason for the act, mama, had been late coming home from the store. Utah and Megan had been with her. Mama's delay that day could not have been more valid. An unprecedented craziness started while waiting in the checkout line to pay for their groceries.

"Sixty-nine dollars," muttered the clerk to a customer.

Static air hummed through the venting system of the store.

"That's highway robbery!" yelled the man. "What did I buy that would cost that ridiculous amount of money?"

Utah remembered the man. She remembered the hum.

He'd reached into his pocket to pay the bill, but in anger, he withdrew a wad of money and threw it at the clerk. It was more cash than her mama would ever see.

"I have three bags here!" he shouted.

The checker stood there, "you put them in your basket, mister. I didn't, and I don't make the prices!"

"You may not make the prices, buddy! Though, by the look on your face, you don't give a damn."

The angered man grabbed the wad of money and shoved it back into his pocket. His brown hair turned shiny black, and beads of sweat had gathered on his brow. Mama acted as if she knew something horrible was about to happen. Utah sensed it too. Something seemed different today.

Suddenly, mama pulled them away from the line and toward an end cap and hid them behind some Snickers Bars. Far away enough to avoid the knife but close enough, Utah could still see. Utah watched the man withdraw a knife from somewhere under his sweatshirt.

Then the shouting started, and packaged jerky, candy, and gum crashed to the floor. Multiple voices screamed out for what felt like an eternity.

Others joined as if the frenzy excited them. Men and women lunged past them at the knife-wielding man. Through many items hanging in front of Utah, she saw people take the knife-man to the ground. Another person joined in, and then another. Grunts of agony filled the air, which had turned eerily electric. Mama grabbed their hands, bypassing the cries of bleeding people. She pulled so hard Utah thought they might fall. Empty-handed, they ran.

For Utah, the entire chain of events seemed more like a movie than real life. As soon as they got home, those minutes passed too quickly. Utah wished she could've predicted what might happen next. Maybe, just maybe then, she could've saved her mother.

"Where the fuck are the groceries, Amy?" screamed Steven. He flailed his hands around like a wild man. "Jesus, can't you do anything? I'm hungry!"

He grabbed mama and pushed her against the wall. She landed with a thud breaking the drywall behind her.

As Utah always did when mama and Steve fought, Utah grabbed Megan and hid her in the hall closet.

"Don't open this door until I come to get you. Understand?" Megan shook her head. Her sister's body trembled. Tiny fingers clung to one of mama's coats.

Her memories went dark. Megan stirred under her hold. The little girl mumbled something in her sleep, so Utah pulled her closer to feel the comfort of her sister's heartbeat. Megan's life depended on her, keeping the monsters at bay.

Somewhere deep in her troubled mind, Utah fell asleep. Both sisters, swallowed up by the blanket of darkness, coldness, and hunger, held on tight to make it through another night.

3

RILEY & MAX
AFTER THE APOCALYPSE-CURRENT DAY... 2016

Riley kept to the shoulder of the road, one hand holding the strap of her backpack, the other, her pistol. Walking off the hill, she headed toward the abandoned town on the 101. She didn't expect to see that anything had changed since her last venture out for supplies, but one never knew. The stillness of the day did not trouble her. It was, after all, a post-apocalyptic world now.

Walking behind her was a stubborn and often feisty gray tabby cat that acted more human than a feline. She affectionately named him Mad Max after the movie. Almost a year old, Max doted on Riley as if she were his mother. He never strayed too far. Now, he pussyfooted through the wet grass, keeping to a more straightforward path but far enough that he could still see her.

The smell of last night's coastal rain lingered in the air, thick musky with dampness that never seemed to dry. Morning left her feeling battered after evil chased her in merciless dreams deep into the night. Finally, with the car that got her here broken, Riley packed her belongings, leaving the house she'd squatted in for almost two years on foot. It was time to go.

It had taken time for her to remember what happened the night she tried to leave the city. Five bullet wounds and a few surgeries later, the memories of that full moon night trickled back like one of the many nightmares that haunted her. A stranger transferred her to the third hospital. Only then, she remembered the night of the apocalypse, now called the Shift. She had no recollection of the stranger who saved her.

"Where is that nice man who came to see you?" The inquisitive nurse with thick hair and moved like a bull in a china shop had asked weeks before she escaped the hospital.

NOT ALONE

At first, Riley didn't remember what unfolded the night of the Shift. Hell, she didn't even remember stepping out into the night toward the parking lot or the pack of bad guys that executed a family. All those weeks in and out of consciousness were a blur. Until one night, she had a dream. However, it wasn't a dream. Instead, the vision was a concise rendition of what happened that night she tried to leave her husband, Mark, all those months ago.

Reflecting back to the day she left the hospital in California, after having stayed even though she'd made a full recovery to help the doctors and nurses with the patients. At the same time, Riley utilized the physical therapy equipment to strengthen her body.

The staff had kept the hospital secured for so long, but it fell under a hostile attack one day. Riley, along with dozens of others, left the shelter of the hospital only to enter a world without electricity and water. The staff and those well enough to run, ran for their lives.

The infected infiltrated the hospital with an intense hunger forcing the ones unable to leave to die. Then, like hyenas, the infected attacked and killed the weak and wounded prey. After witnessing the hospital's takeover, Riley feared not much of the population survived. However, if anyone could survive such chaos, her twin brother Eric could.

That day, Riley stole a paint-peeling Dodge Neon sitting in a parking lot with no choice but to run. With keys hanging from the ignition, the car contained a half tank of gas, a car seat that she tossed, and a six-pack of Diet Coke. Rolling down the windows and cranking up the heat, she gulped in the fresh coastal air and heater's warmth. Then, with only the clothes on her back, she left the fallen city.

Thief and stranger to the unfamiliar town she'd landed in months ago, she silently thanked the stranger who'd saved her the night she'd been shot and left for dead. The coastal Oregon town she landed in was abandoned. Framed in sidewalks marked with brown splatters of dried blood covered in debris, acted as a path leading to the empty streets. Cars and trucks were piled in heaps, some burned into twisted metal, others bashed beyond recognition.

Riley stumbled on the first bodies outside the hospital in the second-hand store's women's section, where she found warmer clothing. She encountered two adults and one child. Their bodies stuck to the worn carpet imprinted for eternity.

Once a fish and game officer, she faced death, animals, not people. The distinct overpowering smell of decay permeated the air. Smearing Vic's Vapor under her nose, she covered the bodies the best she could and then shopped fast for clothes. Scoring big, she found a case of water in the backroom, a bag of unopened chips and, a canned deodorizer for the car.

NOT ALONE

Bundled in someone else's thermals, a faded American Fighter Hoodie, and brandishing a stolen gun or two, she followed the 101 along the coastline. On the western coast, the Shift created towns void of people. The passing of time, weather, and foliage only amplified the destruction.

Heading toward the place, she agreed to meet her brother months prior. When the Neon died, Riley replaced it with an old Oldsmobile she found in an abandoned hotel parking lot. The tuna boat, as she later referred to it, started without a stutter. Her gain was unlucky for the rotting man who was petrified in place and stuck to the front bumper in the early stages of decay. She said a silent prayer and then threw up.

Treasures had been plentiful that day, finding cigarettes, a sealed bottle of wine, and some cash. All but one cigarette she tossed, drank the wine, stashed the money, and started toward Bandon to Eric's cabin, which she found abandoned and mostly destroyed. Maybe he left, or he'd never made it. Both were disappointing. Tired and still healing, Riley was forced to find a place to stay until she could get stronger.

Now with memories scrambled, the only place left to go was Arizona. If Eric never made it to the cabin, he'd be in a town called Prescott, Arizona, where he'd made his home after she married Mark.

The coming of fall was upon her and Max, and it seemed like a good time to hunt for a truck that could tackle the roads ahead. Taking on positive thoughts, she sang "Something Bad," remembering all the words. The weight of the Shift grew heavy, and keeping sane became difficult. Something terrible was happening.

Ahead, a tangled SUV's red mass reflected a scene in a horror flick, staged and surreal. The decayed body hung halfway outside the driver's door window, still held in place by the seat belt. An arm, missing a hand, bleached from the sun, and stripped by rain, hung from the side window.

Death, death, and more death, she sighed, wanting so much to see a live person.

About to turn away, a flicker of metal under sunlight caught her attention. Jogging to the opposite side of the road, she stopped and brushed dead leaves away from the fallen sign with her foot.

She followed the lane which led to what had once been a cranberry farmer's home now free for the taking? Overlooking the yard, two windows resembling eyes turned inward at an eye-like angle.

"Great, clean out of Amityville Horror!" Unmoving, she stared at the house, knowing she would be going in. "Seriously, what were these people thinking?"

An empty swing battered against a carved tree hung from one chain, screeching to the rhythm of the wind. People once lived here. Kids had played in this yard, and now, if she were to guess, death took up residency. To the left, a two-car garage, both doors open, and both stalls empty.

"No car?" *Someone had left in a hurry and never came back.*

Considering the buildings, Riley studied the scattered items in the yard. *Disconnect all emotion and take what you need. Go to the house.*

The wooden steps groaned under her weight while a dark unknowing of what was behind the slightly ajar door igniting her fears. The hinges creaked as the obscurity combined with a natural light called her forward. Inside, her eyes adjusted to the contrast of dark and light obscured by silence. Then a humming haunting tune began. Emptiness swallowed her. Tugging at her bandana, she covered her mouth and nose to keep out mold particles.

The abyss cloaked by heavy draperies hindered her vision. She pulled the curtains back, causing dust to fly. Beams of natural light flooded through as visible specks of dust rose, dancing midair by an unknown breeze upsetting the undisturbed. Old school ranch décor exposed the tenants' tastes, and a pungent bad smell of black mold similar to a wet dog rose. With the slightest movement, particles took flight. The spores were the only life left in the house because death lived here.

As the dust settled, the fresh footsteps leading toward the kitchen became visible. Her heart thumped, listening for movement, a breath, or a hiccup in the day's silence, but all stayed quiet. She followed the trail. The small footprints revealed one set smaller than the other pair. Opened cupboards showed bare-to-the-bone shelves, and the dust-covered countertops held evidence of children at play.

"Messy little thieves."

The sudden movement of a bag of dog food next to the back door caught her interest. A furry head poked a hole in the side without warning. Dog food fell through the opening, sending several mutant-sized mice tumbling to the floor. A protest of frenzied squealing rose. Riley, somewhat humored, chuckled as the creatures scurried in all directions, trying to escape the falling chunks. Dust crept through her bandana, and she fought off the urge to sneeze.

"Keys?" she whispered as she moved down the hallway. She'd caught a glimpse of other buildings on the property.

Several coats, a few aged baseball caps, and an umbrella hung on a coat rack on the hall wall. Riley grabbed the first jacket, and more dust rose. Fishing through pockets, she found a wad of twenty-dollar bills, a pack of gum, and old tissue.

"Please, let there be keys?" she pulled both jackets off the hooks. Hearing a jingle, she reached in and said, "Bingo."

NOT ALONE

In a moment of delight, the wind pressed through the house, catching the door resulting in a long-drawn-out creak loud enough to wake the dead. Goosebumps layered her skin, raising the fine hairs on her arms and neck. Somewhere in the depth of the abandoned home, where spirits rested, Riley felt the dead warning her to go.

Another push of the wind and the front door clicked closed. *Hurry up.* Picking through the wallet, Riley took out more cash, leaving the credit cards. Death lingered all around her.

Her imagination began to wander.

Unseen voices trickled through the air.

Riley shut them out and moved to the bathroom, hoping to find supplies for a first aid kit. As she did, an aroma grew with intensity. Unable to switch off apprehension, when she caught sight of her reflection in the mirror, her heart fluttered.

A thin layer of dirt covered every space in the bathroom.

Another creak sounded, but this time longer and louder. She did a clean swipe of the medicine cabinet, letting all prescriptions drop into the bag. Then she hurried out, not opening the closed torn shower curtain blanketing the bathtub.

Nearly stumbling over a Browning 12-gauge shotgun lying at the base of the stairs, she added it to her findings despite its rusted barrel. Stepping out into the open air away from the clutter of death, a crow squawked above, adding to the already creepy cloud cloaking the house. Called in by an unknown entity, hundreds of crows swooped to the electric lines gathering on the edge of the roof. Riley ignored the terrible squawking as she headed for the outer buildings.

4

THE SHIFT

Jack Colton never claimed to be a social butterfly, especially with the women. He wasn't looking for a woman, and he little time to be around many people.

Jack kept his family and friends close. The amount of effort he spent reconstructing their town and others was time well paid out. After serving ten years in the military, which he served eight of those years in a special ops unit, he returned home to the chaos of the Manic Shift. A few days after the first onslaught of violence, Jack, and his brother, Ryan, formed a paramilitary group focused on stopping the violence and continuing destruction. Their goal was to salvage law and order for themselves as a community and then assist others.

Thirty-six years old, Jack's social network and career, other than his family and the ranch, comprised a handpicked team of men and women with tactical skills. As time passed, survivors heard of the Colton men and their achievements, making them people to be revered. Having regained control of smaller cities, highways, and ranches within a three-hundred-mile radius of Prescott, Prescott Valley made people think again.

News of Jack's recovery methods reached others, and his plight encouraged people to look for resolutions to restore order. The substructure of life needed rebuilding. The movement happened with the help of Jack's elite team, which survivors named the Fighters.

The remaining population believed the apocalypse was due to a rare (once every 125 years) Honey Moon that rose on Friday the 13th. Jack thought that to be horseshit. People named that phenomenon the Shift.

Years ago, the Colton's inherited the land from Ben Colton's (Jack's father) side of the family and house a sizeable healthy herd of black Angus cattle. A profitable business, the ranch had a wealth of remaining stock that fed much of the town.

A few months before the Shift, Jack made the sales of his stock private and more profitable, heading them toward millionaire status. Two months later, the Shift happened.

Now, post-Shift, Jack worked with other surviving ranches to get Arizona feedlots clean, so local people could get healthy meat to feed their families and cities. The Colton's would help provide beef to local meat markets for those in need. With the FDA gone, standards still needed to be met. Ranchers would have to be required to show that their beef was of excellent safe quality. Money made no comeback, and progress barely trickled forward. People were hungry, and they went to all extremes to gain food, even stealing and poaching it. Ranchers needed supplies just as much as the community, so bringing back the barter system was working for now.

Julianne Colton (Ben's wife, Jack's mother) passed away during the Shift's first weeks. All who remained were Jack and his younger brother Ryan, their sister Lynn, and Ben Colton, their father.

Nick Roberts, a respected surgeon in Phoenix, was Lynn's husband. Nick traveled back and forth to Phoenix and also saw patients at the ranch. Between Lynn and Nick was their beautiful and spirited 5-year-old daughter, Lily, whom Jack adored.

The family lived together in the main ranch house. Ryan often stayed in the bunkhouse and Ben in the barn's apartment for added security.

Home to ten working horses, five pigs, adopted ducks, a small herd of sheep and goats, and several cats named "Kitty." It also included two Rhodesian ridgeback dogs (Sadie and Tank), a handful of unruly and sometimes nasty chickens that produced enough eggs for six hardworking hungry family members. They had everything a family needed to survive, food, water, solar panels, and a little extra.

However, keeping trespassers off the property and safekeeping the herd required time and workers. Hence, Jack's younger brother Ryan slept in the bunkhouse. A big part of their ongoing work was protecting the family from home invaders. Once a week, Jack and Ryan took turns riding the property's perimeter, all 200 acres. Because of poachers, cattle were no longer safe to graze on open range and heard, and fencing needed checking daily.

Lynn's weekly tease came in the form of, "while you two are out patrolling, a handful of women stopped in asking if you're still single?"

Both the Colton men were desirable catches, and in a world minus thousands of people, bachelors were rare.

Physically, Jack had inherited his father's looks, height, and strength in being soft-spoken (dark silent type). He'd inherited thick, salted curly hair and green/blue eyes that could melt snow in the North Pole. While Lynn and Ryan almost looked like twins, they'd inherited their mother's blonde hair and witty, charming, and playful character.

The two brothers differed in physical traits and characteristics but not in their skills. Both Colton men had heart and an unsurmountable will to survive. They lived for action because sitting still for too long meant big trouble was brewing.

Prescott and the Prescott Valley had been quiet for over a month. Too quiet, making Jack restless, his gut telling him unrest teetered on the horizon. Jack headed out to fetch Sam. The quarter-thoroughbred bay gelding, big and stout enough to carry the like of him, waited into one of the larger paddocks.

Bundled in a military-style jacket made for extreme temperatures, Jack Colton carried a stainless steel cup of hot coffee in his right hand and a Beretta 1873 Renegade 20" Carbine in 45 Colt rifle in his left. He favored the Beretta rifle, one of his many in a private arsenal collection he kept in a safe room for its balance and efficiency. Jack laid the gun on his shoulder, about to cross through the double doors of the barn before he heard the drumming of a horse's stride. Ryan came in fast from an eight-hour property check for squatters and trespassers. By the sound, he pushed his horse Moe hard, approaching the barn hot.

"Trouble?" Jack grabbed hold of Moe's reins as the horse skidded to a stop.

Ryan jumped off the bay, gelding with the same amount of energy he'd left with hours ago, and turned his blue eyes on his brother. Even in the predawn grayness, Jack could see a dark bruise forming on the skin around Ryan's left eye. A long stream of white frost flowed with Ryan's breathe into the morning air.

"I caught a few markers on the south end near Granite Creek, trying to set up camp." Ryan paused slightly out of breath, pulling his rifle out of the holder. "They put up a little fuss."

Ryan loosened the cinch on the saddle to let Moe know his ride was complete. The horse fidgeted, nudging the two men to hurry because hay and a warm stall awaited him.

Because Ryan wore no blood and appeared unhurt, Jack took it as a sign his brother was alright. Inherited, the characteristic, handed down from generation to generation, not to complain. The Colton way demanded strength and determination even in the weakest moments.

"Check the south end while you're out in case they give it another try." Ryan pulled his pack from the saddle. "I watched them until they hit the boundary."

"How many?" Jack did not want this trouble on the ranch. He hesitated for a second and then looked back at his brother.

"Three. Maybe two more," guessed Ryan.

"They may head this way."

Ryan gave him a nod. "I'll tell pops. I'll catch a few hours of sleep and then head out to make sure you don't need any help."

"Let Lynn know where I'm going first. Just in case. Nick went into the city." Jack was a sonar for trouble, and he had a bad feeling. "Let them know you had a problem. Tell Lynn to stay alert."

"I'll let her know."

Jack and Ryan took extra precautions, rarely leaving Lynn and Lily alone for too long. Lily, Lynn's daughter, proved to be the driving force of Lynn's dedication to her daughter, and Jack knew her motherly instinct was strong. Lil was the future, and Lynn had vowed to see that Lily grew up healthy and intelligent.

Homeschooling Lily at three, Lynn molded her into a more advanced child than most children at age six. The responsibility lay on the entire family to make sure Lily grew up socially adjusted. Everyone would have a part in molding the new world post-Shift.

Jack's mother, Julianne, adored Lily.

"Just look at her, Jack, all those dark curls." Julianne would say. "Her smile lights up the cloudiest of days."

He coveted those memories of Julianne watching Lily. That day, her summer dress, painted with lilies, flowed with the Arizona breeze. Jack kept that image in his heart, saving his life more than once. He held his family close to his heart.

"Lily Bean," the family called her because she looked as small as a bean and beautiful as a spring Lily. Her blue eyes sparkled like liquid sunshine, and her pink lips pushed out into a pout when she failed to get her way. Light locks of dark auburn curls framed her heart-shaped face. Jack adored her. No one knew how many children had survived the Shift or were out there fighting to live, but that would never be Lily.

Filing his emotion to the side, Jack let out a soft whistle. The clatter of hoofbeats sounded as a tall bay gelding appeared. With head held high and ears forward, the horse approached the gate. Jack let the gelding pass through without a lead, watching him trot off a few feet and then stop. He turned his head, looking at Jack.

"Time to go to work, Sam," he told the horse, receiving a neigh in return.

NOT ALONE

Jack gave Sam a playful slap on the rump, putting the horse into a trot heading him toward the barn.

He and Sam headed out as soon dawn broke through the Arizona skies. Jack steered Sam in the direction of Hunter's Creek. He wanted to be sure the markers left without incident. Afterward, Jack would head north and check on the herd. He'd wanted to stay a night at the lake cabin, but knowing Lynn and Lily would be alone until Nick returned gnawed at his stomach.

Several livable buildings sat on their land, enticing squatters who often were up to no good. To the north sat a beautiful log cabin overlooking Colton Lake and a smaller place at the south end on a chunk of land the family called Hunter's Creek.

The Hunter Creek cabin, built years ago for family and friends to stay in and hunt on the property, wasn't far from Granite Creek. The lodging provided a comfortable shelter during the colder hunting seasons. A wood stove for heat and a water bucket for washing fueled Hunters Creek, old-fashioned, but it served its purpose. Hunters Creek sat closest to the highway, and vandals often mistakenly found the shelter and abused it.

Jack favored the lake cabin, hidden and far less accessible and built to keep visitors safe. The stellar view, secluded location, and safety hardware enclosing all openings with roll-down shutters made the cabin a fortress. From the beginning, Jack designed the construction to withstand more than natural disasters. He made the place sturdy enough to survive an apocalyptic fallout.

The chalet hugged a thick tree line and mountainous terrain, camouflaging it from outsiders. Tall timber and extensive meadows covered the land splitting the rocky creeks and unusual rock formation in half. The ground rose and fell with hills and peaks, which created a maze.

Jack let Sam, who knew his way by heart, have his head. The horse moved into a smooth lope. In the distant Arizona sky, dark clouds were gathering off to the north.

5

The house, buildings, and property contained a tomb of ghosts—unhappy ones. There was no other choice but to stay because soon night would close in on her, and already dangerous roads would become more treacherous. The abandoned property was the last place Riley wanted to spend the night. She moved from one building to the next, fishing for supplies and hoping for a lucky break. She reached the third and largest building as the sun descended, trying each key under shadows until one fit.

Entering the tomb, a pungent greasy odor of diesel and metal greeted her. Small cracks of sunlight penetrated through the slits of the giant doors allowing little to no light. Something significant settled inside the tin building, causing her to jump. The silence returned, and then a slight scratching noise began. A Rat, opossum, raccoon, and any other creature looking for a place to scavenge could be an unfriendly slumlord.

Max waited outside the door, hesitant to enter.

"Damn the dark," her words were heard by no one other than herself and Max.

She traced her fingers along the edges of the door, searching for a latch to open the bay doors. She found the lever, lifted the door, quenching the darkness in dim light. For a moment, she faced the long meadow leading to the ranch house, but she realized her luck had changed when she turned.

The front grill of a truck shone under days of dust and grime.

"Score! Double score! Now Max, let's say a prayer that with a new truck came new batteries."

The truck, a new, white, 2500 Dodge Diesel Ram, sat ripe for the taking. The toy hauler connected to the hitch caused a light to go on inside to brighten her brain fog.

"Max, look. A rolling motel. No more searching dark creepy abandoned, and did I say creepy houses!"

She climbed into the cab of the truck, took note of the manufacturer's sticker on the passenger side window, and inserted the key into the ignition. Saying a silent prayer, she turned the key, hoping the glow plug and dash would light up. When the Cummins started to purr, a rush of tears filled her eyes.

"Trailer keys," she said, rummaging through the center console.

"Bingo!" The keys in plain sight now in the palm of her hand felt like a million dollars. "I feel like a millionaire. Let's see what we have inside the trailer."

Riley opened the door to find a UTV, tags still attached. The profitable cranberry farmer, if he could have, had handed her a checkered flag. His misfortune was her gain, and she thanked him silently.

She searched for batteries and a flashlight under a candlelight dinner consisting of expired cold bean soup and stale crackers. Max gulped down some dried rabbit and agreed to share the double bed. For the first time in months, Riley would sleep on a mattress. With her pistol tucked under her pillow, she slept until the breaking of dawn.

Leaving the property by early morning light, Riley pinched her nose to close off a smell not noticed the day before. "What is that smell? Is that you, Max?" She rolled down the windows and looked at the cat, who, in her mind, looked guilty as hell.

The rough highway produced enough rough driving to shake teeth loose and rattle the gray matter held captive in her skull to shreds. Pieces of cement had risen pushed up by land movement and growing grass out of control. The pace started steady, but fourteen minutes later, she braked to a crawl. Mother Nature had jackhammered the road, and the truck's stiff suspension made for a rough ride. A few hours later, and concerned about her rolling motel, Riley pulled over near an abandoned store to check for damage and search the building for supplies.

"You want out, Max? Max?"

He yawned.

"Okay," she shut the door. "Something stinks!"

The manmade structure looked damaged, overgrown with flora, and exposed. Broken windows, the siding of the building wrecked, wires visible, and chunks of old installation hung in pieces. Shards of glass sat scattered around the entry while some had slipped between the warped boards, but once inside, she shut out the destruction, finding left behind supplies. Arms loaded down. She took what she could use and hurried back to the truck.

NOT ALONE

"Time to go."

Once again, Riley smelled the rotten aroma as it wafted to the front of the cab, stinging her nose and watering her eyes. She looked at Max.

"Phew," she gasped. "You better not have. I know you wouldn't!"

Max looked at her, letting out a high-pitched meow as something in the back moved.

"Rats," she sighed, holding her pistol. She leaned over the seat only to find what she could have thought to be aliens from another planet. However, what appeared were two small dirt-smudged faces. Surrounding their thinning frames was long unruly locks of dark hair. Through the dirt, green eyes sparkled, and cherry red lips formed into fearful frowns.

"Don't hurt us," whispered the smaller of the two, her nose smudged with grime.

Confused, Riley stared at the first faces she had seen in a long time. Feeling their presence and the release of air in their breaths moving past the skin on her neck, she decided they were not ghosts. Her voice caught in her throat. She wanted to reach out with her hand and touch their cheeks.

"I'm hallucinating? Right?"

Tears the size of nickels formed around the corner of the littlest girl's eyes and rolled down her cheek. She tried to hide behind the other girl, but both were so thin that it was impossible.

"She might be a monster," the smallest pulled in closer to her sister.

"I'm not a monster!" Riley stared at the girls.

The older of the two pressed her brows together. Riley wondered how long they'd been crouching down to stay hidden. Their torn shirts, stained, hung on their bodies one size too big, and then she realized the aroma she smelled came from the two of them.

Max looked at her as if saying, "I tried to tell you twenty miles ago."

"How... did...? How long...?" Riley fumbled for the right words. Her social skills were as rusty as the humidity plaguing the ocean air.

"We waited until you were asleep," she said, adjusting herself in the seat. "You should have checked the backseat before you left."

"Yes, I should have" Riley's tone lowered. "I can't keep you."

The youngest girl shrank back.

"Sorry," Riley said, her eyes peeled on both the girls as if they were ghosts. "Parents? Where do you live? I can take you home."

"We won't be a problem. We promise," the older girl wrapped her arm around her sister's shoulder.

Riley said nothing. They looked so small and pale. *Not ghosts, but children.*

"What are your names?"

NOT ALONE

Max stared at the two humans.

"Utah."

"Megan," The smallest one rubbed her eyes, trying to wipe away the tear, leaving a smudge of dirt. "What's your name?"

"Riley, Riley Collins." Seeing their blue eyes widen under long eyelashes. Lord, it felt refreshing to see another person.

"Your parents?" She sounded like a cop, but she needed to know.

"Dead," Utah's tone was so soft as she glimpsed out the window. However, Riley heard the pain.

Riley's experience with children, none. "I'm sorry." Riley sighed softly. "Relatives?" The answer was as expected. The two children had found her because everyone and anyone who might take care of them was dead. She understood because her circle of remaining friends and family included a feral cat. She owned nothing and lived nowhere.

"Everyone is gone."

"Where are you going?" Megan cocked her head to the side, looking like a curious puppy waiting for a treat would.

Riley looked out the window. "I'm going to Prescott, Arizona, to find my brother."

"Is he dead? Can we come with you?" Megan's face lit up with excitement. "How far is Arizona?"

"No, he's not dead! I can't take you guys. I'd be kidnapping, and I...," then she realized it all sounded odd.

"I don't think anyone is left," Utah frowned. "You wouldn't be kidnaping us. You would be saving us."

"Was the cranberry farmer your father?"

"No. We lived in Grants Pass. It was bad there," Utah shook her head.

Another agonizing strand of silence followed, and Riley feared the worst. The two children had become her responsibility. She sighed deeply, allowing her doubts to simmer. "I don't mind the company if you don't mind, Max."

"We like all animals," Utah said.

"I can feed Max," Megan said, raising her hand. Utah grinned at her sister, pushing her hand down gentle-like.

With that said, Max jumped onto Utah's lap and purred. The girl settled into the seat, expressing an expression of relief. Max looked at Riley with an "I tried to tell you" look.

Finding two lost children was not in the plan. It meant every move she made involved careful consideration for their safety!

"There are rules. One: do not, and I mean it, do not touch any of the guns. Two: stay away from the guns. Do you two understand?"

Wide-eyed and straight-faced, they said, "do not touch the guns."

"That's all the rules?" Utah asked.

"Yes. Maybe more as we go. Now, buckle up. There are goodies in the box if you're hungry."

In the rearview mirror, she witnessed two smiles. After all, she spoke the golden words. Goodies! A bag rustled, and a soft squeal followed as Megan reached over the seat. Before returning to her sister, she put her hand out to Riley. Riley took a dark truffle from her dirty palm, ignoring the grime, and slipped the candy into her mouth. The chocolate fixed everything for the moment.

6

Chocolate was a great icebreaker, allowing room for a lighter conversation. Megan, with Max curled up next to her stomach, took a brief nap. Utah, wide-awake, watched her, saying little. The quiet in the cab gave Riley the concentration she needed to keep the truck on smoother highway sections. The stiff suspension forced her to work the wheel nonstop and keep an eye on the trailer. By noon, regardless of who needed one, a pit stop was required because her legs and hands felt like broom handles.

"You have to pee, girls? Now's a good time."

Megan woke, crawled from the bench seat, swaying as she slid to the ground. Big sister clasped her hand, steadying her. Riley waited, unsure of what to do next. Seeing Riley's hesitance, Utah pulled her sister toward a clump of trees, disappearing past shrubs.

"Don't go far," Riley watched them for a moment and then went the opposite direction. "I have no clue what to do," she said softly in frustration. "They've been doing this for a long time by themselves. Right?"

A minute later, the girls emerged from the brush. Riley leaned against the bumper, watching Utah, half dragging and half pulling her sister in a full sprint.

"Come on, Megan!" Utah was shouting orders. "Hurry!"

"I'm not going to leave without you," Riley shouted, waving at them.

The two girls, sprinting, brushed past Riley and jumped into the back seat. Stepping out of their way to avoid a collision, Riley raised her hands in surrender.

"Okay," Riley said, climbing into the truck.

"Let's go, Riley. Why aren't we going?" Utah's voice, louder and urgent, quivered and cracked.

"What's wrong? What did you see?"

"A huge kitty," Megan smiled, out of breath but amused, unlike her sister.

"How big of a kitty?" Riley twisted to see the girl's faces.

"A tiger!" yelled Megan, fearless and in awe.

"Seriously. A tiger?" Riley chuckled and then paused, remembering the wild animal park, "shit!" The refuge was small but still contained a few exotic cats and bears.

"Riley, we should go!" Utah begged.

"Yeah. Good idea." Wrestling a tiger dining on human remains didn't sound like too much fun. Anyway, she was no longer on that payroll. She turned the key, waited for the glow plug to turn red on the dash, but got no light, no nothing. She tried again. Riley sat there for a minute, trying to think. "Utah, come to the front."

They both climbed over. Megan's body pressed next to hers. Riley felt their warmth.

"I have to go outside. It's probably a loose connection. Where was the tiger?" Riley pulled out her pistol. "Tap on the window if you see something."

Utah pointed, but all Riley could see was the grass pushed by a gentle breeze and many trees.

"Be careful," Utah pressed her face to the window.

"I can't believe I forgot about the animals in the park?" Riley swore under her breath. She'd dealt with bears and cougars in the past, but never a tiger, especially one eating God knows what?

The wind turned up a notch, swishing the tall grass to the sides of her. The hairs on her neck rose. Something felt amiss. Looking at the window, Riley saw two small faces peering past her. She looked back. Nothing. Her heart raced. She lifted the hood. The engine sat as a maze of high-tech engineering and wiring. There were covers and caps for everything.

"Sweet Jesus, where is the engine?"

Not a mechanic, Riley guessed the problem to be something simple. The wind shifted. Her senses heightened.

Unable to see the girl's faces because of the hood and not hearing a warning, she turned her attention back to the truck. One of the battery cables had jarred loose. Replacing and tightening down the battery cable, she prayed she fixed the problem.

Just about to slide down off the truck, a throaty rumble sounded behind her. Knowing she resembled tiger bait, she turned, gripping her pistol. As she turned, the cat went to a prone position, not a hundred feet from her. Sliced by dark, jagged stripes, the rest of his coat shone gold in the afternoon sunlight. Greens eyes shimmered in her direction, golden circles wrapped around pupils, and fixed. She was the prey.

"I'm in trouble."

Having little to no options, a sudden rush of adrenaline skipped the beat of her heart.

Tap, tap, tap, tap, and tap. Then silence. The cat turned, studying the cab of the truck. A long pink tongue slid across white whiskers. Then the tiger turned to Riley once more.

Tap, tap, and tap.

Riley, now frozen in place, fought off the urge to move. If she fell, the tiger would be on her in seconds. She needed a distraction.

"Think girls," whispered Riley.

Her calf muscles began to cramp from standing on the front bumper, leaning into the engine compartment. She had no choice but to take the risk and make a run for it. Riley kept the tiger within her field of vision and readied for an escape.

The ground was a cushion of tall grass and wet soil. As fast as she could, Riley pulled the hood down and heard it click. Utah pitched something out the window, which distracted the cat. Riley sprinted toward the door. Saying a Hail Mary, Riley scrambled into the cab, slamming the door behind her. Startled, Max did a hop with his back arched and a tail fluff.

Max glared at her as if saying, "What the hell was that?"

Outside, the tiger sprang forward, swatting at the air, and then settled into slow strides as he sniffed the air. The cat, as healthy as one could be, radiated a dangerous beauty. One Riley felt good about leaving alone.

Hopefully, you've been eating deer, not humans?

As if one cat presented enough trouble, another tiger trotted out of the brush toward its mate. Riley sighed.

"The hunter."

"That was close," the color in Utah's face turned ashen.

"Wow! Thank you, girls. We are going to make a good team."

"I've never seen a tiger," Utah looked at Riley, color beginning to return to her cheeks.

"Let's get going." Riley eyed the cats while realizing she could count on the girls to think at a moment's notice.

7

Lily looked at her mother. "Mama, where do baby horses come from?"

"From the mama horse," Lynn said, smiling. Lynn knew her daughter's question would lead to more.

At the age where there was unlimited storage of questions, Lily waited and looked to Lynn for answers. Lynn handed Lily a tablet of paper and a box of crayons.

"What are you going to draw today?"

"Um, maybe a baby horse and a baby duck. Why don't we have any baby ducks, mama? Why not?" Lynn forced herself not to laugh. Lily's questions came quickly, and her speech patterns were continually changing, growing her use of words.

Full of life and sheltered from how brutal the world could be, Lily's curiosity grew. The need to know made Lynn worry about her daughter's future.

Lily turned five years old in August. She remained innocent to the disorder of the new chaotic world. Lily, like all other surviving children, was the future generation. The importance of raising them right shaped the upcoming population.

Lynn didn't like the days when Nick traveled to Phoenix. Lily's arrival changed Lynn and Nick's priorities. When he moved his practice to the family ranch to be available to the townspeople, she understood how vital family could be. The choice to leave Phoenix was a wise decision. One in which Nick was never sorry. However, the city of Phoenix needed him too.

Less than a week after the beginning of the Shift, the townsfolk decided to be active and vigilant in attempts to save the businesses they could. The Colton's spent long hours assisting others with medical and burying the dead. In between, Jack found space on the ranch so Nick could be the doctor he was, caring and compassionate in every way possible.

Medical supplies were tough to get, but Nick had everything he needed for most medical situations, thanks to Jack's team. The town needed a doctor, and the city expressed how fortunate they were to have a Nick

As the violence slowed and the patients became fewer and fewer, Nick reopened clinics in Phoenix with a few other doctors. Twice a month, he traveled, with a small group of peers, to the city to volunteer. Today Nick took a group of nurses to Surprise to visit a pediatrics clinic.

NOT ALONE

Lynn stared at Lily. She couldn't help but think how much Lily looked like Nick, with dark hair, green eyes, and a smile that could lighten even the darkest of rooms. Lily, not only smart, most times entertained herself. Lynn taught her how to read by the age of three, simple words, of course. By the age of four, Lily could do basic math.

While Lily sat drawing a house, a sun in the background with a smiley face, Lynn sat back and studied her daughter's work. The barking of their dogs pulled her attention away. No visitors were expected but often occurred when an extra pie or casserole happened. Ryan, who was asleep in the bunkhouse, would intervene. Then there was Ben, who napped near the barn and would welcome any pie or two.

Once the two Rhodesians ridgeback hounds accepted their known visitor, the barking would stop. If they didn't, they were warning them.

She would have never have carried a gun in past times, but this new world was much different, lawless.

Lily hummed as the two Ridgebacks barked again. The alarm system Jack installed was enough to wake the dead, and yet she felt a slight shiver of fear anticipating its sound.

"Quiet," Lynn told Lily.

She moved to the window, scanning the yard. The dogs reappeared, running back and forth, barking. The ridges on their backs rose to full height. They darted to the opposite side of the yard and disappeared. The barking seized. She motioned for Lily to stay and then grabbed up the papers and crayons, tucking them away in a cupboard. With her pistol in one hand, she motioned Lily forward with the other.

Snatching the hand-held radio off the table, she went to her knees, pulling Lily with her. They crawled past the windows toward the center of the kitchen. Lily's fingers wrapped around Lynn's shirt, her small body pressed into her mother's back. Pausing at the double glass doors, Lynn searched for the two Ridgebacks. Nothing. Maybe Ryan woke up and met whoever was out there? Lynn pulled Lily toward her. One dog yelped and then went silent.

The sound of glass shattering, and then the alarm's high pitch beep cut deep into the house's silence. Lynn jumped. Out of the corner of her eye, she saw Sadie, the female ridgeback, run toward the house but never came back around.

Lynn half crawled, hurrying to the fake electrical outlet that hid a keypad near the refrigerator. Sliding the access door to the side, she entered the code into the safe room. A section of the paneled wall opened, and Lynn motioned Lily through the door. The little girl obeyed her mother.

"Don't be scared. I'll come back and get you," Lynn kissed her forehead. Lily knew what to do. She moved into the opening and out of her mother's sight. As the door closed, it also disappeared.

Lynn pressed against the wall as the alarm wailed in her ears. "Where are you, Ryan?" she whispered.

If her brother were there, he would silence the alarm. Lynn broke into a cold sweat. Her stomach knotted up.

She never had the chance to turn. The intruder clamped a hand over her mouth and hooked both of her arms into a hold. Lynn, trapped against his body, tried to wiggle free. The weapon dropped. She tried to scream, but her throat went dry. Unable to breathe or move, Lynn's thoughts went to Lily.

8

Jack felt a knot in his stomach. Something felt wrong. The chalet sat within sight, but his family felt further away than he wanted. He nudged Sam forward, but the horse already sensed his anxiety and stepped out on his own. Sam knew where to go, stopping near the small four-stall barn, and waited. Jack slipped the saddle from his back and then turned him loose into a small enclosure.

The path leading to the front door weaved in a pattern of soft turns around cactus and boulders. On the outside, the chalet-style log home had a southwestern flavor. Big smooth poles created a tall archway that led to the front door. The twisted antler handles added a twist of country flavor to the cabin's already rustic look. The place built like a fortress kept intruders from entering.

Jack slid his finger along the cement siding, up and under the lip made of rock. From there, he pressed a well-hidden latch releasing the door.

The lake house Jack called home away from home. He understood every intricate detail taking pride in his secret place. The cabin sat camouflaged in the Arizona timber. Now, daylight sprayed a beam of light inward as he accessed a hidden panel releasing metal barriers blocking the windows. Streams of sunshine poured into the chalet, snuffing out the blanket of darkness.

The cabin lacked nothing in size or quaintness. There were three floors total; the first floor sat under Jack's feet. The living room, small dining room, a wet bar, guest bedroom, small office, bathroom, and laundry room took up the second floor. Jack's room, the master bedroom took up the entire third floor. Every window overlooked the lake. Electricity powered by solar worked year-round thanks to the Arizona sunshine. To be safe, Jack had hauled over two Honda generators last year and a generous supply of gas for backup. The chalet, off the primary grid, was a hard find.

Jack looked out the window to the lake, trying to shrug off the uneasiness eating at him. Unease wore away Jack's comfort of being there. It'd take him several hours to get back to the ranch, and already he cursed the ride. Letting out a soft sigh, he shut down the windows of the chalet. Disappointment and worry consumed him. Sam's back would still be wet. Jack peeked at his watch, knowing he'd already too long gone.

9

The intruder stood behind Lynn, driving her backward. He'd stashed her gun underneath his shirt and was now overpowering her with his hands. As he locked her head against him, her lips pressed hard against her teeth. The tender skin tore, and the taste of blood trickled into her mouth. She went to her tiptoes as he pulled her upwards.

"Turn off the alarm," he demanded.

She felt dizzy from the lack of oxygen. A haze developed in her eyes, making it impossible to see. She tried to speak but couldn't.

"Turn off the alarm," he screamed into her ear. She could smell stale cigarettes and liquor on his breath and old blood on his skin.

Lynn pressed a few keys, and the pad flashed "error. Retrying the code, she forced herself to focus on the keypad. The alarm went silent, but the ringing in her ears continued.

For no reason of hers, the man's hold tightened. The thought of Lily growing up without her caused her to struggle. The man holding her was bigger than her, but her thinness came with advantages. Light-headed, she sucked air back into her lungs, making her rib cage and stomach even thinner. When she felt the gap, she wrenched free. Lynn spun and brought her knee up hard, connecting to his groin. As he buckled, she sprang away from him.

Over the pain, the attacker leaped forward, bringing her off her feet. One pull brought her face to face with the stranger. With little effort, he spun her around and clamped his rough hand over her mouth. The force pressed her teeth into her lips, creating a deep cut in her lower lip.

"You're a feisty one. I like that," he growled, intentionally sliding fingers across Lynn's breasts.

Any promise of escape seemed to be fading, and she'd rather die than let this two-bit loser touch her any longer.

Where was Ryan? Was Ben dead? How long could Lily survive in the room made to keep her safe?

"Everyone has guns, but I think there's a lot of them here?" he growled. "That son of a bitch took mine after he sucker-punched me. Hell, I might take the entire ranch and call it my own. What do you think?"

Lynn squeezed her eyes shut, praying for Ryan to show. The gun hunter tightened his hold, forcing her head against his chest and restricting her movement even more. The pungent smell he wore on his of death made her gag.

NOT ALONE

The silence she produced enraged him as he spun her around, yanking her hard enough to cause her skin to burn.

"Speak, woman!"

The man caught her gaze, and he smiled. Seeing evil intent reflecting in the iris of his eyes, Lynn prayed for help. Jagged scars crisscrossed the left side of his face to the corner of his eye.

"This ranch is looking better and better all the time," sneered the trespasser, his jaw clenched. "How about I ask the little one?" He pressed his lips to her ears, whispering.

The quietness in her soul slipped away. Getting to Lily would not be easy. The intruder would fail to find the false panel. He'd have to know the code to open the door or bypass it.

"You're going to die," she muttered.

"I don't think so," he spun her around, pulling her like a rag doll.

Seconds seemed to turn into minutes as the panic inside her rose. His fingers unbuttoned her jeans. He was about to reach inside, his hand sliding down as he licked her ear. His fingers were scraping against her skin.

The more Lynn resisted, the better he liked it, and with one pull, he ripped the sleeve of her shirt, a threat.

Then she felt his hold loosen enough for her to escape.

Like a snake, he struck out, catching her on the cheek.

Another burst of heat and a bright light flashed stars in her eyes as she fell backward.

"You want to play rough?" shouted the intruder.

Disoriented, she shoved the pain away, shifting in time to see the toe of his boot coming in her direction. The hit came too hard, too fast. Before she could try to stand, he planted another hard kick into her side. The impact sucked the wind from her lungs, and she felt an unbearable pain as ribs popped.

Lynn heard her attacker, but she could not see him. Her vision blurred, her breathing labored, and a searing pain ripped through her entire body. She curled into a fetal position with painful movements and recovered the knife hidden under her pant leg.

He reached out and swept her off her feet.

Consumed with hatred, which fed her newfound strength, the fog cleared. Her abductor unbuttoned his pants. Lynn smiled, wanting to look into his eyes when she plunged the serrated knife into his heart. With her feet almost dangling, he locked his fingers around her hair and the back of her shirt. He pulled her head back.

The blade opened easily with one pull of her thumb.

NOT ALONE

The sharp edge sunk deep into the flesh inside his arm above the elbow, ripping muscle, tissue, and tendon. Lynn gave one last push of strength, pressing harder and going deeper. Blood squirted into the air as the blade hit bone. He let out an agonizing cry.

"What the...?" Scarface yelled, yanking his arm away.

The hand around her neck loosened, and in a panic for air, she struggled to free herself. The man shuddered but remained standing. Grasping and clawing at his arm, the wounded man attempted to stop the bleeding.

Lynn gulped in a deep breath when she saw Ryan

Ryan pulled the trigger on his pistol, bypassing her and hitting the trespasser in the shoulder.

Lynn stepped to the side.

The man glared at her with darkened eyes shuddered.

Ryan shot again. This time the bullet hit the man in the chest. The bullet exited through his back and into the splash guard behind him. Blood splattered across her face. It felt as if it took minutes for the trespasser to fall to the ground, but Lynn stepped over him toward Ryan when he did.

"There's more. You okay?"

She nodded, eyeing the red liquid covering his shirt.

"Two more...," he hesitated, "out of the five that I saw, anyway," he grinned, clutching his side. "I'm all right."

Lynn reached out and took her gun from the trespasser. The sharp ache in her side was unbearable. Ryan took her hand and guided her from the kitchen.

"Lily?"

"She's safer in there than with us," Ryan reminded her.

He nodded and then pointed at the dead trespasser in the hallway. Blood pooled under his body and onto the hardwood floor. Lynn stepped around the puddle. The stale smell of death hung heavy in the house.

"Jack's going to be pissed about all the blood," grunted Ryan.

Lynn chuckled but stopped abruptly.

"Marty! Marty! Where the hell are you?" another trespasser yelled.

Glass shattered.

Lynn jumped.

"Stay here."

"Be careful, Ryan."

She leaned against the wall. The pain produced a fine layer of sweat across her brow. More than anything, she wanted to get to Lily. Unknown and hidden, Lily remained safe.

Lynn looked around the corner, checking on Ryan.

Ryan stood holding over another trespasser, clenching a knife in his hand. A stream of red trickled down the blade and rolled down onto the trespasser's face. Ryan looked at her. His face paled.

Lynn scrambled forward, seeing her brother covered in blood as another trespasser appeared in the hallway.

Lynn felt a sudden sense of control. Fluid and determined, she swung her pistol up and pressed the trigger. With the trespasser's focus on Ryan, not Lynn, her target was unmoving, and the bullet hit center mass. Strands of shirt material exploded outward. The trespasser staggered back, looked at Ryan, and then moved toward her.

The second bullet hit a centimeter from the first bullet. The trespasser's body tumbled backward. The muscles in his gun hand contracted, sending stray rounds into the air. Sprinting, Lynn and Ryan scrambled to the side. One of the multiple stray bullets sliced into the doorframe splintering the wood into toothpicks. Ryan fell to the floor.

"Ryan!" Ryan!"

Lynn rolled him over. His eyelids flickered, moaning as she tore away his shirt. On the left side of his chest, a bullet hole gaped open nearly three inches in diameter. She pressed her fingers over the wound and whispered, "No."

She scrambled, fell, and in a painful try, she climbed to her feet, rushing toward the guest bathroom, grabbing towels and a box of medical supplies. The adrenaline surpassed her pain as she hurried back to Ryan.

"Hurry home, Nick," she shouted. "Please hurry."

Jack wouldn't be home until tomorrow, and Lily would be getting more scared by the hour.

Kneeling beside Ryan, she checked for secondary wounds. The first bullet entered through the front of his chest and exited his back, but the flowing blood suggested another problem. Needing to stop the bleeding, she pressed a towel to the back wound and then rolled him on top. Taking several more, she pushed hard against the front of his chest. Her teeth turned numb from pain as she bandaged the shoulder wound.

Lynn was frightened Ben was hurt. She needed Nick to walk through the door and be her hero. Lynn needed him to stop Ryan's bleeding and keep him from dying. She needed to get to Lily.

The stack of towels soon turned crimson red. Fighting through the pain in her ribs, she pressed harder on Ryan's wound. The rare silence inside the house taunted her as Ryan's pulse slackened and her worst fears heightened. Tears formed and rolled down her cheeks. Minutes crawled by.

"Please come home, Nick," she felt warm tears slip down her face. "Please."

NOT ALONE

Except for the refrigerator's occasional hum and lingering shards of glass falling to the floor, the house was silent. The late morning passed, and early afternoon approached. It was then that Lynn heard a sound, so soft and near inaudible, she thought she imagined it. Lynn strained to listen. Through blurry eyes, she watched and waited. The shadows changed and flickered beyond the broken glass, suggesting movement. Lynn gripped the handle of her gun with both hands.

"Lynn," the voice moved in her direction. "Lynn."

The silhouette of her husband appeared through the sunlit fog, and before she could say a word, he moved to help her. He shoved aside furniture, stepping on broken glass, taking the stairs two at a time.

"Any more?" asked Nick, bending down toward Lynn.

"I don't think so," she said, relieved. "Lily is in the safe room?" A crackle broke her words into pieces as she gave in and cried.

He holstered his pistol and took hers. Nick touched her, but Lynn said nothing.

Nick lowered his voice as he knelt beside Ryan, "Lynn, I need your help."

She reached up to wipe away tears, leaving streaks of blood on her cheeks. Nick touched her face brushing a fingertip across the swelling. She heard him take in a deep breath.

"Can you help me, Lynn?"

She nodded.

Nick pulled Ryan away from her. "Everything will be all right, but I need more towels, my bag, and sheets. I'll meet you in the surgery room."

Weak and in pain, she left to gather what Nick requested

Life turned to near death in a little over two hours.

10

"Where've you been staying?" Riley asked, Utah.

"The school. Do you know what month it is?"

"November. I think. Where did you live? I mean before what happened.

"Grants Pass. You?"

"Sacramento."

"Were there any monsters there" Utah lowered her voice, looking downward.

"Yes. Do you two understand the danger of guns? I need you to understand because I have to keep them close to me, out, and in the open."

"Yes. We understand. You're our protector now. Mama told us not to trust anyone." Utah smoothed out the dirty creases in her jeans. It was the first time Riley saw a glimmer of fear in the girl's eyes. "We won't touch the guns. We promise."

"How did you get to the farmer's place?"

"A truck, and then we walked some of the ways."

"Utah, what do you mean by monsters?"

"Crazy people." Utah looked over at Riley. "They have dead eyes."

"The infected?"

Utah said nothing, which meant the ping-pong conversation ended, or maybe she was regressing on the reality of it all. The skies darkened in front of them. A gray line of thick clouds mixed with black thunderheads forming to the east foreshadowed forgotten tragedy.

With the threat of rain coming, a new set of problems became apparent. Riley needed to find a water source for the trailer, a lake, or a creek with enough fresh water to fill the holding tanks. Then she and the girls could shower.

Reaching the turnoff to a lake, Riley parked where she wanted despite the tow-away signs. The lake water was for showers and the bathroom only. They had plenty of bottled water until the next city.

Riley backed the trailer over the park's green grass close enough to siphon water from the lake into the tank. In little under an hour, they had water for Utah and Megan to shower. While the girls scrubbed away dirt and odors, Riley stood patrol outside.

"Mama puts conditioner in my hair," Megan said, lifting long, dark curls in her hand.

"Yeah. I can see why," Riley looked at all the tangles. "Have your sister do it, Megan. Riley needs to keep watch."

Riley heard giggles as she gathered a few boy's shirts and pants found in the cupboards. Make-do clothing until they could find a place where the stores were plentiful. T-shirts weren't going to keep the girls warm in this weather.

In the distance, a soft roll of thunder echoed a warning of a brewing storm.

Riley slipped a smaller t-shirt over Megan's head, who wiggled to adjust the fit. The two sisters looked in the mirror and started laughing. Megan's shirt, decorated with a Superman logo, brought out the blue in Megan's eyes, and the pants were a size too big, but they were clean. Utah faired a little better with the Batman t-shirt, and with some adjustment, the pants fit. Wearing Superman and Batman t-shirts, the two little superheroes stood side by side, smiling.

An hour later, they pulled into the Walmart parking lot under a dark gray sky.

"Riley, why are we here?" Utah looked at the building.

"Supplies and clothes for the two of you."

"We should stay here." Utah shook her head no.

"Monsters," said Megan moving closer to her sister.

Utah wrapped her fingers around one of Megan's curls and twisted it into a ringlet. No longer dirty, the girls looked angelic.

"I don't like monsters," Megan whispered. Her small heart-shaped lips pursed forward.

"I can't leave you in the truck," said Riley, pulling a pistol out from under the bench. She gathered a second magazine and the shotgun secured under her seat.

"What if there are monsters in there?" Megan asked.

Riley said nothing as a gust of wind blew through the parking lot, pushing litter across the ground in a giant sweep. In the flurry of wind, loose paper caught, took flight, and danced.

Riley and Utah climbed from the cab. "Come on, Megan. I'll hold your hand."

"Okay," she said, climbing down from the truck.

The three of them faced the store.

"You stay with me no matter what, okay?" Riley said to Utah. She surveyed the darkened depths of the entry while feeling a tidal wave of apprehension. "If I stop, you stop and be real quiet. Sometimes it's best to listen."

"Utah told me that," burst out Megan, wrapping her fingers into Utah's palm.

NOT ALONE

Riley took out her Vic's and wiped it under her nose. She looked at Megan and Utah and then lowered the jar to their level, getting curious looks from both girls.

"Vick's Deep Heating Rub," Riley lifted the jar into the air and turning the label so they could see. "For the smells."

Utah took a swipe and rubbed it under her nose.

"It's like when you had a cold, Megan. Mama used to put it on your chest, too, when you were sick? It smells good." Utah took another dab and rubbed it under Megan's nose. Megan scrunched up her nose at first and then smiled.

"Smells good, but it makes my eyes burn," smiled Megan. "What about Max?"

"He doesn't need any," responded Riley. "He's going to wait for us here."

Riley sighed, looking around the parking lot. A mass of clouds cloaked the sun, leaving them in complete shadow.

Frowning, she locked the truck and took slow steps toward the Wal-Mart opening. Shattered doors and broken windows layered the entry, a dark abyss made for an unwelcome entry.

"Welcome to Walmart."

11

Glass crunched under their feet, and no senior Wal-Mart greeter offered them a cart. Containers of hand sanitizer littered the ground, empty.

So much for clean hands, thought Riley

Decorated inside the entrance was a unique statue made from shopping carts. The display reached the ceiling and cascaded outward in a ceremonial show of debris. Riley took the closest cart standing.

Welcome to Walmart.

Smells, sharp enough to sting the inside of their noses, permeated the air. Rotting mold and God knows what made for a foul odor.

Stay focused, Riley.

The girls needed clothes, more water, food, and batteries and the superstore was the best place for all of the above. Finding salvageable and unopened cans might be challenging. Riley flicked on the flashlight, casting a splash of dim shadows on the checkout isles. The light bounced off the edges of decaying bodies as Riley shuffled the girls forward, aiming the beam for a clear pathway.

The store was an exhibition of destruction, contents strewn in a chaotic mess. The aisles, short of a retail store maze, had no purpose or direction. Sorting by shapes and shadows, Riley looked for anything they could use. Impossible to shield the sight of bodies from the girls' view, Riley kept them moving.

"It smells bad," Megan pinched her nose, glancing down at form that no longer resembled a human. "I want more rub."

"Breathe through your mouth." Utah plugged her nose, too, ignoring the corpse.

Were they desensitized to death? Riley thought sadly, guessing they'd seen their share of violence.

The shopping spree's primary goal included clothing and food, so Riley led the girls further into the store, trying in vain to avoid the horror movie scenery. Heaps of items covered the floor mixed in with the wrong departments. No longer were the departments broken up into sections. Instead, the isles were utter chaos. Weights, bats, and bicycles lay atop broken glasses and plates, diapers, and paper towels, which soaked up and dried liquid seeping from containers. Only a few things held to hangers. It seemed safer to toss the stuff they did not need and search only for what they needed. The problem, Riley had no clue about shopping for children.

How hard can this be? she thought.

"She's six, but she wears a small," Utah read Riley's thoughts. "what does desensitized mean?"

"Size small," repeated Riley. "How...?

"Just pick out what you'd wear." Utah interrupted Riley and looked at her like she should know this.

Utah stepped over to a pile of clothes, picked up a pair of jeans, kept them under the light, checked the size, and then tossed them off to the side. She found another pair and held them up.

"Here."

Having tossed the old stinky clothing did little to dissuade Megan from deciding what clothes Riley kept. If Megan hated it, she would shake her head no. However, a far too bright fluffy pink skirt fluttered in the air like an astronaut claiming his stake on the moon. Megan, hugging the skirt, had found her treasure and starting searched for a shirt to match.

As Utah picked through clothes, the stack in the cart grew. They edged their way to the shoes, Riley assessing the girl's sizes tossing in socks and underwear. She even threw in a few coats, gloves and caps, an umbrella or two, and rubber boots. They grabbed clothing in the dark bypassing essential wear hidden under rubbish. The cart was full.

A roll of thunder rattled the roof of the building. Lightning cracked as flashes of light flickered through broken windows. A large bird rose awkwardly into the air from a darkened corner, squawking and flapping its wings. Megan froze in place. Her hands balled up into tiny fists.

"It's a vulture," Riley said, placing her hand on Megan's back as they watched the vulture search for a way out. Wal-Mart felt like a giant tomb filled with dark and scary things.

Take what you need and get out! Batteries and candles. "Hold this." Riley handed Megan the flashlight. "Stay right here."

Maneuvering over several decayed bodies, Riley searched for candles, lighters, and bags to hold everything. The dim glow of the light was close enough for her to reach if needed quickly. Megan's silhouette stood attached to her sister.

Riley turned when she heard metal on metal. Another round of thunder echoed overhead, then to a series of rumbles. Lightning popped in a repeated sequence, making the hairs on her neck rise.

"Not normal," she whispered. The sky growled, clearing its throat with bursts of rumbles that grew closer. It was about to get loud.

She turned back to where the girls were. Utah and Megan were gone. Riley sprinted toward the cart and dropped her bag on top of the pile.

"Utah, Megan," she called into the dark.

Minus the flashlight and camouflaged by the montage of overturned displays, she walked down the aisles unseen. The stores scattered stock looked more like graves. The flashes of light eerily outlined dismembered bodies constrained to the floor.

An unnatural shadow splashed down on the dead, leaving the imagination to fill in the story. The smell of rotting flesh and food thickened the air as Riley wandered to where the store's frozen food section had been. As far as the eye could see, a sea of moldy unpreserved foodstuff lay scattered. She could hear the bugs writhing under the rot.

A fresh death was beginning to ferment smelled foul. Similar to a wax figure laid out for Halloween, it looked surreal. The lividity of death odors permeated her clothing, and the sight crawled into her memory, squatting forever. A small bead of sweat formed on Riley's brow. Her heart thumped in her ears.

A voice boomed through the overhead speakers, making her jump.

"Welcome, Wal-Mart shoppers." The voice was that of a man.

The weight of the shotgun felt heavy as Riley froze in place, listening. Wherever the girls were, they were quiet.

"Pick up on aisle eight," he said.

Riley had little doubt that the maniac would kill her, and then he'd find the girls and kill them. The proof was laid for eternity on the floor. She waited for the thunder to mask her movement and then stepped back away from the bodies into the deep recesses of no light, hiding, ignoring objects under her feet. False shadows reflected an invisible outline of twisted souls lost.

The figure, now named the Monster, leaped from a darkened hole. Riley spun, bringing the shotgun to her shoulder. She pressed the trigger. As if matching the blast from the barrel, thunder exploded overhead. Cheese puffs and several canned objects took flight mid-air, then fell and scattered onto the floor. There was a grunt, shuffle, and then a thud. A hit!

"Bad management here," she growled.

Sounds erupted from the opposite aisle and then moved further away. The thunder stopped. Riley, hoping to make a no-bull-shit warning, reloaded the shotgun.

As she withdrew into the safety of the darkness, footfalls, too soft to be a man's, sounded to her right. "Utah, Megan?"

Two small silhouettes came into view.

"Is the monster dead?" Megan asked, clinging to a stuffed animal tiger.

Riley took the flashlight from Utah and stepped around the corner.

The man was down and bleeding profusely but breathing. More than likely, he'd bleed to death.

"Judgement day," she said aloud.

Returning to the girls, she gestured for them to get moving.

Let's get out of here. No, wait. We need to get our stuff."

"Bags! We need bags," Utah whispered.

Riley shoved the cart into a checkout lane. One ailing tire caught, stopped rolling, and then gave up the second they reached the counter. Riley yanked out a handful of extra-large bags from under the broken register.

"Let me know if you see any movement," Riley said in a low tone as Utah and Megan hurriedly started bagging their treasures.

Utah nodded, watching Riley toss sodas and sealed food onto the pile.

"Good, let's go!"

Together they moved toward the entrance. The cart, filled to the brim, screeched. The damaged wheel caught and then broke free.

"Shopping sucks sometimes," muttered Riley balancing the cart on three wheels. "And thank you for shopping at Wal-Mart."

The natural light outside shone not seventy-five feet away. Almost home free, a bloody hand clamped down on her arm, flesh twisting under the monster's hold. Megan screamed.

"Run!" shouted Riley.

Utah and Megan took off.

Utah looked back as Riley hurled the truck keys into the air. Utah caught them and grabbed Megan's hand.

One swift jerk from her captor caused Riley to lose hold of her shotgun. She pitched her body hard to the left, and when she did, she brought out her pistol. The monster lost his grip. She broke free and fired, but the giant, overly graceful killer dodged the shot. There one minute and gone the next.

Holstering her pistol, she grabbed the shotgun. "What the hell?" The man was gone. "Freaking psychotic ninja!"

By the look of the trail of blood, she had hit him again, and yet he'd slipped away. The edge of a bag of M&Ms rested almost hidden behind the debris.

Snatching the bag up, she shouted, "Mmmmm... Time to go!"

Grabbing the bulging bags, Riley made her way out the entrance, escaping the tomb, monster, and trouble. As she moved through the exit, a splattering of raindrops dotted the parking lot under darkening skies.

Walmart appeared to be busy with the vast sea of the carnage of abandoned vehicles that framed the parking lot. The truck and trailer sat amongst them as a welcoming sight.

NOT ALONE

The girls pressed their cheeks to the window, watching her toss most of the bags into the hauler.

Riley opened the back door of the truck to hand Megan her bag when Utah screamed at her.

"Riley!"

Megan screamed.

Riley spun around. A fist the size of a softball connected with her face knocking her backward. She scrambled to keep her feet under her, not wanting to scrape the pavement with her face.

The monster, covered in blood, laughed. His hardiness to survive being shot made her think the monster was infected.

Again, her shotgun fell, but this time, several feet from her reach, clattering on the concrete. Stars spun and swirled in her eyes, but Riley saw the girl's faces. She died. They died.

"Let's see what you got." Her shotgun rested under his shoe.

In a whirlwind of trouble, she reached for the nine. At close range, the pistol would do some damage. Training kicked in, but at a noticeable disadvantage, she doubted she could take the man down. Instead, she twisted away.

He swung the second time.

Riley pulled the trigger. Being big did not give him a disadvantage to being fast. The monster dodged the shot.

Ironic, here she stood in a parking lot, fighting for her life. He lunged at her. She thanked God for adrenaline because the surge racing through her veins allowed her the strength to go midair.

12

A rush of fresh air intertwined with the wind forced a handful of orange-colored leaves into a colorful miniature swirling tornado. Above, a push of wind shook the tree line as it pressed through limbs and into steady gusts. Some remaining foliage rustled in playful harmony, holding onto their branches in some unseen magnetic pull. The sound of a horse's hooves hitting occasional rocks joined the chorus of forest chatter. An occasional snorting and breath expelled from Sam added tempo to the melody.

Jack pushed the horse, fighting back the sick feeling in his stomach and taking pleasure out of the ride. Hooves under long strides struck the dry ground, crushing dry leaves underneath them.

The gelding's ears laid back in irritation. Jack placed no blame on the horse's attitude as steam rolled off the still damp coat from the unplanned return journey. He urged Sam on passing places they stopped not a few hours ago. The horse sensing Jack's unease, pushed forward, dodging rocks and branches, keeping steady quick footing.

Clouds increased overhead. Thunder sounded, and the smell of rain filled the air promising the coming of a storm Arizona style. Jack looked upward, seeing the deep blue-gray moving fast over the horizon beyond the ridgeline. Thin fragments of lightning clapped overhead.

They were making good time dipping in and out of trails making the distance shorter than the way he'd come. Nevertheless, as the sun disappeared, the trail darkened, making it hard to see. Sam slowed, ears pricked forward. Jack never saw her until it was too late. The woman stumbled from behind a mound of boulders. Her bare feet scraped over the dry grass as she collided with man and horse. Sam's front shoulder brushed her side, and a mass of brown tangled hair slipped past him.

The horse scrambled to keep his footing, blowing hard through his nose, excited. Jack moved with him, and then Sam stopped lifting his head high and snorted again, but this time much louder.

The woman held her position, her hands up over her face, not five feet from the horse's hooves. Sam calmed, and the woman slowly climbed to her feet. She did not say a word but instead put a finger to her lips, asking him to be silent. He gave a slight nod.

NOT ALONE

"Bitch..." A man's voice boomed, then a long pause followed. "I'm not done with you!"

Long strands of brown hair hung in a tangled mess covering the woman's dirt-stained face. Blood flecked her lips, and bruises branded her face. Wide-eyed with fear, she shifted, pulling on her bloody torn shirt. Thin, far too light for her height and frame, the woman clutched the material of her shirt in her hands. Jack raised his hands, gesturing he would not hurt her, thinking the woman might flee.

Jack dismounted. "How many?"

She said nothing. Jack stepped away from her but stopped when she grabbed his arm. She held up three fingers.

"He's coming," she whispered. "You'll need more than that." She stared at the rifle in his hands. A slight drop of blood formed on her lips and rolled down her chin.

"I don't think so."

In the distance, the trespasser whistled as he made his way through the trees. Thunder rolled overhead. The woman trembled and stepped to the side. A long strand of lightning split off into several fingers, far from the ground. Jack pointed at her and then to the boulders. Not in a position to argue, she crouched down behind the largest.

The trespasser, whistling, grew closer. Once in view, Jack could see the rifle in one hand and a chain in the other. He wore a stained and torn dark hoodie.

Jack frowned. The quiet streak was over.

A camouflage baseball cap worn low over his forehead kept the stranger's face shadowed. His size was apparent the closer he got to Jack. A worthy opponent. Without any hesitance, the man stopped twenty feet from Jack.

"This is private property," Jack said. "Pack up and get off."

"Nothing is private anymore, partner. Haven't you heard?"

"I heard there are no more laws. And I'm not your partner."

"My point exactly. Have you seen a kitty running through here? It seems I've lost her?"

"Get the fuck off my property!" Jack said, patience growing thin.

The sun peeked through a bundle of clouds casting light on the man's face. Deep scars ran the length from his chin to his brow bone. Another crack of thunder released as a black cloud engulfed the sky, shadowing the man's face once again.

"You don't want this trouble," the trespasser warned. "I'm not leaving without her."

"Then, you're not leaving. As you can see, I have plenty of room for growing daisies."

More thunder. Jack raised his rifle, irritated. His property was becoming a graveyard. A twisted strand of white light popped from the sky, snaking. Jack ignored Mother Nature's fireworks and waited for an answer.

The shot came from the timber. The bullet hit Jack in the shoulder, spinning him around. Jack aimed his Beretta at the tree line and fired. While at the same time, he pulled out a pistol to keep Scar Face, who was now aiming his rifle in Jack's direction, at bay.

"Where is she?"

Jack said nothing.

Scar Face waited.

Today wasn't Jack's day to die.

The trespasser focused on the blood soaking through Jack's shirt, but Jack's expression remained steady.

"Man, you're hit," Scar Face said sarcastically.

"Last time, get the fuck off my property."

Scar Face turned his attention past Jack and onto the vast desert. "Here, kitty, kitty. Time to go home to your papa." The trespasser fixated his gaze back on Jack. "I'm tired, and I want the woman."

Jack didn't feel like digging a hole today. Though he felt one coming when the man began to swing the heavy chain in his hands. The movement to the trigger would be delayed by momentum, giving Jack time to avoid more bullets. Not in the mood for game playing, Jack was about to give him a taste of the .357 when another shot rang out. Scar-Face swung the chain. Jack pulled the trigger, and Scar-Face dropped all weapons.

Whoever was shooting from the mound of boulders was a horrible shot because the shooter's bullet, intended for Jack, hit Scar-Face in the chest. Blood sprayed, and material exploded. The man fell dead against him. With one push, Jack let him fall to the ground, and then he sprinted behind a set of smooth boulders, tearing off his long-sleeved shirt to keep the trespasser's blood from soaking into his open wound. It'd be a chilly ride back with one sleeve missing and his coat on the woman. One last detail before they headed for the ranch, he planned to make sure there were no return visitors.

Jack scanned the area where the shots had come, catching a glimpse of blue and black running in the opposite direction. Jack stood and watched the figure disappear and then returned to the dead man on the ground. He wanted to be sure this one was deceased. When he felt no pulse, he searched him for any other weapons only to find an old piece of candy, tobacco, and a wad of cash. Jack tossed the chain, took the trespasser's rifle, and walked away.

"I'll put asshole on your headstone." Becoming an expert at digging graves and trying to keep the property secure, Jack knew he'd have to bury the dead later. For now, the woman was more important, and this guy wasn't going anywhere.

He heard Sam fuss, and as the gelding stepped into sight, Jack knew why. In the saddle, the woman kicked and urged Sam forward, but the gelding refused to move. Going nowhere fast, she slid from the horse, almost falling to the ground, and started to stumble away. Jack slipped the rifle into its sheath.

"Wait."

He withdrew his pistol and moved toward the woman, but she darted into the brush, scrambling to stay upright. She faltered, caught herself, and ran. Looking upward at the darkening sky, Jack sighed. The storm would not be as kind as he had been, and the temperatures were sure to drop.

Swearing under his breath, he just wanted to get home. Irritated, he kicked rocks with the toe of his boot but stopped, hearing footsteps behind him. The woman stepped out into the open, took a step, and then fell to the ground.

"Can you ride?" He looked down at her.

She pushed herself up, but her arms failed. Jack learned a long time ago not to trust anyone, especially a wounded woman. He winced as he picked her up and carried her to Sam.

"Put this around you, he said, trying to wrap his coat around her."Rin..." she muttered.

Once on Sam, she was dead weight in his arms. He struggled to keep them both from falling to the ground. His shirt, wet with fresh blood from his wounds, was another cause for discomfort. Worse than the trouble in his arms, the feeling there had been trouble at home remained.

The ride back quickly became fast and awkward. The load of the woman restricted his movement, and the sound of Sam's hooves flicking rock and sand pounded in his thoughts. Even with the additional weight, the horse never broke his gait. The beat of his strides joined the clamor of the thunder above. The wind picked up several miles from the ranch making the last part of their trip a cold one. Fingers of white light struck near the path they were on, exploding treetops into tiny shards of kindling. As rain fell, lightning subsided, and the thunder uncorked one last rumble. They were about to get even wetter.

They rode the last mile in a downpouring of rain. Nothing on Jack, the woman, or Sam seemed dry. The first red flag, Sadie and Tank, failed to meet him at the fence. The two Ridgebacks were good guard dogs. They should have heard Jack coming, regardless of the storm. No barking was the indicator he didn't want.

Dismounting, Jack slipped down from the wet horse first. Gathering the woman in his arms, he moved toward the double doors of the barn with a gun in hand. Sam followed. His reins still looped around the horn of the saddle. The woman wrapped her fingers around his neck while long strands of wet, tangled hair hid her face.

He'd lost blood, causing him to misstep. Kicking the barn doors open, Jack stepped into the breezeway straight into the barrel of the end of a rifle. As Ben came into the light, Jack saw the anger in the old man's eyes.

"Pop," Jack lowered his voice.

His father lowered the rifle, all the while wearing a worried expression. Then, he swung the gun around and pointed it at the woman.

"No, pop, it's okay."

"Ryan's been shot. Lynn's hurt pretty bad. Nick's doing his best." Ben's voice crackled. "Who's she?"

"I don't know yet. Are you okay, pop?" asked Jack, stepping past the old man. The air smelled of leather, ointments, and hay.

"Yep!" Ben rubbed his head. "Got a good lump on the head."

Jack laid the woman down and covered her. As much as he wanted to sprint to the house, he needed to handle one thing at a time. Ben moved aside while Jack pulled some canned food from the cupboard and handed it to the old man.

"I knew something was wrong," Jack looked back at the woman curled into a ball on the couch. "I should've stayed home. Can you feed her if she wakes up? I have a feeling she hasn't eaten in a while."

Ben nodded, keeping his rifle in his hand.

"Men were chasing her. I got all but one."

Their father grunted. Ben's cantankerous character typically kept trespassers at bay, but he might scare the woman when she woke to find the old man's face glued to hers. She might try to run again.

Jack reloaded both the rifle and pistol and then stopped. "Don't scare her."

"You're bleeding," Ben pointed at his shoulder. "Get in line. Nick will stitch you up too."

13

Riley could not breathe. Something dense and bitter smelling held her down. She opened her eyes, seeing a fuzzy outline of someone or something moving over her. Riley withdrew her pistol. A small voice, angelic and soft, spoke to her.

"Riley, help me push him off," Utah tugged on the man's arm.

Riley heard material rip as the man's body shifted. "Careful," Riley choked, setting her pistol down to help.

"One, two, three," Utah whispered. The monster's thick, foul-smelling body rolled off Riley, and air rushed into her lungs. She choked a few coughs back, fearing she might lose the cranberries in her stomach.

Utah knelt next to her. Riley saw Megan pressed to the inside the cab window though everything looked blurry.

"Shit, he smells like sh... poop," Riley stopped. Utah's gaze held hers, holding onto every word she said, keeping Riley's words proper.

"Are you all right?" asked Utah, pointing to Riley's face.

Riley reached up, her fingers connecting with blood and flesh.

"I'm calling the manager. This store is not customer friendly." Riley said, trying to kneel, but the world spun around her. Swaying, she reached out to catch herself, but Utah knelt to help her. *An angel,* Riley thought as she climbed to her feet, leaning against the truck for support. The ground slowed down, and the merry-go-round stopped. "Let's get out of here."

Riley's fingers shook as she recovered the shotgun and found the truck door. The air inside the cab warmed her. The day turned to late afternoon, and night closed in too fast.

"You stink," Megan leaned forward. Her big blue eyes had traces of tears. "Can I have some more of that minty stuff?" she asked.

Riley brushed a curl away from her forehead and handed her the Vicks vapor rub. "You okay?"

"We've seen monsters before," remarked Megan.

"I'm sure you have." *I didn't want to fight a monster today and not in front of you girls.*

"We know," said Utah.

Riley looked at Utah in curiosity before she turned away.

"It's okay," whispered Utah, finding something to press against the cut on Riley's cheek. "It's bleeding pretty good."

Retracing the path to the 101, they drove a short distance before turning into a town nestled near the ocean. Below steep mountain walls, rows of torn tents and canopies lay strewn and ripped apart in state campgrounds. Weather battered camping gear, and everlasting RVers sat entombed in their million-dollar worlds and expensive motor homes.

"Free camping for life," muttered Riley.

The sheriff's hub was large enough to hide them from the road while allowing them easy escape if need be. She parked under the eaves of the building nestled to the rolling doors far away from any more carnage. Close to the sand, Riley unloaded the Wildcat. Hurrying to beat the dark, Riley gathered a sleeping Megan into the trailer. At the same time, Max leaped from the cab toward brush to do some much-needed business.

"We can rest here tonight."

Megan mumbled something and then nestled closer to her. The cold coastal air held moisture like a sponge. Riley found herself hugging Megan tight, sharing body warmth. Inside the trailer, it felt like a refrigerator until the furnace caught up, and they began to feel the heat.

Under soft light, Riley analyzed the wound on her face. The gash on her cheek looked to be a good four inches of opened flesh and in need of stitches.

"I can help," Utah poked her head in through the door motioning Riley to the table where a steaming hot pan of water, a washcloth, and first aid kit sat. Pressing the warm cloth on the wound, Utah began to wipe the blood away.

"I found Peroxide in the bathroom," Utah poured the peroxide on the wound. The liquid hit the injury, producing a hot searing sensation, causing Riley to jump. Then the door rattled. Utah jumped.

"Max," grimaced Riley, catching the bottle before it fell to the floor.

Utah opened the door. Max leaped into the trailer, bypassing the steps scrambling to keep his feet under him.

"Pussy," grinned Riley.

Twenty minutes later, and with Utah's help, Riley had four butterfly stitches keeping the gash closed. Even with the blood gone, the rest of her stunk, and her head ached. Taking a shower would tap their water supply, but a washcloth cleanup might erase the blood covering her.

Riley shivered as she scrubbed on her skin, exhausted and sore. Rethinking a better way to clean up tomorrow, she slipped into fresh clothes before sitting down at the table. Three aspirins, tomato soup, bottled water, and a bottle of wine sat on the table, waiting for her.

Curled side by side, Utah, and Megan snuggled under equal blankets. Riley smiled, wincing at the pain. A child had taken better care of her than her husband ever did. Hell, Mark would have told the girls to get out of the truck the moment he saw them. He would have left them there, alone. She poured a glass of wine, drank it, and then poured another. Max, no longer angry, kept the side of her leg warm.

"Mark would have never allowed you," she stroked the cat's soft fur while resting her head on her hand.

"Riley. Go lie down with Megan. I'll stay awake." Utah sat down next to Max and looked over at a boxed puzzle sitting on the table. "Megan's warm. She won't mind if you curl up next to her."

Riley's legs and hands tingled from sleeping in such an awkward position. Megan never stirred as Riley pushed her way in behind the little girl and laid her head on the plush pillow. Her head ached, and as fast as she fell asleep, someone woke her to morning.

"It's dawn," Utah's face came into sight as her eyes adjusted to the light.

The glow of morning filtered through the windows. In Riley's fuzzy mind and deceptive dreams, she heard a motorcycle. For the first time in over a year, nightmares escaped her.

"You still stink," Megan stood dressed and ready. "You need a bath."

"Okay then," Riley looked at Megan, trying to focus on the bright t-shirt and a neon green skirt. To add to her chosen wardrobe, Megan wore purple tights and glowing pink tennis shoes. Riley smiled.

"You like it?" Megan twirled around.

"Oh my, yes," laughed Riley, taming the stinging in her face.

Riley grabbed fresh clothes, feeling as though she'd endured the complete cycle of a commercial washer.

"I found these," Utah handed Riley a black case.

"This is a great find," Riley thumbed through the CD case. The girls did a little happy dance knowing the DVD player in the truck would pass away miles of boredom. To make the day even better, Utah handed Riley a cup of coffee.

"Thank you."

"She used to fix mama's coffee for her. Mama said she made the best coffee in the world," informed Megan. "I tossed your jacket. The monster's blood was all over it."

"Well, I agree with your mama! The good news is there's a fresh lake. The bad news is we'll have to cross the sand to get there." Riley waited. What kid didn't like sand? Megan's heart-shaped lips formed into a smile.

"Can we take that black spider?" she pointed out the window. "Looks like a spider."

"It's a Wildcat."

"Why is it, wild?" she asked. "It looks like a spider."

NOT ALONE

A ride on the sand would be a treat for the girls and her. More than likely, having never experienced anything like the coastal dunes, but Riley had and not so long ago. Having some fun would not kill them, or at least she hoped it wouldn't but not before swallowing three more ibuprofens and eating a handful of jerky.

There was no sign of life. There were no tracks on the sand, no other riders. Riley gambled the truck, and the trailer would be safe. Once they hit the sand and minus thousands of people, she felt an incredible sensation of what used to be. One person who kept tugging on her memory was Eric. She missed Eric.

14

Jack felt Lynn's body tremble under his hold. Hot tears spilled down her cheeks onto his t-shirt. She pulled back, drying her bruised eyes, and looked up at him. Thinking about what might have happened to his family made him angry. He'd taken several men out only hours ago, and already he sought to kill another. Jack had never seen his sister bruised and battered, and her condition made him sick. His family was his priority, and he felt deep guilt because his absence had come at the wrong time.

Kneeling next to her, he placed a hand on her knee. "How many?"

"Five, Ryan said he got three out of the five. Six?" Her voice trembled. "They wanted guns."

"I should've been here."

"This is not your fault, Jack, and you're bleeding." She reached up and pulled back his shirt.

"I'm okay."

"I got Lily into the safe room in time." Lynn closed her eyes for a second. "Ryan."

"Nick is with him." He took her hand. "Lynn, you need to be strong now, for Lily. She needs her mama. I need you. I brought a woman back with me. She's hurt and needs some help."

"Where is she?"

"She's with pop."

"Jesus, Jack." Lynn sprang to life, climbing to her feet. "Bring her to the main house. She can stay in the spare room."

Jack nodded. "Okay. I need to see Ryan and Nick first. Will you be okay?"

"I'll get the room ready," she answered and then stopped. "Ryan saved my life."

Jack stood up, taming his anger at what could've happened. Nothing he could say would make either of them feel any better, but he knew a distraction for her would help. He stopped at the doorway.

"Nothing happened." Lynn knew to ease his assumptions before he left.

The quiet in the house hummed like a million ants marching to their last dinner. Hidden in dark spaces, the smells of a hospital stung the family with a sterile reality of the passing violence. Jack covered his face with a mask, gloved his hands, and feet with sterile fabric before stepping into the room dedicated to surgeries.

Nick stopped when Jack entered and dropped several bloody gauzes into a bag. He then looked at Jack with concern.

No movement came from Ryan, only the soft beep of his heartbeat echoing from the wires hooked from his chest to the heart monitor.

"He's stable. The bullet missed his heart but broke a piece of a rib, tearing his lung. He has some broken ribs and a gunshot wound to his right shoulder. He'll have the chest tube for a few days. He was lucky. Damn lucky."

"Thank you, Nick. I had a feeling something was wrong."

"Unless you're psychic, you can't predict these things. We've taken precautions, and until now, it's worked."

"Lynn?" Jack rubbed his chin.

"She'll be okay, Jack."

"If they would've... " Nick stopped his brother-in-law mid-sentence.

"She's a Colton. Stronger than you or I know," Nick tossed another handful of bloody gauze into the bag. "You had better get used to it. There's more riffraff than good out there. Whatever caused all this could happen again." Nicked grabbed a package of sterile instruments. "Now, I need to stitch Lynn up."

"I wish I'd been here."

Nick patted Jack on the shoulder and sighed, "I wish I'd been here as well."

"I need an army to put this place back together."

"Don't give up the fight, Jack, because of this. We need you, and this town needs you. Build an army. If anyone can do it, you can."

"Thanks for the confidence, Doc."

"You're welcome. Now, where is Lily Bean?" asked Nick, changing the subject.

Something rustled behind Jack, and he turned. Lily was tapping her lips with her finger. "Uncle Jack." She rushed to him and put her arms around him tightly. "Bad men were here, and Ryan and mama got hurt."

"It's okay, Lily. Your daddy fixed them all better." Jack winked at Nick. Nick shuffled Lily to the door.

"Hey, Doc, I have another patient for you. I'll bring her over to the house after you're done with Lynn." Jack turned to Lily, brushing the tight curls away from her face. Her cheeks puffed up into a pout, and her small fingers pointed at his shirt.

"You're hurt, too," she murmured.

Nick turned to Jack. "I'll see you shortly."

Jack smiled at Lily, blowing her a kiss. She caught it and blew a kiss back to him. Nick stepped out the door with the medical bag tucked under his arm and Lily at his side. Jack turned to his younger brother, who began to stir.

"I got all six of em," reminded Ryan. "Pops?"

"Pop is more cantankerous than ever," Jack grinned. "Rest, buddy. I need you back on your feet."

"Pushy son of a bitch, aren't you?" snorted Ryan. "Lynn?"

"She's fine," but Ryan had already fallen back asleep.

Jack often forgot how kick-ass Ryan could be. Looking at him here asleep, engulfed with IVs and bandages, gave way to his vulnerabilities as a human. The bond between the two of them was strong. Ryan was the charmer in the family, smooth with the women, and always there to lend a helping hand when someone needed it. However, Ryan, a better long-distance shot than Jack, also had an unusual knack for taking on guys twice his size and usually coming out unscathed. Not today. Ryan would make it through this round, but he'd need some time to heal.

Stepping into the hallway, Jack slipped into the guestroom, leaving the door ajar. The woman he'd brought home lay in the bed. Her face, free of all blood and dirt, appeared delicate. She wore an expression of peace, not terror he'd seen earlier, as she slept. He stepped to get a closer look. She looked different than the woman he'd ran into on the path. There were stitches in her lip and soft yellow bruises forming under darker ones.

Tossing a blanket on the chair next to the bed, drained and a little light-headed, Jack stood. Between the dim light and the warmth, he felt some comfort under all the pain.

Nick would be looking for him. He had replaced his bloodstained shirt with a new one, but it turned red too. Uncaring, Jack slipped down into the chair, gazing at the woman sleeping. For a moment, he forgot the hurt. Not realizing how much blood he had lost, he closed his eyes and fell into a sleep where dreams often became nightmares.

15

Clean, recharged, and ready to get the hell out of Oregon, Riley and the girls were back on the road by noon. A black bear and her cubs held up traffic for a few minutes, and then a five-car pileup in the northbound lane blocking the southbound lane. No one waited in front or back of her, so Riley played demolition derby until she cleared the road, which included ramming a sheriff's car. She apologized silently and steered the truck and trailer through a small opening, taking them to another wreck. A blanket of spilled contents, bottled water included, littered the highway free for the taking.

Riley found the middle lane driver, torso, and limbs ripped apart by wild animals. Before Riley could cover the grotesque scene, Megan, paying no attention to the dead man, ventured into the debris a few feet from him. Turning her back to his upturned face, she knelt beside a box of toys. Occasionally, she glanced back to be sure the dead failed to walk. After careful inspection of the toys, Megan stood up and held a Barbie doll in her hand for Riley to see. Riley felt a deep sadness, children walking among dead people, surviving pit maneuvers in cars, and looting in stores full of corpses. All the while, Megan seemed unaffected. Riley planned to change that.

The girl's resilience and self-sufficiency astounded her. Having bounced back from misfortunes, the girls needed to feel safe again. Most of all, they needed to be children.

With each town entered, Riley hoped to see life if only one person. The small city of Florence, on an average day, would be bustling with locals and tourists. The town looked dead, literally. Riley took the exit leading toward bigger cities. So far, the only troubles they had faced were exotic animals and a store with a monster.

Riley believed the freeway would lead to an extensive set of problems depending on where survivors fled. It was possible and reasonable for people to turn to populated places for supplies and companionship.

Leaving the coastline where ghosts lingered and an occasional infected squatted in shopping centers, they began the trek toward Arizona. The days on the coast grew colder, and night temperatures dropped into the mid-forties. They needed a place to stay, a place safe enough where they could rest. They needed propane for the trailer for the lengthier sections of desolation between towns.

"Girls, start looking for a road or lane."

"There," Utah pointed.

The paved road ended where a dirt one began, but the truck pulled the toy hauler with little effort. It would be a blessing if the trailer got them to Arizona, but even without it, they could find shelter in abandoned homes and barns along the way.

They came to a ground-level log home, nestled and hidden, in the timberline bordered an RV garage. The cabin, concealed by a messy yard, revealed a chimney. The place appeared uninhabited.

Yes, warmth for the night! Riley thought, looking at the chimney.

"I need to check the house out. You two okay here?" Riley asked the girls. They nodded. Riley tucked her pistol into her holster and then reached for the shotgun, a few more shells, and a mini-flashlight.

"We'll honk if we see anything... monsters mostly," Megan said. She climbed to her knees to see over the dashboard.

Riley grinned, enjoying both the girl's company. "Lock the doors."

It'd be dark soon, and Riley wanted to secure the house as fast as possible. She moved from the garage to the side door. Nothing would open. Climbing over limbs and debris, she stepped to the front of the house only to find a locked door. Riley sighed, road tired and leg cramped. She wanted to get some rest.

Where is the hidden key?

The rocks near the porch produced no key. Next planters and doormat, but Riley saw nothing. When she glanced back to check on the girls, Utah pointed at a tilted sign on the side of the house. It read "Welcome."

"It couldn't be that easy," Riley spoke in a soft tone.

Leaning across unruly hedges, she lifted the wood. Hanging on the nail, a single key attached to fishing line.

"How did Utah know, or was that just a good guess?" Riley said to herself as she unlocked the door.

As the sun lowered, the light from her flashlight lit up the foyer, surrounding rooms, and into the living room. The floor plan and the furnishings hinted at careful planning and meticulous decorating. It smelled dusty, but everything inside appeared untouched. Her guess, it was a vacation home, now abandoned and not used in a long time. There were three rooms, which included the master bedroom and two bathrooms. Outfitted with the best appliances money could buy, the kitchen opened into a modern dining room. A large stone fireplace held a large flat-screen TV facing a sectional couch. It all looked expensive as it did comfortable. Inside, towels, extra bedding, and a well-equipped kitchen were treasures for sure.

Riley started a fire with the complimentary wood stacked inside the house. She headed out to the garage with the keys to get the girls and park the truck and trailer.

A throaty rumble from the line of growing shadows of timber stopped her short of the truck. Standing to the side of the garage, camouflaged in overgrowth, stood a pair of black bears. The bears were plump, packed with solid fat, with thick fur necessary for winter warmth. The bigger of the two bears grunted, swiping paws against the ground. The bears lifted their noses, catching Riley's scent.

The sow shifted and sent a warning snort.

That's when the cubs bounded into view, becoming Riley's worst nightmare. Wore out and hungry, a chilled breeze infiltrated narrow openings in her clothing, causing her to shiver. She thought of the fire.

"Great. Tigers and bears!"

Her finger rested on the trigger of her shotgun, not wanting to have to pull the trigger. "Keep moving. I have no beef with you.

The mama bear reared up, standing on two legs, ready to protect her cubs. When the truck door opened, Riley scrambled to safety. The girls, entertained, cheered for her, which distracted the bears, buying her time.

The bears, curious to the noise, stood watching but for one cub who bolted forward. Mama bear would be right behind the youngster. Riley bounded toward the truck. She tucked the shotgun close to her as she dove into the cab, escaping an inevitable attack. As the door shut, the cub collided into the fender, rocking the truck slightly.

The sow closed the distance between her and the truck, rising on hind feet to peer into the driver's side window. Frosted air floated from the bear's nostrils producing a circular pattern of fog on the window.

"That was close," Utah's expression of astonishment faded into relief.

"Too close."

"You should've seen your face," Utah grinned.

Megan stared at Riley with wide eyes.

"Scared, huh?" Riley saw a flicker of a smile on Utah's face, and she nodded. The bears grew uninterested, moving back into the timberline. "Let's park this beast and go get warm."

Sometime in the night, Riley woke with Megan curled under her arms and Max burrowed between them. Riley listened to Megan's breathing and Max's snoring, keeping the pistol under the pillow and the shotgun next to the bed for safety.

The girls were changing her, forcing her to rethink priorities. Mark had been a game-changer when it came to having children. In the beginning, she felt the desire to be a mother, but then she met the actual Mark, and she became dead set against it.

Megan stirred under her arm, a small cry escaping her lips. Her legs jerked in slight movements as if trying to avoid monsters chasing her in dreams. Dreams had their way of staying alive, especially with all the horror witnessed days before the Shift and now post-Shift.

"It's okay, Megan," she whispered.

Megan stopped, and Riley pressed her face closer to Megan's curly dark hair, closing her eyes. The mere fact two children survived months without an adult made her head spin. They had walked the same path she had, alone and afraid. She wanted to keep Megan and Utah, but the girls belonged with surviving relatives if there were any.

As if sensing her thoughts while sleeping, Utah moved a little closer to her. Riley felt a heightened sense of security. For the first time in many years, she fell asleep feeling complete.

16

"Good morning, Jack."

Jack woke to Lynn's voice. His last memory found him sitting in the chair next to the woman's bed. Now, he lay in his bed surrounded by pillows and warm to the core. He shifted, remembering yesterday's events, feeling his wounds.

"I didn't want to wake you, but Nick said you needed to eat," Lynn said, setting the tray on the nightstand. The smell of bacon and coffee filled the room.

"I smell the coffee. Bacon, eggs, and toast."

"You've got a good nose on you, Jack Colton," she teased, pushing the coffee closer to him. "At least that isn't broken."

"And you make an excellent nurse. Mom always said...," Lynn cut him off.

"I should've been a nurse," she finished the sentence for him. Her voice steadied, and her eyebrows creased. "Well, I got a house full of patients now. She's probably smiling down on me. She must be. The sun was out for the better part of the day."

"How long was I asleep?" He turned toward the covered window and then to the bright glow coming from the fireplace across from his bed. "It's still night."

"Nick took the bullet out and put you back together. Then you slept through the evening and all day. You're not Superman, Jack."

Jack's stomach growled, and the smell of the food made his mouth water. He used his uninjured shoulder to prop himself upright. The bandages on his wound crinkled under pressure, and the surgical tape pulled on his skin.

"Nope! I'm not Superman."

Lynn lifted a pillow setting it behind his back. "I thought you might enjoy the breakfast more than a sandwich."

"How's Ryan? The woman?"

"Ryan's on the mend. He won't be up and around for a few more days. Nick has him getting up, but just to the bathroom and back, and Shay is remarkable."

"Shay?"

"The woman! Shay. She's lucky you found her." Lynn sat down next to the bed, her fingers holding her side. The bruises on her face were already taking on a change of colors.

"You? Is anyone taking care of you?"

She smiled. "Ben is doing the bloody laundry, and I do mean bloody. Nick won't let me lift anything over a pound, and Lily cooked your eggs, so I'd watch for shells."

Jack grinned. "You're just like mom."

"Did Shay tell you why she was running?" Lynn wrung her hands, and Jack could see she wanted to talk about it.

"I'm assuming it has something to do with the fertilizer I'll be planting between here and the lake house."

"The night after the Shift, she and her fiancé were in an accident. Someone rammed their car. Those men took her, and she never saw her fiancé again."

"Where is this going, Lynn?" Jack sensed there was more, and he'd hear it whether he wanted to or not.

"She was five weeks pregnant when a man named Ringo kidnapped her and held her prisoner with other women during that time she had a son?"

"Where's the kid?

"Ringo has him. He believes Jonah is his?"

"Why didn't she take the kid when she ran?" Frustrated, he tried to piece together the puzzle.

"Ringo wasn't there. He left one of his men in charge, and they decided they wanted something to hunt. The way she tells it, hunting humans is a game to them."

Jack said nothing because hearing the name Ringo brought back a ring of familiarity. Still, he could not put his finger on it.

"So six other women are being held as prisoners. Three of them are under sixteen."

"Six?"

"Six plus, Jonah," she repeated.

"Jonah?"

"Her son."

Another strand of silence followed before Jack spoke. "Where's the house?"

"I didn't ask, but she's going back for her son."

Jack set his fork on his plate, not as hungry as he first had been. The warmth of the room engulfed him, and still, he felt a chill.

Lynn stood, looking at Jack's plate. "Done? You had better get some rest. Oh, Lily wanted me to give you this. She came in a few hours ago, but you were still asleep." Lynn said, handing him a paper.

NOT ALONE

The drawing showed seven people holding hands, and a big sun shone over what looked like a ranch house with stick horses and cows, all comprised of an array of colors. Jack smiled. His sister knew him well. With a full stomach and thoughts playing in his head, for now, he melted down into the pillows. He watched the glow of the fire until sleep took him once more.

17

The fading contrast of morning light darkened under Jack's troubling thoughts. The team's job was to help people, which included trying to rescue the women held captive.

With Ryan down and Lynn wounded, they were going to need help. Nick and Ben picked up the slack on the chores, but even they would struggle to keep up. If they wanted to keep their stock, he'd have to beef up the security and find some help. To add to his list of concerns, Christmas loomed days away. Though the family had suffered an attack, holidays remained a constant on the calendar, and Lynn would expect a Christmas tree.

Jack sat with Ryan, who looked no worse for what he'd incurred. Wanting to tease him, Jack thought twice about it, not wanting him to bust stitches. Thankful to see him awake and talking, his brother's eyes already held a hint of mischief.

Nick stepped into the room, smiling. "I swear your sister makes the best damn coffee."

"No one will argue that," agreed Jack. "So, Doc, it seems the youngest Colton is trying to get out of his chores."

"Bring it on," Ryan grimaced.

"You won't be running any races, kid. I stitched you, inside and out."

"Chicks dig scars. Right?" he kidded. "Awe, get me the Superglue. That'll hold me together."

"I used Superglue, but that doesn't mean it won't rip open. You were lucky! I swear you Colton's have nine lives." Nick looked at the two men and frowned. "What's going on, Jack?"

"A rescue plan."

"Your sister told me you'd probably do it."

"I want to talk to the woman, Shay, first."

"Be gentle, Jack. She's wounded inside and out."

"Despite what other women have said about me, I can be sensitive."

"Ryan can't go," Nick added. "Just in case you're thinking about it, Ryan."

"I know," Ryan looked at his brother. "Call in the boys. Be sure to take Blake. He's a good kid."

Jack nodded. "Good idea. I also want a few extra men here while I'm gone."

"Ben won't like it," Nick remarked, knowing his father-in-law well.

NOT ALONE

"He never does." Jack glanced at his brother. "We've built a good team over the past couple of years, you and me."

"Maybe you should run for Mayor. That'd make pops happy." Ryan grinned. "Hell, you'd have my vote."

Nick chuckled. "It'd be one way to meet a nice woman."

"Speaking of women, Nick. Is Shay up?" asked Jack, changing the subject quickly.

"She's with Lynn and Lily."

Jack patted his brother, soft like, on the chest. "Rest. One day at a time, okay."

The desert skies greeted Jack as he stepped out into the cool morning air. Lavender and blue streaks dipped and swirled through a current of gold on the horizon. The sun, barely crested over the mountain line, promised yet another cold day. Around him, silhouettes of deep canyons carved in sand and stone crested toward the illuminant sky.

As the chilled breeze caught his breath, a cloud of frost beat him to the barn's double doors leading to the breezeway. Sam neighed, hanging his head out the stall door opening. Much warmer inside

Jack set his coffee next to Sam's stall and rubbed the horse's forehead.

"Thanks, friend, for getting us back safe," he said, scratching behind the horse's ears. Sam closed his eyes and stretched his neck out. An older tomcat jumped down at Jack's feet, interrupting them. The horse reached down, nudging the cat with his nose. Jack chuckled.

"You keeping the mice at bay?"

"Best mouse hunter on the ranch. I'll be sorry when he passes." The old man said from somewhere inside the barn. He heard several whispers and then a slight giggle. "He dropped a mouse at my door this morning. A gift. You want it?"

"No, thanks, Pops. It's for you."

Lily's voice touched his ears before she appeared atop Ben's shoulders. "Faster, grandpa, faster."

Ben grunted, setting the girl onto the ground. The gruffness in his face returned, and he frowned at Jack.

"Feedings are done," grumbled Ben. Lynn and Shay appeared from behind. "I think the women get it done better than you."

"Thanks, pops. I'm sure they do."

"Papa, be nice," Lynn took the carton of eggs from Shay. "I'm going to get breakfast started."

"I'll help." The woman Jack now knew to be Shay started to move.

"You stay."

Shay stiffened.

"He only looks scary. It's okay." Lynn patted Shay on the shoulder. "He doesn't bite."

"Okay, Lily, let's go help your mama with some breakfast," Ben scooped the little girl back onto his back.

"But I want to stay with Uncle Jack," she squealed.

"I need some pancakes," chuckled Ben, giving the girl a buck like a horse. She bounced up and down, giggled, and held on. Lily's laughter trailed them as they headed out the door toward the house.

The space between them got uncomfortable and quiet. Jack looked at Shay.

"Coffee?"

She nodded.

She looked different this morning.

Her hair brushed out, looked longer. There was also a sparkle shining in her almond-shaped eyes. With the swelling decreased, her skin reflected an olive color. The bruises hid her beauty within, but he could see it. He led her to the studio apartment.

Jack handed her a cup of coffee before he sat down across from her. At first, they said nothing. He found it was easy to look at her, but he shifted his gaze, not wanting to frighten her.

"Lynn told you?"

"Saving the world is on Lynn's to-do list," he sipped his coffee.

"I have to get my son."

What mother wouldn't try to recover her child? Shay would go back and fight to rescue her son, and she would die trying.

"Jonah is all I have left."

Jack said nothing.

"If I hadn't run, they would've killed me. He won't hurt Jonah because he thinks Jonah's his, but he isn't."

"I believe you?"

She lowered her eyes. "You killed Ringo's best man. Ringo will come after his property if only to kill me and for revenge."

"You're someone's property?"

"No, but he thinks I am. He really only wants Jonah."

"What do you know about this, Ringo?"

"I've been imprisoned by him for a few years now. He's nothing but a maggot to me." She wrapped her hands around her cup. "This may sound odd. Make me sound crazy, but he's not like you or me. He's different in a scary way."

"How?" Jack took a deep breath. He'd already put his family and the ranch at risk by getting involved. He wished he and Shay never crossed paths. He found it hard to walk away from trouble when it came to people, but this was all part of putting things back together. "Some helpful information, please," Jack felt a wave of anger rise within him. "Like you, my family means everything to me. If I'm involved in a fight coming this way, I need to know everything to stop it. Are we clear?"

She looked at him, her eyes filling with tears. It set him back a few beats.

"It's almost like he's not human," she lowered her voice.

"Not human?"

"I didn't ask you to kill anyone. Hell, I didn't even ask you to bring me here. However, you did. I can't do anything about that."

"You're right," he answered. "However, I'm not one to leave a hurt person to the vultures. You were on foot? Hurt!"

"I ran until I reached that dirty little town. Idiots left the keys in one truck, so I drove it until it ran out of gas. I was nearly free."

"Without your boy?"

Jack could see the anger shine in her eyes. She was going to need that for what he had planned.

"I was going to get help. I had no idea. Everyone, in the real world, if that's what you want to call it, had gone completely insane," Shay paused.

"What highway were you on when you and your fiancé were attacked?"

"Route 66 and then 89."

"Town?" His anger subsided. She needed him, but now he needed her to protect his own family as well.

"I think it was Seligman."

"What did the house look like?"

"Log home. No one around for miles," she whispered. "They kept us in cells below the house."

He kept his eyes on her, reading her, watching for inconsistencies in her story, but none stood out, only fear.

"Ringo, he's in charge?"

"Yes. Ringo's three times more dangerous than the ones you killed." She leaned forward. "I stayed alive because he thought Jonah was his, but those girls back there won't be as lucky. He'll take Jonah when he feels threatened, and then I will never be able to find him."

Jack watched her, cursing her vulnerability because it made him want to help even more. He shoved his thoughts to the back of his mind, annoyed at the distraction.

"It was Ringo's boys who rammed our car a few days after the Shift occurred. I didn't know about the baby yet, so my fiancé never knew he would be a father. Those men left him to die. They took me to Ringo, and I've been a captive ever since." Unfortunately, he liked me. " I did what I needed to stay alive. He keeps a supply of women for his men."

"How many men?"

"15-20, maybe."

"How many, Shay?"

Her lips relaxed, and a hint of sophistication shone through. Jack could see she came from education as well as sophistication.

"I'll recover the women and your boy," Jack turned away from her. "But I need to know details to keep my team safe."

"I'm going with you," she whispered, "I don't think you can stop him by yourself."

"I've never failed a mission, Shay. Not going to start now."

"He wants what he can't have."

"What's that?"

"Jonah. Unlimited power."

"Why? The world is lawless. A person can have whatever they want, for free?" Unlimited power sounded supernatural, and for a moment, Jack thought maybe the blow to her head might have scrambled her thoughts.

"He's crazy and dangerous."

Jack disliked what he heard. He remembered the night of the Shift, and he never, before that night, thought a phenomenon like that could occur, but it did. Jack felt the strong unnatural pull when it happened. Since then, he'd seen many things, doing battle with the wickedest people, but he'd always turned the odds to his favor while hunting down the hunters.

"If we can find the town where you found the truck, we might be able to start there?"

She shook her head yes. "When those men kidnapped me, I'd only been to Prescott a few times. All I know is it's a little town out in the middle of nowhere. I'd never seen it before."

Jack stood up. "You need to write down everything you can remember on paper."

"Paper. Okay."

"We'll talk later. Breakfast should be ready, and you need to eat."

"I'm not hungry." She stood up, positioning her too close to where he stood.

The light of morning broke through the glass of the living room window revealing the secrets she could not hide. The scars on her face were visible under the glow and reflected abuse. A slight smell of lavender touched his nose. He held his ground, not interested in that way. She was younger than him, and she seemed vulnerable.

"Do you think your son is still at the house?" At the mention of her son, a spark ignited in her eyes.

"Yes."

"If you're going with me, you'll eat."

"Breakfast sounds good, then. Thank you."

"My pleasure."

"Do you believe in miracles?"

Jack stood still. Shay waited.

"I suppose so."

"We're going to need one," she whispered, stepping in closer.

"You don't owe me."

"Maybe I like you, Jack Colton," she said, turning away from him, reading his body language, she disappeared through the door.

Jack trusted few people, but Shay, being the boy's mother, needed to be involved in the rescue. Shay knew the hostages personally, which would be helpful if any of them became difficult. She knew where she was taken and by whom—another asset. His thoughts turned to the young boy. A child without his mother or father living in this broken world was cruel enough.

After breakfast, the Colton family gathered near the fireplace warding off the cold from the morning temperatures. Though the injured appeared rested, external as well as internal wounds took time to heal. Jack could not help but think how little he knew of Shay and her injuries. He hoped his gut instinct about her was correct.

"What's the plan, Jack?" Nick asked, sliding his arm over Lynn's shoulder.

"You're going after them?" Ben's voice came from the hallway. His white hair seemed whiter as he stepped into view.

"We don't have a choice pops." Jack lowered his voice.

"She going?" asked Ben, pointing at Shay.

"Ringo expects me to go back for Jonah," said Shay. "He'll be looking for me and looking for Jack. If we're gone, you're safe."

"John and Jeremy will be here to help," Jack reminded them. "We leave tomorrow."

"Do you even know where to start?" asked Lynn.

Jack spread out a map on the table.

"You left from here, right?" Jack drew a circle around Prescott. "Headed for Vegas."

Shay nodded. "We spent the day hiking and then camped overnight." She pointed, "somewhere in here. My co-worker called it the ghost stretch."

"Coconino National Forest?" Ryan leaned over them. "I'm guessing it was Seligman. Lots of old signs and mannequins?"

"Yes," Shay shook her head.

NOT ALONE

"Take the Hummer," Lynn stepped in next to them. "It's a good ride on and off the road."

"I like to ride Baily," announced Lily quietly, brushing her doll's hair through the entire conversation. "Mama says she's as smooth as Bailey's and cream." Lily struggled as the brush tangled in her doll's hair. She sighed, frustrated, and handed the toy to Lynn for fixing.

Jack turned to Nick. "You're in charge."

"Thanks."

"We leave early." Jack folded up the map. "You better get ready for six more guests."

18

While the girls slept, Riley admired the glass-framed shower doors with etched elk standing in timber. Black and gray marbled stone lined the floor and walls. Two extravagant showerheads hung from the sides with a third wide-mouthed waterfall-producing faucet in the center. Wanting nothing more than to stand beneath a warm shower, she imagined scrubbing her skin clean, soothing aching muscles and flesh. Expensive bottles of shampoo and conditioner lined the built-in shelf. She tugged on the band, holding her hair in a braid between her fingers.

She could not remember the last time she took a long hot shower. Yearning to feel the water, she opened the glass door and stood under the showerheads staring at the handles. She missed such luxuries so simple and often taken for granted. The imaginary smell of soap combined with water filled the steam-free air. Closing her eyes, she lifted her face to where the water would fall if working. She let the memories soothe her.

What if?

Expectant, Riley wrapped her fingers around the knobs suspecting time had frozen them in place, but the faucet handles turned, eliciting a longing for something ordinary. Then, a slight drip of lingering water flowed from the tap. About to turn away, a steady stream of lukewarm water flowed from the showerhead. Startled, Riley stared.

I'm dreaming.

Warm water, transparent as glass, cascaded to the floor, streaming into the drain lost. Not muddy and cold as expected from a faucet not used for several years but clean, clear warm water.

The water isn't real. I'm asleep.

The water rained down on her. Hungry licks of steam rose to the glass, creating a blanket of fog.

"Impossible," she cupped her hands, trapping the water and then letting it fall between her fingers. Her nightshirt, now soaked, clung to her body, and the long braided strand of hair wrapped around her shoulders. She undid the tie, letting wet strands fall free.

She stood under the hot waterfall while the magic fingers of heated liquid eased tight, aching muscles. Riley surrendered, uncaring as to how this happened or if she was dreaming. Pulling off the wet shirt, she lathered her body and hair with rich shampoo, the cocoa-scented soaps smelling good enough to eat. She moved between the two showerheads, not wanting to waste time and risk waking. Several of the butterfly stitches fell from her face.

Then the steam pulled away, and through the milky mist, two little faces appeared. She grabbed a towel, stepping out, she reached out to the girls.

"Hurry. Before it goes away."

Utah, asking no questions, guided Megan through the ghostly steam curling toward the cracked door. She helped her sister escape the nightshirt as long strands of curly hair twisted away from the material. Riley knelt beside her, untangling the hair with gentle fingers.

"I'll be right outside the door."

The girls nodded.

Riley shut the door.

If children could shine, Utah and Megan sparkled, and after several bouts of giggling, they decided they were hungry. Hugging the fire, Utah braided Megan's hair back, fighting unruly curls springing free and falling onto her forehead.

"That was weird," Riley touched her wet hair seeking proof.

"What?" Utah thumbed through her trail mix. The girls separated the orange M&Ms from the others. Riley learned some miles back orange M&M's meant something to her.

"The shower." Riley handed an orange M & M to Utah, who smiled and placed it into her mouth. Riley watched her. Utah looked beautiful. A few days with Riley and already, the tone of their skin had brightened. Utah's eyes shone a cream hazel with swirls of gold. How could any mother not protect her children? But then, Riley guessed, she had.

"We should get on the road," Max bounded in purring and rubbing against Riley's legs.

Before leaving, Riley checked the rooms for their belongings. She paused by the shower, wondering but then thought it best to leave questions unanswered.

19

A cold sweat broke out on Riley's skin when she saw the highway's amount of traffic. She'd been wrong. There were more than a handful of people alive. There were hundreds on the road right now.

A new hope rose in her as well as newfound anxiety. Her social skills, having hibernated for too long, gnawed on her nerves.

With law enforcement extinct, people became their own worst enemy. She's only been driving on the highway less than five minutes, and already the speed limit had turned limitless.

Traffic moved at a steady uncontrolled pace except for the occasional tapping of brakes. With no speed limits, she witnessed aggressive driving, making tempers rise. Brake checking, swerving, and horn blowing happened all around them. Dumbfounded t this new uncontrolled way of life, her knuckles grew white around the wheel and then loosened with a few deep breaths. In possession of the girls kept her emotions in check.

The safest act was to keep her distance, alter her speed, and ease the truck and trailer to the right side. She watched in the rearview mirror as drivers switched lanes driving at too high of speeds to pass.

"Mad Max at its finest!" Riley said.

Temperatures dropped into the low thirties, turning rain into delicate snow. A flatbed truck carrying twisted chunks of material fastened down by thick rattling chains slipped sideways in the left lane. Debris was trapped momentarily and then took flight. Riley eased out of the throttle, keeping a steady but slower pace well behind the wreckage. With her gun on her lap, they crested over the highest summit with no more altercations as many drivers had to stop to keep from slipping off the highway.

The falling snow turned to near whiteout conditions. Riley continued to push the Cummins diesel up hills and through narrow valleys bypassing cars parked to the sides.

As dusk closed in, they dropped down into a valley and found a side road outside of Yreka where they could sleep for the night.

"Can we make snow angels?" Megan said excitedly, straining to look out the window. "I've never made a snow angel. Mama used to tell us about the ones she made when she was little."

"Tomorrow, Megan, I promise."

NOT ALONE

Megan pressed her cheek harder to the window, watching the snowfall from inside.

Max turned his nose up to the canned cat food, stared at her, and then blinked one eye. Not moving from his empty dish, he looked down at the pureed chicken and swatted his bowl.

"Okay! I give," teased Riley. "Rabbit for you, hot chocolate, and a movie for us."

Age and preferences separated their ideas of which movie to watch, so Riley took three straws, shortened one of them, and enclosed them in her hand. Megan, easy to entertain, squealed with excitement, prancing about as if never seeing snow. Utah smiled a winner's smile.

"Goonies," blurted Utah.

"Goonies," Riley repeated, looking at the box. "That's not scary, is it, because I don't think...?"

"It's not scary," cried Megan. She pointed at the box. "See, it's about a pirate ship and treasure."

"You've never seen Goonies?" Utah asked as if everyone should have seen the movie "Goonies."

"Nope! I never saw it."

Megan giggled. "Everyone's seen, Goonies."

"Pretty sure not everyone," Riley grinned, taking out the movie. "Now, prepare for bed or walk the plank."

Megan giggled, her fingers curling into a ball. Megan pulled off her shoes and ran to the sink to brush her teeth. Riley grinned as she readied three cups of hot chocolate before settling in for the movie.

Halfway through and before discovering the treasure, all four of them were sound asleep.

"Come on, Riley, you promised," Megan said the following day, pressing her fingers into new pink gloves. Kneeling, Riley straightened the beanie scrunched down on Megan's face. Long curls bounced around her rosy cheeks.

"Okay, Megan, let's go make some snow angels," Riley said, reaching for her hand.

When Riley opened the door, a perfect Christmas card scene greeted them. Sparkles shimmered off the snow like tiny diamonds and the cobalt blue-sky outlined mountaintops. The quietness past the crunching of snow under their feet caused them to stop short of the third step. Max meowed impatiently behind them, pushing through their legs, dropping off the steps only to disappear into the white powder. Megan raced after Max, who bounded through the snow like a deer. Half of Megan vanished under

NOT ALONE

the blanket of snow as she twirled excitedly with palms reaching outward, catching falling flakes. Utah joined her sister, and for a moment, it seemed as if nothing in the world was wrong.

"Snow angels!" Megan fell to the ground.

Now, this is children having fun! Riley thought, remembering her and Eric doing the same thing.

Megan dipped under the layer of white powder. Riley watched as her arms and legs flailed back and forth. Snow shot into the air in tiny puffs of powdered ice. Riley and Utah giggled, joining Megan. Riley played with the girls forgetting, if not for a little while, the hundreds of miles still left in front of them. They had a snow fight, laughed, and then built a snowman before getting on the road.

"Here. I found this inside," Utah handed Riley a disposable camera.

"What is it?" Megan stood on the tips of her toes to get a better look. She pulled Utah's hand down toward her.

"A disposable camera," Riley held it for Megan to see.

"What's dis... poo... sable?" Megan always asked questions while tugging on her lower lip.

"You think it still works?" asked Utah.

"Worth a try, girls." The button lit up. "Go stand with Megan next to Frosty."

The girls grabbed the snowman's hands and posed. Riley clicked the button setting off the flash, thinking she'd find some way to process these keepsakes.

20

At first glance of Redding, California, from the I-5, everything looked desolate except for the madness moving on the freeway. Parking lots overflowed with wrecked cars; some shoved to the sides, and others locked together on side streets left behind as symbols of destruction. A remote section of the city appeared to have survived hard times though it had taken one hell of a beating. Every other building appeared broken, marked, and or vandalized. An occasional structure sat in skeletal remains, burned and charred, fragments protruded like spears crudely and meticulously placed. They looked like weapons to ward off possible flying demons. Even with so much destruction, several dozers weaved back and forth through the mess, attempting cleanup.

Few people scurried about on sidewalks, while the amount of moving vehicles crowding the city streets numbered less than a handful. Noon came and went while the Northern California skies of Redding began turning a stormy gray. A new surge of traffic emerged onto the freeway, clogging lanes and slowing traffic.

The experience at Wal-Mart supported the infection was real. The man who attacked her was willing to kill or be killed without any forethought to the consequences. Is that why she'd seen so many deceased when she escaped from the hospital?

Whatever the reason, the virus still existed. In Riley's opinion, no place looked safe, and the lunatic behind her showed signs of being infected now. The driver stayed on her tail, matching both speed and distance while the car in front of her slowed, forcing her to tap the brakes. Because of the probability that a collision was about to happen, she tensed.

The driver of the black truck displayed his agitation by tapping the trailer, causing it to sway. Riley, pinned in her lane with the trailer swaying from the impact, had nowhere to go. She watched in the mirrors as the truck appeared and then disappeared from her view. Pulling over to the shoulder wasn't an alternative, and even if she could, a debris barrier sat between it and the road.

"Go around me, asshole!" she said aloud. Remembering the girls were present, she finished by saying, "don't say bad words. It's not nice for girls to…" Her sentence stopped short when the gap between all vehicles around her tightened. The black truck now brought up the rear.

NOT ALONE

The car next to Riley began to speed up. Riley, sensing trouble, wanted no part of the trouble building. The black truck started to move to her left, which would force her off the road. Instead, he gave the trailer a hard tap.

Riley laughed aloud, feeling the rise of anger. "Right! Like I'm going to pull over. Here's the truck, the keys, and everything else I've almost died for." The weight of the trailer whipped from side to side. Fighting the steering wheel, reacting like a serpentine, she held tight to the gun in her hand, hoping the newfound trouble would find someone else to mess with instead of them.

The left line of traffic cleared, allowing her to move over two lanes. The tailgater moved over, so Riley went right and decreased her speed. Her pursuer shifted to the opposite lane and then throttled it, driving inches next to them. Tinted windows hid faces from view, and as other cars pulled away, the black truck gained ground.

"What does he want?" Utah asked, craning her head to see.

"Everything we have. Stay down," Riley told the girls.

"What're you going to do?"

Riley looked behind her. Megan held Max tight.

"I don't know yet." Riley lifted her foot off the throttle.

Utah sat back in her seat. For a scary moment, the truck slipped away from their sight. Riley turned to the opposite mirror and saw it moving fast to the left side. The driver slammed into the trailer with his front fender, and the toy hauler fishtailed, making tires squeal. The driver of the black truck sped up. Sensing this guy wasn't going to leave them alone, Riley reached for the shotgun lying under the seat.

"Utah, climb in the backseat and hold on."

Utah obediently crawled over.

"I like this truck and trailer," Riley said, rolling down the window.

Setting the barrel on the window's edge with one hand, Riley drove with the other. Behind her, Utah told her sister to clasp her hands to her ears and duck down to the floorboard. Lucky for them, Riley's instinct was right. As the black truck pulled up next to her, the passenger had a sawed-off shotgun pointed in her direction. In danger of being shot at, Riley fired the 20-gauge Browning semi-auto expelled a shotgun shell full of pellets into the door of the black truck as a final warning.

The man jerked the wheel, which sent his truck into theirs. Tapping the brakes, Riley swerved to the left. The trailer swayed to the right. Underneath them, tires chirped from pressing in the opposite direction, causing a bouncing effect. The truck started to level out, but the driver behind them continued the chase.

The passenger, a rough-looking woman, smiled, exposing a mouthful of rotten and broken teeth as she handed a gun to the driver. Riley feared the trailer would weave out of control and into a rollover, taking them with it. Trying Jerking the wheel, she whipped the hauler into the black truck, metal scraped metal, sending sparks flying.

Riley glanced in the passenger mirror. The entire fleet of vehicles behind them stopped on the highway. It faded into the distance, everyone except the black truck. He came up fast, too fast for her to make a game-changing move. The trailer broke free from the ball of the hitch. The Dodge shook as the chains caught, jerking the trailer forward. Swaying out of control, the metal motel whipped sporadically.

Stopping was no longer an option. Exhausted from fighting the truck and trailer's movement, Riley saw the tailgater coming up fast, too fast. In seconds, he was rolling alongside her. The nasty habit of drugs had boiled the skin on both of their faces. Riley grimaced at the lunatic's condition.

"Keep your friends close and your enemies even closer," murmured Riley.

The trailer and all of its contents were about to be lost. By now, gallons of diesel, kerosene, and several propane tanks had broken free. It was a rolling time bomb.

"Pull over!" screamed the woman, shaking her fist in the air.

Megan peeked out the window and screamed, "Monster!"

Road raged, and out of control, the man slammed into Riley again, but this time, the impact shoved the Dodge forward. Riley's cheek hit the steering wheel, reopening her wound. The time had come to take him and the toy hauler out of the equation.

"Objects may appear closer than they are," shouted Riley.

Riley waited until the black truck's front fender was visible. Then she fired a round into the hood. A crack, like the roar of thunder, ricocheted between both vehicles as the hood folded and then lifted, taking flight like a bird but not before crashing into the windshield. Glass shattered.

"Hold on!"

The trailer bucked sideways. Riley felt a pull. Tires chirped as clouds of dirt and rock detonated into the air. The back of the trailer swung around, slamming into the black truck. Momentum pushed the moving vehicle hard to the right side of the road. The front tires dug into the shoulder, sending the driver and passenger into a rollover. Metal scraped cement and dirt puffed out into the air like powder.

The Dodge sprang forward when the safety chains broke, free. Riley watched the trailer sway and then roll, cartwheeling, tossing materials, and thrusting them across the highway. The Wild Cat tore loose from inside the trailer and rolled out, bouncing between the center lanes in pieces. The second cloud of dirt puffed into the air as the trailer hit the shoulder, smashing into the meridian. A giant ball of flame exploded behind them.

"There goes our diesel."

Another ball of fire climbed into the air, igniting propane and kerosene. Several more blasts rocked behind them, and a black cloud lifted upward, shrouding the evening sky. People scrambled to steal what they could.

Utah climbed up to the front seat, looking backward. "Wow!"

"Are you guys okay?" A deep ache settled in Riley's heart and then in her stomach. She wondered if the man upstairs had chosen the right person to take care of these two little souls. "I don't like hurting people."

Megan clutched Max with both hands. Her face paled.

"We know. The bad man would have hurt us." Utah's finger wound around a long curl. "It wasn't your fault."

"The school was cold and dark at night. It smelled of monsters," Megan looked down as she spoke. "I like you, Riley."

"Thanks," grinned Riley. "I like you too."

"I have to go potty."

"Okay," Riley looked down at the fuel gauge. "We need fuel."

Riley spotted several buildings just ahead and sitting off to the side of the highway. Lights shone from what looked like a convenience store. The letters on the neon sign, glowed "assino." Someone had spray-painted in the extra letter s to make a statement. The casino survived the brutality of man's violence highlighted through the hand-painted artwork splashed on the exterior walls. The structure escaped vandalism of a more damaging caliber, leaving behind a post-apocalyptic sinners paradise. Not a gambling girl, she hoped the market would have supplies and or diesel to get them to the next stop.

The building, riddled with bullet holes, exposed plywood covering significant gaps and broken windows. Besides appearances, the store grew into a welcoming sight. Riley parked in the front, where she could see the girls.

"You two okay out here?"

Utah looked at her with a matter-of-fact gaze.

"Right! Lock the doors." Riley said, reaching under the seat, withdrawing a hidden handful of twenty-dollar bills. She stuck the money inside her bra.

Evening light caused the outside lights to flicker on, creating a buzz followed by a high-pitched beep as she passed through the door. Everything seemed loud and neon light. Bright. Even the woman standing behind the counter was colorful. The woman gave Riley a compelling smile with fuchsia lips and then pointed an AK-47 in Riley's direction. Directly over the woman's head hung the store's policies handwritten in red ink. "I reserve the right to refuse service to anyone."

"Understood?" The woman flashed glowing white teeth smeared with red lipstick.

"I need diesel." Riley laid down a twenty.

"Water and food I have, sweetie, diesel is another story." She pointed over to the empty shelves and said, "prices are on them. If it doesn't have a price, ask, and I'll make one up for you. I hope you have more money than that. You'll need it when you do find diesel."

Riley nodded, inspecting the half-empty shelves. She about fell over at the prices as she picked up several jugs of water marked twenty-three dollars apiece. Peanut M&M's were ten bucks and twenty-eight dollars for a large bag of jerky. Riley inhaled a deep breath making several trips back and forth to the counter. The woman smiled.

"You must be hungry, sweetie, and a sweet tooth at that."

"Yes, hungry."

The woman added up Riley's items with such a methodical slowness, Riley could hear the clock above the doors ticking.

"Is there anywhere to stay... that someone could sleep through the night without out getting her throat cut?"

"A hundred and forty-eight dollars, sweetie, no credit cards." Her fuchsia grin widened, revealing hot pink streaked teeth. "We got rid of coins a year or so ago. No more penny for your thoughts." She shifted her feet, keeping her hand on the gun, waiting for Riley to pay. Red Lips left her question unanswered. Instead of pushing the matter, Riley reached into her shirt and handed her the money.

"You shouldn't carry there. It's the first place they look, especially the men."

Red reached into a bag, withdrawing change in dollar form. Setting a box on the counter, she waited for Riley to load her treats. Red's perfume mixed in with the smell of old cigarettes made for an unpleasant odor making Riley load the items quicker. She tried in vain not to wrinkle her nose, but the scent grew stronger, making her eyes water.

"I know of a place you can buy diesel and stay for the night." She took out a pen with a pink feather pink end and wrote on a piece of paper. "I assume you're not from around here, so I won't confuse you." She spread out a detailed map, highlighting the turns.

"Thank you." Riley took the paper from her.

"How long you been gone?"

"Two years."

"You listen to me now. Only a few troopers are left, and there aren't enough of them yet to keep control of the uncontrollable. You being a lovely woman, you need to be especially careful. That address is a safe one. It's my son and daughter-in-law. Tell them Shirley sent you and flash a little cash. I hope you have more of that cuz the diesel's going to cost you." She smiled and tossed in some gummy worms. "That's for the little one. Welcome to the new world!"

Riley grabbed the box and made her way to the girls. "Let's go get some diesel."

Utah took the box from her, pulling out the gummy worms.

Megan looked at the candy. A big smile formed on her face. Forgetting she had to use the restroom, she screeched, "yes!"

21

Predawn light revealed a hint of color on the horizon, promising an explosion of colors of dawn. The temperatures were down in the low thirties again, freezing freestanding water and making the ground crunchy under footsteps. During the first week of December, the weather changed for the coming holiday season, making the coming of Christmas more Christmassy.

Jack and his family gathered in the adjoining building near the ranch house. He watched as his family gathered around, Nick wearing a look of concern, Lynn expectant, and Ben quiet while watching everyone. Shay appeared calm.

Yesterday, Shay proved she could handle a weapon, and by the day's end, she shot with accuracy and without fear. This morning, he saw a fire in her eyes and confidence in her movements. She was going to need it if the rescue was going to be a success.

Jack packed the last of the supplies into the back of the Hummer. Built for tactical purposes, off-road-ready, and dressed with bulletproof glass, the vehicle had the makings of a Military vehicle. Packed with gas, water, a spare tire, tools, and guns, it was ready for travel.

"We'll be back tomorrow," Jack said. He loaded the rest of the supplies. "Don't come looking for us if we aren't." He looked at Ryan, who was still on the mend. "I'll be back."

Ryan looked away from his brother, apprehensive. "I should go with you."

"Yep. Damn you for getting shot, anyway. Take care of the place." Jack gave his younger brother the Colton handshake and then pulled him in for a brotherly hug, careful not to hurt him. "Don't break anything while I'm gone."

"Asshole!"

"Go sit down before you bust a stitch or something," Jack said. "Oh, and Pops, try not to shoot any of the good guys, okay."

Ben reached out with his hand, and Jack took it. The old man drew him in, patting him on the shoulder. "I'm proud of you, son," Ben spoke in a soft but firm voice. "Weathers acting odd. Be careful."

"Thanks, pops," Jack felt a softening in his heart at his father's words.

"You're burning daylight." Ben's voice dropped a notch.

Quiet, Lily leaned across Lynn and latched onto Jack. Her fingers laced behind his neck. He glanced at the pink winged fairies on her sleeves, wishing he could stay and hold her a little longer. "When you get back, Uncle Jack, can you take me for a ride on Baily?"

"Yep! A ride on Baily for Lily Bean."

Nick took one last look at Jack's shoulder and then, with a gentle hand, patted him on the other. "It's healing, Jack. Try not to tear the stitches."

"Okay, Doc. Take good care of our family," Jack slid into the cab of the Hummer. He nodded at Shay, who sat in the passenger seat.

Leaning in so Jack could hear, Nick said, "Ryan is doing good."

Jack nodded. "He's in good hands, Doc. Just make sure he stays put." He hesitated for a moment. "John should be here anytime."

"Be safe, Jack, and get back here as soon as you can."

Jack looked at his family under the dim glow of the cab lights, waiting for him to go. He wanted these missions, needed them, but he struggled when it came time to leave. Once on the road, he would settle down into an old rule of mental preparation before the mission.

"You ready?" Jack turned to Shay.

"I'm ready," Shay nodded. "Let's go get Jonah."

22

The sun ascended into the sky, bringing with it a crimson red streak. The jagged mountain base shadowed by tall-ridged peeks hid while the sunny side exploded with color. Atop one of the highest peaks, a torn American flag lay unmoving in the morning stillness. The high desert appeared unchanged, existing as it had for centuries. A vast animation of space and weather carved sand and stone. Jack cherished its isolation, its serene beauty, and its endless skyline. Undisturbed by infected troubles occurring in its realm, the splendor of nature and her fixtures remained steady. Jack and Shay were making good time, being as they were the only travelers on the road.

"The desert is so beautiful," Shay gazed outward, growing silent, closing her eyes. She dropped the sunglasses down over her face. The sun, rising into dark clouds, tried to shine through the front windshield. "Why aren't you married, Jack?"

"Who said I'm not married?"

"You're married."

"Was."

A long strand of silence fell.

"Is she alive?"

"No," replied Jack, almost too quick.

He watched Shay bite her lip. Having not spoken of his past in a long time, he learned it was better to keep emotions locked away where they belonged. He said nothing else.

"Were you together when the Shift happened?"

"No." Pause. "She was at a meeting in Phoenix. There were only a handful of survivors, and she wasn't one of them." The words tasted bitter because they were.

The death of their connection happened a while ago. Still, sometimes, Jack could smell Kate's expensive perfume and feel her fingers on his face. Her materialistic greed had ruined his impression of her beauty, and they'd had some beautiful moments. His friends and family had warned him, but he only saw what he wanted to see. Women came easy to the Colton men like honey to a hive. Kate had seen herself as a trophy, and Jack had accepted the win.

"I'm sorry."

"Don't be."

"Destiny?"

"I don't believe that."

"What do you believe?"

"I don't think about it."

"I wonder if anyone knows."

"You mean why some people were infected, and others weren't. It doesn't matter." Then Jack thought twice. It mattered. He knew things she would never understand, seen things too.

"There's something else I forgot to tell you," Shay turned to him. "We've heard a helicopter there. He always seems to be present shortly after we hear the helicopter."

"Good to know."

Outside the cab, the scenery remained unchanged. The highway continued as a straight line of pavement with soft curves and roller coaster dips that monsoon seasons flooded. They had miles of rolling sand and rock to look at, and at the same time, desolate whistle-stops abandoned by man lay broken. Morning light showered strands of violet across the jagged rocks making their depth and height deceptive. A few soft streaks of white clouds reached across the sky. Pollution dissolved from lack of man and vehicles, and with no airplanes, the skies held a profound silence.

As they approached Ash Fork, the land changed to a high desert. Behind them, a truck and van closed in on them fast. The driver clicked his headlights on and then off, signaling.

"Blake is behind us. I've already filled them in on the details."

Shay straightened in her seat. "There," she pointed, hearing him.

A rising yellow gold broke across the sky, spraying light on the valley floor. A portion of a vehicle with no tires, glass, or seats sat in desecrated ruin on the side of the highway. The wreckage was a monument of what was to come.

"That used to be the SUV. Seeing it now, I can almost remember every detail right down to the song playing when we wrecked."

The heap of torn, twisted metal represented a piece of her past. Deep scratch marks engraved the pavement where tires had split from the rims and dug in, causing the metal to grind into the asphalt. Even the skid marks remained stuck to the highway. Jack pulled over and climbed out of the Hummer.

"Take your time," he told Shay before he turned to greet his team.

"Blake," Jack outstretched his hand. "Found a van, I see."

Once a rising star quarterback for Arizona State University, Blake Harris had been paving his way to the NFL when the Shift happened. Handsome and broad-shouldered, dark hair, blue eyes, and the kid had more talent than one man should own. He played like a pro and looked like one too.

"Jack," he grasped Jack's hand in a firm shake. "Things have been somewhat quiet until now. I hear Ryan's on the mend?"

"Yes. Quiet before the storm," Jack glanced back at Shay, who stepped in to join the group. "This is Shay. Her boy's name is Jonah. Blake Harris, Dan Manning, and Matt Cooper."

"I appreciate your help," She extended her hand to Blake first.

"I have to be honest, Shay. I have a personal interest in this mission," Blake said. He pulled a photo from his shirt pocket and handed it to Shay.

Seeing the photo, an expression of recognition touched her face. "Terra. That's Terra!"

"She's my girlfriend. She came up missing about a month ago. She's alive, then?"

"She was when I left. Those aren't gentlemen holding her. Sorry." Shay handed the photo back to Blake. "She spoke very highly of you."

With a slight smile, Blake returned the photo to his pocket. "Terra is a fighter. I expect her to be alive and well. Recognize any of the others?" Matt handed Shay a few flyers.

Shay nodded as she thumbed through them. "No," then she turned her gaze to the van. "I hope they will all fit in there."

"Shay thinks they're somewhere in Seligman. Any ideas?"

"Seligman is small, but if a person wanted to be off the grid, Seligman would be ideal," Blake took out his cell phone and showed her some photos. "You see any mannequins positioned around town or a burger joint," Blake pointed at the screen.

"That's it. More mannequin's now. Eerie then," more so now," Shay frowned at the pictures. "Does your cell phone work?"

"No, I keep it only for the photos. It's about 25 miles ahead," Blake put the phone away.

"Marilyn Monroe?" Dan joined the conversation for the first time.

"Yes. Marilyn Monroe," repeated Shay.

"Burger joint used to have the best-damned cheeseburgers," Dan patted his stomach.

Out of the team other than Jack, Dan stood as the oldest of the three men and the quietest. He'd graduated several years in front of Blake and Matt and had become one of the youngest deputies in the State of Arizona. Climbing the ladder to become a detective, the Shift took his career away. The guy had an instinct about him and always was as dependable as hell.

"Oh, please don't say anything more about cheeseburgers," Matt said, rubbing his stomach. "Awesome milkshakes too."

Not related, Matt could have been Blake's brother. Matt, aka "Coop," wanted nothing more than to join the military in his senior year in high school and follow his father's example of serving his country. Because of the Shift, he would never see boot camp, but his drive to become a soldier remained intact. Matt got his training, and he'd seen more combat from the Shift than if he'd gone into the military. The kid, resilient, and a gifted sharpshooter, impressed Jack even at his young age.

Jack and Ryan handpicked this team, knowing each man's skills and abilities. While most were learning how to survive, these young men, the fighters, trained to protect and restore order. Standing there together, dressed in dark clothing hidden by desert camouflage, and armed, they looked like fighters. Weapons were drawn, checked, and replaced. Each of their weapons was handpicked and was an individual preference, and they all had personal favorites.

Jack's team watched Shay and being a stranger to them, they saw her as a liability. Maybe accurate, but Shay would be the best asset when it came time to walk those women out to their freedom.

"We'll get as close we can. Hold back until nightfall." Jack looked at Shay, "you got anything else?"

"Ringo's boys start drinking early. By nine or so, they're liquored up. The rest will be in town. They keep Jonah at the Casita. Once we get there, I should be able to lead you back to where they are."

Jack nodded. "We go at ten."

23

Once night fell, the temperature dropped into the low 30s. The only sound between Jack's team and the darkness was that of their footfalls.

"I used to bring Terra out here to ride," Blake said, concealed in the shadows. Their vehicles were hidden behind a strand of permanently parked buses.

"Terra's been strong for all the girls." Shay leaned against the Hummer. "She'll be okay."

"Hot Wells Dunes. Hell yeah! That was a great time," reminded Matt excitedly. "We tore it up."

"I haven't been over this way in a while." Dan, leaning against a boulder, said in a quiet tone. "Wonder what the town looks like now."

"Spine-chilling," muttered Shay. "They have those creepy mannequins posed all over town. They use them as targets."

"Used to bring tourists in by busloads headed for Vegas," added Blake. "Anyone left?"

"No. The townspeople put up a good fight, but in the end, they were no match for Ringo and his men." Shay shook her head as if disgusted. "They make it look scary to keep markers away. They're the only ones left. The men! They talk a lot when they're drinking. They run a town now."

"They got a favorite hangout?" asked Blake.

"Roadkill Café," answered Shay. "Motel."

"Do they patrol at night? Security?" Matt was barely visible in the void of light.

Shay chuckled with sarcasm. "Hardly ever. People know not to come here. Anyone who enters rarely leaves."

"Be alert. We'll be hiking in," said Jack. "Hope you brought some good hiking boots."

"Danners." Blake lifted a pair of boots for everyone to see.

"Dan, you okay here?" asked Jack ignoring Blake's proud choice of boots.

"No problem. Call when you're in position."

"They're Danners!" Blake held the boots out further.

"Did you steal those?" Jack pulled out two vests, tossing the smaller of the two to Shay. She caught it, turned it, and then sighed.

"Bulletproof. I hope this thing keeps me warm too. Did you get a pair of those boots for me? They look warm," shivered Shay.

"Put it over your t-shirt Shay, the rest of your layers on top," instructed Jack.

"I'll be a Christmas present. All wrapped up and no one to open me."

Jack chuckled and then looked over at the others. "You guys have protection?"

"Fits like a glove," Blake said.

"That's not what she said," Matt teased. He ran his hand down his side, turning from side to side. "Look, dad, no lines."

"Great," Jack said, holding four headsets. He handed them out. He looked at Shay. "You'll be able to hear everything we say, and we'll be able to hear everything you say." He put her microphone and earpiece into place. "Ten minutes, guys. Pop was right about the weather."

The Seligman sign, broken into kindling wood on the highway's shoulder, was almost invisible under their feet. They had no choice but to keep to the open until they reached the town making for more comfortable walking. With no moonlight, the darkness of night camouflaged them. The slight breeze gave a small warning to the storm overhead. Without the moon, the town ahead fell into an abyss. They eased forward, surveying the cookie-cutter buildings while closing in on the historic city as a team. They used dead trees and fence lines to weave in and out of, using tall weeds as barriers. Tumbleweeds rolled past them, catching on broken chain-link fencing, claiming permanent residency.

"Let's do a quick sweep," Jack instructed. "We don't want any surprises."

"Wouldn't hurt," nodded Matt. He and Blake peeled off to the right.

The first home Jack and Shay approached appeared to be nothing more than a shack. The rough front porch hung broken, splintered wood, and exposed nails sagged underneath their weight. The door fell when Jack tried to open it.

"So much for being quiet," Shay grinned, following Jack around the door into a studio-type apartment. "What is that smell?"

Jack knew, but he adjusted to the obscurity, separating colors into shapes, and opened the bathroom door aiming a dim flashlight, which exposed the contents in the tub. "Let's go."

The second house looked no better. Shredded curtains, like translucent dancers, blew from the inside out, flapping in the night wind. Each roll of the thin material produced a perfect choreographed act. Glass lay in heaps near the big windows, and the porch had gaping holes as if someone had taken a hatchet to the boards. In red spray paint, someone left the word "warning" in bold lettering.

Jack slipped through the window, bypassing the worn outer door. In the darkness, hidden by sunshine, the house felt depressed. He felt the thick layer of sand under his feet, and the floor moaned underweight. Jack withdrew his second pistol from its holster.

"This is a hellhole," he breathed.

The destroyed master bedroom contained upturned mattresses and broken furniture. The child's room was robbed of everything cheery, drowned in an eerie shadow of dull tones. Taking his light, Jack saw a small form of what used to be a child. Cursing under breath, he glanced at the rotting teddy bear clutched under her arm. Crumbling on her body, the dress half-eaten by moths, and body decay lacked contrast, leaving bones protruding through leathery skin. He thought of Lily. He glimpsed at Shay, who closed her eyes and looked away.

"Shit," whispered Jack. "The devil's spawn."

"I told you," Shay whispered.

Innocent people like the girl influenced him to find justice for both the living and the dead and those dying without reason. They found no other bodies in the house, leaving Jack to believe the child had died alone. It is hard to fathom a little girl left alone at night and wake to morning hungry without anyone to protect her.

"Behind you." Blake appeared, "found a few dead, maybe a few days."

"Could be Markers too," replied Shay. "They come here looking for trouble, and they find it when Ringo's men use them for hunting."

"Hunting?" Matt looked at Shay. "What for coyotes?"

"No. Ringo's thugs hunt men, women, or children. Whatever they can get."

"I'm surprised. Why?" asked Matt. "Jesus."

"For the fun of it," Shay said softly.

Jack nodded, not wanting to think any more about what might have happened to Shay or the little girl. It was his job not to analyze but to stop the bad stuff from reoccurring.

The town resembled a graveyard of both humans and history. They moved further into town, stepping carefully to avoid broken glass and debris. Adjusting to the darkness, a line of cars and trucks from the 50s served as roadblocks on the main streets. Mannequins sat as drivers and passengers. Some dressed others naked. Warped ply boards spray-painted with the words "NO TRESPASSING" lay destroyed and riddled with bullet holes. The iconic gas pumps, broken and faded by gusting sand and intense heat, remained icons. Dozens of fragmented signs swayed in the wind, humming in a chorus of creaks and moans. The mannequins looked to be in better shape than the humans left behind for scavengers to eat.

Shay hesitated. Jack stepped up next to her, waiting for her to calm whatever she fought internally. He felt it, too. The abnormality of where they stood lay evilness unleashed.

24

"What do you think, Jack?" asked Blake. Jack stepped away from Shay toward Blake and turned off his mic.

"I think we need to get the women and Jonah and then get the hell out of here. If any of Ringo's men are hanging in town, they'll tell the others and head that way."

"This place used to be so cool," Blake pulled his jacket up closer around his neck. "Shit, it's starting to snow."

"Maybe the cold is keeping them in for the night. Might be to our advantage."

"Yeah, spotted the tavern from afar." Blake looked down the street. "A few rigs parked outside."

"It's a dirt road most of the way," Shay said from behind them. Jack failed to hear her footfalls. "Oh, and if you like classics, Ringo's got a beauty in the garage, but it'll only hold three people at the max."

Jack nodded, switching his radio over. "Grab the Hummer and pick us up. Copy."

"Affirmative. Beautiful night for a run. Copy."

Blake grinned, hearing Dan fall back and take off in the opposite direction. "Man's a beast."

"Thanks," Dan said, his voice reaching their earpieces.

Twenty minutes later, they were rolling out of Seligman toward highway I-40 West. Shay pointed them in the direction the best she could. Seeing the turn-off for Anvil Rock Road, she gathered her bearings.

"We're close."

"Which way?" asked Jack.

"Go right. It's a few miles ahead," Shay's words soft. "It's starting to snow harder."

Jack found a spot to pull over further up the road. The snow fell in a steady blanket of white, promising to cover his tire tracks, making them disappear. They geared up and hiked the rest of the way, leaving Dan with the van.

"There," said Shay, breathless and stepping in close to Jack.

"Off the grid," Blake stepped in behind them.

The unique log home built into the hillside camouflaged and separated from the outside world. A steep jagged cliff framed the house's front, the perfect getaway house for someone who wanted to be off the grid. Even the helicopter pad minus the helicopter would give a person in a hurry a quick exit.

"Security cameras, Shay?" Matt set his pack down beside Jack.

"I wouldn't be surprised, but I don't know for sure."

"I don't hear a generator running," Blake raised his head above a boulder to take a better look and listen. They sat several hundred feet from the house, enclosed by foliage and trees.

"They're always running out of gas," Shay shifted uncomfortably. "It'll be getting cold down there for the others. We need to hurry."

"Pretty quiet," Jack stared at the house. "No vehicles."

"They park in the garage on the other side," Shay kept her voice low. "They play poker and drink until they're stupid."

Jack raised his glasses to get a better look. "Good, let them drink a little more. We go at midnight."

"This area, the house, it all seems a little too thought out, don't you think?" asked Blake. "I'd like to know what's on the other side."

"So find out," grinned Jack.

"Okay, old man," teased Blake. "Let us younger guys go in. You gotta be on the tired side. Right, Matt?"

"You need to rest."

"Tired my ass. I'm just getting started," Jack promised.

"Better pull out your big boy skirt." Blake grinned, tossing Jack a punch.

"Can you two do this on another day," Shay's words gentle yet worrisome?

"Sorry. We'll meet you back here by eleven." Blake looked down at his watch. "Eleven."

Matt glanced back at Shay and Jack? "Can you read me? Copy."

"Desert Four, Check." Dan's voice crackled.

"Big boy skirt," Blake pointed to Jack as he disappeared into the timber.

The radio chatter consisted of Blake and Matt giving small details of the property and the house as they circled the compound. They were able to chat openly without concern someone may be listening. At one point, Blake's signal dropped and then picked back up. Close to eleven, both Blake and Matt appeared through the brush.

"Three floors. Five bedrooms, maybe six, three baths, two living rooms. Lights are on in the game room. Generators are running the inside lights. They've looped razor wire around the perimeter. The front gate's locked as well as the two side ones. The back gate isn't locked, though, but faces two sliding glass windows." Blake took off his gloves, unwinding a bloodied piece of cloth off his arm.

"What happened?" asked Shay, moving to look at Blake's arm.

"Hooked up with a wild boar,"

Shay grabbed bottled water rinsing off the wound. "Right."

"Got me pretty good. Razor wire's a son of a bitch." Blake winked at Shay.

"Put this on it," Jack tossed a flask to Shay. "Is the problem solved?"

Blake nodded. "They've got a few traps set out. There's a side door off to the left. That'd be a good way for us to go in."

"This is going to hurt," warned Shay.

"Bring it." Blake smiled.

Shay opened the flask and poured the alcohol onto the wound.

She rummaged through Jack's backpack and pulled out a t-shirt. Before he could argue, Shay ripped the material into strips. She wound the cloth tight around Blake's arm.

"You brought whiskey with you, Jack, but not a first aid kit?" Blake leaned over the backpack, trying to look in. "What else is in there?"

"First aid kit is in the Hummer, and you can thank me later for the whiskey," replied Jack. "Hope there was no rust on that wire."

"The road looks good but rough. The casita is lower down on the south side," informed Matt. "There's no easy way down."

"How did I miss the other house?" asked Blake helping Shay wrap some dressing around his cuts.

"It's a square thing with a roof and pretty hard to miss," chided Matt. "They're both occupied."

"We hit them both at the same time," suggested Jack inspecting Shay's patchwork on Blake's wounds. "Good job."

Jack turned to Matt, "You and Shay take the lower house. Blake and I'll take the main house. Whoever finds Jonah needs to send for Dan. Copy that?"

"Copy," answered Dan.

"Meet us back at the main house for some housecleaning." Jack glanced over at Shay. "If we tell you to go, you make for the road until Dan finds you. Don't play the hero."

"I won't play the hero," Shay repeated back to Jack.

25

"I bet that was heavy," Jack watched Blake pull a set of lock cutters from his bag.

"Bet you're glad I brought them," replied Blake.

They did a second check on their weapons. Blake nodded an approval to advance, stopped, and leaned the Smith and Wesson M&P 15 Tactical against the fence. He cut the links, dropped the lock on the gate with one cut, pulled out a miniature can of W-D 40, and sprayed the hinges. Jack would have teased him about the can of lube in different circumstances, but the gate swung open without a sound. Blake entered the house first.

"Honey, I'm home," waved Blake, gesturing to Jack to move forward.

Unnoticed, the voices rambled, and the scent of stale cigars, cigarettes, and booze taxed the dry air.

"You son... a bitch, Larry! The dark-haired one is mine for tonight."

"Have another drink, asshole." Glass shattered. "Sit down... hon... ey. I don't bite." From some unseen space, a woman cried out, topping off her cry for help with a bloodcurdling scream.

"There's plenty to go around, you idiots! Boss said we could have whatever we want."

"Boss, don't know you lost mama."

Blake started forward, but Jack put a hand on his shoulder, stopping him. "Wait."

"Toss me another bottle." Words slurred.

Jack tapped Blake on the shoulders three times, indicating three different voices.

There was a crash and then more laughter. "Boss was pretty pissed off when Grant didn't come back with his bitch."

"I thought he was gonna pop a vessel," a round of laughter broke out again. The voices were induced by alcohol and muffled.

"He'll find... her." One of them slurred. "He was head... ed in that direction."

Jack tapped Blake one more time. Then he methodically searched the smoke-filled room. "Ringo's not here." Jack turned and spoke into his mic. Ringo was out hunting, and one of the trophies he hunted was right here in his palace. "We go on three."

They crossed the line between light and darkness at the same time. Like the mannequins out on their streets, the men sat with their concentration solely on their cards in hand. When they saw Jack and Blake standing side by side, the men at the poker table dropped their dealt hands and rose from the table in a moment of utter surprise. Too shocked and drunk to react, the men fumbled, using chairs as crutches. A man dozed in a corner chair, oblivious to any intrusion.

"Room for one more?" Jack activated the red laser on his weapon. Blake, holding the impressive firepower, was ready to unload a magazine on anyone who moved. In reality, they could have wiped them out right then, but they believed in play fair.

Jerked to awareness, drunk and slow, the men turned and reached for weapons hidden near the table, others holstered under clothing. Cards fell, cigars and drinks dropped, and chairs toppled as men lunged in all directions. Knocking over the card table, they sought refuge from Jack and Blake. The woman, forced to sit on one man's lap, fought to escape her captor's grasp. With her screaming, the sleeping man woke and dove for the floor. Jack attempted to grab hold of her, but she slipped through his fingers and took shelter from the fight about to begin.

Chairs splintered the wood flooring ripped apart from the first spray of artillery cracking through the room. Money on top of blood splattered the floor. Jack dodged, dipping down, taking cover behind the bar. He waited for a pause in the gunfire, not risking being wounded or dead this early in the game.

A man too drunk to run stumbled across the room, shooting aimlessly until catching one of Jack's bullets center mass in the chest. He fell with a thud to the floor.

"One down."

Jack crawled to the end of the bar. He slid to the doorway leading to the living room. Wood exploded overhead, sending shards of giant toothpicks into the air like miniature missiles. Jack fired multiple shots into the door and to his left, which detonated into a flurry of return gunfire. Muddled and unprepared, the men scurried like rats retreating from Jack, and Blake came prepared.

Blake unloaded the M&P on the thugs. As the aftermath of the shots simmered, the air filled with gunpowder, smoke, and metal, overpowering the aroma of cigars and whiskey.

"Four down. Are we done here?"

"We're not so lucky." Jack hugged the doorway.

Four more groggy-eyed armed men staggered into the room from another part of the house. Jack swung away from the doorway, bolting across the room. He grabbed hold of the girl curled up in the corner, hiding, and pulled her toward him. "Stay behind me," he told her and then fired. The high-pitched "pop, pop, pop" echoed, followed by a thump.

Jack looked at Blake.

"Impressive."

"I'm just warming up," grinned Jack, assessing the situation. "There's more."

"Where are they?" Blake asked the girl. She pointed.

"We have Jonah." Matt's voice crackled over the radio.

"We're not clear. You all okay, Coop?" asked Jack.

"I'm hit, but don't come for me. Get them out first."

"Negative." Jack refused to lose or leave anyone, ever. "Stay put."

"Keep going."

"Send the bus," commanded Jack.

"Copy," answered Dan. "Hang in there, Coop."

"Let's finish this," Blake said.

"Copy that." Jack turned to the woman. "Follow the road down. A white van will pick you up. Do you understand?"

She nodded tears, staining her face. Before Jack could ask her where the women were, she bolted out the front door.

The card table now smoldered with hot cigarettes and cigars, having found fuel, filling the broken room with toxic smoke. Jack grabbed a container of water and tried to douse out the flame. More smoke.

"Shit," he swore, tossing the plastic jug. Blake moved in to help, but Jack stopped him. "Leave it."

They did some quick house cleaning, sweeping, and clearing each room one by one. When they reached the master bedroom, the compound fell eerily quiet. Jack anticipated the whirl of helicopter blades, but none came.

Three sliding glass doors framed the room leading to a wraparound deck facing westward. Beyond the glass, a passing shadow darted into an abyss of unknown. Jack skimmed the wall to one door and then slid it open. The decking sat twenty-five feet wide and several stories high. In the daylight, he assumed it was one hell of a view.

Through the obscurity of light, Jack caught sight of the movement again. He slid back inside, raising a finger to Blake.

Jack waited.

Ringo's man slipped past the slider, drawing his pistol in full stride. Simultaneously, Jack stepped out, sweeping his forearm up and across the man's throat, pressing him backward. Jack squeezed, tapping off the blood racing through the man's carotid artery. With his free hand, Jack swept the gun from the man's hand for Blake to retrieve.

"How many more?" asked Jack, feeling the man's heartbeat under his fingertips. Silence. Jack pulled him to the edge of the rail, and the man squirmed. Cold air connected with the man's breath creating puffs of moisture swirling from his mouth.

"Go... to... hell," the man stuttered.

"No can do," Jack held steady. "Not tonight. Where's Ringo?"

The man moved his lips, but his voice caught in his throat.

"Jack." Blake stepped forward, facing the man with his M&P. "He can't talk because he can't breathe."

Jack loosened his hold. The man's body relaxed. There lingered a moment of nothingness, and then, all hell broke loose. Ringo's man slammed his elbow hard into Jack's rib cage, connecting hard enough to rob the air from his lungs, but Jack stood solid. The man flashed a knife inviting Jack to fight.

Jack glanced at the knife and grinned.

"I don't have time," said Jack as the muscles in his jaws tightened.

"At least make this fight fair." Ringo's man grinned.

Jack lifted the man's pistol rolling it over from side to side. "Nighthawk Talon.45 the perfect weapon for creatures of the night, men included."

Jack handed the pistol to Blake, who laid it down a few feet away, making it so that the man would have to be fast. Jack could have ended it right then, and justice would be served, but Jack also understood the dynamics of playing fair.

"Now it's fair."

The man rolled the knife over in his hand, "let's see what you got, asshole."

Jack went silent. The smell of cheap whiskey and the stench of old cigarettes wafted his way. The man's eyes darted from the tip of the knife to his pistol. Jack stood unmoving, wondering what choice the man would make.

"You die. I get your gun. Your move." Jack saw the tremor.

The man dove, landing on one knee, sliding across the wood, decking for his weapon. Overestimating his speed, he overshot his ability to stop, grabbed for the gun, shoving it forward as he skated toward the rail. The gun went midair and then disappeared below. Realizing his mistake, the man rolled to his side.

"Son of a bitch." Withdrawing a pistol from under his pant leg and rising to his feet, he pivoted to face Jack.

Jack, no more amused by all the theatrics, waited for him to wrap his fingers around the grip before he pulled the trigger of his 45. A flame ignited a flash of light into the blackness. The echo from the blast bounced off the canyon walls disappearing into the depth of the night. *"Poker, call them when you know you catch them in a lie."*

The bullet shattered the bone in the man's shoulder, and the impact shoved him against the sides of the railing, which splintered in half against the weight. He was going over. Scrambling to find a grip while keeping a hold on his pistol, he grabbed hold of the post. The knife flew across the deck, landing short of Jack's feet. The wounded man dangled over the side of the decking. Below him, shadowed by the floorboards, was a steep drop. No matter the material that lay under him, the fall would be too steep to survive.

Jack moved closer to the edge, keeping his pistol aimed at the man. He looked down. "I'll show you the same courtesy you showed the women." With his foot, Jack kicked the post.

The man screamed out, "you fucking asshole!"

As he plummeted downward, several rounds echoed against the rock walls. Blake moved next to Jack, peering down over the balcony.

"I wonder how steep that is, Jack?" both staring into the dark space.

"Let's go."

Inches past the slider, another explosion of repeat automatic gunfire filled the room. The glass doors exploded into tiny fragments blasting out a cloud of raining glass.

Blake twisted around from the outside wall, sending a barrage of rounds into the room. Casings rolled off the deck's edges and made a soft ting between the slats as they hit the rock.

"Three men," reported Blake. "A few ran."

Gunpowder permeated the air while distorted shadows danced under the moon's blue light. Wafts of smoke rolled down the hall from inside the house and from somewhere outside. Jack pulled one of the dead shooters from the room into the hallway.

"He won't be needing this," he picked up the dead man's rifle and slung it over her shoulder. "Let's go."

Crunching over blankets of glass and empty casings, Blake cleared the hallway, allowing them to walk toward the kitchen. Time ran short; they needed to find the entry to the cellar, searching cabinets, counters, and walls cut out as an entry or holding a device that might open a door.

"Here," Blake tapped a section of the wall with the butt of his gun. "It's hollow."

"That's it," Jack stepped back, shining his light on the spot. Tracing the wall with his fingers, he felt a hairline separation. "Look for a switch."

Precious minutes slipped by. The women weren't far, and Matt needed help. More of Ringo's men were barricading themselves outside, and additional men would be on their way. They needed to recover everyone and get out before all hell broke loose.

"We're in," Blake opened the door. "You still with us, Coop?"

Jack moved past Blake, stepping through the opening that looked like nothing more than an abyss of oblivion. Blake stood at the entry, pressing his body into the wall, and waited.

NOT ALONE

"Affirmative. Mother and son are en route," Coop's voice not sounding right.

26

Riley and the girls reached Bakersfield around three in the afternoon. The city felt as though a cloud, the kind that dampens the soul, not the ground, had accumulated, filled with lost souls lost. Hiding in the dust devils that rose off abandoned dry fields were fragments of life that once existed here. Broken billboards highlighted hometown heroes like Kevin Harvick and Casey Mears had begun to fade.

In her mind, Riley could hear some old country song her dad listened to when she was a small child. After seeing it with her own eyes, she understood why Bakersfield had been so popular with country singers, racecar drivers, and cowboys. She smelled the pungent aroma of dust and fertilizer. It was where dirty boots, dusty jeans, and cowboy hats were the norm. She imagined a hole-in-the-wall bar where the mechanical bull was Friday night's entertainment right after the homegrown singer under the dim lights and smoke-filled curtain. Gone were the visitors listening to rising stars. Future performers lost never to see fame or fortune.

So far, the directions for safe places to stop had been reliable, and Bakersfield made a good stopping point before wrestling the road to Prescott. To keep her goal fresh, Riley replayed Eric's voice. Hell, she replayed many things in her mind. She believed she would find him alive. That hope kept her forging forward. The girls were asleep, giving her unwanted time to think about the night she left Sacramento or tried to go anyway. Seeing the execution of a couple and watching their little girl run into the dark and disappear. Riley would never know the child's fate.

What happened to the little girl? She called out my name.

Too many unknowns remained in the parking lot that night.

Mark would have eventually killed me or hurt me so bad I'd never wake up. Was the man who tried to kill me in the parking lot there for me? Maybe Tim and his family were just in the wrong place at the wrong time. And who was the person who saved me?

She thought of the gun taken from under her pillow, the phone lying on the floor, dialing Eric. That was enough to convince her to get far away out of town. After leaving the house that night, she went to the office to give Jackson her Service weapon and ID before leaving town. Instead, she almost died.

She often had memories of the hospital, and they weren't pretty.

The cries of help burned into her mind. She'd been ready to leave the hospital for days. Instead, she decided to stay behind to help the overworked team until they at least caught up. After all, they had helped her. Then, the day she did leave, the hospital fell under attack. As she searched out a clear exit, she stumbled into a gurney holding a wounded woman. The woman turned to face her, and Riley's heart sunk. Due to her injuries, nothing about her resembled that of a human. Riley would never forget. Even if the woman lived, she might never look human again, and she doubted she lasted through the hour. Tears poured from one of the woman's eyes while the other hung from its socket. All but one finger was gone from her hand. On the other hand, she wore a bloody bandage of crimson red strips wrapped around stubs. There was so much blood.

Somehow, Riley escaped infected people who broke into the hospital just to kill.

"I was lucky," she said aloud. "You'd better be alive, Eric."

She and Eric shared a solid connection with the other. Being twins, she hoped to go to college together, live in the same town, and spend every Christmas together with their families. In their senior year, Eric enlisted in the Navy. Riley enrolled in college.

Their bond remained strong, calling the other at least once a week, often more if the feeling arose. Some years later, after a trip back to the states, he told her that he'd advanced in his training and had become a Navy Seal. He often disappeared for months at a time, unable to discuss where he'd been.

She saw the change in her fun-loving brother, as he became a warrior overnight. Because she knew her brother, her anxiety about his well-being grew. Pushing away any more memories or preconceived thoughts, Riley brought her thinking back to the here and now. A surviving sign was just ahead, and she hoped it might be their turnoff.

"Historic Ghost Town ahead," Utah said from beside her.

"I can't believe they sent us to a ghost town."

In reality, they passed many ghost towns. This one smelled like Bakersfield, mixed fertilizer, dirt, and cows. The wind stirred in time to welcome. Riley stopped the truck. Several dirt devils swirled in the street's center, dancing and spinning as if choreographed by some unseen spirits. Everything in front of them looked like it was a western movie set.

"Cool!" Utah pressed her face to the glass. Megan woke and joined her. "What is this place?"

"A ghost town."

"Where are the horses?" asked Utah.

"Better yet, where are the cowboys?" Riley murmured.

"Is there a school here too?" asked Megan.

"Probably. Someone has done a nice job preserving the buildings."

"What does pres... ubing..., mean?"

"Pre-serv-ing. It means to keep something nice." Riley explained to Megan.

They didn't drive far until they found the motel. A gray-haired man stepped out into the street, motioning Riley to stop. His old and once tan cowboy hat sat low on his forehead, shielding his eyes from the fading sun. His button-up cowboy shirt hung loose enough on his thin frame to flap like sails in the wind.

"There's a cowboy," Utah pointed.

Riley grinned. "Not exactly what I meant."

"Is he a ghost?" Megan stared.

Riley chuckled, "no, silly."

"He looks like a ghost," Megan pressed her face to the glass to get a better look.

As the grey-haired cowboy approached the truck, his sky blue eyes met hers. He lifted the rifle and then lowered it, possibly seeing the girls.

Riley rolled down her window. "Shelly and Brian, Shirley's kids, sent us. Said this was a safe place."

At that moment, Max jumped from the back seat. His claws grazed the back of Riley's neck. She shrieked as he made a flying leap out the window onto the ground. The cowboy swung his rifle and aimed at Max.

"No," she yelled, jumping out of the truck.

The old cowboy shifted, legs bowed, to face Riley, who found herself staring into the end of the rifle.

"What are you saying girl," he yelled out.

The saving angel stepped in from behind, a gray-haired woman as lovely as a spring flower. The heel of her boots clicked on the wood below, but she stopped and put a hand on the old man's shoulder. Yelling, she said, "Hank, she said, Shelly and Brian sent her."

"Oh," he nodded, lowering the gun. "Sorry, I'm hard-of-hearing. Hell, I thought that gray thing was a giant rabid squirrel or something. What was that?"

Megan giggled. Riley took a deep breath, grateful for Max's speed.

"A cat," Riley used her loudest voice. "A healthy cat."

"You travel with a cat, ain't heard of no such a thing," he frowned, waving his gun.

"Park in the rear. The left stall is open. There's a back door to the hotel. Just come on through there when you're done," the woman said.

"Thank you," Riley squinted, searching for Max. The way he darted from the truck, he needed to potty. He'd find them before he got too hungry and maybe after all the shouting stopped.

"He'll find his way to you." The woman said before she stepped through the entry and disappeared.

After they parked, Riley and the girls headed through the back door with their bags. They passed through the back door of a saloon into what turned into a modern-style hotel. Polished wood and granite countertops framed the reception space adding a western flavor. Western-style rugs blanketed the floors, and on the walls were photos of movie stars, famous animals, and unforgettable movies filmed from the 50s to 2013. Over the river rock fireplace hung a large portrait of John Wayne, completing the room.

"I'm Rose. Hank, over there is the cantankerous one," she pointed at the old man. "He usually wears a hearing aid but misplaced it this morning. We're all hoping he finds it soon."

"We?" asked Riley. "Are there others here?"

"We always have a house full," she said.

"I didn't see any other cars?"

"If they like you, they'll show themselves." She continued talking as she stacked towels and wash clothes onto the counter. "I think you'll like room 224," she said, looking down at Utah. "Up the stairs and down the hall. It'll be on the right."

"224", Utah smiled at Rose.

"I didn't see any other cars," Riley repeated, confused.

"Dinner is at six, breakfast at five." She handed Riley the towels and gave the key to Utah. "The lights are a little tricky in that room, but I think you'll figure it out."

"Thank you," Utah's cheeks flushed, and her eyes sparkled.

"Chow hall is just around this corner here."

"Chow already, woman!" growled Hank.

"No, Hank, I was just telling, oh never mind," she yelled. "Find your damn hearing aids, would you?"

Hank mumbled something as Riley and the girls went to find their room. Riley wanted a quick run before dinner, but she didn't want to leave the girls alone. Hours in the driver's seat left her feeling stiff.

Their room for the night consisted of a small living room, kitchenette, and a dry bar. There were two bedrooms, one being the master suite and the other a guest room. The matching wood tables adorned with horseshoes added a southwestern flair, reflecting careful handpicking of decor.

"Can we help Rose in the kitchen?" asked Utah. "You want to go for a run, right?"

Riley looked at her.

Someone knocked on the door. Riley jumped.

Utah opened the door. Rose stood, wiping her hands with a dishtowel. "I forgot why I came up here," she said. "Oh well, how's the room?"

NOT ALONE

"Perfect," Riley said. "Come in, please."

"Thank you. I'm glad you like the room. I thought maybe the girls might like to help me in the kitchen?" tossing the towel over her shoulder. "Hank's got a hankering for some peanut butter cookies, and I could use some cookie helpers."

Megan squealed.

"Looks like it's a great idea," Riley raised her eyebrows a touch. *Eerie.* "Maybe, I'll take a short run then."

"Take your time, honey. We're not going anywhere," Rose replied. "Keep in mind, though, that this is a real ghost town."

"Real ghost town. Got it! I won't be long."

The girls followed Rose out the door. The woman, refined but strong, reminded Riley of her mom. She found herself wanting to hug Rose.

I love you, mom.

Outside and under the descending sky, a purple and orange crisscross of streaks filled the sky, casting a splash of shadow as Riley settled into a steady pace. Her footfalls soft as she connected with sand and dirt, and with the rhythm of breath and stride, she fell into a steady pace. As she passed through the streets, so did her time alone, bypassing the straightaway that'd take her back to the motel, she circled back for one more lap.

Riley slowed to cool down. The pause gave her a moment to reflect on the buildings in front of her. On her right sat an old post office and several older buildings to the left. The buildings casting fall shadows appeared more extensive than the barriers creating them. A soft hum stirred as the wind started an eerie conversation between air and sand.

She stared at the old buildings for a time. Somewhere down the line of weathered doors and rusted nails, and fragile door hinges, something clattered. Then as if all her senses heightened, she heard a creak, a moan, and the stir of the wind cast shadows of abandonment, drawing her forward.

27

A layer of sweat trickled down her neck and then rolled down her back, dampening her clothes.

Keep in mind that this is a real ghost town. Roses' words replayed in her mind. Those words to Riley only fed her curiosity even more. She was not fearless, but she was adventurous, and walking away without exploring wasn't an option.

Worn wood and weathered planks led the way into the general store. Behind her, footfalls left prints in the dust-covered wooden sidewalk, which creaked under each step taken. Riley bypassed captured tumbleweeds trapped against the wall siding and covering faded debris. Overhead a hand-lettered sign read "Hardgrave General Store." A sun-faded closed sign hung sideways in the window. Another teaser to enter.

Therefore, she did.

The door creaked loud enough to wake the dead. The wind pressed through open cracks whistling eerily from different corners. The wooden floor whined under pressure, soaking into the darkening shadows of the building. Empty shelves and loose barrels remained long since abandoned, remained as relics of the past. Inside, Riley felt a powerful pull of energy, a wrenching of good and evil. A waft of cool air brushed past her, raising goosebumps and fine hairs on her arms and neck.

Riley took heed to the warning and started to turn away. In the blink of an eye, the store came alive. Wooden barrels were full of fruit, bins full of rice, beans, flour, jellies, and pickles lined the shelves. Hard candies lined a shelf behind the front counter. The scent of fresh bread, cinnamon, and coffee beans scented the air.

Holograph? It looks so real!

Riley reached out to a pair of century-old boots, expecting her hand to find nothing but air. Instead, the leather folded under her touch soft and supple. Riley jerked her hand back.

Not possible. Then Riley thought about the water in the shower. *That, too, was impossible.*

The smells inside the store made her stomach growl. The cookies on the counter smelled like *peanut butter.*

Still trying to figure out how Rose and Hank were doing this, she reached out to see if the dish felt warm.

Warm to the touch, Riley traced the plate with her fingers.

The woman entered through a side door, the material of her old age dress swishing under her steps. Slender ivory hands swept blonde ringlets away from her face, illuminating swollen blue eyes that shifted with uncertainty. She looked in Riley's direction, and their gazes held.

"Uh... sorry....I..." Riley, taken back, fumbled for the right words.

"Good afternoon." The woman's voice held such softness, Riley barely heard her.

If they like you, they will show themselves Rose's words.

A thin beady-eyed man with thinning hair appeared behind the counter. Riley blinked. "Actors?"

"Don't just stand there, Ellie," the storekeeper wiped off sweat lining his brow. His eyes focused chest level on the woman in ways not acceptable.

Placing a hand on his hip, and with purpose, allowed his elbow to brush Ellie's back. The worn material of the dress hung in soft folds, hugging Ellie's slender body. She made the dress, which was thin as a spider's web, delicate and beautiful.

Ellie shifted, trying to free herself from the weasel's touch. He moved closer to Ellie, his eyes searching over her shoulder and down to the front of her dress. Riley's stomach churned.

What the hell was going on here?

No more than a shadow at first, a tall man entered from the side door, his body brushing past hers. Immediate first impression, Riley didn't like him one little bit. He brought with him an evil presence that Riley could not explain. The scent of tobacco and whiskey lingered after him. Then he stopped midstride and turned. Riley tried to slide behind an aisle to hide and watch, but the man's voice stopped her cold.

"Stop!"

Riley stopped. Interaction with the customer, *a good twist*, she thought. *Frightening but convincing.*

"Actors. You're actors," Riley said.

"Who are you?" he asked.

Ellie dropped the container she held, cringing as it crashed to the floor. The tall man, forgetting Riley, approached Ellie, glass crunching under his feet. Ellie froze. He reached across the counter and, with slow movements, stroked the neckline of her dress with his fingertips. The thinner storekeeper man scurried backward.

"What do you think you're doing here, Ellie?" Pause. "If you want to work, I'll put you to work," he said.

Everything about him felt dark to Riley. How did one play a part so well that even Riley could feel his sinister aura?

"Please, Spade," she took several steps backward. "You have no reason to keep me."

"But I do, Ellie, if not only because you are his."

Ellie's face flushed red as she tried to ignore Spade. Ellie and Riley trembled.

Riley looked from Ellie to Spade. Something rang familiar and troublesome after hearing the man's name. The room did a quick spin, and Riley appeared in another place. Riley no longer stood hidden. Instead, she faced Spade. The unthinkable became possible. Riley became Ellie. Another blanket of goosebumps rose from her skin when she realized the weight in her right hand hidden under the folds of Ellie's dress was a gun, her gun.

"I'm part of the game."

Warmth crept in where cold should have been, and it eased across her cheeks. Spade laid his hand on Riley's arm, and the vise-like grip pinched her skin. Underneath, awkward undergarments pressed into curves. A surge of anger rose. Having survived the cruelty of Mark, living after being shot multiple times, surviving the Shift, she lacked the appreciation or understanding of this fear-inducing game.

"Let go of me," Riley grimaced.

He gave her a hard yank.

Furious, she looked into his eyes, seeing two tunnels of blackness encircled by a rim glowing orange-red. Those eyes mirrored a man she'd seen before.

Her skin burned as she tried to peel his fingers away.

"Rose, Hank, end this now," she shouted, searching for cameras but finding none.

"Who the fuck are Rose and Hank?" Spade clenched his teeth. "I told you, Ellie. You're not going home, and if he comes looking for you, I'll kill the bastard."

"Okay, I tap out. Now get me the fuck out of this game."

Spade, the actor, or the devil, maybe both, wore an expression of rage. His silver-blue eyes rimmed in an orange glow turned to blue fire. Long jagged scars twisted around his high tensed cheekbone, up and under his eyes. Her throat constricted. All saliva left her mouth, turning it dry. Unable to swallow, she choked out, "enough,"

"I don't have time for this."

He ground his teeth hard enough for her to hear. She sensed she feared him before and would again in the future. An enormous heat radiated from his body, and the smell of sweat mixed with the scent of old perfumes touched her nose.

Riley stood still, knowing any reaction would trigger him to blow. Spade's broad shoulders loomed over, and as he grabbed her by the shoulder, Riley lost footing. The tip of her shoe caught the bottom of the dress, and the material tore. He pulled her through a side door where they entered a smoke-filled saloon.

Remember, this is the real thing — Rose's words rung in her head. *Not actors!*

Everything appeared before her. Scantily clad women in saloon dresses laughed, and drunken men fondled them. Shots filled with whiskey and full jugs of beer sat on tables. An old cowboy with a bullet-riddled hat pounded on the piano. The beer sitting on top sloshed beer down onto the key as two old poker faces waved guns at the other, shouting.

"Cheater," he yelled. "You cheating, son of a bitch."

The devil loosened his hold.

A young woman, frazzled, rushed past them, nearly colliding with Riley. Slade reached out and grabbed her by the arm.

"You'd better straighten out, Liza. Go clean yourself up." Spade said. "You've got a cowboy waiting upstairs." She looked at Riley, the fear in her eyes gleaming through her tears. Riley could see the bruising on her skin. Comfort came with the gun hidden in the folds of the dress.

"Sorry, Spade," she cried. Escaping his hold, she ran off.

Spade turned to Riley, "I warned you. It's time you learn a lesson. Should I have one of the girls teach you?" A smile formed on his lips. "You'll think twice about leaving my house after spending a few rounds with these animals." He dipped his face close to hers. Close enough, she could draw a map of the scars on his skin.

"I don't think so," Riley told Spade.

The slap came hard, stinging the skin on her cheek. The blow sent her backward. Riley saw flashing white lights and then darkness as she clutched the gun tighter in her hand. Riley slowly climbed to her feet, not bothering to dust the dirt from the dress.

A loud moan from the hinges of a door invaded the stale air.

The room fell silent.

Everything stopped at once. Even the cowboy banging on the piano paused.

Men parted, women moved across the room, and thin streams of smoke twirled like little twisters from lit cigarettes and cigars toward the ceiling. Dust rolled inward, catching beams of light, joining in the last of the fading sun. A shadow of a man appeared, and the cowboy held presence.

"I should've helped the girls bake cookies," she muttered.

This circumstance screamed trouble. Maybe she suffered from a concussion caused by the Wal-Mart monster. This place could all be a dream. Or a nightmare? Riley blinked, running her finger over her lips, tasting blood. Her hand and the side of her face stung. Remembering the cut on her face, she reached up. The cut was gone. If she wasn't asleep or dead, what was she?

"Lucas." Spade smiled, revealing straight white teeth.

"Spade!" The man's voice touched her ears with a safe familiarity.

The man called Lucas entered. His silhouette blocked most of the early evening sky, trying to shower inward through the saloon doors. As he stepped into the light, Riley thought him to be ruggedly handsome. Dark features, olive skin with blue-green eyes. Lucas glanced at her. Riley felt a soft jolt of electricity as Lucas's eyes met hers. The immediate warmth she felt indicated he was the good guy.

Riley took a step forward. Spade clamped his fingers around her arm even harder. The heels of her boots caught in the planks of wood, forcing Riley back into Spade's hold.

"Spade!" Lucas shouted.

Spade raised his pistol and aimed for Lucas.

"Stop this, Rose!" Riley stomped her foot.

No answer came.

No Hank. No Rose.

The hand of the devil snaked out, and his fingers locked around Riley's neck. She spun, slipping away from him. With fierce intensity and not an ounce of hesitancy, she aimed her pistol at Spade's heart.

He smiled.

Riley pulled the trigger.

"Click."

Never had her gun failed her. She cleared the jam quickly.

The weapon made a chick clunking noise.

She aimed and fired.

"Click.

Lucas approached fast.

Riley turned to face the footfalls.

Spade latched onto her throat, squeezing down until her breath locked closed.

"I'm going to kill you both," Spade spit out.

"Let her go!" Lucas shouted, closing the distance between them.

"It's a good day for you to watch her die." Spade laughed. "She's got fire. I'll give her that."

Light-headed, Riley closed her eyes, thinking the game might end here.

Riley dug with what nails she had into his flesh, forcing Spade to lighten his hold. When Lucas attempted to step forward, Spade stopped him.

"Don't!" Spade squeezed down on her flesh.

In an air-deprived panic, she dropped her gun. Clawing, she felt flesh peeling away from Spade's arm. Riley could barely see that he still held his revolver aimed at Lucas.

Lucas locked onto her gaze. A flash of white light flickered in her eyes and then a passing moment, like a slow-motion scene in a movie of Lucas aiming the barrel in her direction.

An explosion of flame shot out the barrel. The shot rang in Riley's eardrums. Lucas's bullet hit Spade in the chest. A warm spray of blood splattered across her face.

Spade's grip loosened as Lucas's hand grabbed hers. He pulled her from Spade as a rush of air filled her lungs. Lucas held Riley at his side, pressing her into him. For a short moment, Riley felt his heart beating. Lucas pulled her, and she followed without reservation.

A red stain spread across Spade's chest. "Time for you to join your brother." Blood dripped from between his lips, and as hard as he fought death, Spade could not run from the blackness standing behind him.

"Go to hell," Lucas sneered.

"If I go, you go." Thick red liquid pooled on the floor beneath Spade.

"We aren't going the same direction," Lucas informed Spade.

The room was silent. Again, everything went into slow motion. Spade's eyes, mirrored by an evil shadow, penetrated the connection to Lucas's soul. He attempted to infiltrate an unwanted ugliness into her, making her heart physically ache as she fought off his energy. Riley closed him off as Lucas wrapped his arm around her waist, pulling her close to him, reconnecting them. Blood oozed from his shoulder, soaking his shirt. The smell of finely aged oak and whiskey lingered on his breath.

Spade, taking his last breath, steadied himself. He raised his pistol to Lucas. Riley cried out, but Lucas already anticipated his enemy's next move and held his Colt 45 on Spade.

"Live," Lucas told Riley.

Lucas grabbed her, and for an instant, Riley thought they would leave through the swinging doors together. Instead, he shoved her outward, causing her to fall on the wooden walkway. Two gunshots echoed and bounced off nearby buildings. Screams gushed outward. Then everything went silent.

The sunlight started to disappear, leaving long finger-like shadows on the ghost town's base. Darkened shapes weaved around streets cast by the dying light. Riley sat upright, trying to think. Looking down, she once again wore the running clothes she left the hotel wearing. Close to her lay a pistol, her pistol. Twisting around, she looked at the saloon doors, nothing but silence. One lone dust devil swirled in a sequence of touchdowns and liftoffs. Riley jumped at the push of the wind, catching and moving tumbleweeds. As she climbed to her feet, the gun disappeared. The weight under her shoulder told her the pistol was still in its holster where it should be.

Walking toward the hotel did nothing to help her sort out what just happened. Her throat itched, and the sounds of the ghost town woke by way of the walking dead. She started to run.

She may have rushed inside a little too quickly. Rose, Utah, and Megan looked at her with curious faces. Hank shuffled in from the front desk, giving her an eye. Setting a carrot into his mouth, he took a bite and then pointed the tip at her as you would a finger.

"I see you met Spade," he took another bite. "By the looks of the handprint on your neck, he had a good hold on you too. He must have liked you."

"That's a horrible game," she said, glancing over at Utah, who had grown quiet. The girl's face had gone pale.

"That wasn't no game misses. That was a warning," Hank said. "Best to learn by what you saw as you see fit."

Riley rushed off, looking for the nearest mirror. The girls and Rose followed, but Hank stayed in the kitchen. A set of Spade's fingerprints branded her neck. Dry blood spotted her lips. She wiped off the blood, but they only bled again.

"Premonition?"

"It's a long story. It sounds as if Lucas found the one he was looking for," Rose started to leave and then turned toward Riley, "best one saved for dinner."

Rose and Megan turned back to the kitchen, but Utah hesitated, moving in close to Riley.

"It was real, Riley. Like the water. Spade is evil," she said, patting Riley as a mother would on the arm. She turned and followed her sister.

A child warned her. If only she would have listened. Riley stood in front of the mirror, pondering what Utah had said. Her heart fluttered as Lucas reappeared. Something drew her to him without knowing why. He reached out and touched her shoulder, sending instant warmth throughout her body. As he moved closer to her, the soft fabric of Ellie's dress swished against his leg. Riley leaned back into him as his lips brushed her face. Then the air turned chilly, and he was gone.

28

Jack heard the women's voices from the top of the cellar stairs. He took the stairs, two at a time, downward. Coldness seeped through his boots into his socks, making his feet turn suddenly cold. The hand-held light lit up space in front of him, but further down into the abyss, he saw the flickering of fire coming from a candle. Not paying attention to the conditions of the chamber, he moved forward.

A woman appeared behind a set of steel bars. Her skin smudged with dirt, her eyes sunken and dusted with a bluish tint smeared under her eyes.

"Help us." She reached her hand through the bars toward Jack. He moved forward but too quickly. She retreated in her cell to a shadowed corner where she was too hard for him to see.

"Shay brought us here," he said, keeping himself visible in the light. "The keys?"

At the mention of Shay's name, the woman took quick steps toward Jack. She reached through the bars and pointed.

The keys hung far enough away for the prisoners to see but too far to reach. Jack grabbed the keyring and moved back to her.

"What's your name?"

Her clothes were dingy and torn. The long-sleeved shirt hung from her body, paper-thin and a size too big.

"Sherry."

Small cells, only fifteen by twenty feet, connected to make a single row. The space provided little room for the makeshift toilet and provisional bed that sat against the far wall. The smell of urine, feces, and mold hung heavy in the air. The brutal reality of the isolation inflicted on these women was cruelty no human being should have to endure. These women were nearly in too poor of shape to wait outside for Dan's pickup, but Jack didn't want to wait even a minute more than he had to. He wanted to get the hell out of here as quickly as possible.

"Hurry," she whispered. "Did you kill all of them?"

Jack set any emotion to the side and focused on sorting through the keys one by one. "

Sherry pressed her face against the bars of the cell. "We thought Shay died?"

"She isn't dead," he replied. "She came back for Jonah and all of you." He tried a key and then another. "Amy, Sadie, Holly, and Terra, are they here too?"

NOT ALONE

"The men took Amy."

"She's safe," he slipped another key into the lock. The lock clicked and released open. It meant one thing, freedom.

"Here, over here." Voices called from the folds of the cellar.

Jack stepped toward the row of cells while Sherry kept her distance behind him. Searching faces, he stopped at the furthest. Fingers white from clinging to the bars. Jack recognized Terra from Blake's photo as she pressed her face to the bars.

"Is Blake here?"

"Yes," Jack said, unlocking her cell and handing her the keys.

"What's happening, Terra?" a voice called out.

"You guys do whatever they say, understood?" She stepped out of the cell and took the twins by the hands.

"Is that everyone?"

Terra nodded. Four pale faces pressed together, locking fingers and steps.

"Coming up. Copy."

"Copy," Blake answered, but Jack knew he'd been listening via radio.

Terra led the women up the stairs and into the flat light of the smoky kitchen. She stopped short of where Blake stood, and he gave her a reassuring nod. Jack urged them on.

"Have Terra drive the Hummer," Jack called after them.

For the first time in months, the women stepped out into the open air, free. Jack hurried them through the falling snow. Worried hypothermia might happen fast in their weakened conditions. Jack stopped, and the women clung together for warmth as Jack reached for something hidden underneath brush and snow. He handed the full duffle bag to Sherry and Terra.

"There's clothing in there." He turned away to allow them to dress concerned about Cooper. "Coop, you okay! Coop, answer me if you can?"

"I'm a nurse," Sherry stepped up from behind him, listening.

"We're going to need you." Jack knew a treasure when he found one and a nurse numbered at the top of the prize list.

Blake reloaded his pistol glancing at Terra.

"Get them moving," Jack commanded Blake.

"I gotta go get Coop," said Blake.

"I got Coop and the makings for a good fire," Jack said. "Get them going before they freeze to death."

"Desert One," Dan reported in, "winds picking up."

"Copy," Jack headed back toward the house.

29

Jack went into the garage from the house. The generator was sputtering down below and wouldn't last much longer. The best way to get what he wanted out was to use the emergency release kit on the garage door opener and open the doors manually. There was no way in hell he was going to drive the Chevy through the barrier. Jack worked fast, pulling down on the emergency release handle. The cord disconnected the garage door from the trolley, allowing him to pull it upward.

When the door held and remained stationary, he stepped back. A wide grin formed on his face as he turned around and faced the restored red fifty-six Chevrolet truck that would get him and Coop down the road.

A classic in its right reflected an era of time lost and returned. The old classic shone candy apple red against the white walls. Cherry wood panels polished to a high gloss finish lined the bed.

Jack scowled at the rusty gas cans stacked in the bed. He lifted them out and set them to the ground. "Fuel for the fire," he said.

He ran back into the house with the fuel cans leaving one in the entry hall and another in the furthest cell. Then he planted a small bundle of explosives next to the can in the cell. If timed right, and with Matt in tow, he'd take the Chevy and detonate the bombs on exit, blowing the house into toothpicks and get Matt to Nick quickly.

A screen of smoke from the smoldering poker table blanketed the interior. Jack stepped over the dead, toward the guesthouse, where a faint but visible light shone from a window. The front door was open. Matt sat slumped over on the living room floor. No movement and no sounds came from within the house. Jack knelt and felt for a pulse. The slight beat of Matt's heart thumped under his finger.

"Coop," Jack said, lifting Matt's head away from his chest. He then ripped Matt's shirt open, pulling aside his bulletproof vest. "Where are you hurt?"

"The ball... game... I... smell... gas." Matt stirred, talking in riddles, but speaking just the same.

Jack found several wounds leaking blood. One of the bullets missed his bulletproof vest entering his side and exiting his back. The third bullet hit him near his armpit.

"Damn it, Coop. Hold tight. I got to find something to stop the bleeding."

Jack found the bathroom quickly and started gathering items to stop the bleeding. He went to work using a sheet and the only thing available, sanitary napkins. By pressing the makeshift bundle into Matt's side, Jack was able to wrap strips of the cloth around him and secure the pressure. He was losing and had lost a lot of blood. Jack hurried. They'd already overstayed their welcome. He picked Matt up and laid him across his shoulder.

"Hold on, Coop."

Jack moved toward the house and then into the garage. He placed Matt onto the Chevy's front seat carefully.

"I'll be right back, Kid," said Jack.

Inside the house, he soaked the couches with the last can of gas. Void of remorse, he struck a match and tossed it onto the center cushion. A hungry hot flame ignited, spreading across the sofa and onto the side table. The fire, hungry, joined the smoke already floating near the ceiling. Now the smoldering card table responsible for all the smoke disappeared, and a full-fledged fire resulted. The red-hot blaze licked upward, spreading to the floor and then crawling toward the draperies. Jack sprinted out the door, not looking back.

"Stay with me, Coop," he said to Matt as he slid him into the driver's seat, telling the truck, "keys or no keys, you're mine." He reached under the seat and heard the jingle, which was magic to his ears. "Meant to be," he sighed.

Jack started the Chevy as smoke began to seep into the garage through cracks in the door. A fire alarm overhead chirped and then screeched. Jack put the truck into reverse.

The Chevy's tires made tracks in the thin blanket of new snow as he headed down the drive. Behind them, a loud explosion rocked the house, shaking the ground. In the rearview mirror, Jack watched dancing blue flames rise overhead. Snowflakes the size of a half-dollar combined with ash descended from the still night sky.

Giant plumes of fire and smoke reached upward as the fire found fuel and gained momentum. Jack was a good hundred yards down the drive when the second detonator exploded below the cellar. The blast's force propelled debris and projectiles made from the house and its contents into the air. A small fragment of burning wood fell on the hood of the Chevy, sliding off as they made a turn.

"Jesus, Jack! What the hell are you doing up there?" Blake's voice crackled in his earpiece.

NOT ALONE

"Blowing up Hell on the Hill! On my way down. Have the nurse standing by." Driving the hell out of the Chevy twisting back and forth on narrow switchbacks and hairpin turns, Jack slow drifted the corners on the snow, keeping control of the vehicle. He gave the Chevy more throttle on the straightaways until the storm intensified. The windshield wipers, unable to keep up with the falling flakes, failed. Now Jack slowed, fighting to see past the white out in front of him.

"Standing by," answered Blake.

When Jack neared the bottom, he gave the gas pedal more throttle pushing the truck hard toward the high desert's flats. A layer of snow already several inches thick formed on the ground as he brought the Chevy to a sliding stop behind Blake's truck. In the distance, Jack saw the van and Hummer's taillights heading toward the highway for the ranch.

Before Jack could say anything, Sherry opened the passenger door. Snowflakes gathered in her hair as she pulled off her gloves and pressed her fingers against Matt's wrist. Shay stepped out of the shadows, her eyes catching Jack's expression of disapproval.

"You should've gone with the others."

"Sherry is going to need an extra hand."

"Unbuckle him."

Jack did as Sherry asked. She untied the makeshift bandages letting the blood-soaked materials drop to the ground.

"We need to get him to a hospital. Now."

"There are no hospitals," Sherry looked at Jack, disbelieving.

"What do you mean there aren't any hospitals?"

"How long have you been at that cabin?"

"Too long."

"Things are different now," Jack said. Hey, what about Pam's place."

"Good idea. What's your experience?" Blake asked Sherry.

"I worked in the ER in Phoenix."

"Good, you can assist Pam. Move him over to my truck." Blake pointed over to the 56. "We can't all fit in that truck."

"Okay. I'll be behind you," Jack said. "Can't see shit out of this ole girl."

They lifted Matt to the backseat of Blake's truck. Sherry jumped in beside him, keeping pressure on the wound. "Hurry."

"That relic won't make it in this weather," Blake looked at Jack with concern as he climbed into his truck.

Jack would be back to bury the girl they'd found in town, gather the remaining gasoline, but not tonight. He turned to the red truck and then to Shay, who climbed in, ignoring the blood on the Chevy's seat. Jack looked straight ahead into the blizzard, saying nothing.

30

Riley tried to focus on the goal at hand, which was to find her brother Eric alive. So far, that was proving to be challenging. The morning conversation rolled through her mind as Arizona's desert loomed in front of her. The hum of the Dodge's diesel hummed as Rose and Hank's story repeated in her mind.

"You're not the first one to see Spade." Rose leaned in closer to her. "The others never made it past the plate of cookies. But no one has ever seen Lucas."

"Lucas and Jason Evans were Texas-born brothers. The ranch belonged to their father," Hank said, biting into a cookie. "Wish I had cold milk to dip this in."

"The brothers ran the ranch, but Lucas also worked with the local sheriff. When he turned twenty-two, he was the sheriff," Rose continued. "They say he was a handsome man."

"Who is Spade?" asked Riley. Utah set her cookie down on her plate slowly, looking up as if she knew the answer.

"When Lucas left town on business, a motley crew out of Mexico killed his brother, burned the ranch house down, and stole all of their cattle."

"Spade?"

"Spade wasn't his real name. Honestly, I don't recall his real name, but he had no clue who he fucked with," Hank said, letting his fist fall to the table. The bang made them all jump.

"Hank Jenson! There are young ladies at the table," shouted Rose. "And you scared the be-Jesus out of all of us!"

"Sorry, girls," he mumbled, grabbing another cookie. "Lucas searched for months, vowing to kill the men who murdered his brother. He searched for well over a year, killing one bandit at a time, riding hundreds of miles to track them until there was but one left, Spade."

"A year later, Lucas met Ellie. Ellie was the daughter of a wealthy banker in California, beautiful, compassionate, and smart. Lucas wasn't looking for a woman. Instead, he was out for revenge. But Ellie changed his fate when he fell in love with her," Rose smiled, setting a fresh pot of coffee on the table.

"Bittersweet." Riley wished she had found a hero like Lucas. Instead, she found an animal like Mark. "So you're telling me that ghosts abducted me and that what I saw was another world. Their world?"

NOT ALONE

"World or realm? Lucas and Spade, spirits, you might say, inhabit that place. Lucas is good, and Spade is evil," Rose looked down at her coffee, perhaps feeling silly about what she'd just said.

"Spiritual manifestations?"

"They married, and Lucas rebuilt the ranch bigger and more elaborate than the first one. He came back stronger," said Hank.

"He must've found Spade?" Riley asked.

"Lucas and Spade never crossed paths before, so Lucas had no idea what Spade looked like. He'd been chasing a ghost all along. Fast forward a few years ahead. Spade returns to Bakersfield. Changed his name to Spade, bought the local saloon, and filled it with girls barely old enough to well, you know," Hank flushed.

"I don't know," Megan said and rolled her cooking over in her fingers.

"When Spade saw Ellie, he had to have her," Hank said, leaving Megan's remark unanswered.

"Spade waited for an opportune time to kidnap Ellie," Rose added. "Lucas was out assisting his hired hand with a cow who was having trouble birthing."

"Lucas didn't know he'd be confronting the one man he'd been looking for all those years." Hank tapped his hearing aid, which prompted a high pitch squeal. Utah plugged her ears. "It was a violent battle. Both men fought to their deaths."

"Lucas shoved Ellie out onto the boardwalk."

"Lucas not only saved her life but also the life of their unborn child," Rose said, looking at Riley. Their gazes met. "Elli buried her husband on the hill overlooking their ranch. She rebuilt the house after giving birth eight months later to a son. The legend says the town was never the same. Ellie was never the same. She mourned her husband's death and vowed to have her revenge on Spade in the afterlife."

"What happened to the child?"

"Their son grew up to be a strong, handsome man assuming his father's role by later becoming the town sheriff, and then the town's Mayor."

"What does this have to do with me?" Riley looked at Hank, then Rose.

"I have a feeling you'll someday find out," nodded Rose.

"I can't wait," Riley spoke with reservation. Lucas and Spade were something else for Riley to ponder in the quiet moments of their travels. Apparently, unbeknownst to her, the future held answers to all her forthcoming questions. Riley, unable to answer why the encounter between herself, Lucas, and Spade occurred, decided to push it as far back in her mind as she could. For now, anyway.

NOT ALONE

Riley looked at the girls, then Max sleeping beside her. The hum of the tires brought her mind back on the road. They were closing in on the Arizona state line, now getting closer to Eric. They traveled from the coastline to central California's arid land to this mysterious place of rock-formed peaks and Arizona's endless sand. The desert's beauty held such captivating landscapes. Road signs were riddled with bullets reminded her that this new world was the product of violence.

While Kenny Chesney sang about sunny, sandy beaches and margaritas, the sky overhead grew dark.

"Where are we?" Utah yawned, rubbing her eyes.

"I'm not sure," Riley pulled over. "Signs on the ground. If you need to pee, now's a good time."

"It's cold!" Megan pulled her lap blanket up and around her.

"Hurry up then, Megan," Utah tugged on her sister's arm.

After the girls were back in the truck, safe, Riley turned over the sign, fighting the frigid cold stealing her breath. "Needles, twenty-three miles."

She looked toward the sky. Having weathered some severe storms in Oregon, she stared at the one they faced now, but this one looked blacker than anything she'd ever seen. The world had gone crazy, and Mother Nature was following its example.

Highway 40 might turn out to be both their friend and enemy. She wanted a smooth ride to Ash Fork and then onto highway eighty-nine to Prescott, where she hoped shelter would be plentiful.

Easy, right? Riley shivered, feeling a biting cold. They'd be heading into a storm.

31

Riley could not push the truck any harder. If she did, she risked damage to the truck because of the condition of the highway. The wreckage spread out across the pavement and onto both sides of the road. Nails, metal, and other objects were tire destroyers and lay scattered on the ground. She could not risk blowing a tire or putting the truck in a ditch, and without the rolling motel, there'd be no place to shelter.

Dozens of wrecked cars, twisted in gruesome angles, framed the shoulder, making her think twice about applying any more pressure to the throttle. Several miles ahead, Riley saw the reason for the carnage.

Chunks of commercial airplane debris were spread over miles of road and sand, forcing Riley to slow and chose her path with care. Bleached seats, large pieces of the cockpit taller than the truck, suitcases, and sifted and separated clothing lay adrift. She made out a few resting bones, but predators of the desert had disposed of the rest. The scene manifested into a sinister, creepy mess better made for the movies. After seeing so many other horrors, this one, for some reason, made her feel lucky.

In and around, Riley maneuvered the truck, the tires passing over objects best left unknown as they pushed in the direction of Kingman, bypassing Route 66 best saved for another time. It took three hours to reach Ash Fork from where they'd gotten to, and when they did, six inches of fresh snow lay on the ground and building fast as the storm increased with a dangerous intensity. Closing in on Prescott, the snowstorm kicked into a near whiteout.

Self-entertained, the girls quietly watched movies as Riley kept an eye out for barriers blocking her way. The temperature outside dropped to the low thirties and wind pressed against the truck with power. Nothing was visible on the highway as visibility lessened, and the dark gray-blue canopy above turned invisible.

Riley stopped in the road, needing to refuel the truck from the cans in the back. Layered up, like the Michelin Man, she still felt the bitter cold biting her skin. A known fear crept back inside of her head. If they lost control or ran out of gas, they would freeze to death. Her only goal now was to find shelter long enough to ride out the storm. She pulled cans of diesel from the back and started filling the tank, praying it would be enough to get them someplace safe.

She looked up when she heard the window roll down, and Megan's tiny voice found its way through the gusts.

"Can we do snow angels, Riley?"

Riley shook her head no. A bad feeling built up inside her, making her anxious. She silently wished they were back at the ghost town with Hank and Rose.

"Close the window before you freeze."

The girls rolled the window up.

Riley, feeling the cans lighten as the diesel ran into the truck's tank, looked up to where the girls had their faces pressed to the window. Megan's gaze wasn't on Riley but instead fixated on something behind her.

"What?"

Megan pointed.

Riley looked back. Nothing. She shook her head.

Several hairs rose on the back of her neck, knowing an overactive imagination brought to life such things as monsters and beasts hungry to harm. Riley knew kids were so much more intuitive. Riley emptied the last of the diesel. Powerless to shake a feeling that someone or something lurked behind her, she hurried. Through the magical hush of snow falling all around her, Riley heard a metallic sound. She tossed the empty cans into the bed then climbed into the truck. Heat blew from the vents, making her cold fingers burn.

Utah leaned against the window peering outside. "Riley. Something's out there."

"I need your help, Utah. Any towns ahead of us?" Riley asked, handing Utah the map.

She pressed her finger to the map tracing the highlighted road. "Ash Fork."

"Okay."

Riley felt the tires fight for traction plowing through mounds of fresh snow and sliding from side to side. Even in four-wheel drive, they were moving at a snail's pace, but they had escaped the long stretch of highway unscathed. If there were some chainsaw-wielding serial killer behind them, he'd be crazy to challenge Mother Nature and follow them. Relentless and not ready, nightfall rode the skirt tails of daylight in a hurry. A long hour later and exhausted, Riley searched for both roads and signs to lead them to shelter. They had to stop. It had taken Riley several years to get here. What were a few more hours?

The girls dropped to their knees, pressing their faces to the windows assisting in searching for shelter.

Between storm and dusk, the dim light left Riley with a feeling of dread. According to the truck's reading, the outside temperature dropped. If stranded, they would freeze to death for sure. If they found shelter, they'd be taking one hell of a risk of the unknown.

The snow hypnotized her, making her struggle to keep the truck on track. Through the white curtain of snow, she caught a flash of green under the headlights.

"There," Riley said, bringing the truck to a stop. She jumped out and tossed a rock at the sign. A blanket of snow fell from the metal. "Two miles," she whispered.

A swishing sound caused her to turn as the storm shifted. The truck's headlights looked dull, sending another wash of fear through her. She took her gloved hands and wiped the buildup of snowfall, shielding the lights. Riley jumped in as the wind shifted, slamming her door shut. An invisible force inserted urgency in her to get moving. Visibility went from five feet to not being able to see past the windshield. The last two miles felt more like ten.

"Get your bags ready. Grab all the water you can, food, and stuff that into the bags," Riley said.

She followed the fence line keeping the truck tracking to the center. In four-wheel drive, she steered the diesel on a blanket of white. Gusts of wind pounded the side of the truck, rocking it back and forth.

"Put on everything you can."

"What about Max?" asked Megan.

"I'll put him in my bag." Utah said, "see, plenty of room."

Riley had her doubts, not knowing where the road started or where it ended. Inch by inch, they pushed through.

"Look," Utah pointed. "You see it?"

"No," Riley asked her, straining to see.

"Buildings. We're in a town!" Utah said.

"Okay, you're my navigator," Riley said to her.

"Go more, more...," she paused and then said, "Stop, turn left."

Riley listened, letting off the throttle to keep the truck moving in a straight line.

"Find us a building," said Riley as another gust of wind blasted the side of the truck.

"There!" She pointed again. "Go straight... turn right."

The edge of a building appeared as the wind blasted from all directions. Riley maneuvered the truck through the parking lot around white mounds of snow-covered cars. The headlights, covered, turned dim, and of little use.

"I see a door!"

Tearing up due to exhaustion, Riley scanned the side of the building until she saw the faint outline of a door. She shut off the engine, and the sounds of the storm intensified inside the cab.

"Holy shit," Riley whispered, leaning forward. She peered upward, but there was no sky. There was a daunting void. "We need to get inside quick-like. Grab your bags. Put on your beanies and gloves. Double up?"

"It's too dark," Megan pulled on Riley's coat.

Lifting a flashlight into the air, Riley said, "not dark."

Grabbing pistols and the shotgun, she layered on clothing while the girls did the same. She stuffed the remaining water and food into one bag, clothes, and ammo into another.

"Ready?"

"Max," Megan cried, looking scared. "He'll get cold."

"He'll be okay, Megan, I promise," Utah said, opening the bag. Max looked up at Megan, licked his paw unworried, and then burrowed deep into her clothes.

"Let's go," Riley said, searching through the raging storm outside.

"Megan, climb over here, sweetheart. Hold my hand, and don't let go." Riley checked on Utah as she gathered her and Megan's bags. She nodded.

Not thirty feet from them, the building appeared engulfed by the body of a storm thirsty to kill. Riley waited between gusts to open the door. They scrambled out of the truck. The door slammed shut behind them, almost catching Utah's jacket. She let out a faint cry and scurried forward as another gust of wind swept across the parking lot, sending them several feet backward. Utah pushed forward behind Megan, clutching both bags, trying to keep on her feet. The hurricane-force winds made it almost impossible to walk. The numbing cold air slapped against their faces leaving a stinging sensation. Riley's concern for the girls increased, tiny with bodyweight well below average, they would freeze too fast. Pushing through the snow together, gripping hands, they advanced into the wind.

Then as if summoned, the wind stopped. Riley felt a chill on the back of her neck as thundering crashes ensued. Something big and cumbersome ripped objects apart. Megan's grip tightened. Whatever the thing was, it traveled in their direction.

"Run," yelled Riley stumbling forward, catching Megan. Separated by gusting snow, Riley had to let go fearing she might pull Megan's arm out of the socket or worse. Riley landed face-first into the snow, the wind whipping past. Unable to see anything, Riley struggled to stand, searching for the girls.

"Megan!" Riley screamed out, "Utah!"

"Riley," Megan cried.

Everything turned to an instant gray, Megan appeared only as a ghost-like figure, but Riley reached out and pulled the little girl into her arms, shielding her from the wind.

Utah appeared beside Riley, reaching out to take her hand.

"Good," Riley saw both her and the bag holding Max.

A release of wind propelled several objects into the air, slamming them onto the roof overhead. Riley pulled them toward the door. A large metal body flew past them, slamming into the side of the building. The sounds of the wind pushing objects and propelling them into the air sounded like thunder. Riley turned the handle, willing the door to open while holding tight onto Megan. The locked door held them captive outside.

"Can you open it, Riley?" Utah hugged the duffle bag and Megan, her teeth chattering.

Riley reached into her pocket and removed a small container. Her fingers, already frozen through her gloves, made for stiff and clumsy lock picking. She dropped the wire twice before she could press her device through the keyhole opening.

The girls pressed into her, searching for warmth. On the third try, and with something moving toward them at high speed, Riley unlocked and opened the door.

"Get inside."

They dove inside as debris slammed into the door. The sound echoed inside the abyss of space with a loud crash, making Riley wonder if it might be a car.

Don't move until I get back. Understand?" Riley told them. They nodded.

Riley waited to make sure the flying object had landed and then went back outside, pushing her way back to the truck. The cold air bit through her clothing, freezing skin and muscles. Someone or something had pissed Mother Nature off, and she reared her ugly head in retaliation. Frantic, Riley gathered the rest of the bags, half carrying, half dragging them in the direction of the door.

Entering through a realm of a place unknown to her, Riley stopped beside the girls. The cold latched onto exposed flesh, chilling her to the core.

The door trembled as the storm's strength increased more, sending a sharp whistling sound underneath the threshold. Forced air pressed through pinhole gaps. To Riley, the building felt like a giant freezer.

32

The newest building, Ash Fork Veterinarian Hospital, was well equipped and had a ton of supplies. Jack only knew this because he'd helped find the men to build it and the supplies to stock it. The compound sat a quarter of a mile off a drainage road that ran parallel to the highway nestled against a massive chunk of land hugging a deep valley. There were three buildings beside the largest one. The freak storm would be wreaking havoc on power lines.

However, the hospital contained several backup generators for nights like tonight. The main center building included examining rooms, surgical rooms, office space, and even a compact apartment, all of which needed power.

"Where are we?" asked Shay peering out the window.

"Wait here." Jack stepped out of the truck as a surge of wind pushed him back a step, slamming the door closed. Jack wasn't paying attention to the snow-driven wind. He was looking at the outside lights that should be lighting the place up.

"No power," he said aloud.

Jack unlocked the door to the building and then motioned the others over.

"Sweet Jesus, it's cold in here," said Jack, flicking on a flashlight. "I'm afraid to know why the backup generators aren't on. Take this." Jack handed Shay the light. They stepped into a long hallway that looked more like an abyss of space and blackness. "Something's not right," Jack muttered, wishing they'd taken their chances on the road.

"Hurry," said Sherry. "He's too quiet. Where's the doctor?"

"There's a surgery room here." They moved together until they reached two swinging doors, which led into ice-cold blackness.

"Don't touch anything." Sherry's voice trembled. "It needs it to be sterile in here." Blake and Jack set Matt down on a stainless steel table.

Shay stood quiet. Several sizable stainless steel sinks lined the countertops, and several cupboards lined the walls. There were plenty of supplies stacked on shelves, a few on the floor unopened.

"Eerie and cold. Where's Doc?" Blake asked.

"Good question. You have never been here, Blake?" Jack asked.

"No, Doc's made a few house calls. Never been here. It's spooky."

Jack grinned, but Sherry reappeared, pulling on scrubs, turning his smile to a frown. She handed them surgical gloves too small to fit men. "Can you get him on the other table?"

They lifted Matt, moving him carefully.

"I'm not a surgeon," Sherry told Jack.

"No, but you're a nurse, and no doctor is a doctor without a nurse."

"Shay," Sherry said, taking Shay's hand pressing it into Matt's wound. "Press hard. I'm going to need the key to the medicine cabinet?"

Jack handed the key to Sherry. "Get what you need. You okay here?"

"Where are you going?" Blake asked.

"Going to try and find out where Pam went and see if I can get some power."

"Should we expect the doctor, or should I try to get the bullet out?" Sherry asked, reaching into the medicine cabinet, taking several vials out.

"Her truck's here," Jack said, holding back his concern.

"She might be out taking care of an animal," Blake said.

"Maybe. Maybe got caught out there in the storm. No technician either?" Jack had a bad feeling. He knew Pam, and this wasn't like her.

"What kind of animals?" asked Shay. "Horses?"

"Large ones," Jack nodded. "Don't leave this room."

"Cows?"

"She takes care of those too," said Jack, trying to avoid any more questions. He rummaged through his pack, found a key, and unlocked a larger cabinet, withdrawing a tranquilizer gun and some vials.

As if on cue, a loud cry resonated down the hall, causing Shay and Sherry to turn. The sound, shrill and terrifying, did not come from a horse. The scream bounced off the walls, echoing through the doors and into the darkness. Several mixed shrieks followed. They all turned to Jack.

"Holy shit!" whispered Blake. "What was that?"

"That my friend is Bermuda or Elmo. If I remember correctly, Elmo is out on the conservatory," Jack said, tossing him a tranquilizer gun. "You know how to use one of those?"

"What is Bermuda, Elmo?" Sherry asked with a tremble in her voice.

"Point and shoot," Blake said, ignoring Sherry.

Blake inspected the gun, clicking open the chamber. "Awe," he said.

"Should we be worried?" asked Shay.

Jack glanced at Shay and then stepped past Blake. "Lock the door behind me." Jack left all questions unanswered. He needed Sherry and Shay to keep their attention on Matt.

Jack knew his way around the hospital, even in the dark. He knew where he needed to go and did it with little light to guide him. Whoever was out there could see him just as well without the light as with it, if not better.

The power's backup system came out of a hospital three times the compound's size, and when powered up, it could run all three buildings. There was no reason it shouldn't be powered up now unless Pam was in bad trouble or someone had intentionally turned it off while she was gone.

Jack and his friend, since childhood, Scott restored Drake's power many times. Still, Pam needed an emergency backup, especially being so far from Prescott. Jack brought in the generators as a dependable backup. In return, the Doc took care of him and the locals as well as their animals. The relationship worked for both of them, with no strings attached. He knew Pam would not have left the hospital or the animals without heat or light. Worried, Jack hurried down the corridor to the room housing the generators.

The reception area, located in the hospital's center, had corridors that branched off and led to different sections of the building. The exception was the waiting room, which faced the front parking lot and was part of the reception area. Slipping down a hallway, Jack turned down a stairwell through another locked door. Tapping the flashlight up a notch, he aimed it at the monstrous generators he and Pam named Godzilla.

Another infinite cry rose, and the sound was confined to the walls in which it echoed. Fine hairs on the back of Jack's neck rose. He thought again of Pam, seeing the power levers locked in an off position. Godzilla hummed a deadly silence. A different kind of fear intercepted his concerns for Pam as he flipped on the large generators.

A soft glow of red, then green light appeared on the panel as the generators powered up and motors started. The furnace clicked on, and overhead safety lights flickered as they warmed. Heating the building would be slow. Time neither the team nor the animals could afford.

One situation was fixed while another one let out a shrill cry that trickled down the stairwell. The sound reached a high pitch and then slipped into silence. Jack holstered his pistol, withdrawing the tranquilizer gun. He made his way back out into the cement jungle. He'd rather face a man than a lion.

Jack paused at the reception room, hugging the wall to listen. "Where are you?"

A series of claws tapped on the linoleum floor. The cat's senses outdid his a hundred to one. Jack knew the big cat might smell him long before she saw him.

The tan outline came into Jack's view, taking on an orange glow under reddish emergency lamps. Cutting the corner at the opposite end of the hall, the cat moved slow and confident, stopping only to raise her head upward, smelling the air. He watched as her ears dropped down against her head. An irritated hiss followed and then turned to a deep guttural vibrating growl. She stepped toward Jack. Her tail twitched. The stride was one intended to stalk prey.

"Bermuda, not Elmo."

Bermuda, a ninety-pound resident female cougar, trailed her prey, Jack. Jack glanced down the line of examination rooms. Several of the doors were open. If she went into one of them, he could trap her. If he raised the tranquilizer gun now, she might be able to reach him before the drug took effect and maul him to death. Bermuda paused, sniffing the air again. The instinct to hunt exciting her senses, but also her curiosity. She passed the first opened door uninterested. Jack, not comfortable having the cougar so close to him, leaned into the wall. Jack could now smell her. She stopped at the second opened door.

Something caught her attention.

The wait was excruciatingly dangerous, and the capture would depend on timing. Bermuda was three-quarters of the way in the room before he risked sliding forward. The cat, balanced, spun around but not before Jack had the door halfway shut. The edges of the cougar's cheeks lifted, exposing long stained pointed feline teeth. She hissed a series of angry growls.

The cat backtracked a few steps, ready to pounce, and as she did, Jack slammed the door.

"Gotcha."

He had no qualms with the cat. Through the window, he watched the cat's tail and back twitch, reflecting agitation.

"Jesus, you're a big girl."

She reared up on her haunches, sniffing the window. Jack had a bird's-eye view of her bloodied muzzle now, and his skin prickled.

"Whose blood are you wearing, Bermuda?"

The cat pinned her ears against her head, swatting her paw into the air. Bermuda, one of many residents living on the property, and Elmo, a Siberian White Tiger, an impressive big cat, resided on the property. Beautiful and dangerous, both cat's deserved man's respect.

Because of the Shift, wildlife in zoos had either died or been set free. Pam dedicated herself to save and protect as many as she could. Most animals lived outside in natural habitats, but a few of the sick or wounded stayed contained inside. Why was Bermuda loose, he didn't know? He'd seen the cat last week in her habitat built just for her. All he knew is that Bermuda wouldn't have been in the hospital if Pam wasn't here to watch over her.

Jack moved toward the hospital's south wing under shadows and distorted light, his imagination playing cruel tricks on his vision. He wanted to see if he could make heads or tails out of the questions that kept popping into his mind. When he came to the messes of overturned boxes that lie scattered on the floor, he paused.

Heat pumped through the vents overhead. Jack looked down, shining the light on the floor only to find red paw prints leading around the mess. He drew his pistol close, keeping the tranquilizer gun even closer. As he moved around the boxes, a rusty scent rose in the air.

Pam lay hidden behind overturned supplies, her body twisted and lifeless. Her coat, once tan, was soaked reddish brown. Dry mud clung to her boots. Strands of sandy brown hair matted with blood and brain matter lay stiff and flat against her head. Curled strands of hair and strips of clawed flesh were visible from teeth and claws. Pam lay facing the opposite direction.

Staring yet cautious not to turn his back to the hall, Jack knelt beside her, laying a hand on her arm, feeling the coldness of her death. Not squeamish of blood and body matter, Jack rolled her over. Grotesque mauled flesh between her cheeks and nose made her unidentifiable open bite marks on her neck, exposed vein, and bone. Broken bones, deep claw marks, and blood loss were all reasons for her death, but the bullet hole was the tell-all reason. Pulling back the fabric, Jack found the hole.

"Shit, Pam," he said softly. Reaching in her pocket, he took her keys. He stood, watching the corridor, listening to the sounds coming from the cages.

33

Kid, a name by his high school peers, kept to himself for a long time, trusting no one. He'd witnessed the effects of the Shift, the infection, ruthless killing, and the struggle for some to survive. Hell, he lost everything he ever loved, so laying his life on the line for others felt right. Kid took on an undercover paramilitary role himself months ago, and today seemed no different. Post-Shift, he delivered supplies to those in need, traveled up and down the long stretches of highway, covering miles of broken land. He'd reached out to a few isolated people and made some valuable connections, never saying too much or staying too long. Kid was doing what the Colton's were doing, only by himself and on a smaller scale. Like many survivors, he did whatever was necessary to keep his stayer status and helped those in need. However, Kid believed the time had come for him to join forces with the Colton's.

He'd been helping others alone for so long that he felt ready to be a part of something bigger. Jack Colton's team continued to make a difference by intercepting and preventing further violence. His efforts made a difference not just in Prescott but anywhere there was a call for help.

Kid heard through the grapevine that Colton was on another mission to save some kidnapped women. They needed a hero, and his name was Jack Colton. Kid had a particular interest in the situation after hearing a woman trespasser claimed a handful of women were hostages at some remote location.

Accompanied by a Rhodesian ridgeback, he named Shift. The puppy was the one positive thing that came out of the Shift. Shift stared out the window of the truck while letting out a soft whine. Well-bred and obedient, she and Kid worked well as both partners and friends. The dog turned her sweet honey-brown eyes on Kid seeking attention.

"What's wrong, girl?" He rubbed the dog around the neck up and under her collar. She lowered her head while not taking her eyes off the road. "You know we're going to Doc's, don't you?"

Kid felt the storm coming, but like most warnings, he ignored it. Another storm raged inside him, far more substantial than the one in the sky. Chasing demons regardless of the weather gave him newfound strength. The dark grey canopy above him did little to discourage him. Unlike most, he kept prepared for anything, even this coming storm. With the truck's back loaded down with supplies, he drove toward Ash Fork after stopping to drop off medical supplies in Chino Valley. Facing the dark sky and billowing white sails entombing the Arizona heavens, a mysterious dark shadow took daylight and shut it down. Kid felt a twinge of excitement.

Ash Fork, an isolated town comprised of barren grass, vast meadows outlined by rolling hillsides, and endless miles of railroad tracks, appeared abandoned. The first of the snowflakes fell like soft specks of loose cotton, twirling and spinning. Before long, the dancing flakes turned into a steady downfall of snow. As the storm increased, the ground became a thick blanket painted in contrasting white and blue colors. Mother Nature had a way of interrupting plans. Today she was unleashing her fury.

Kid locked in the four-wheel drive headed to his first of five stops. Four hundred and fifty souls populated Ash Fork before the Shift, and only thirty-four remained. In the bed of the truck were medical supplies and three drums of gas. The weight of the supplies kept the truck from sliding on the snow-covered road. He did a quick check on one family and then made deliveries to the elderly before stopping at Pam's place. Kid maneuvered the truck down the drainage road with little visibility and mostly memory to the back of the hospital.

Trading with the beautiful Doc, Kenny brought pleasure to both him and Shift. Pam got medical supplies, and he had a doctor and a vet when he needed one.

He'd met Pam after the Shift. His Great Dane, Duke, grew sick, dying an hour after arriving at the hospital. After Duke, he had nothing left. Devastated, Kid was walking back to his truck when Pam caught up to him. She set a moving bundle in his arms.

"Listen," she said, fighting back the tears, "I know what Duke meant to you, but this little girl needs a good home, and she needs one now. She lost all her siblings and her mama. I don't have time to cuddle her. Take her, and if you don't want her after she's a little more grown-up, then I'll take her back."

"I can't," Kid had said, trying to give her back to the Doc.

"I'm asking a favor of you," she turned her back to him. Somehow, Pam knew Shift would become his dog. After that, he spent more time at the hospital, and a friendship formed and a partnership.

The building sat further back from the highway, isolated from the center of town. The compound looked more like an industrial park with a ten-foot chain-link fence framing the property's perimeter. Above, four strands of twisted razor wire, security lights every sixty feet, and heavy locks on all the gates kept the compound secure. The property and its structures looked intimidating, similar to a full-fledged prison-like environment. The aim involved keeping animals in and people out. The sign at the entrance read, "Warning, enter at your own risk."

Kid strained to see the buildings through the falling snow. The flurry of flakes sped by him so fast he felt as if he was sitting still. Throttling through the gates, Kid saw the wind shift and the strength of the storm increase. Shift rose to her feet, excited.

Several cars sat in the parking lot, prompting Kid to place his weapon of choice, a 45 Kimber 1911 R1, on the seat next to him. He pulled on his ski jacket, gloves, and a stocking cap facemask. He gathered extra ammo and magazines. A gust of wind hit the truck hard.

Shift, no longer just excited, shivered.

"I know, girl. I've never seen anything like this before." Kid gave the dog a reassuring pat.

Kid grabbed the 308 semi-auto. Besides the Kimber, Kid favored the weapon as an extra. Hoisting the rifle across his back, he and Shift stepped out into the storm.

A truck blocked the back entrance to Pam's office. Concerned, he swept a handful of snow off the hood, exposing a blue fender. Pam drove a black SUV, not a Dodge.

"Blake Harris's rig."

Man and dog slipped through the door, finding little comfort from the cold. The backup lights were on, and the heating unit hummed, but still, the building felt like a giant freezer. Kid crept through the office, studying the trail of blood on the linoleum. Shift already on the scents moved with her nose to the ground, the dog's claws tapping on the floor. Kid followed her through the exit and into the corridor.

You're hiding something, Kid. Pam once told him. *If you ever need to talk, I'm a good listener.*

"I'll stop by," he promised.

Shift stopped, lifting her nose into the air. The smell of the animals caused the ridge on her back to rise. She pressed against Kid's leg for both comfort and warmth. He reached down, patted her on the top of her head, and then gestured her to move forward. She stepped out in front of him, leading the way.

The smell of cleaning chemicals hung in the chilly air, growing strong as they passed examining rooms, closets, and empty stacked animal containers along the corridor.

"Hey Doc, you here?" he called out.

No one answered, but the silence inside of the hospital wasn't a reason for concern yet. It was a giant cement maze with lots of rooms and divisions. Pam could be out of hearing distance and unable to hear him.

NOT ALONE

However, these days Kid remained alert for trouble. Like the night of the Shift, things appeared to be life as usual until it wasn't. From that full moon night forward, Kid walked as if he were walking into a fight.

This hospital also held creatures of the night and day, prey, and predators that could rip a man or animal apart with one fatal swoop or strike of a claw or tooth. That alone made Kid weary.

The red lighting played tricks on his vision, producing shadows that appeared and disappeared. When the cry of an animal broke the silence sending a slight chill down his spine, he knew something wasn't right. The animal crying was angry. In the animal kingdom, that meant hunger.

This place, Kid thought, was always somewhat creepy. To think lions, bears and badgers lived here made for a warranted accelerated heartbeat. Tonight, the silence made the hairs on the back of his neck stood on end.

The glowing light spilled from the split doors at the other end of the north wing hall. He and Shift headed for that way.

34

Riley kept her voice at a mere whisper. Experience dictated every space had its monsters, and here there was ample room. The storm outside lashed out with a supernatural punch making it hard to decipher one sound from the next. Eeriness pierced the walls, and from somewhere deep within the tomblike building, Riley heard an animal cry. The hair on her skin prickled. To go back out into the storm would be a certain death sentence. The outcome alone was reason enough to stay.

The wind howled outside, searching for openings. Riley shivered from the currents of cold air passing through the halls as it sliced into the dimness with a bitter bite. She feared using a flashlight would just make them an easy target if an infected occupied the building. So it was become a target or remain in the dark. She chose the latter of the two.

Inside, the outside noises echoed with soft thuds.

Thud.

This place, whatever the purpose, felt uninviting to Riley. No person in their right mind would think to step foot through the door she and the girls just entered through.

Thud.

Riley imagined that this is what it might have sounded like in a time of war. Trying to be brave for the girls, Riley pretended to ignore all the factors happening around her, trying to calm the unrest in her mind.

"It's dark, Riley," Megan took Riley's hand.

"I know, Megan." Riley bent down. "Rub your hands together."

Another cry so agonizing it terrified Riley because she, experienced as a wildlife officer, knew the sound wasn't coming from a human.

"What is that?" Utah stepped closer to Riley.

Before Riley could answer Utah, she heard the soft hum of the heater hum through the vents. Then, as if lighting their path, a dim glow of reddish lights that looked like something out of an end-of-the-world movie flickered on every twenty feet. However, there were dark spaces in between.

"We need to keep moving into the building away from the doors." Riley took the girl's hands, leading them forward.

Cold open space consumed the heat passing over them. Then another cry rose, this one far different, a cry Riley recognized as the call of a wolf.

"No way?" Riley slipped out aloud.

"Coyote," Utah answered, her teeth still chattering.

"Wolf," Riley said.

NOT ALONE

Max stirred inside of the bag, his feet and claws attempting to find a way out. Utah held to the bag, but Max, the Houdini he was, discovered an opening and jumped out of the bag. Instead of running, the cat stood up, rearing like a horse, and hissed. His tail inflated to three times the size.

"You're not helping, Max!"

Megan clutched onto Riley's jacket with her other hand. Riley grabbed the bags she could carry and led the girls down the hall deeper into the structure. The load was heavy and made her walk with awkward steps. Riley paused to heave the heaviest bag on her back, hung another around her shoulder, and then retook Megan's hand. She wondered how her mother ever did anything with twins.

The emergency lights continued to flicker and then held steady, showering enough light to see at least direction. The hallway led to an open area, where the cold seemed to be less frigid. The vents continued to pump warm air out, raising the temperature slowly.

Riley paused, unable to see but a small percentage of the area. The girls remained close to her side as the wind's pressure seemed to bend the building inward.

"Stay put, okay?" The girls nodded, Utah latching on to Megan to share warmth.

The word hospital was running through Riley's mind as she moved to the reception area to sift through the loose papers, animal magazines, and files littered on top of the L-shaped desk.

Chairs and boxes covered the floor, messy as if a struggle had happened there. That's when she felt an icy chill. Riley hopped up on the counter and slid over and through the darkness to the waiting room. A light overhead buzzed and then flashed an orange glow, casting a shadow across a frozen fish in a tank. Riley stepped closer. Glass crunched under her feet as another safety light glowed, revealing the broken window which lay in fragments under her feet.

The freezing temperatures pressed inward.

Riley needed to build a barrier to keep the cold from coming in. Whoever broke the window was inside the hospital now. She worked fast, tossing, as quietly as she could, pamphlets, stuffed animals, and bedding to block its entry. She slid a bookcase in front of the window in a final effort, blocking most of the cold air.

Riley hurried back to the girls who huddled with Max. The hum of the generator shifted tone. Then a flow of warmer air flowed from the vent above her head.

"Here, stand here," Riley said, pulling the girls under the vent.

NOT ALONE

Two of the three hallways become somewhat visible but not inviting even with the steady glow coming from the backup lights. One corridor they entered through, and the other two, Riley, had no wish to explore. The dim splash of red glowing lights added to the ambiance of the horror show setting. Further down, at the south end, a brighter white light spilled out into the corridor.

"Probably Doctor death," Riley whispered.

"What," asked Utah?

"Nothing," Riley answered. "Nothing. I wanna see what this place is."

Riley took a mini-mag light, clicked it on, and put it between her teeth. She picked up the first file on the desk and started thumbing through several pages, reading as fast as she could. Distracted by her findings, she jumped when another cry shattered the calm. Her fears intensified under a terrifying realization of where they were, and the hairs on her neck stood on end.

"Puma, Siberian Tiger." Riley reached for another file. "Mexican gray wolves, black bear, and badgers. What, the...?"

"Riley." Utah's voice caught her off guard. "Where are we?"

Riley wondered if this wasn't a safe place at all. The maze of rooms and hallways and the cries coming from within meant one thing, trouble. This building she chose to shelter in was a cement jungle for exotic wildlife.

"Are you two warming up?" Riley tried in vain to hide her fears.

"Yes," cried Megan.

Riley nodded. "Okay, no tears. We're just going to find a spot to nestle up in until morning, okay?"

Okay," Megan said, wiping her eyes.

She shoved their bags into a closet, pushing past a doctor's coat and a woman's purse. Besides another weapon, Riley tucked several loaded magazines into her jacket.

"Put your bag in there," Riley told Utah, patting the girl on the shoulder. "It's okay. Really."

"Okay," Utah said.

A full wet cry cut into the cold. Utah craned her head in the direction it came. Max growled, making a guttural sound, and then continued with a long hiss. Megan clamped her hands over her ears, shutting out the daunting noises while hugging her sister's jacket.

"What is that?" Utah asked in a soft tone.

"Let's go." Riley moved, not answering Utah.

Riley, about to take a step, sensed they were not alone. Max let out another hiss. She set her foot back down, and the stink of an old cigarette and campfire overrode the medicine smell stinging her nostrils. Worst yet, she smelled blood. With nowhere to go, Riley saw the outline of a man and then another. A third figure stood under the safety lights and off to the side.

Riley pressed her hand back toward the girls and then waved them away. She lowered her pistol close to her side as Utah quietly took Megan away from Riley's side.

Outside, the storm roared.

The lights flickered.

For a moment, Riley thought they were about to be engulfed in complete darkness. Not good conditions when three strangers were no more than a few feet away. She heard the footfall and should have known that exact moment. Things were about to get worse.

Through the contrast of casted shadows and deep space, Riley stared at the end of a sawed-off double-barrel shotgun. A mountain of a man stood at the end of the shotgun. Taller and broader than she'd ever seen. The cast of orange glow outlining his broad shoulders and face made her legs feel like cooked noodles.

Max hissed. He arched his back up and lunged over the desk, landing on his feet, and then sprinted down the hall, feet churning to gain traction. Running would not be so easy for Riley and the girls.

"Hey, did you see that, Ringo? That was a cat," the other man said, aiming his gun at Max.

"You act as you've never seen a cat before, Dave," growled Ringo. "You ever see a cat before?"

Riley strained to see their faces. The glow of light danced like a flame around the big man's features, distorting and skewing her perception. Her eyes fell to the side barrel of the gun. His finger stroked the metal, index finger reaching for the trigger.

The barrels aimed at her head, if ignited, promised to be ugly. It all depended on what kind of shell he'd loaded into the gun, birdshot pellets, buckshot, or slug? They all would render different horrible, devastating effects. Death being a given.

She took comfort in the weight of her gun. Her finger slid to the trigger guard.

Prudence caused Riley to strain, wanting to see the face of the one who intended to kill her. Then a red shimmer circled his eyes as if sparking, igniting, and sputtering out. Riley tensed. It was as though she'd been here before, death. She felt his evil, tasted it, and could even smell it.

The man, called Dave, stepped in behind her, pressing a gun under the base of her neck. The soft click of the revolver and the cold barrels sorting between hairs found flesh. Her heart raced.

"It's my lucky night," smiled Ringo.

"Lucky," Riley lifted her chin. "Why?"

"It's rare these days to find a woman such as yourself."

"You don't want this," muttered Riley.

"It depends on what's under all those layers?"

More layers, asshole.

The cold metal of her gun pressed against her thigh.

Lift and pull the trigger.

"Come out here," Ringo commanded. "Now," he bellowed out.

Utah stepped out first, her arms encasing Megan.

Keeping the gun on Riley, Dave ordered the girls to stand near him. She felt the slight wisp of Megan's fingers as she tried to grab her jacket. Riley shifted but stopped feeling the gun press harder into her head. Terror surged through her, and for a split second, she remembered the family in the parking lot, the little girl running for her life, and the voice telling her to get up. She moved her gaze to the man's eyes.

"Dave won't mind stripping you down, would you, Dave?"

"Uh-uh," he grunted.

"Yes, he will," said Riley.

"What?"

"Yes, he will mind," Riley repeated.

"Why is that?" asked Ringo with a grin.

"He's not stripping me down," she said, emphasizing the word stripping.

Riley knew what he wanted, what he wasn't going to get, and if he tried, she would kill him. The tossing of threats back and forth between the two played out like a game she'd play. He'd pay. She would die protecting herself and the girls.

Ringo took a step forward, the dim light falling past his frame casting another eerie glow. His face remained hidden from her, but she could smell him, both of them. Her sense of smell had gotten extraordinary through the months, and right now, Dave smelled like a wet dog, and the devil smelled like blood.

"Strip her down," roared Ringo.

"Un-fucking believable," swore Riley.

That same day and only hours ago, she prayed for no more obstacles. She chose the one building occupied by wild animals and evil trespassers hunting human flesh.

Lucky me, she thought.

"She's got a mouth on her Ringo," chuckled Dave. He reached up and stroked her hair, his hand brushing her skin.

Riley shivered.

NOT ALONE

Dismissing his touch, she focused on the real threat, Ringo. The hood of his jacket shadowed his face. Hiding features best saved after his cold body no longer moved. Her fingers tightened around her pistol.

They thought she wasn't a threat.

They were wrong.

35

Jack and Blake progressed down the hallway. A continuous tapping sound outside the building disguised their movement allowing them to move faster. From a fork in the corridor, they saw a woman trapped by two men at gunpoint, neither of which had good intentions. Voices were sharp. Words fell lost to the chaos outside.

"Markers," Jack watched from the dark hallway.

"They're going to kill her."

"Probably."

"We can get to her."

The man who advanced on the woman towered above her, making her look small. He leaned downward, putting his face close to hers. The conversation between them, from what jack could see, was unfriendly. Then he saw a flash of a child, making the urgency of the situation worse.

When the big man shoved the woman backward, he hit her with the butt of his gun. From where Jack and Blake stood, Jack could hear the hit. That cheap shot and the little girl was the deciding factor.

When the little girl cried out, Jack watched the direction that she ran. For a moment, Jack felt a wave of panic, thinking about Bermuda. If the cat found a way out, human trouble would be the least of their worries.

How quickly the scene exploded into chaos was par for the course Post-Shift. Multiple gunshots popped in the room, the sound of bullets ricocheting off the cement walls amplified, overriding the fury of the storm.

Jack motioned Blake forward, hugging the wall. They moved further away from the soft glow of light and back into an examining room. The smell of gunfire, hot metal, and smoke permeated the air. A prelude of silence followed except for the solo player, the storm. Two shadows, further down the corridor, moved in their direction. A man and his dog had arrived in time to help.

"Someone to the right," Blake pointed. "Not one of us."

"Friend."

"How do you know?"

"He was shooting at the bad guys too."

36

"You smell familiar to me," said Ringo. He leaned in closer to Riley. A rusty smell of old blood touched her nose, making her stomach roll. "Who else is with you?"

"Seriously?" Riley said sarcastically. "My husband and the rest of my people are outside." Riley took a step forward, but the pressure of the barrel on her head forced her to stop.

"Come out, come out wherever you are," Ringo called out. His voice was taunting. He stopped, and as he moved, Riley could see the rim of fire in his eyes again. "You're alone. Men don't send women and children to do their work. Especially the little ones. Do they Elle?"

"No," said the woman.

The strong scent of hospital cleansers hung heavy in the air, the emergency lights bounced off the woman's pale complexion, making her look ghost-like. The woman stared at Riley with a stern expression of contempt or boredom. Maybe it was the mix of dark colors applied liberally below and above her eyes that made her face appear so angry. Piercings decorated the woman's eyebrows and lips. Colorful tattoos too far away for Riley to see did little to brighten the woman's appearance.

Lady Goth might be a new person with different clothes, a cut and color job, and piercings eliminated. Everyone made poor decisions at one time, or another and Lady Goth's poor choice was hanging around Ringo and Dave.

Ringo pressed his nose to Riley's cheek, and as he did, she held her breath. He inhaled deep. She expected him to smell toxic and stale, and she was right. He pressed his mouth to hers, but she pulled her head to the side. His tongue landed on her cheek. Dave was now two inches closer to her.

Riley found it hard to breathe. Her personal space invaded. Unacceptably excited, Dave touched her hair again as he laughed in her ear. "What do you want to do, Ringo?" The gun moved. "Can I have her?"

Ringo gave Riley a slight push backward, moving her even further into Dave's space. "No way, this one is special."

"Special?" Elle took a step toward Ringo, but he stopped her with a mere raise of his hand.

Before Dave stepped back, he knocked the gun from Riley's hand.

"Don't run, kitten. It would be a bad decision," said Ringo seeing Riley was without her weapon and ready to run.

NOT ALONE

He's reading me like a book," she thought silently.

Ringo raised his gun hand and knocked her across the face. The force threw her into Dave. The sight of Ringo's pistol caught the flesh on her cheek. A cloud of white stars sparkled over her as she struggled not to blackout.

The ground beneath Riley was cold as ice. Blurry-eyed, she saw Ringo looking at the gun that lay on the floor only a few feet from her.

"Well, well, what do we have there," he remarked. *What are you waiting for? Take the gun.*

Riley trembled as she climbed to her knees. If she was going to die, one or all of them were going to go with her. Riley regarded Ringo with great distrust as she recovered her weapon.

Riley rested her sights on Dave and then Elle, not saying anything.

"You don't get this game, do you?" shouted Ringo. "Kill, Dave. Poor bastard is as dumb as a tack. Elle, she is the walking dead. Look at her!"

Dave chuckled.

Elle's expression darkened.

A chill passed over Riley.

Ringo's voice lowered. "I don't want to kill you. I want to...."

"Not while I'm breathing," Riley interrupted. She widened her eyes, wiping the blood from her face. She moved the pistol from Dave to Elle. Riley's adrenaline hit the rev meter, and the anger boiling inside of her gave her newfound strength.

"You won't need to be breathing," Ringo took a step forward.

"Fuck You!" yelled Riley.

The girls bolted to the right. Riley lunged to the left. Holding her pistol out, she aimed for Ringo's chest. He dodged the bullet, which shattered the wood behind him. With light steps too quick for such a big man, he leaped towards her.

The rounds of gunfire sparked from the ignited primers in the dim light as bullets splintered wood, plastic, and computer screens. A shower of exploding debris shot into the air. White foam blew from office chairs as the force of bullets sent them crashing against the counter. Now Riley wished she had the state-issued bulletproof vest she left behind the night she turned in her badge. Dropping to the floor, she crawled off to the right under the edge of the counter. Rounds sprayed in all directions missing flesh and bone. Ringo could only fire so much until his rounds ran dry.

Megan and Utah disappeared within seconds at a sprint, and only the distant sound of their footsteps remained. Riley prayed for time, time to allow the girls to hide. The bursts of explosions ricocheted inside the building, echoing down the empty corridor. Then it all stopped.

NOT ALONE

Riley, in the melancholy of the silence, drew on Ringo first and fired. This time the bullet caught his shoulder, shoving him backward but only for a heartbeat. He was advancing towards her in a fit of fury.

"That didn't feel good, Kitten," he slammed a chair against the wall. The sound of his footsteps grew faint, but his voice boomed loud and clear. "You're the first to put a bullet in me. I'm not finished with you yet."

"Where did Lady Goth and Dumb as a Tac go?" she whispered to herself.

The hospital grew quiet except for the pounding outside. The best solution, vacate the building even with the fury of the storm raging outside. However, now the girls sat hidden, making leaving impossible. Even the animals surrendered to the exterior calamity, stern warnings as cries fell to a soft moan.

Riley sprinted over the counter, landing softly on her feet. She saw no movement nor heard any voices. The storm once again took center stage, grasping the building and shaking it with fury.

The ringing in her ears subsided, and the cold combined with fear made her shiver. The building felt like a walk-in freezer. She could not stay here long.

She slid inside another doorway. A stiff gust hit the building, putting a strain on the roof and siding. Somewhere within, not made of concrete but wood, material moaned under pressure. Then his voice trickled down the long walkways, eager to scare.

"You've been out there hiding for a while," Ringo sneered. His voice twisted with sarcasm and into pure evilness. "What are you made of Riley Collins? Run and hide, Kitten. But if I find you, you're mine."

His laughter made her shiver. Even worse, he knew her name.

Riley felt slow-burning anger build inside of her. Rage wouldn't do any of them any good, but a plan to get her and the girls to safety would. Survival mode kicked in as the sound of doors opening and shutting echoed down the hall. Ringo's voice and a woman's irrational laugh taunted her.

The breaking of glass mixed in with the sounds of the storm created a chaotic chorus of destruction. Riley jumped. The roar continued and then grew closer. His actions were nothing short of insane induced by either insanity or drugs. Find the girls and get the hell out! They would take their chances on the road.

"Anything is better than this," she said aloud.

Riley stood still, willing her body to conserve body heat. Frigid air surrounded her. The floor was so cold that it penetrated through her socks and boots, freezing toes.

NOT ALONE

Riley waited. Then Ringo stopped. She heard him swear then he popped off a handful of rounds. Riley closed her eyes, jumping at each shot fired. Then she heard rebounding gunfire, and she knew someone else was in the hospital beside herself, Ringo, and his people. Regardless, she considered them all a threat.

"So you aren't alone. I'll be back?"

"I won't be," Riley answered, taking a deep breath. Find the girls and get out.

"Son of a bitch," someone said, but it was a different voice. Riley paused mid-stride, straining to listen.

"Where'd they go?"

"The woman went that way." Both men spoke above a whisper, but the hollowness of the building amplified every little sound.

"I don't think they're here to see the Doc." One of them said.

"No," the other answered.

"I don't think it's a good idea to go looking for them, Jack." Their voices lowered.

"Where'd the kid go?" There was a soft shuffle of feet.

"He's here," she heard him say. "Watch out for Bermuda. She's on the loose. There could be others."

What the hell does that mean? Are animals running free? "Shit," Riley said, thinking of the girls. She just turned them loose in a petting zoo of lions and tigers.

She crossed paths with mountain lions, bears, and a coyote or two in the past. All hunters, all predators, were searching for prey. With that said, an animal cried, sending an even deeper chill through her body.

"Great!" she murmured.

37

"What was that?" Shay asked, turning to Jack as he and Blake slipped through the doors.

"Cougar and a tiger. Mexican gray wolf. Five of them."

"In here? Who were you shooting at, the animals?" Shay went to her tiptoes and looked through the surgery room windows.

"Someone else is taking up shelter here," Blake moved his pack, grabbing more ammo.

"I forgot to tell you, stay away from room six." Jack pulled Shay away from the doors.

"What about Pam, Jack?"

"The Doc is dead."

"How? What's in room six?" Sherry stood quiet.

"Bermuda's in room six. Someone shot Pam." Jack said nothing more about Bermuda.

"Sweet Jesus," Shay shifted her weight in discomfort. "Are the animals lose?"

Jack moved, glancing out the eyehole of a window with his rifle tilted outward.

"I'm not sure who's lose and who's not," Jack searched the hallway, looking for movement. "Pam has an apartment across the hall. "We'll move Matt there."

"Why are the animals making so much noise?" Sherry asked, pushing her limit of questions Jack wanted to answer.

"They're hungry," said Jack. A high-pitched scream echoed down the corridor, causing him to pause.

"What's Bermuda?" Sherry kept picking through supplies.

Blake tried to hide his concern, "didn't Pam have a technician living here with her?"

"She does," Jack, knowing Bermuda wasn't the only cat on the property, stepped back. "Is everyone done asking questions now?"

Sherry had a mound of supplies stacked on top of Matt's legs. "Okay, we can move him."

"Good job on Matt!" Shay said, patting Sherry on the shoulder.

"Thanks. I'm pretty sure I just stepped outside my legal boundaries, though."

"No worries there," Shay grinned.

"He's stable, for now anyway."

NOT ALONE

The good news about Matt was lost as the pack of wolves began to howl. The sound floated its way down the brick wall siding into the surgery room.

"You were kidding about the tiger, right?" Blake looked at Jack and shifted his position.

"Where's your big boy skirt now?" Jack teased, trying to lighten the mood. "We only have to go twenty feet."

Blake shook his head, "I'm not wrestling a tiger."

"Better than a hospital full of infected people," Jack wondered after he said it if he agreed with that analogy. "Anyway, she's a cougar. Elmo is the tiger. I'd rather take my chances with the animals."

Jack cracked the door open, hearing nothing more than a peaceful silence that fell across the hall. He pointed, motioning the women forward. It was twenty degrees cooler outside the surgery room, and the cold stole the warm air as it drifted through the opening. The women guided Matt through the door, slipping through the next. The sound of the gurney wheels bending the quietness until the high-pitched scream of a cat commanded attention. Everyone stopped.

"Keep going," Jack said, leading the others into the studio apartment, which was dimly lit and warm, but Jack and Blake wouldn't be staying.

"Don't open this door unless you're positive it's Blake or me," Jack whispered. "Understand?"

Both Sherry and Shay nodded.

38

As Ringo disappeared, Riley started to search for the girls keeping to the folds of shadows. The hospital was much larger than she first thought. Sectioned off and separated by doors and windows for exams, the rooms were perfect hiding spots. She looped back around, searching through the glass for Utah and Megan while paying heed to her back. Coming to the last room, she turned the handle looking for the girls. Instead, something bulky and pissed off slammed into the door. Jumping back, she caught the scream that almost escaped her lips.

"What the hell?"

Slowly, she moved away, not wanting to upset whatever was on the other side. Now team evil had gone silent, and that left her more skittish than when she could at least pinpoint their location.

The gunshot came from the darkness. The bullet ripped past Riley's head, grazing her hair as it passed. She turned and sprinted down the hall, speeding past several doors to the end of the corridor. Ringo moved behind her. Riley could feel his presence, intense and chilling. Hearing footfalls coming fast, Riley veered left, stopping at the double doors ten feet away. The smell of the hospital changed. The stench of urine and feces intensified. She could hear claws shuffling behind the barrier.

"Oh girls, please tell me you didn't go in there."

The hallway forked. Moving right, Riley kept within the shadows peering through the windows as she passed. The building resembled a giant maze, and she'd done a full circle.

"Listen," yelled Ringo in a theatrical tone. "Sounds like Bermuda!"

Riley jumped at the sound of his voice.

"You'd be a mere morsel for a hungry cat," he said, moving closer. "I like this place. Holy Hell. Here, kitty, kitty." The slight scent of cigar stirred. He was stalking her while smoking a cigar.

"Riley," Utah said softly.

Riley squinted, peering through what looked like a deep hole. She could make out the slight outline of Utah and Megan. Riley nodded. Utah had a hold of Megan behind boxes almost camouflaged from sight. Just behind their silhouettes, another person lay sprawled out on the floor. If not terrifying enough, another shadow appeared. Riley's mouth went dry. Holding her breath, the cat stepped out into the open, stopping thirty feet from the girls.

Letting out an angry cry, Bermuda dropped down into a stalking position. Megan saw the cat and screamed. Startled and confused,

Bermuda reared back. Utah pulled her sister behind her, pinning them both against the wall. No time to think, Riley lunged out of the darkness and aimed for the cougar's head, but something caused her to redirect her aim.

Dave stepped into the corridor, his pistol aimed at her.

The bullet grazed Riley's shoulder, stinging the flesh. The gun in her hand loosened.

The cat bolted from the sound of the gunshot. Riley fought off a slight shudder as the cougar ran and then stopped. There was no training to prepare a person when facing a wild animal such as this one.

The feline snarled its lips showing bloodstained teeth. Bermuda lowered herself to the ground.

Laughing, Dave fired, making the animal scramble into boxes past Megan and Utah, where it slid to a stop, spun around, and faced the girls. Megan screamed again, but this time, the cat stood her ground, confused, buying Riley precious seconds. Chances given, none of them would survive a cougar attack, but even less doubt, Dave would kill Riley first, leaving the girls alone.

Riley set her sights on Dave as he fired. The first bullet whizzed past her catching the wall and upsetting the cougar. The cat, now outright frantic, turned and faced Riley, ready to defend herself.

Megan and Utah started to run in Riley's direction.

The red dot from a laser caught Riley's attention as it came to rest on the cougar's chest. Riley tried to stop the girls from crossing paths with both the cougar and the line of fire, but it was too late. The girls were unobstructed moving targets.

Riley sprang forward to grab them, but Ringo fired before she could reach them. The bullet made full impact with flesh and bone, but not Riley's. Megan's body shot backward, and the round slapped her small body. Riley screamed, sliding to the floor while emptying the magazine where Ringo stood.

Bermuda, confused, dodged to the side, her claws tapping on the floor away from the spray of bullets.

"Come on now, Kitten," shouted Ringo.

With clenched teeth, Riley crawled toward Megan.

Dave and Lady Goth were a good twenty yards from her when they stepped into view. Riley replaced the magazine with a loaded one.

"Stay behind me, Utah," Riley said as she gathered Megan into her arms.

Utah nodded, grabbing hold of Riley's jacket.

Riley pulled Megan up to her shoulder and prayed silently that the girl was still alive. One-handed, Riley fired.

NOT ALONE

Two high-impact shots echoed down the corridor. Holding the girls behind her, she waited, straining to see movement. It was the woman she saw first, her hands grasping the long black jacket she wore. The woman shuddered, eyes wide. She fell.

Riley pulled Utah inside one of the exam rooms, holding both girls tight to the inside, keeping them hidden. Megan already grew heavy in her arms, but she could feel the steady beat of the little girl's heart. Riley pressed her fingers to her lips through the shadows of light and dark, gesturing to Utah to sit and be quiet.

Teary-eyed, Utah nodded as Riley placed Megan in her sister's arms.

"She's alive, Utah," Riley whispered, searching for the wound. When she felt the sticky warmth of blood, she paused. Blood oozed between her fingertips. Riley pressed, and the blood stopped flowing.

Resting a hand on Megan's chest and tears streaming down her cheeks, Riley felt the slight rise and fall of the little girl's breath. "I need to get help."

Utah laid her hand on Megan's chest, afraid.

"Hold your hand on the wound and press." Riley tried to clear her voice, but her throat burned. "Put your hand here." Riley took Utah's hand and placed it where her hand was on Megan's chest. "Don't be afraid. I'll be right back."

"There's so much blood Riley," Utah's hands already shone red with blood. "I can't fix this."

"I know, sweetie. I've got to find some help."

"Riley," Utah's voice was a mere whisper.

"Don't make any sounds." Riley took off her sweater and placed it around Utah. "I'll come back to you. Press on the wound. Can you do that? Can you press hard on the wound?" she asked, Utah. Utah wiped the tears away from her face as she nodded, her fingers leaving a bloody red streak on her cheek.

Riley stepped out of the room and was about to find the two men she'd seen earlier when someone spoke to her.

"Over here," said the man.

The stranger's words, neither Ringo nor Dave, came from the folds of darkness. Riley turned around to see a tall silhouette step out of the obscurity into the dim light. He was tall and broad but different than Ringo.

Riley started to tell him that she needed help when he pressed his finger to his lips and then pointed. Riley looked in the direction he pointed. Someone or something was approaching. Already the stranger was attempting to protect them.

"Shoot to kill," he said in a whisper.

NOT ALONE

Riley turned as the stranger disappeared, replaced by the big cat who stepped out of the shadows. Riley stepped backward into the shadows to shelter herself from sight. Bermuda lowered her body and moved slowly toward Lady Goth lying on the floor. The cougar was more interested in blood than in live prey.

"Here, kitty, kitty," Ringo called from the hidden space.

"You son of a bitch," Riley whispered. *Step into the light so I can shoot your evil ass.*

The cat froze mid-stride. Bermuda licked her bloodied whiskers and then began cleaning a paw. Riley could smell the cat, the woman, and the distinct odor of body fluids pooling in blood. Called on by the scents, the cat sought the smell's source. In a stalking stride, the hunter slunk low, seeking the treasure lying on the floor.

The big cat placed a paw on each side of the woman's head and then sunk her teeth into long strands of tinted hair.

Riley felt a sudden excess of saliva rise into her throat as the cat effortlessly lifted the woman with sharp teeth and shook her like a rag doll. Riley closed her eyes. The woman's body scraped the floor in front of her.

Go away! Riley screamed silently.

"I'm getting bored too." Ringo sang out. The cat dropped the woman and climbed to her feet, hearing the voice.

"Good kitty. Good kitty," she repeated. *Kill the devil.*

Bermuda was on the move once more, slipping through a doorway and into the dark folds of the cement building. As the wild cat disappeared, the two men dressed military-style reappeared. A third man had joined them but only for a brief moment.

39

Riley hurried to the room where the girls were hiding. Utah and Megan hadn't moved. Both girls look fragile to Riley, but Megan's face was as pale as a doll's, and she feared the worst.

"Hurry," Utah whispered.

The two strangers were at the door by the time Riley had Megan scooped up in her arms.

"Come on," the tallest man said after seeing Megan's condition. He laid his fingers on her neck to feel her pulse, and Riley hoped to God that he had some medical experience.

"He shot her," Riley said in a low tone.

"We've got someone with us who can help," he answered. "We need to move fast."

Riley nodded. "Let's go!"

Riley held Megan close to her as they moved through corridors and past the reception area, which now looked like a battleground. Nearly falling over debris, Riley sidestepped furniture and files cluttering the floor. She struggled to keep the pace, almost dropping Megan for the second time. The wounds on her shoulder and face stung.

The taller man stopped Riley, taking Megan from her and into his arms. She started to argue, but he stopped her.

"You're slowing us down," he said.

Riley followed. They stopped at the door at the far end of the hospital. The man knocked twice, paused, and then knocked three more times. The door opened, allowing them entry into what felt like another world. It was a world of light, warmth, and a pungent odor of blood and medicine.

"Sherry," the tall man said.

A thin pale woman rushed forward. "What happened?" she asked, gesturing to set her on the table.

"She was shot," Riley brushed everything off the table with one swipe. The woman pulled Megan out of Riley's jacket gently and started searching for the wound.

"Here! Just one shot?"

Riley lowered her pistol, "Yes."

She moved quickly, stripping away Megan's layers. Megan wore the butterfly shirt they'd gotten at Walmart, but the material was soaked in blood, making Riley's heart hurt. Sherry ripped the shirt away from Megan, exposing the child's wound.

Sherry stepped back, looked at Riley, and then tossed the taller man some gauze and iodine. Riley felt a rush of warmth burning her cheeks and the sudden thought of escape, which meant fighting the demons still alive outside the door.

"That's Shay, Jack is the tall one, and Blake is the puppy," Sherry said, never looking up. She tossed bloody pads into a bag and then grabbed another bundle. "Matt is the other patient on the bed over there."

"Riley, Utah, Megan," Riley said, softening her voice.

The woman, introduced as Shay, stepped forward. "This is Sherry," she said, patting her on the shoulder. "Your daughter is in good hands, Riley."

Sherry inserted an IV into Megan's arm with the ease of an expert.

"The bullet hit her here," Sherry said, pointing. Blood continued to seep out of the wound. "Press here," she said, taking Riley's hand pressing it on top of a thick towel lying over Megan's wound. She checked her vitals and sighed.

"Can you get the bullet out?" Riley asked.

"I don't know if that's such a good idea." Sherry looked at Jack. "I'll do everything I can here, but we need to get her to a surgeon."

"A surgeon?" Riley's voice quivered. "Oh, you don't want to go to any hospital. Finding a surgeon would be like trying to find a needle in a haystack. Over half the population is dead. Doctors included. Hospitals don't exist anymore, not to mention there is one hell of a blizzard outside and a maniac trying to kill anything that moves."

"Trust them," Utah wrapped her fingers into Riley's hand. Riley felt a hot tear roll down her face as she sighed, "She's right. Megan needs a surgeon."

"I don't think it's a good idea for me to take the bullet out. There's no exit wound, so the bullet's still in her. If it's lodged in or near her spine, I...," Sherry stammered.

"Can you stabilize her so we can get her to Nick?" asked Jack, looking at Sherry and then at Riley.

"I believe so," Sherry answered.

"Do it. We'll get her to Nick," Jack patted Sherry and then pointed at Riley. "You're bleeding."

Riley reached up and took off her beanie. "Dammit!" she said.

Tears and blood flowed free, and as much as Riley tried to gain some composure, she failed gracefully.

Jack pulled off his mask, and a moment of awkwardness occurred between them. Riley's cheeks flushed. For an instant, she thought she saw Lucas, so handsome, tall, and dark. His light green eyes held yellow gold splashes under lashes as dark as his above shoulder-length hair. The ends curled and close to a two-day shadow showed on his face, and still, he looked like he'd stepped out of a GQ Magazine. Then a hint of recognition happened.

"How do I know you?"

"We still have a few problems," Blake pulled off his mask and beanie. "There are still other people somewhere in this hospital and an enormous pissed-off cat."

"One of those cats is mine," Riley said. "The small one." Jack moved closer to Riley with gauze and peroxide.

"That needs to be stitched," Sherry pointed at Riley's cheek, and then she saw the blood on her shoulder. "Is that you or Megan's?"

"Mine," Riley touched her shirt. "It's just a graze."

"Who is the third guy out there?" Shay asked.

"A loner lives in Prescott." Jack set his pistol down on the table. "You need to take your shirt off."

Riley struggled, her arms stiff and aching.

His voice seemed so familiar, smooth, in control tone, making her feel as though everything might be all right. Still untrusting, she hesitated to set her pistols down.

Jack saw Riley's hesitance and said, "it's okay. We're the good guys."

"How come the third guy isn't in here with all of you?" Riley looked at Jack, who reached up and helped her peel away a layer of clothing, leaving her in a thin black t-shirt.

Jack looked at her, his eyebrows raised ever so slightly. "You ever consider a bulletproof vest?" He signaled for her to sit down. "He's one of us. He just doesn't know it yet. He shot the woman who almost shot you?"

"You both saved our lives," Riley felt the goosebumps layer her skin. "The cat?"

"That's a big cat," Blake whistled. "Matt's going to be pissed he missed that."

"Bermuda." Jack took off his jacket, draped it over her shoulder, and then leaned forward, observing the gash on her cheek.

Jack was so close to Riley that she could smell spiced soap.

"I've already had a run-in with a tiger, but I draw the line at monkeys. No monkeys, though, right?" Riley asked.

Jack looked at her with a familiar grin.

I know you. I've loved you before, Riley thought.

"I'm not fond of monkeys," Riley tried to keep her thoughts on course. "Never want to meet one."

"No monkeys."

"I thought since the asshole trying to kill us is called Ringo, there might be a circus in town."

Sherry and Shay turned in her direction. "What?"

"Ringo. Big guy, looks like a demon," Riley watched the expression on both of their faces change, so she changed the tone of her voice. "Do you know him?"

Jack sat down next to her, wiping the blood from her face as Sherry set a sterile stitching pack on the table and returned to Megan. The room turned to an eerie silence.

"Demon might be too kind of a word," Jack murmured, picking up a needle. "This is going to hurt."

"Have you ever done this before?"

He smiled, "Yes, but not on a woman."

Blake chuckled.

Max appeared from behind a chair.

"Awe, you did squeeze your way in unnoticed, didn't you?" Riley moved forward, but Jack stopped her with his leg. She could feel the heat from his body pressing into hers.

Max's tail went fluffy, and his attitude angry. His senses were already on high alert with all the big cats and meat-eating wildlife. He entered the room, meowed, and then made his way over to Utah, who remained at Megan's side.

"Hey, little fella," Blake said, kneeling next to Max. The cat purred and rubbed against his hand. His tail flattened back out as he calmed. "You're out of your league here, fella. This one belongs to you?" Blake asked, looking at Riley.

"Yep," The cat looked up at Riley, and she grinned. "That's Max."

"You brought a cat with you?" Blake rubbed Max's head. "Seasoned traveler, huh?"

"He had a choice, get in the truck or get left behind. He chose the latter of the two," Riley grimaced as Jack pushed the needle through her skin.

"This is pretty bad. Healing gash, new gash." Jack leaned in closer. "Hey, Sherry, you got something to numb this with?"

"It's okay," Riley didn't want Sherry to leave Megan's side. "I'd rather her focus on Megan."

"Megan's stable," Sherry appeared and applied something cool onto her cheek. She felt a slight poke. "How's that?" She pressed on the skin.

"Good."

"You're going to need a sweater or jacket of some sort when we get ready to leave," Sherry said.

"How'd you get the first gash?"

"Bad shopping experience at Walmart."

Riley felt Jack's breath on her, noticed his tanned skin, and the slight wave in his hair, holding a shade of gray. Playing up to the distraction, he leaned in close to stitch up her wound.

Jack raised his eyebrows. "Walmart?"

"I disagreed with a purchase," Riley jumped as the needle hit a nerve. "Ouch!"

"Don't jump."

"Don't go so deep."

He paused, grinning. "Hey, Sherry, how about a little more juice?"

It looks a little on the angry side," Sherry handed Jack a small syringe. "Nice stitch job, though. Douse it with iodine afterward."

Riley looked at the needle and pulled back.

"You want me to deaden it or not?"

"Yes," she leaned toward him.

The needle going into her skin hurt like hell, but after a few seconds, the pain subsided. She feared she might be drooling as Jack fed the needle through her skin, but this time, Riley felt nothing.

40

Jack and Blake stood quiet. Jack's shoulder pressed close to the door, locked and loaded, and Blake behind him. The sound of metal tapping on steel echoed inside the apartment.

Ringo's unwarranted laughter filtered inward. The hunter enjoyed the vicious game of survival, but his intended prey did not. Sherry pulled Riley back down onto the chair to finish what Jack had started. With the needle and thread between her fingers, she began stitching the wound with gentle fingers.

Riley felt for her pistol, letting her gaze fall on Jack and Blake.

"Hurry," Riley whispered to her.

The taunting continued, but Sherry, steadfast, finished the last of the stitching. "That's going to hurt later," she breathed, slipping a few Advil's into her hand. "For the pain. Now let's see that shoulder."

"Nerves of steel, Nurse Sherry," Shay stepped up behind Sherry. "We would have died without you."

"How do you know, Ringo?" Riley asked. Afraid of the answer because she was scared of the man, but she wanted to know.

"It's a long story," Sherry's face paled, giving way to first-hand knowledge of Ringo. "Long story short, he held us captive."

The monster behind the door stopped taunting, and a hushed silence fell. Riley looked back at Utah.

"You're going to have to take your shirt off. I can't get to the wound," Sherry said. Riley looked down at the black t-shirt, now blacker with blood, and then at the two men standing in the room. No way in hell she was going to take off the t-shirt.

"Ah, no!" Riley shook her head.

"It'll get infected. Guys, give her some privacy." Sherry looked back. A loud crash occurred outside the door in the corridor. She and Riley jumped simultaneously. The vial jumped out of Sherry's hand and fell to the floor.

Ringo, who was trying to rattle cages, was doing an excellent job.

Blake and Jack both grinned at Riley, waiting. Jack tapped Blake on the shoulder, and they both put their backs to her. Riley pulled her shirt over her head, exposing a black lacy bra.

Sherry smiled at her.

"Shopping spree at Victoria Secrets," Riley recalled, looking at the wound on her shoulder.

"Very pretty. Glad to see some things are still available out there."

"Can I see?" Jack started to turn.

"No!" Sherry and Riley said at the same time.

"Then don't talk about it," Blake's voice almost child-like.

Sherry cleaned the flesh wound, but this time Riley didn't complain. Jack peeked over at her more than once, but she ignored his gaze. Sherry's stitch job was neat, and her bandaging job snug. Riley dressed while being careful not to brush material across stitches.

Shay handed Riley a military-looking sweater and then grinned. "This will tell you a little bit about Jack's taste in apparel."

"We need to get them out of here." Riley heard Blake tell Jack.

Riley wanted to get Megan somewhere safe. Everything else fell secondary, including finding Eric. The Ringo roller coaster of terror went quiet. They listened for movement, waiting for the next round of threats to begin.

Getting in from the outside would prove to be more than challenging since the windows and side door was made of steel plates, making the room a prison or a safe place.

"Someone planned for the worse," Riley brushed her fingertips over the cold steel.

Somehow, the protective layers did little to ease her fear of Ringo and Dave. Also, outside the door, a blockade of intricate mazes and corridors held various wild animals. Meat eaters, to be exact. Yet somehow, the wildlife seemed trivial compared to the evil play of the two devils on the other side of the door.

"If they wanted to get in, they would," Shay said, rubbing her hands together. Riley sensed her anxiety.

Kissing Megan's forehead, Riley fought off exhaustion. "We're near to Prescott, aren't we?" asked Riley.

"Fifty-five miles," replied Blake. "The problem is the weather."

"Ringo will kill us before the weather does. Either way, some of us won't leave here alive," Sherry said softly.

"She's right," Shay said.

"What did you guys do to piss this guy off so bad?" Riley asked.

"I killed his brother, and then we took his women. Oh, and burned down his house," Jack replied.

"More like Jack saved my life by killing Ringo's brother and saved my son and five other women before he burned down Ringo's house but not before stealing his truck," replied Shay.

"Thank you for that analogy, Shay," Jack responded.

Fear mixed with exhaustion made Sherry's voice falter. "I'd rather die than go back."

Riley listened. She'd spent the past two years thinking about finding Eric. Until now. Her main objective was getting Megan to a doctor.

"I think I may have pissed him off, too," Riley said. "Strange though, he called me by my name. My full name."

"That is odd," Jack said.

Riley studied his face, seeing not even a hint of knowing something she didn't.

"Whatever happens, don't let him take you," Sherry whispered to her.

"I'm not going anywhere with that man. And neither are you," Riley replied in a low voice.

"There's two of them and five of us. I say we shoot our way out and get the hell out of here," Blake said, glancing over at Matt.

"There are seven of us and two of them," Riley reminded them.

"That we know of," Jack rubbed his chin deep in thought.

"You think he has more coming?" Riley asked, now worried.

"He seems like that kind of guy." Jack's voice softened, exposing a hint of concern as well.

Riley scrutinized their faces, strangers only an hour ago. In over an hour, they'd become a part of her moment. Pacing the room, she analyzed expressions and voice tone. She took in every word, filed every emotion, and she could not stop thinking she'd been here before. Riley believed they were all a part of a bigger plan.

The warmth of the room had spoiled them because when the generator stopped shutting down the power, all light, and the heating unit, Riley felt an instant chill. Once again, they were at Ringo's mercy. The hunter would make nothing easy.

"He's trying to draw us out," Shay said.

"Unfuckingbelievable." Jack jested in the obscurity of the room, and Riley couldn't help but grin at his choice of spoken words.

41

The wind came in steady gusts all night, hammering anything not nailed down. One in the morning, a full-blown white out occurred, leaving the ranch and property snow white. Outside, temperatures dropped to a chilly twenty-eight degrees. Inside, Lynn stroked the fires and kept the team supplied with hot coffee.

Ryan's concern for his brother and the team started the hour they left the ranch. The youngest, Colton, was not good at sitting back and waiting. No, he was better when he was on the mission. Wounded, the family expected Ryan to stay at home and proceeded to drive everyone at the ranch crazy. If the mission had gone as planned, the team would have returned with Dan. Jack and his team were in trouble, and Ryan knew that. When Dan delivered the four women, a three-year-old full of energy, and the Hummer to the ranch minus the others, the unknowing left the youngest Colton on edge.

Ryan was about to go out and toss hay to the cattle gathered under the shelter when Nick intervened.

"I got it," Nick said, pulling on his jacket and gloves.

"Great. I'll look for the keys while you're gone."

"Good luck," Nick nodded, slipping out the back door.

Ryan growled a few words at Nick and then checked on the horses for the tenth time. His fever was gone, and the drain in his chest was keeping the infection out, not to mention the antibiotics that looked more like horse pills he took every five hours. Capable and more than willing to find his brother, Ryan continued to stew. He returned, seeing Nick sitting at the table. Lily walked in, holding Jonah's hand.

He woke up, and I can't find mommy." Lily stood with a sleepy yawn followed by eye rubbing.

"Lily Bean," Nick knelt to her level. "You're still sleepy."

"Daddy," she murmured in a sleepy breath while rubbing her eyes again, but then she out the window. "Oh my gosh!" She wailed in excitement. She forgot her sleepiness and rushed to the window. "Can we make a snowman?"

"Oh, sweetie. It's nasty cold out there," Nick said, but then he saw the disappointment in his daughter's eyes. "Later."

"I love you, daddy," she said, wrapping her arms around Nick's legs.

"I love you back, Lily Bean."

Lily grabbed Jonah's hand. "We're going to make a snowman today, Jonah."

NOT ALONE

The two disappeared up the stairs.

"Lily's up already?" Lynn asked, stepping into the kitchen.

Ryan jumped at the sound of her voice behind him.

"Jumpy," she asked?

"Bored," he said, pouring more coffee into his cup. "Both kids are up."

"It's still dark out there," she said, switching off the porch light. "Jonah's cute," Lynn handed Ryan the cream.

"Want another one, huh?" Ryan said, kissing his sister on the cheek.

"No word from the others yet?" she asked, throwing him a slight punch and changing the subject.

"No. The winds are picking back up. Crazy damn weather!"

"They're riding out the storm," Lynn said. "So should you. Geeze, it's really blowing out there."

"Yeah. Where is everyone?" Ryan asked, pressing his fingers around the cup for warmth.

"Sleeping," mumbled Lynn. "It's three in the morning. It's horrible what those women went through. I rounded up clothes and shoes, but I need more. I need to look at our supplies from the truck we recovered a few months ago. It's loaded with clothing." Lynn sipped her coffee.

"I'll gather some up for you," Ryan said. Nick glared at him, and his response, "what?"

"No, lifting Ryan. You'll bust those stitches," Nick said, shaking his head. "You do, and your brother will kill me."

"Lily likes having Jonah around," Lynn said, changing the subject yet again.

"We need a boy in the family," Ryan winked at Lynn.

"Who's the lucky mom?" Lynn snapped a towel in Ryan's direction.

"Hilarious. We need a boy in the family," he said, dodging the towel. "I'm a little way off from having kids seeing as how I don't even have a woman, and then there's Jack. Hell, Jack may grow too old before he has children, let alone a woman."

Lynn laughed. "Sounds like you have this all figured out."

"What's going on here?" Ben said, peeking through the doorway.

"We're talking, kids," Lynn chuckled.

"Awe. You're pregnant?" Ben asked, pulling off his jacket. "We need a boy in this family. The girls are starting to outnumber the men."

"No, dad. I am not pregnant." Lynn said, grinning at Nick. "Yet."

The conversation got quiet.

"He'll be back," Nick said, but Ryan disagreed. He had a feeling Jack had run into some trouble.

"Jack could be stranded or worse?" Ryan said, trying to get them to agree. If he knew where the keys were, he would have been out of there hours ago.

"Jack would've got them to shelter. More than likely, they took Matt to Pam." Lynn lowered her voice a notch.

"Dan said Matt was in pretty bad shape," Ryan said.

"Dan said that Sherry is a nurse. Pam is a doctor. It made sense to pull over in Drake."

Ryan sighed, feeling trouble looming on the horizon. Tempted to hotwire one of the trucks, he waited for someone to cave.

"I feel like I'm back in high school," Ryan dug a little deeper. "Just give me the damn keys before I have to call someone to pick me up. I'll go straight to Pam's place!"

"I can't let you go. You know it," Nick said, trying to sound convincing.

"You promised Jack," Ben pointed a finger.

Ryan glared at Nick and Ben. "I never promised! For God's sake, Nick, it isn't as if I need your permission or yours, pops. If they're at Pam's, then they're only fifty miles from us. I never promised."

"I'll get the truck ready," Ben sprang out the door with the steps of an eighteen-year-old before Lynn or anyone else could say anything.

Lynn faced Nick saying nothing. All three, Jack included, knew Ryan would come for them if they failed to return home. Nick took a sip of his coffee as reality settled in between all of them.

"I want to look at those stitches before you go," Nick demanded.

"Take the Hummer," Lynn added.

Ryan looked down at his watch, anticipating the handing over of keys.

42

The sounds of the animals crying for food made Kid feel bad. As soon as the lunatic that killed Pam Kenny either died or left the property, he would be sure to take care of every one of them. Until then, Kid needed to lay low. He found a warm space in the hospital's southwest section while the sad song of hunger continued. Shift's ears moved back and forth as the dog listened under the umbrella of red safety lights. There was no better partner than the Ridgeback. Athletic, dedicated, and an excellent protector were much-needed traits on a night such as this one.

Kid closed his eyes, trying to erase Doc Kenny's image lying on the floor and the trespasser, the little girl who appeared to have taken a bullet.

Not long after Colton and his team moved in, he heard voices coming from the corridor. Kid overheard the one called Ringo radioing for backup, assuring that more trouble would head their way. However, Kid was willing and able to help Jack's team out when they were ready. With his eyes closed but awake, the storm intensified, and the clattering from the wind seized. Now in the obscurity of shadows, he waited.

The lights in the corridor flickered once and then twice. Then a familiar failure in power and the building went black. It had only been a matter of time.

"Game on," Kid whispered.

Ringo's voice trailed down the darkened space separating the rooms and doors as if the words were lyrics to a song. "I see you."

Colton had gone stealth, making the enemy even thirstier for the hunt. Kid laid his hand on Shift's back to make sure the dog remained quiet. Animals sensed things humans couldn't, and Shift disliked Ringo's voice. The scents of the cats were keeping her alert as the ridge on her back rose. The dog would get her time, but Kid played the game safe, for now, keeping Shift at bay.

Unmoved, he separated the sounds trickling down the corridor. A gust of wind slapped the sides of the building as if announcing that Mother Nature's fury re-festered. The force sent a long howling sound through the hospital along with a cold draft of air. Then as if hell had broken loose, a loud explosion rocked the foundation. Shift lifted her head, letting out a deep growl.

"I hope that wasn't our ride."

43

They took two shifts until all of them could rest at least a few hours. They could not see outside, but the sun began to crest over snowcapped mountains. Riley hoped dawn might shower light on the dark and brighten the dreary hospital walls, but the breaking sun didn't. The giant concrete building warded off any predawn light, keeping them buried in cement dullness. After huddling near the propane heater for most of the night, they agreed to make a stand. Bitter silence hastened over overactive imaginations, as it seemed only the storm had calmed. The hunters on the other side of the door roamed the hospital, keeping them aware they had not left.

"It's time," instructed Jack.

The others were readying themselves when Utah rushed over and wrapped her arms around Riley.

"Be careful, Riley."

"I will. You'll be safe here," Riley held her close. Utah rested her head against Riley's heart, listening before stepping back.

"Ringo is not good," Utah whispered. "He doesn't care about anything but himself." Riley bent down to her level and forced a worried smile.

"I know, but these people are good. I'll be back. I promise."

Even now, in this craziness, Riley saw a unique purity in Utah. She saw the innocence in her eyes and characteristic. A glow Riley wondered if anyone else could see. Riley felt comforted in her presence, but her words seemed all-knowing.

Jack and Blake checked their weapons while Riley got herself ready. The lantern sitting in the center of the room flickered on occasion, lending little light to prepare. The heater, a midnight warrior, clanked noisily.

"Antiquated piece of....." Jack said, giving the metal casing a slight hit with his hand. The machine hiccupped and then hummed on.

Jack turned to Sherry extending a pistol out to her. "You ever handle a gun before?"

"No," she said, taking the gun. She pressed her fingers around the grip.

"It's ready to be fired. Keep your index finger on the guard. Don't touch the trigger unless you intend to shoot. Point to kill. Got it?"

Sherry nodded.

Riley watched Sherry's headshake as she listened to the slam course in gun handling 101.

"I'll be here," Matt slid to a sitting position, his voice strained.

"I don't think you should be standing," Sherry said.

"I need to stand. You can't carry both of us out of here."

"You've lost a lot of blood, and I don't want your stitches to bust," Sherry reminded Matt.

"Give me a little more of that good stuff and let's get the hell out of this place," frowned Matt. "How can anything break? I'm wrapped up like a human burrito?"

Shay handed Riley a bulletproof vest. "You're going to need this. Jack brought extra."

"Thank you, Shay," Riley took the vest, slipped it on, making a few adjustments. Jack moved next to her, brushing his shoulder against her upper arm, and handed her a facemask.

"We're not robbing a bank," she frowned, staring at the mask.

"Put it on. You'll thank me later."

"I don't think so."

"Are you always this tenacious?" he asked, now standing near enough for her to feel his body heat slipping past layers of clothing. Through the light, Riley could see a ring of gold in his teal eyes. The color, swirling like a circle of honey, made his eyes look green. She turned the facemask over and stared at the skull printed into the material. She felt something deep within her stir.

"What's wrong?" Jack asked, watching her.

"Nothing. It just reminds me of something." Riley said, suddenly feeling a slight pain in her head. In her mind, and with her eyes open, she saw people dressed in dark clothing pressing through a blizzard. Almost invisible, a white tiger darted past them. Riley followed first and then the others. They were all wearing the mask she held. As quick as the vision entered her mind, it faded, as did the pain in her temple. She looked up at Jack, who stared at her.

"You good?"

"Do you know cats can see in the dark," Riley informed him as he placed the earpiece into her ear. His fingers touched the edges of her earlobe, sending tiny bolts of electricity across her skin. He slid the mask over her hair, careful not to disturb the earpiece. He connected the radio.

"Yes," Jack looked into her eyes.

"Is there a white tiger here?" Her inner voice asked silently. She felt invisible under all the layers of clothing.

Their gazes met, and the sounds of the hospital quieted. They both turned and looked at the door, waiting. "You'll be able to hear us, and we'll be able to hear you."

"Okay," Riley understood the underlying truth in what he'd said. *Don't say anything you don't want everyone else to hear.*

He took in a deep breath, and she heard, *"You don't remember me, do you?"*

"What?" Riley asked.

"I didn't say anything yet." He stepped back, keeping his eyes on her.

Warding her attention off Jack, she checked her pistol and ammo then looked over to Shay, who struggled to get pieces of her hair back into a braid.

"I can fix that," happy to be released from Jack's hold, Riley stepped behind Shay and ran her fingers through the thick tresses of auburn hair.

"Shave it off," teased Blake rubbing his hand over his head.

"Good advice," smiled Shay. "Have you ever seen an onion with ears, eyes, and a nose? That's how I'd look if I shaved my head."

Riley let out a soft chuckle. She did a quick reverse braid tucking the unruly strands under before winding a band around the end.

"Thanks," Shay said, pulling her beanie over her head.

"Be ready to go?" Jack turned his focus on Sherry, who nodded, and then he turned to Riley once more. "I need you to partner with Blake."

Riley nodded. She stepped over to hug the girls one last time.

Predawn, the sun began a slow ascent into the December sky. The protection the storm provided them would soon be lost. They were about to become visible. A rush of cold air greeted them as they stepped out of the studio. Riley grew grateful for the full-face mask covering her face. A slight amount of light filtered through the corridor, promising nothing more than a shade lighter than night.

The snow had pushed the bookshelf forward in the reception area, letting an enormous amount of snow pile inward. Blake and Riley split away from Jack and Shay moving toward the east wing. Mimicking Blake's pace, Riley stayed close without tripping him up. With the coming of morning, the animals though even more hungry, grew quiet. The stench of feline urine filtered outward, forcing Riley to cover her nose. Clearing room after room, they saw nothing other than shadows reflecting off the examining rooms' windows, making illusions and tricking the eye.

They backtracked and headed toward the maze of corridors passing the room where the dead trespasser lay. Like a bad rendition of a wax figure in a horror museum, Lady Goth joined the smell of death permeating the air. The sound of the dead woman's bones breaking still fresh in Riley's mind. Blake stepped up the pace until he reached the back of the hospital, where he stopped. The sound of metal grinding metal sliced through the quiet.

Jack and Shay appeared as if shoved through from another dimension.

"Bermuda's in her run. I couldn't find Elmo," he informed them, "all the animals are loose outside but the smaller ones."

"Who's Elmo?"

"Rare White Siberian Tiger," said Jack looking at Riley. "I didn't want to scare you off since you have a thing about white tigers and monkeys."

"A white tiger?" repeated Riley, remembering the image of the cougar. "I never said anything about a white tiger."

"Any sign of them?" Blake's question brought Riley back to the present.

"No," Jack shook his head.

The sudden and fevered pitch of Ringo's voice crossed into the conversation, apprising them that he hadn't left. "Awe! You put one of the kitties away."

"That pretty much answers the question," Blake said, hoisting his gun a little closer to him. "Asshole's like a snake."

"Not a snake," Ringo called out. By the sound of his voice, he closed the distance between them.

Jack took out a piece of gum and casually slid a piece into his mouth. He chewed slow-like glancing down at his weapon. "I don't give a fuck what you want," he said in a calm tone.

"Sure you do." There was a long pause, and then, "I want to kill you, take the women and all your guns. Repayment."

"Repayment?" mocked Blake mimicking Ringo's voice.

"Asshole has a sense of humor," chuckled Jack, unmoved and unaffected. "Time for some payback."

"Oh, hell. I'd take just you and the blonde." Ringo's voice traveled as one sentence came from one direction, the next coming from another. "She's an excellent little pussycat."

"Gee. Thanks! I'm flattered, but not." Riley's harsh and unreceptive words faded. "Take drugs, much?"

"Only the best," whispered Shay loud enough. Riley heard her. "If he wants her, he'll have her in the worst ways possible."

"I feel better," Riley said. "This is a bad rendition of Bird on a Wire."

A burst of gunfire sent them scrambling in different directions. Riley sprinted after Blake toward one of the examining rooms. They dodged spraying bullets thudding into cement walls, spraying white mist under explosion. Riley crawled on all fours through the double doors behind Blake, following him into the cement jungle.

Thick shadows fell around her, boxes and debris blocked her path. Riley kept moving, shoving hospital supplies to the side while trying to keep up with Blake. When they stopped, Riley was pressing against cold steel bars. For a minute, she felt trapped in a cage, but instead, she was leaning against one.

"What the hell?" Blake strained to see through the cages.

"Welcome to the jungle," she said softly.

NOT ALONE

Blake grabbed her sleeve, pulling her to him, the last rounds thwacking closest to her head. The emergency lights flashed on, making the lighting dramatic. Now with the generator on, the heating system pressed not yet warm air through the vents outward. Ringo changed the rules again, and the players were about to come full circle. The devil wouldn't stop until he won.

44

The reddish glow of emergency light returned, showering a pale contrast that shimmered through a festering tide of nonentity. Sitting center stage, stainless steel tables, and large monitors lined uniform on a U-shaped desk in the oversized room. Lining the walls were medium-sized, much larger cage, neat and spaced appropriately, to house the more dangerous animals. Some of the larger cages reached as wide as they did high and framed the sidewalls.

"Holy shit," Riley cursed.

In awe, Riley considered the purpose for the lighting, cages, and medical equipment until an angry hissing sound came from behind. Riley froze and then spun around to face the noise. The badger pressed his nose through the bars, hair on end, hissing. Gleaming bloodstained teeth threatened attack while reflective eyes caught the light and turned a wicked red.

"Can anything look scarier?" she stared at the animal and then turned to Blake, disbelieving.

"Uh, yeah. Ringo!" Blake said.

With barely time to breathe, another short burst of gunfire rang out. Riley and Blake scrambled away from the cages looking for shelter from stray bullets and falling debris. Riley and Blake nestled themselves between a more extensive section and the wall near the larger steel enclosures.

"How does he move like that?" she asked.

"No fear. The man doesn't care if he dies."

"Sorry, I asked, then." She peeked around the container.

"Hold your position." Jack's voice came across the radio. Blake nodded. "Copy that."

Riley heard the occasional scratching of animals, a growl, a hiss, but the one that caught her attention was Bermuda. Having already met, Riley strained to see inside the giant cage. The big cat's eyes followed all movement as she paced back and forth.

"Let's talk," Ringo laughed. "I have coffee."

"Oh God, I'd love a cup of coffee."

Blake looked at her. "I'll ask him if he wouldn't mind bringing us over a cup or two." He rose, but Riley grabbed his sleeve, pulling him back down. She smiled, appreciating his effort to ease her fears. She'd forgotten how nice it was to have a partner.

NOT ALONE

They waited for the next round of gunfire, but none came. Ringo might not have been in the mood for talking, but he continued to agitate with an unwanted talk. "I've got a little surprise for you," Ringo said. An extended silence followed, and then he said, "Boom!"

"He's bluffing, right?" Riley felt a twist of nausea.

"Explosions are your field, Jack," Blake said into his mic. "Go get 'em."

"Too late. Brace yourself."

"What does he mean?" With her words lost, Blake pulled her to the floor, her face thumping on the cold cement. She glanced back to see him pulling his gun close to his body, and with lightning speed, he nestled close to her wrapping one arm around her back. They covered their heads as the entry exploded, sending a gust of debris over them. The hard surface drove numbness underneath her body while Blake leaned over her, warming her backside.

The loud blast vibrated her eardrums. The door, wall, and surrounding objects broke into pieces becoming projectiles, launching into midair with such force they traveled across the empty room like missiles. Particles blasted through open spaces exploding above their heads. Chunks of ceiling and building material rained down onto the floor, debris hitting their backs.

Riley lay with her face pressed to the concrete, waiting for the shower of debris and snow to stop raining down on them. Something popped. She waited for impact, keeping her hands enclosed behind her head, covering her ears. Seconds later, the roar softened to a ringing. Blake tapped her on the shoulder. A cloud of fine dust filled the room. Wires and metal hung broken and ripped apart overhead as water flowed through pipes onto the floor. Riley looked over at the big cage. The cougar was no longer visible. A large mass of bars pulled apart in a tangled mess.

"Are you listening?" Ringo yelled out. "That was one."

Riley scrambled to her feet and whispered, "Megan and Utah!"

"Down!"

Blake reached out to grab her. Riley never saw the other stranger shoot from the folds of shadows. With Ninja-like speed, he took her to the ground. The impact from the man forced her forward, throwing her to the ground. Riley hit the cement hard, taking the wind from her. The mask on her face bit into the new stitches creating tiny bolts of pain. The high-pitched hiss of a bullet grazed by them midair, missing and lodging into the wall. Her friend, the badger, hissed.

Riley covered her head, drowning out the sound of the gunfire. Casings fell, rolling on the floor close to her. Through the chaos, Riley made out a set of black boots and four paws. The dog pressed its nose to her mask, and then the canine disappeared. She fingered her pistol but then heard retreating footsteps. She stayed down for several more seconds before crawling behind the crate. Riley moved, testing limbs for breaks or bullets or both. She sat up and searched for Blake.

In a hurry to get nowhere fast, Riley moved over a pile of snow that had fallen through the broken roof. Brick and twisted metal blocked her from getting to the hospital's center. The smoke-filled air also sought an exit. The glow from a small fire intermixed with the blinking orange backup lights made for eeriness unwelcomed. Then through flickering light, she saw an opening.

Trembling and with clumsy steps, she moved over debris. On the other side, Blake and Shay were moving towards her.

"You okay?" Riley asked them.

"You?" Blake asked, reaching his hand out to her.

Riley nodded her head, "yeah." Without forethought, Riley moved on. Blake reached out and grabbed her arm, stopping her.

"Let Jack do this. He's trained for it. We stay together." Blake's voice held firmness. "Ringo brought more men."

"Megan, Utah."

"Jack knows what he's doing," Blake gave her arm a reassuring squeeze. "You're no good to anyone if you're dead."

"Where's the man, the dog?" she asked, looking around.

"He went to help Jack," Blake moved forward. "We need to get to the trucks."

"How are we going to do that?" asked Riley. "If he has more men, the exits will be blocked."

"Jack's brother, Ryan, is here. He brought help." Blake looked at Riley. "Let's go get the others."

"Okay."

Ready?" Blake asked them both.

"Ready." Shay and Riley spoke at the same time.

They slid through the door in a line, slipping into the dim orange glow of yet another corridor. The dimness above flickered and then fizzled back into the hole where no light could find them.

Riley played Hide-and-Seek when she was a kid. She knew how blackness plays on the imagination, creating monsters out of shadows. The game played with Ringo resembled a twisted version but with deadly intent.

Sensing the monster hid nearby, Riley felt him everywhere, waiting. The hairs on the back of her neck rose, causing her to be cautious of all space. Shay and Blake stepped up their pace, causing her to fall back as she weaved through the maze blind, all the while searching for a hint of his presence. Awareness rose inside her, old destiny redefined.

The minute she took hold of what she must do, Ringo grabbed hold of her and pulled her into a black opening. For Riley, the darkened space might as well have been hell. Unseeing, he yanked her to him, pinning her pistol against her chest. The tip of the barrel pointed upwards under her chin. If only she could be the one holding the gun, Riley would have pulled the trigger. Ringo clamped one hand over her mouth, pulling the stitches on her cheek, ripping away the facemask.

"Old habits die hard, don't they, Riley?" he whispered in her ear. "How more perfect can this all be?"

Ringo held Riley so tight she could not inhale or move.

Riley closed her eyes, trying to focus on her breathing. *I've been here before, and I survived.*

Then his fingers parted, allowing her to take in some air. With his mouth, he took her earpiece and spat the mechanism out. Repulsed by his touch, Riley shuddered and then sucked in a stream of air.

He wants me alive.

An animal-like quietness blanketed his strides as he pulled her further away from the corridor, slipping through doors and hallways, taking her with him. His fingers pressed down on her lips, capturing her breath and her voice. Riley struggled to find more air.

"It is my lucky day," his voice warmed her ear. "I've waited a long time for you."

His words were hot. His mouth pressed to her displaced facemask. Stopping only to allow her to breathe, he pulled her deeper into the confines of the hospital to places she never imagined existed. Every movement Ringo made was deliberate and precise. Then he turned, keeping the gun pressed under her chin, dragging her backward. "What's behind door number two? Could it be the little girl?"

Ringo paused, his tone lower and his breath even warmer. "I will blow this place to up with everyone in it if you do not cooperate with me. Do you understand?"

Riley nodded, tears forming in her eyes.

If she fell unconscious, she would never know where he took her. Thick fog swirled in her head, and it got harder to fight the dizziness off and stay awake. He'd set off the explosives regardless if she surrendered or not, but Riley needed to buy some time for Jack and the others. If Jack survived, Megan and Utah survived.

Don't let him take you. Utah's voice sounded in her head.

"Good. Awe, I think we're going to get along fine."

Terror surged through her. Riley wanted to throw up, but his hand made that impossible. She had her fingers wrapped around his, pulling and prying with desperate fingers taking pieces of flesh with fingernails.

NOT ALONE

The barrel of her gun pressed harder under her chin, and she struggled to keep pressure off the trigger. The fog and the imbalance of her equilibrium wanted her to succumb to unconsciousness. She feared her muscles would contract, and her finger would slip. As much as she tried to pull her body away from his, he only held her tighter. If he took her from the building, she might be lost forever. Riley's knees buckled as dark, and light flashed in her head. Under Ringo's hold, her trigger finger at risk of slipping. Then her world went black.

45

A few hours prior.

The coming of dawn and the calming of wind brought odd tranquility in the ruins of the storm. Prescott to Flagstaff had received unprecedented record amounts of snowfall overnight. Dan called in his uncle Randal, who cut a path through the white powder with an old snowplow he called "Snow-White." With Snow White's help, Dan and Ryan reached the hospital in a little over an hour.

"There's Blake's truck." Dan pointed, but all Ryan could see were mounds of white.

"And a few others. Boy, did the storm dump here?"

"Hey boys, you got a pack of bad guys tracking your path fast through the snow," Dan's uncle's voice sounded over the radio. "One passed me going the other way. Watch your backs."

"Copy that," said Dan.

"Park in there." Ryan pointed over at a building with three large bay doors. He checked for the red flash of the security camera that sometimes recorded the front, the driveway, and a gate. The building appeared empty, save a few large cages and supplies, a tractor, and a smaller pickup.

Dan slipped out of the vehicle and lifted the bay door. Ryan slid over to the driver's seat, backing the Hummer through the opening. Darkness hid them as soon as Dan lowered the door, shutting off anyone approaching.

"You should've had one of those on at the ranch," Dan flipped on a dim flashlight and tugged on the bulletproof vest Ryan slipped over his head. "You wouldn't be gimpy now." Dan teased, tightening the Velcro on his jacket.

"I was ripped from my sleep," Ryan tapped Dan's vest, "you sleep with yours on?"

"No, but I'm bulletproof without it."

What sounded like a diesel engine made them pause. "Bad guys?"

"Yep. Let's give them a minute." Without argument from Ryan, Dan said nothing more, adjusting his radio.

"Desert One, what's your position. Copy." The radio crackled. "Desert One, I got a pup in tow. Do you copy?"

"Pup?" asked Ryan. "What the fuck does that mean?"

"It means we watch over you. I can't believe you never heard us say that."

NOT ALONE

The two men moved in the direction of Blake's truck past open spaces and between buildings and cars. A dark blue-gray sky showered a brilliant glow of dark and light downward onto the snow, making it shimmer. The temperature hung in the mid-twenties, freezing their breath. Seconds after leaving the safety of the building, a burst of gunfire forced them into a run. The blizzard left a barrier past their knees, creating resistance slowing their strides. Under their feet, objects lay imperceptible, creating human hazards dangerous enough to break a leg. Bullets whizzed past them, slapping metal and snow. Fleeing moving projectiles and fighting the cumbersome path, Ryan tripped. Dan, not but a step or two behind him, grabbed his arm, pulling him to his feet. Together, they plowed forward, finding safety behind a snow-covered car.

"Hey, pup. Nine o clock on the roof."

"Got him," Ryan spotted the shooter, laying his finger on the trigger, the firing pin connected with the primer detonating the charge, sending the bullet at its intended target. The shot hit, sending a spray of blood and flesh outward, turning the snow below red.

"Good shot," Dan said, ducking down as a short burst of gunfire broke out overhead.

The car shielding them took on a hammering of bullets. Windows exploded, sending tiny pieces of glass into the air. Ryan hugged the front tire, facing outward. He sent a warning to the shooter hiding behind a ground-level air-conditioning unit. Reloading, the man gave Ryan and Dan a chance to run to the next car. They stopped at Blake's truck. The shooter fired, sending glass exploding into the air and snow.

"Shit!" Dan ducked under the door of the truck.

Only twenty feet from the hospital's back door, a thump sounded and then a hiss as rounds connected with a front tire. Several bullets sunk into the truck's fenders, making a plinking sound. All four tires were about to become flat.

Ryan crouched down low, popping off a few shots of his own. "Blake's going to be pissed."

A new shooter on the roof was making it hard for Ryan to get a good shot. "Get the shooter behind us?" he told Dan.

"Move to your left. On three."

All Ryan needed was one chance, and he'd send the man to the ground. The front windshield shattered, and the second shot sent it into a cloud of fragments. Ryan covered his head.

"Mother, fucker."

"One, two, three," Dan sprung to his feet, twisting around, shooting several rounds at the marker.

The man jerked backward, dropping his gun, disappearing, but another replaced him. Ryan swung to the right aiming at the roof. The replacement shooter disappeared. Ryan hurried for the back door, leaving Dan to cover him. Two more shooters closed in.

"To the left."

"Get the door open, Ryan. Get it open now!"

Gunshots rang out from their right side. Dan held them off. A body fell from the rooftop, hitting one of the snow-covered vehicles breaking the windshield. Dan fired as Ryan worked the key into the lock. One of Dan's targets dove past them tumbling into the snow.

"Doors unlocked, but it won't open," Ryan muttered, pulling the steel door feeling the stitches in his chest pull. Still, the door would not move.

"Doors jammed," Ryan said, shaking it.

"Marker on your right."

Another truck, between themselves and the marker, acted as a shield buying Ryan time. Dan disappeared. A spray of dry snow floated from overhead. Ryan stopped pushing on the door as another marker stepped around the other side of the building. The man looked upward to signal his friend, but Ryan aimed and shot through the windows of the truck. His bullet slapped the man in the chest.

"Shit!" The voice came from overhead, followed by the sound of retreating footfalls.

Ryan pulled on the door again, but it stayed wedged. About to find another way in, Dan stepped up next to him.

"You lost your touch or what?"

"You want to give it a try?" Ryan said, stepping aside.

Dan turned the knob, pulling. "The door's jammed."

"Really?"

"Yep."

Ryan rolled his eyes. Being the youngest Colton did not come easy. Ryan was continually watched over and scrutinized, while Jack was never questioned no matter the circumstance. Ryan had big shoes to fill, being Jack's younger brother. Jack was a hero these days, and Ryan was right behind him.

"The front," Ryan turned away from the door, moving to the other side of the building only to meet a retreating shooter. They dodged behind several overturned dumpsters using the metal containers as shields. They waited, but the man's only intent was to run.

"What, did they bring a busload in?" growled Dan.

They moved quickly to where the snow had piled up several feet high. Both entrances and windows had at least a two-foot barrier. A broken window allowed access via an opening at the top. Ryan, not waiting for direction, slipped through the hole unheard.

"Can you fit?" Ryan asked from the other side.

Dan snorted. "If you can, I can."

The building's interior emitted cold air, which concerned Ryan, knowing neither man nor animal could withstand such temperatures too long. Papers and product littered the floors. Pieces of furniture rested upside down and scattered. The reception area looked like a bomb went off. They stood quiet until someone cleared their throat behind them, causing them both to turn at the same time.

The man, camouflaged by enclosure, directed his gun at Dan and then shifted to Ryan, moving it smoothly from side to side.

"Don't move." A dog appeared from around a corner, halting beside the man.

Ryan said nothing, raising both hands upward. The gun in his left hand intact but aimed up toward the ceiling.

"I'm looking for my brother," Ryan, still not all the way healed, struggled to keep his arms up.

The man was not a part of the cavalry outside. Otherwise, Ryan and Dan would have already been dead. He leaned in closer. His facemask was separated by the whites of his eyes, which glowed through the dark. He searched their faces.

"Colton?" asked Kid.

"Ryan Colton."

"Kid. I know your brother, Jack."

"I know," replied Ryan, recognizing him from town. "The dog gave you away." A shimmer of light penetrated the top of the windows, promising warmth non-existent in the cement jungle.

"How many did you get outside?" Kid raised his mask a little.

"Depends. A handful. How many were there?" asked Ryan.

"Storms been so aggressive. Hard to tell." Kid rubbed his cheek. "Your brother's alive. They've got a few wounded people. One's a little girl."

The dog let out a slight whine.

"A little girl?" repeated Ryan.

"Doctor Kenny and her technician are dead." Kid stepped in a bit closer. "You can lower your hands."

"You've been here all night?" Dan asked, relaxing.

"All night. I was out making deliveries when the storm hit." He kept his weapon drawn but had it resting on his arm.

"How many men inside?"

"Two bad guys, but you might want to count Ringo as five in one?"

"Where's Jack now?" Dan asked.

NOT ALONE

"Good question. They scattered when the bomb went off."

"Bomb!" Ryan raised an eyebrow. Kid lowered his gun. "Who's Ringo?"

"The devil with a circus name. I think your brother pissed him off. Either way, he's pissed off."

"I'm not surprised," Dan smiled. "Jack has that gift."

"Jack had a little run-in with a few men on our property this past week."

"Well, let's go round up your brother." Kid moved forward. "he'll be glad to know you're here. Watch your back. Animals are running free."

Ryan and Dan followed the man and dog. Partway down the corridor, Kid paused, pointing at a body on the floor. "Pam Kenny."

"Sweet Jesus," exclaimed Ryan. "Poor Doc."

They passed through double doors stepping over large chunks of broken cement. The blast had destroyed the door, leaving nothing but a dark gaping hole.

The sound of water trickling from somewhere in the room resonated off the cement. Wires hung like giant snakes dangling from a rip that extended well up into the beams of the roof.

The sound of claws tapping on cement pulled Ryan's attention to the cage.

"Bermuda." Above the carnage, Ryan made out the silhouette of a cat pacing back and forth.

"I got her back into the cage. She was scared." Kid said, restless but alert. "Stay here. You're brother's working on finding and disarming the more explosives."

"Nice!" Dan said, distracted by the cat rather than the word explosive. "I knew Pam Kenny had some exotics, but...."

"We're missing a cat or two," Ryan said in a soft tone.

"Are you serious?" Dan looked at the cougar.

They moved closer to the cat but paused, watching the animal lick her heart-shaped nose stained with blood. She flattened her long white whiskers back with her tongue, never taking her eyes off them. A hiss came from her throat more than threatening. Displaying her displeasure, she flattened her ears tighter against her head, pressing her nose hard against the bars, watching them. Ryan turned around to say something to Kid, who had disappeared.

"Where's the rest of the cats, the Mexican Wolves?" Ryan stepped forward, searching the cages for the bigger animals. The hairs on the back of his neck rose to see the deep animal tracks under his feet, leading inside the hospital.

Dan lifted his rifle a little higher. "I don't like this."

"Be ready."

46

Jack met Kid in the hallway. Not wasting time to exchange greetings, they moved in step with the other.

"Your brother is here." The dog walked with Kid as if anticipating his next move. "They're in the south wing. They took out a handful of markers."

"What the hell took him so long?" Jack mumbled. "You know how to disarm a bomb?"

"I'm not a pro, but I can work my way through just about anything," grinned Kid as Jack handed him a headset.

"Let me know when you find something."

Kid and his dog turned toward the surgery room.

Ringo promised not to make anything easy, so Jack searched in places less conspicuous and out of reach. He inspected shelving and entryways, closets and equipment, and reachable air vents, all the while watching out for Ringo and his sidekick. He ran his fingers around space large enough to hold explosives. Minutes ticked away. He grew anxious. Time was wasted, but if they tried a getaway, Ringo would detonate more explosives.

"Shift found something," Kid's voice crackled across the radio. "Through the surgery room, take a left."

Jack stepped in to find Kid looking down at a container filled with liquid. The explosive looked crude, a mix of hospital instruments and chemicals. It was inventive and crude, something a demented mind would create. As Jack went to work, Kid stood at his back, facing outward. After a few minutes, Jack turned around, giving Kid the okay.

"Just one?"

"No. I'm sure there is more. I think it's time to get everyone out of here," Jack said.

"You'll be moving targets once you leave this building," Kid reminded him.

"It's a big building. Too many places to hide explosives inside or out." Jack mumbled wearily.

They walked toward the studio door, and Jack tapped on the door twice, paused, and then repeated the sequence of knocks. The door opened, Sherry stood in the doorway.

"You ready?" Jack asked. "How's the little girl?"

"Not good."

"Bundle up, and let's get her to Nick."

He helped Matt toward the door. Kid stepped in next to where Megan lay and stared down at the little girl's face. Sherry brushed by him, setting a box of supplies at Megan's feet, unhooked the IV drip, and then nodded. Jack led them to the back office, where they began only twenty-four hours earlier.

"Stay here. Lock the door," Jack ordered.

"Got it." Matt leaned on the doorjamb for support, but in his hand, he held his pistol steady.

Jack and Kid slipped back down the corridor through the double doors to where Ryan and Dan waited.

"Glad you listen," he told his brother.

"Good thing I don't."

Jack patted Ryan on the shoulder, "Glad you're here."

"Where're the others?"

"Close," Jack said, zipping up his jacket. "Tell me you brought the Hummer?"

"Second bay door," Ryan said. "Blake?"

"They should be to the office by now."

Jack looked at the cougar, pacing inside the steel cage. The cat would starve if left behind caged, a cruel way to die. Jack already decided he'd help Bermuda find her freedom. Having been born in the desert, the cat needed to be in the wild where she belonged.

"Careful, she's hungry and pissed off," Ryan muttered.

"I have an idea." Jack looked at the walk-in freezers.

"I wouldn't go in there." Kid warned.

"Why?"

"Ringo must have locked Destiny in there. That or she hid, and he locked her in there," Kid informed them.

Jack opened the door only to face a young girl sitting Indian-style, her hands enclosed around her body in a tight hold as if trying to hold in the warmth trapped inside her. Her skin no longer pale or tanned by the sun, but a blue-gray, her eyes frozen open.

"Sick son of a bitch," Jack knelt beside the girl bowing his head before gazing into the dead girl's eyes, feeling deep sorrow. In life, her young eyes had been a stunning blue. In death, they were a chilling white-coated gray. The team, out of time, wounded and outnumbered, waited for direction. Jack needed to get them out of there before someone else died. He slipped inside the freezer, returning with a large chunk of frozen meat. Dragging the hindquarter of a pig to Bermuda's cage, he laid it close to the bars, teasing the cat's senses. Kid stepped in, taking one end of the meat while Jack took the other.

"Lift the gate," Jack told Dan.

The chute allowed a person to feed without becoming the next meal. They turned the frozen meat loose, watching it slide down the line making a clanking sound on the cement floor. The portion of the pig stopped several feet from where Bermuda stood. The cougar watched and then hissed. Her lips curled upward, pressing lines into its muzzle, baring white bloodstained teeth. The distraction would buy them time until they could set her free.

"Looks like the asshole has no vendetta against the animals," Jack said, watching the cat go to a prone position and sniff the frozen meat.

Jack kept his eye on her, lifting the latch on the gate but not opening it. He moved fast now, unlatching the remaining cages holding the badgers. The animals hissed, stepping sideways out of their cells, scrambling in Jack's direction.

"You ungrateful little bastards," he shouted, stomping his feet.

"You have ten minutes," Jack said to Bermuda as he passed by her cage.

Jack checked his back one last time. Bermuda had left her cage. Unnerved, he led the team down the corridor to the center of the hospital. He saw Shay and Blake standing outside Pam's office door. Their guns pressed forward, and their expressions hidden by facemasks. Jack could tell something went wrong. They were shy one person.

"He took her," Blake said, shaking his head. "Asshole moves like a ghost. Never heard or saw him. He reached out of the dark and swiped her up."

"Where?"

Blake pointed in the direction where they were all together last. "I backtracked. Been looking for her since we split apart. He's gone."

"Get the others and load up."

Ready to vacate the hospital, the team waited for Jack to say something. Instead, he shuffled them toward the office where the exit from hell awaited them.

"Doors jammed, Jack. That's how we tried to get in." Ryan said.

"That's because that asshole's been blowing shit up." Jack tried the door. It wouldn't even budge an inch.

Prepared to make a run for it once they got past the exit door, another detonation rocked the building, stopping them midway. The blast shook the walls sending a spray of fine powder trickling down on them. The echo of the explosion bounced through the corridors, vibrating the foundation under their feet. They ducked, bracing themselves for the roof to cave.

Blake covered Megan with his body, Utah holding beneath him. Jack jumped to his feet, dipping under the sagging doorway to the door leading outside. The door moved but only a few inches.

Kid stepped up next to him.

"It's moving, but not enough to get her by" Jack shook the door again. "Something inside the doorjambs moved."

Kid nodded, together they stepped back, and then with all their weight, they pushed forward, shoving the door another few inches. Dan stepped up, and three men backed away and then rushed forward again, pressing shoulder weight into the door. This time the opening broadened, taking part of the frame with it. The space was now wide enough to allow them to pass. Blake slid past them to the outside to clear their way.

"What about Riley?" Sherry asked.

"Go with Shay," instructed Jack.

"He'll kill her," cried Sherry, her face turning an ashen white.

"I'll find her," Jack's tone rose. "I promise, I need you and Shay to help me with these guys." Jack looked over at Megan and Matt.

"Okay," she nodded, taking the bag of fluids for Megan's IV in her hands.

Utah stood at Jack's side, holding onto his jacket.

"Looks like you got a few," Jack looked at the blood-streaked snow. "You ready, Coop?"

"Yeah. What about the kid's mom?" asked Shay.

"She can't be far," Jack said, helping Matt. "I'll find her." Utah held on to his coat. Jack was taking his team home. The business between him and Ringo would have to wait.

"We'll find her," Kid stepped behind them.

47

Riley shivered when she woke. The cold bit into her flesh like bee stings. The more she tried to relax, the harder she shook. She could not control it, nor did she have the strength. There came a musky odor of dirt rising from the ground beneath. Unknowing how long she slept or where he'd taken her, a deep panic surfaced. The only sound, eerie and hollow, was dripping water. She knew he'd drugged her.

Drip, drip... drip.

Chilling. A drugged mind developed images into dreams.

Drip. Death. Influenced by drugs, the sound expanded. Imagination grated on deep fears, monsters infiltrated her thoughts, holding her mind hostage. Words crawled through her throat like spiders spinning webs. Embracing the lightless hole, she settled with one positive note. She wasn't dead yet.

Moving one limb at a time, she found herself intact. She bolted upright, her head slamming against something hard. Stars flared, and then she felt a cold fear.

I'm in a box! She screamed silently.

The ringing in her head made her nauseous. The thought of him burying her alive supercharged a surge of horror already racing through her body. Wrapping her arms around her chest, she rolled into a fetal position. Tears. A wave of convulsions began in her stomach, causing her to dry heave because there, nothing sat in her stomach. More spiders tried to crawl from her throat. Focus. She saw tiny threads of light sneaking through the wood slats of her prison. Thin strands of hope that she wasn't underground. Not yet, anyway.

"Kitten, are you awake?" A familiar voice boomed overhead.

I want to kill you.

The door creaked. Ringo's footfalls pressing on wood planks made her shiver, but then more light filtered through. Shiver. Riley closed her eyes, hoping he'd leave.

"Hungry?" His tone sounded relaxed.

What edge of insanity are you walking on, and how can I use it to my advantage? She wanted to scream.

He stood above her. A stream of dirt filtered through the cracks, like sand in an hourglass, falling onto her.

I'm not in a box. I'm under the floor.

Panic. More spiders. The light went away. The floorboards groaned under his weight some more. Keys jingled, and a lock was released. The top part of the box rose, and light spilled inward. Ringo appeared.

"I wanted to be clear. Very clear."

Her eyes watered.

Ringo reached his hand out to her. She felt nothing but hatred. She took it, not wanting to remain another second in the hole. With one pull, he put Riley in front of him. He let go, and she swayed, feeling the pins and needles pulsing through her legs. She looked down at the boxlike coffin and went to her knees.

Ringo set a plate in front of her as if she were a dog. He knelt there, and they stared at each other. Never had she seen eyes like his, fire, and brimstone circled the iris. Evil. Fearing he'd dismantle her, something she would make sure he'd regret, but instead, he turned and walked out of the room, mumbling.

"You aren't so full of fire now, are you?"

He'd left the door open, inviting her to follow. She climbed to her feet, realizing they were bare. Without shoes, Riley could not go anywhere, not tonight.

She rose slowly and reached for the plate. To survive, she needed food. Get her mind right. Play the game. She hoped the food might absorb whatever Ringo had given her. Riley hugged the plate and followed him. Refuel.

The warm glow of the fire called her forward. Warmth! The flames cast a spray of light from the center of the room outward. She shivered, unable to control the rattling of the fork tapping the plate. Desperate for warmth, she hurried toward the fire brushing Ringo's knee as she passed.

The table where he sat seemed small in comparison to his broad frame. A large plate of what looked like stew sat in front of him. Steam swirled off the meat. He motioned at the food, but she didn't move. He shrugged and ate. He'd already drugged her once. Maybe he poisoned her food.

"I didn't poison your food. Eat. I want you alive, for now."

She hugged the fire while balancing the food in her hand. As the shivering subsided, Riley got hungry.

Ringo tossed her bottled water. She caught it midair. "Drink."

The cold water washed away the spiders, cooled her dry lips, and even softened the ache in her cheek. He stared.

Riley chewed, swallowed despite his stare. The light of the fire illuminated the scars on his face. The burning ebbs of flame were gone from his eyes and were now a gray steel tint.

"Who are you?" Riley's throat hurt, making it hard to speak.

"Your worst nightmare. Have you ever had bad dreams?" He leaned back in his chair. His eyes turned transparent as if he were controlling the way the color changed.

"Everyone does."

This metaphoric unwanted second round of poker with the devil scared her. Worst yet, Riley was a lousy poker player because she hated lying, and to win, she'd have to lie.

"You have a spirit that's broken."

"You're evil." The words slipped from her, sounding melodramatic.

"I'm not evil," he paused.

"You shot a little girl."

"An error on my part. Right now, your friends are trying to save her life."

She watched him.

His thoughts drifted and then returned. He took another bite of his food.

Riley said nothing. Her first impression of him remained dark and daunting. Whatever drug he took interacted with his body chemistry, making him reach different euphoria and madness levels.

What are you taking, and what did you give me?

"It won't hurt you. I assure you."

He can read my mind.

"Soon, you'll want more."

"Don't count on it. Where are the rest of my clothes, my shoes."

He wanted to say something, but she didn't care, not about him. However, Riley didn't want to go back beneath the floor either.

"You'll have to earn them back. Where were you the night of the Shift? Ringo asked, pausing between a bite.

"I don't remember," Riley lied. Poker.

"Everyone remembers," Call.

"I don't." Lie.

"I'm calling your bluff, Riley. You remember some of it, don't you?"

"Are you sure about that?" Knowing he'd baited her, she took a bite.

He was silent for a spell taking a chunk of meat chewing on it slowly. The sound grated on her nerves.

"The night the Shift happened," he stated. "I was playing poker with some buddies of mine. We were having boy time, smoking cigars, and having a few beers. Life was good, as people used to say. We had jobs and families. Life was good," he repeated. He took a drama-filled moment to reflect. "I made over seven hundred grand every year, that was take home, sometimes more. My wife and my children lacked for nothing. She got her hair and nails done at the local beauty shop. She met her friends at the gym every day at ten. Her wardrobe took up a huge walk-in closet that would make most women jealous. I bought her the car of her choice."

Again, Riley remained quiet and listened but took nothing he said in truth. Ringo neither looked nor spoke like a hillbilly with a third-grade education. He was far more intelligent than that. His sentence structure and manner were of someone educated and well raised. She had a sense that he was an intellectual and smart but domineering man. His real name could not be Ringo but rather Michael or Richard, something intelligent and wealthy. He sat reflecting on his wife as if seeing it in his mind. He waited. Riley knew he was testing her.

48

Blake moved through the door first, taking cover behind his truck while cursing the man who had destroyed it. Jack and Sherry slipped through with Megan, who was a tiny bundle in Jack's arms. Shooters forced them to take shelter before making it halfway to the adjacent building.

The sky overhead opened, and a slight breeze pushed clouds, breaking them apart, allowing a thin stream of sunshine to make its way through.

"Get them to the Hummer. I'll cover you," said Blake, motioning them on.

Using parked cars as shields, they stepped with quick strides toward the building to the Hummer. Jack helped Sherry with Matt and Megan, getting them settled in the backseat, and Ryan started the engine to warm the cab.

After securing the wounded, Jack moved to the driver's side window, "Wait here," he said to Ryan.

Outside, crossfire kept Kid pinned down. Ringo's men were trying to disable as many of the vehicles as they could hit. Stray bullets exploded windows, popped tires, and slammed into metal, but the shooter on the roof ran out of ammo and needed to reload. Jack took the shot.

"One down," Jack said. "Flush him out."

"Make that two," replied Blake. "Copy."

"Copy," Jack waited for Blake to make a move. He placed a bullet into the lip of the roof, forcing a third man to change his position. The man stepped out in the open, and Jack made another controlled shot.

"Looks like Ringo left his men to do the dirty work."

"What that crazy asshole do, bring in a busload?" Blake's voice crackled across the mic.

Another man appeared, but Jack had him in his sights, sending a round into his chest, hurling him backward. There came a long pause.

"Asshole's got an army."

"You see those tracks?" Jack pointed at the tracks, knowing Blake could see him.

"Looks like Ringo's headed to Prescott. You see anymore?"

"Nope, but be careful."

Blake plowed through the snow ducking the shots ringing from somewhere on the south side of the building. Stumbling over debris on the ground underneath the snow, he did a face plant. "I hate the snow," Blake muttered into his mic. "Son of a bitch."

"Stay there." Jack waited for the shooter to come into sight while tapping his finger on the guard of his trigger. "One more."

Jack watched Blake through his scope. Minutes passed. The marker on the roof held tight, making it so Jack could not take the shot.

"Come on," Jack said in a whisper.

Another minute passed. Blake, impatient, moved. Jack pulled the trigger, letting a round of bullets connect with the cement lip.

Overhead, another man rose sporadically, firing shots, and in the rain of bullets and chaos, Jack fired back but missed. The hum of a diesel engine purred as Jack and Blake turned to see a truck advancing towards them. Kid stopped and fired a semi-automatic at the marker overhead. The man froze, shuddered, and then staggered forward.

Jack waved at Kid to get on the road.

Blake climbed to his feet as the wounded man's body twitched. The dead man fell with a soft thud onto the blanket of snow. Random shots sprayed outward, Blake catching one in the thigh, sending him to his knees. All went quiet except for the hum of the engine.

Jack sprang across the snow, reaching Blake, "You okay?"

"He got me in the thigh, but nothing's broke."

"Good. Let's get out of here."

The big bay door of the receiving building rose, revealing the Hummer. Jack grabbed hold of Blake and pulled him toward the red Chevy.

"Not even a bullet hole."

"That you can see." Blake chuckled as he gazed at the truck. "Can you keep this girl on the road?"

"I thought you were driving," teased Jack.

Ryan took the lead as he drove the Hummer through the bay door, steam rolling off the tailpipe and into the late morning sunlight. Kid followed, and then Jack and Blake. The cat emerged and stopped in the center of the road.

Jack stopped the Chevy. Bermuda's tail swayed back and forth, ears forward, nose tipped upward. She was not only beautiful but powerful. Her frosty breath penetrated the cold, sending a cloud of air outward. The cat stared at them, then for an unknown reason to Jack and Blake, she hissed and sprang off her feet. Bermuda sprinted toward the mountains.

"I think she was thanking you," said Blake watching the silhouette of the cat disappear. "You're doing the right thing."

Jack frowned, glancing down at the detonator in his fingers. "It's what she would have wanted," said Jack under his breath.

He took one last look in his rearview mirror, and then he pushed the red button.

NOT ALONE

Jack was ready for it. The percussion from the explosion shattered the quietness inside the Chevy but more so outside. The ground shook as the building ripped apart, first into a ball of fire and then into a dark blanket of black smoke. A hard shock wave rocked under them, rattling the frame of the Chevy. Dan's uncle waited for them past the railroad tracks and was ready to carve a smoother pathway toward the highway.

Nick and Lynn waited on the porch. Lynn's worried expression faded as the trucks pulled in one by one. Jack immediately scooped up Megan in his arms and hurried toward Nick.

"She's been shot."

Lynn's gaze fell on Megan. "What happened, Jack?"

Nick took Megan in his arms.

Ben stepped out of the shadows of the barn holding his shotgun and nodded at his sons.

"Jesus, Jack," Nick said, carrying Megan toward the house. Utah bound her fingers around Lynn's shirt moving beside her.

An hour past noon, the Arizona sun decided to play Peek a Boo, and the frozen white blanket of snow sparkled under the rays of light. Ryan helped Matt as Dan and Shay helped Blake out of the Chevy. A fresh trail of blood formed behind the wounded as they made their way into the house.

Ben moved to the front door, taking watch. Nick took Megan into another section of the house with Sherry and Lynn, eager to assist. Jack followed. They entered the office and then into a compact surgery room.

Nick placed Megan on the bed unwrapping jackets and blankets. His expression remained constant even at the sight of the little girl's condition. Working swift and calm, Nick did what he did best, saving lives.

"We've got her now, Jack."

Jack knew Nick would do everything he could to save the little girl's life, but he remained at the doorway until Lynn closed the door.

49

"There were six of us playing poker that night." A subtle grin formed on his face. "I had a winning hand. We were knee-high in bullshit, smoking, and drinking. Then, the air became thick, and we all kind of stopped. We sat there for a second, down in my "man cave," as she called it. Out of nowhere, we laughed. I mean, laughed."

Ringo set his plate down on the table and stood up. Riley felt the muscles in her body tighten. She couldn't shake that seemed something seemed odd and familiar about him, and the sensation scared her. She stopped chewing. Ringo saw her reaction and smiled. He liked that she feared him, and Riley knew he'd use that on her.

"The door...," Ringo said, pointing to the door, "is bolted with locks." He held up a single key, making it visible to her, and then he slid it deep into his pants pocket.

"I know," she said. Nothing more.

She chewed her food again, feeling the bile rise in the back of her throat.

Riley would have to play along with Ringo until he screwed up enough to allow her room to escape. She looked away from him and gazed at the fire, waiting.

Remember, the key is in his right front pocket.

Ringo picked up from where he left off. "Joe reached for the money, and Charlie, well old Charlie whacked off Joe's hand," he slammed his hand down on the table, mimicking the whack-job Charlie did, which made Riley jump. "like it was nothing. You should have seen the blood! It flew all over the money and us." His voice lowered a notch. "It was ironic strangely, blood and money. In the end, money was our final downfall and the root of our evil. It didn't go too pleasant from there. Within a short amount of time, all of my friends were lying on the floor, but two. I was alive. Tim, my best friend for many years, was missing. For how long, you might ask?"

He paused, waiting for her to ask. Riley grew curious but calmed her curiosity because she did want to know his misery. Ringo lingered there in his thoughts. Pushing his half-eaten dinner away from him, he pulled out a cigar and looked at it for a long moment. Cutting off the tip, Ringo rolled the tobacco torpedo between his fingers with care. Then he set it between his lips. These actions, combined with the pauses of his storytelling, created a dramatic effect. Riley had a feeling he told his story to set precedence for something more.

"We don't know how long Tim was gone. Time played tricks on us. I could see everything around me but felt like something was driving me, something other than myself. It felt like I was turned upside down, and all the blood was rushing to my head." He lit the cigar, now moist with saliva.

Remembering her last night at work, Riley understood what he'd said. She felt it before stepping out the back door of the department. To hear someone else describe what they felt that horrible night seemed strange.

"My wife had gone to bed early that night." He lifted his voice higher to scare her. The increase in volume did. Riley jumped again. "The kids were at a slumber party." He tugged on his shirt to build theatrics to his story. "I was covered in blood. I went upstairs. I had a few superficial wounds from the boys fighting back, but nothing serious. Blood everywhere, carpet, tables, and walls. I moved through a haze, fog. I don't know what it was exactly. The voice, my voice, was inside me, telling me what to do. The blood vessels in my temple felt constricted. My head pounded, but it wasn't painful until I opened the door and saw my best friend Tim fucking my wife. When I say fucking, that's what they were doing. She looked straight at me and moaned, making sure I knew she liked it. Teddy was under her."

"I thought you said his name was Tim?" Riley said, accidentally breaking her silence as well as allowing Ringo to see she was paying attention.

"Tim. Tim was under her. He looked up and saw me. He laughed. How had he gotten from the poker table to my bed so quick?"

Riley chose not to answer. A cold chill rushed through the room as the fire popped, making her jump.

Ringo reached down, and Riley became afraid. Was he going to kill her? Instead, he held her socks and tossed them to her. She caught them midair.

Ignoring the dirt and dried blood, Riley pulled her socks on. Reward number one. She was silent. She looked to Ringo and waited. The softness of the socks warmed her skin.

Ringo lit his cigar. The ring of fire shimmered and then disappeared. Spade. Two black hearts twisted with hatred by circumstance, two souls different, but the same Ringo and Spade, Spade, and Ringo. He studied her, the steel gray around his pupils returning.

"At first, I was in shock by her promiscuous behavior and his betrayal, but then shock turned into rage. Something within me exploded. I went into the room, shutting the door behind me. I had guns everywhere in the house. It's something you do in my line of work," he paused, waiting for a response. She caught the hint but decided not to question his line of work.

"Every detail is as crisp as it was that night. Reaching for my gun, and all the while, I watched them. I shot my best friend first and then my wife. I stayed there for a long time. Hours maybe. I wasn't worried about the consequences of my actions, but theirs, my wife and Tim, justice had been served. Then I thought about my kids."

Riley stopped breathing. *Megan and Utah.*

Ringo stood up again. She felt everything in her body tense. She now lived minute by minute. Her mind could not work fast enough to work out an escape plan. Ringo moved next to her. She smelled the lingering fragrance of the cigar on his clothes mixed with a smoky oak smell. Every muscle in her body stiffened, and the fine hairs on her arms and neck stood up. In his too-calm behavior, Ringo reached down past her and picked up a piece of wood.

"Fires going out," he said, placing the log on the fire. Riley failed to cloak her tension and braced for the unexpected. Ringo's intentions were not good, and the effect it was having on her showed. He wanted to see fear.

"I got in the car." Ringo sat back down and leaned back slow-like. His eyes shone through her, into her soul. His following sentence would have made no sense if she didn't know he could feel her fear.

"It's working," he said dryly.

"I went to the house where my kids were staying. The father had gone offline. He nearly knocked me down when I reached the door. I took his life because I knew he'd taken my children's. I didn't knock. I just went in. My son was still breathing when I got there." Ringo took an exaggerated drag off the cigar. Riley felt a brief moment of sadness, not for Ringo but for the kids. "I held him until he took his last breath and then gathered them both in my arms and drove them home."

The pause this time took much longer, and his attention focused downward. Riley remained dead still. The fire crackled and popped, but her attention went to the window next to the door. Carefully, she scanned the entire room one foot at a time, looking for a weapon of some sort.

"There's nothing there, Riley," he rolled the cigar between his fingers. She hated how he said her name and the expression he made when he said it.

"The kids?" Riley shifted her gaze back on him. Dark and a foreboding evil seeped from his words.

"I put the kids in their beds. I used gasoline to start the fire, and then I stood on the street and watched. Everything I'd worked for, everything I loved, eaten by the flames. I watched as the fire caught from one house to another. Sirens were going off everywhere, but I knew there was no help coming."

She watched the smoke from his cigar form a line, and then the strand curled upward.

"Your story is much different, though. Isn't it?"

"You don't know me."

"I've known you for a long time, Riley Collins," he sighed. His eyes narrowed, and a glimmer of fire caught her attention. "Riley Collins from California, you remind me of my wife. Your personality, your looks, and then there is that different fire within you." The smoke left his breath from the cigar when he spoke.

Riley did not like the fact that she reminded him of the wife he killed. "I didn't tell you I was from California. Who are you, and what are you?"

"Right," Ringo said, looking down. "You're husband doesn't understand what he has or had."

How do you know?

"Tell me." He raised the pistol in her direction and leaned forward.

Riley hesitated, "I left him. I don't know if he survived the Shift or not. You tell me."

Ringo spoke as if he knew more about her than he let on, but how. Riley sure as hell lacked the desire to know him.

He laughed aloud, "poor man, your husband. Oh, come on, Riley, do tell," his voice deepened. "If I were a betting man... I'd say he...," he stopped, not finishing that sentence. "Tell me, Riley, or we end it here and now. Did his cheating hurt you?"

"Yes," she answered. Ringo already knew the answer, and he fed on her misery.

"You left him because he was cheating on you," Ringo grinned.

"I left him because he was an asshole."

"There's that fire I was talking about. I bet you were a handful," Ringo said, pointing at her. "I saw it the moment I met you."

"What do you mean? Met me? Am I supposed to know you?"

"Not, really," he sidestepped the question. "Did you like your job? What did you do for a living?"

"I was a dispatcher." Bluff.

He lurched from his chair so fluid and silent and picked her up as if she were a feather. If he hurled her across the room, Riley would break.

Riley cried out in pain as his fingers pinched her skin and muscle. He pinned her close to the fire. The backside of her pants heated up, burning her skin.

"Don't ever lie to me again, Riley," he said in a whisper. "You understand?"

Riley could see the jagged scars on his face, the zigzag of the lines where the stitching needle had entered and exited. Light gray streaks of color throbbed to his heartbeat. A touch of red danced deep behind the iris.

Ringo stared into Riley's eyes. She felt his malevolence. Rage simmered as his teeth gritted together and his nostrils flared wide. Then he calmed, and his hold softened. He pressed his face within an inch of hers, lifting his nose as if smelling her.

Animal.

"Never lie to me again."

"I was a fish and game officer," she said, gritting her teeth.

Ringo let Riley go.

The backs of Riley's legs stung.

The first of Ringo's schooling was over. He knew too much about her. He'd known Mark, and he'd known he'd cheated on her. Spade kept flashing in her mind, but the how seemed impossible. Any familiarity she felt led back to what happened in Bakersfield, or did it?

"You're wondering why you're here," he said. "I mean, that's what I'd want to know if I were you."

"Yes," she answered, boiling with hatred.

"That's better. I can't make too many promises because I find you exciting. However, I do want the boy back. Your new friends murdered my brother, burned my house down, and took what was mine. That includes a boy. That boy is mine. The women are all very replaceable."

Riley recognized Ringo's unique capacity to use common sense by putting himself in his victim's shoes. He knew her fears. It was all part of the game to him, and he enjoyed every moment.

"Where is the boy?" he asked.

"They had no boy with them," Riley said with honesty.

Ringo stepped near to her. Riley wanted to rip his eyes out. He placed his fingers on her shoulder and neck, stroking the loose strands of hair that had strayed from the band holding it back. Riley thought Ringo's fingers would be as cold as his heart, but they weren't. He wrapped his fingers around her throat. She tried to pull herself away, but his grip tightened as he shook his head no.

He'll kill you.

"Your eyes, they're so blue." His fingers tightened around her neck, squeezing down until the blood flowing through the carotid artery pounded against his fingers. He closed the space between them. "You have no control over your body when you're unconscious."

"That's not your style," she choked. *Now!*

Riley brought her knee up hard between his legs. He buckled, but his grip around her throat tightened. Riley fought to get free.

"You'll pay for that one, Riley," he groaned.

NOT ALONE

Then he closed her off, shutting her down by pressure. Her last thought was the box under the floor.

50

Inside the Colton home, a feeling of tension coupled with serenity fell on the faces of its people. Lynn brewed her best camp coffee on the kitchen stove, hot, robust, and black, a coffee wizard. Jack could smell the aroma flowing from the living room as he waited with impatience while it finished brewing. His body ached with exhaustion, and still, the deep-seated anxiety way down deep within his gut kept him from falling into the chair, slumping over to catch, if even, a minute of sleep. In the far corner of the room close to the fire, Matt slept upright. Blake sat nearby.

"Let's get him to one of the guestrooms," Jack told Shay, but she stopped Jack, putting her hand to his heart.

"You need to rest too."

Jack's current need involved finding Ringo's nesting place. One more warrior needed to come home, one more soul to save. Her soul, who held great importance to him, fell hostage to a maniac. He would not forsake her.

"Come on, buddy," he said to Matt, "let's get you somewhere you can rest." Matt opened his eyes. Between pain meds and loss of blood, Matt's words drifted off unsaid. He draped his arms around the two, allowing them to stand him up and lead him toward the hallway.

"You're next, Blake," instructed Jack after getting Matt settled.

Shay handed Blake a pill for the pain. "Take it. It might be another few hours before Nick can get to you." Jack ripped his pant leg open and looked at the wound.

"The bullet went through?"

"I've never been shot before," Blake clenched his teeth as Shay pressed into the wound. "Jesus, it hurts like hell."

"Suck it up, buttercup," grinned Jack. He patted Blake on the shoulder. "Good thing though, chicks dig scars. Right, Ryan? Where is that brother of mine?"

"Great," replied Blake.

"I heard Terra's parents came and got her yesterday," Amy said from the doorway. "You know she told us you'd come, Blake."

"I'm sorry it took so long," Blake said, shifting his weight.

"You'll live." Shay pressed gauze onto Blake's wound. He jumped.

"Easy."

"Baby," Shay teased.

With the wounded attended to, a much-needed silence rolled through the house. The warmth in the living room came from the roaring fire, crackling and dancing to some unheard song. Shay and Amy helped Lynn, filling coffee cups and handing out sandwiches. Fed and warm, the team grew sleepy. Jack wasn't far behind the others.

A forty-eight-hour no sleep marathon left Jack feeling exhausted. He needed all his strength for the next fight. Dusk settled in, and the night approached too quickly. He settled into the big armchair next to his bed. Time ran short for sleep, and the already exhausted walked a thin line.

As he began to drift into a light sleep, he thought of Megan safe from the storm, but not from possible death. Then his thoughts went to Riley, who had fallen in the hands of a powerful demon far too evil for any woman to withstand. He'd seen the scars and wounds on Shay and then Riley's fear. Now, both child and woman slipped in and out of his dreams.

In a light slumber, Jack heard Lynn long before she turned the doorknob. He let his finger go slack on the trigger and turned to face her as shadows of her hair fell on her shoulders, which meant Nick had finished performing surgery on the little girl. Lynn stepped in closer, looking down at Jack, breaking the silence between them.

"How is she?" he asked, setting his pistol down on the nightstand.

Turning his back to Lynn, he stood up and rubbed his face. If the girl died, he didn't want anyone, especially Lynn, to see his face. She sat down on the bed and took in a deep breath. Jack felt his stomach roll.

"She made it through surgery. She's fighting hard."

Jack nodded, putting his fingertips to his forehead. Lynn stood, setting her hand on his back, rubbing his shoulder. "She reminds me of Lily, too little and far too young to be going through this."

"I know." He closed his eyes for a moment. Her fingers slipped away from him.

"You did the right thing, Jack," she said. "Choosing to get the girl here instead of going after him."

"Yeah."

He heard the door shut, and for the first time in three days, he pulled his clothes off, slipped into his bed. Bombarded with dueling nightmares, one of a demon named Ringo and a woman named Riley, he fought sleep until he could fight no more.

He woke to the sound of closing doors. Mid-day sun shone into the room. He slipped out of bed and peered out the window. Below the twins were getting into Mark Henderson's van with Susan, Mark's wife. On the side, it read "Your Connection. Reconnecting friends and family."

Mark offered a beginning for people who lost loved ones during the Shift. His team placed young homeless kids, elderly folks, and disabled people with residents until they relocated to a home or a safe environment. Susan, Mark's wife, and her team worked diligently to find family, friends, or houses to place them in. Frequently, no surviving relatives came forward, dead or lost. The list of lost parents, siblings, and children was long, and the majority was due to the Shift. In the end, those not able to take care of themselves found a home.

The Henderson's also provided room and board until survivors got back on their feet. Every week, support meetings offered people a chance to gather. Nick provided free clinics for those in need of medical. With an abundance of abandoned homes, families always had a second chance. However, the town of Prescott had a protocol, and it came with a price. Jobs were plentiful, and there was plenty of work available. All of which were essential components to rebuilding their lives.

Jack turned away from the window in need of a shower. He finished and headed downstairs, passing through Nick's office door. Coming to the surgical room, he paused and tapped on the door, waiting. The door opened.

"How's she doing, Nick?" Jack asked, tapping on the opened door.

"It was a long night," he motioned Jack in.

Utah sat in a chair next to her sister. The cat in her lap curled up in a ball purring like a Cummins diesel. Stopping beside Megan, he started to say something and then stopped.

"Jack, you okay?"

"Yeah, yeah... fine," he said, looking at Megan's face pale, but a rosy red replaced the blue tint in her lips from yesterday. Her innocence overshadowed the violence done to her. As Jack listened to his heart, he could almost hear her speak.

"I got the bullet out," Nick said, showing him a jar with a bullet resting at the bottom. "This will make for a great conversation piece for her someday."

"Is she unconscious or sleeping?"

"Both."

"If she wakes up, will you come and get me?" Jack asked, stepping away and then remembered Matt. "Matt?"

"He's good. You guys saved several lives this time around."

"We took a lot too."

"You and the team are taking back what is ours." Nick stepped over and patted Jack on the shoulder. "Cool truck, by the way."

"It didn't seem right to leave it behind."

Nick grinned.

"Nick, thank you. Keep her safe."

"I got this, Jack."

51

Riley woke to a slight sliver of light peeking through a tiny opening somewhere inside the room. Cold to the bone, the gash on her jaw ached. There wasn't a muscle or joint that didn't hurt.

The flickering light coming from under the door teased her, lending little comfort to the current situation. The empty room felt less than daunting. Thick boards and plywood blocked the windows, but the light from the fire snuck through cracks enough so she could see it. Ringo had provided her with a plastic bucket without a handle, a military-style blanket, and a large gallon of bottled water.

Riley tried to stand, but her legs felt like Jell-O. When she finally stood to her feet, she grabbed the blanket holding the material for metaphorical comfort because the thin cover gave no warmth. The muscles in her body were cold and cramped. She needed to move to warm up. Fighting the effects of the drugs he'd given her, Riley tried to clear the clouds from her darkened thoughts, walking around the small room in laps. At first, her teeth chattered, her body trembled, but then on the fifth or sixth lap around the room, she started to warm up. Now, making a plan of escape was foremost on her mind.

Tiptoeing along the wall, she brushed fingertips over the wood, searching for nails. Large unmovable bolts secured the pole siding, leaving her to find nothing but smooth sides. She stared at the dim light under the door, knowing freedom lingered so near to her.

The floorboards creaked, and the boards under her feet sagged ever so slightly. She felt an indent and something metal under her feet and knelt, tracing the outline of the door with shaky fingers. The box. Riley's stomach churned. She fought off yet another urge to vomit.

Make it go away.

God only knew how many miles she was away from the outside world. The cry of a wolf and then another deepened her worst fears. Tears rolled down her face.

Wounded and exhausted, Riley wrapped the scratchy blanket around her, curled up in a ball, and finally fell into a chilled sleep.

In her dream world, the sunshine streamed through the window, warming her skin. *Max purred beside her, watching birds pecking at worms. The grass looked like an endless sea of green. Flowers bloomed brilliant colors under her feet, and with each step taken, more rose. Pedals as delicate as a newborn's skin danced in the breeze between the graves, interconnecting buds with vines. She started to reach down and pluck but instead found herself standing in front of a window. From where she stood, she saw the graves and the flowers still blooming.*

Time sped up. Shadows rolled past her as if in fast motion. Clouds rolled overhead, supernaturally speeding past her field of vision. Then the light faded, and the dark cloak of night fell. Unable to see into the darkness, she felt vulnerable to the glass that separated her and whatever was outside. Before she could turn away, Mark appeared on the other side.

Riley jumped back. He locked his dark eyes onto hers. Then, he pointed his finger to look like a gun in her direction and pulled the trigger.

The material of the black trench coat swirled around him like wings of something dark and gothic. Riley stepped backward and away from the ring of fire, framing his eyes. She detected Lucas's presence before he appeared to her.

"Someday, you will have to face your fears," whispered Lucas. "Look again."

Ringo appeared beside Mark.

Evil stood next to evil.

Max hissed.

"He'll kill me."

"Only if you let him."

"Is he alive?"

Lucas said nothing. She moved from this place in her dream to another, somewhere much darker.

The small apartment, blanketed with a dank depressed feel, held no happiness or familiarity with Riley. Enclosed by stained walls, stained carpet, and musky smell, the room did little to conceal miserable living conditions. The older furnishings, worn out like most everything else Riley could see, lacked luster. Dark curtains stained with nicotine covered the windows, keeping the outside light hidden. From somewhere inside the living room, blown-out TV speakers blared.

A man, not appealing in any way, appeared in a reclining chair holding a beer in one hand and a cigarette in the other. He belched loudly, scratched his ass cheek, and then crushed the can.

The smell of stale cigarettes made Riley's nose itch and her stomach roll.

"He can't see you, Utah whispered. On the television, NASCAR arrived in New Hampshire to race the Sprint Cup series.

"Amy!" he shouted, anger in his tone.

Riley jumped, feeling immediate dislike.

"Who is he?" Riley asked.

"Steven. Our step-father."

NOT ALONE

A floorboard creaked overhead. Riley watched a thin woman with long curly brown hair slink down the stairs.

"I need another beer," Steven shouted.

He sat with his feet propped up, wearing nothing more than a dirty tan shirt and a pair of shorts. The stubble on his face reflected sheer laziness, not style.

Riley's first impression of him fell short of anything positive. Sitting ten feet from the kitchen, he could've fetched his beer. Riley shuddered. She remembered how Mark used to boss her around, tell her how to do things.

"My mom, Amy," Utah said to Riley.

Amy possessed a delicate beauty. Her natural dark eyelashes framed large almond-shaped eyes. Putting aside that her face looked worn and tired, several bruises cast a yellowish-green on her face, and she wore a new cast on her left arm. Traces of scars marred her olive skin leaving remnants of things better forgotten.

In her adolescence, Riley imagined Amy looked just like her two daughters, vibrant and full of life.

Amy sighed, grabbing a beer from the refrigerator.

"You can hear her thoughts, Riley," Utah told her.

Amy hesitated, glancing at the knife sitting on the counter. Next to the knife sat a gun, both of which would do the job. Both of which should not be on the counter where a child could reach them.

I could stab him. Not kill him, but stab him and then pull him outside into the alley. He'd bleed to death.

Amy's mind spun.

I could poison him. Make it look like an accident. The girls, child protective services would take the girls. I'd go to prison. I need to get Steven out of here. How?

"Amy!" he shouted. Riley jumped at the same time Amy did.

Amy closed her eyes, trying to make him go away. How could I've been so stupid?

Passing Riley, she handed the beer to Steven. He took the can but then grabbed her cast and twisted it. An agonizing cry escaped her. Riley heard footsteps running across the floor upstairs, and then two girls scrambled downward, stopping at the bottom step. Utah and Megan crouched in the corner of the staircase, hugging their legs.

"Mama," Megan cried out.

"Mama," mocked Steven. His tone hateful. "Mama."

He pulled Amy down to him and spoke in a whisper, the cigarette smoke making her choke. "Next time I ask for a beer, it better be a little quicker than that, you understand?" he asked through clenched teeth.

Amy shook her head, and Riley felt her hatred for him. Riley was experiencing everything she was.

"I don't think you do," he said, moving the end of his cigarette toward her face.

"No," Riley cried out, but Amy did not try to fight back. She knew if she did, the results would be far worse than a slight burn to her face.

Riley looked away as Steven pressed the cigarette's burning end into the flesh of Amy's face. All Riley could do was witness the events unfolding for Utah and Megan's sake.

"You scream, and it'll get worse. Child protective services, Amy. How about I give Utah another lesson in adulthood or maybe give Megan her first?" he said. This time his tone filled with promises.

"You son of a bitch," Riley looked from Steven to Utah, smelling burning flesh and cigarette.

"Now, hide that," he yelled, pushing her away from him.

She stumbled, falling toward the girls, landing at Utah's feet. The girl stared at Steven long and hard, hatred smoldering through youthful innocence. Utah helped her mother to her feet.

Fingers wrapped around Riley's palm, Utah stood next to her.

"It's okay," she said, tightening her hold. "Watch."

Mumbling something about how lame women were and how he needed to teach them a lesson or two, Steven got up out of his chair. Amy, still holding the beer, stepped aside as he opened the refrigerator. He stood there, looking as if he forgot what he wanted. Then he shouted, "Where the fuck are the groceries, Amy?" Steven screamed, throwing his arms around like a wild man. "Jesus, can't you do anything right. I'm hungry."

"I...," she started. She'd already cowered because she knew trouble stood in line. Riley felt something horrible coming.

"I don't give a flying fuck!" he yelled.

Moving with swift strides across the room, he grabbed hold of Amy and shoved her against the wall. The impact of her body caught the thin drywall with a thud making an indent in the wall. Megan reached out to her mother as Amy fell in her direction.

Utah caught Megan and pulled her away.

"Don't open the door unless I tell you. Understand?" Utah said, leading Megan to the hall closet.

Megan nodded. Her body shook as she clung to one of her mother's coats. Riley wanted to grab them both and run away. She didn't wish Megan or Utah to see the continuation of violence and live with the fear of always having to look back, but they had already done that.

With Megan hidden, Utah moved to face her stepfather.

NOT ALONE

"We don't like you. Leave." Utah screamed, and her hand quivered as she pointed to the door.

"Or else?" He moved toward Amy and laughed.

Bringing his free hand up and around Amy's throat, he clamped his fingers down, making her fight to breathe. Steven was going to kill her.

Amy's eyes bulged.

Utah moved toward her mother, and then she lunged at Steven, throwing all of her weight into his side. Letting out a grunt, he laughed in an uncontrolled fury as Utah pounded her fists into her stepfather's side. With one swift kick, he shoved Utah across the room.

Steven let go of Amy, and she crumbled to the stained carpet, robbed of oxygen, unable to stand. Massaging her neck, coughing, and wheezing, she tried to find the strength to get up. What came next, Amy could've never predicted. Steven darted across the living room, lifting a glass table, flipping it over, shattering the top into a billion pieces. Wild and out of control, he ripped off one of the wooden legs. He swung the wood in the air and chuckled.

"It's time for some schooling, you little bitch," he grinned.

"Utah!" Amy's scream sounded no more than a choked cry.

Steven swung at Utah. Amy fought to climb to her feet, reaching out with both hands to stabilize her body, but nothing worked. Urine slipped down her legs, and she clawed at her neck, trying to allow more air through. Utah's hands tightened on Riley's fingers. Riley felt Utah's warmth, her fear.

The room spun, and suddenly they were no longer in the apartment but in a grocery store. "This is what started the fight."

They stood in a grocery store. Several shoppers brushed past Riley, hurrying to check out. They got in line only to stand behind a man who nervously shifted his feet. The man wore a thin blanket of sweat across his brow and a brown out-of-season jacket. He slipped his hand inside his coat and produced a gun.

"You're dead! You're all dead," he yelled, pressing the weapon outward.

Confused, the checker stared at him. "Hey, mister..." A loud pop sounded and then a surge of panic.

Without forethought, Amy pulled Utah and Megan behind an end cap. Another shopper standing in line lunged at the robber, taking him to the ground. Amy grabbed both of the girls and flew from the store, leaving the groceries.

Riley stared at the cart until Utah took her back to the apartment.

"When was this Utah?" Riley asked.

"That day. The day the world went crazy," Utah answered.

Utah wanted to show Riley the story of what happened to them the day after the Shift. Riley turned to watch as Amy staggered across the room. Steven, now buzzed, swung the leg at Utah, missing the girl by inches. Utah screamed.

No one would come to their rescue.

No one came.

No one cared.

Amy's fear of having her children stolen from her disappeared as she went into survival mode.

Amy rushed Steven.

"You lazy son of a bitch," Amy choked out. Her adrenaline pumping through her veins brought life back to her almost unconscious brain.

Megan slipped unnoticed out of the closet and ran to the kitchen. Riley saw her go to her tiptoes and grab the gun on the counter. The weapon was far too big in her hands and too heavy. The weapon was awkward in her hold.

Steven shoved Amy across the room. Her foot caught on the edge of the couch. Unable to regain her step, she fell. Her head cracked the side of the already broken glass table. The sound of the impact broke bone and glass. For a moment, Amy did not move, and Riley thought this was the end. Blood spilled from under her hair and dripped down the side of her face. She moved, rose to her knees, and then her feet and staggered, disoriented.

Steven charged at his wife. Rage permeated the air, but Amy never saw the blow that ended her life. Utah and Megan did. They saw the last spark of life leave their mother's eyes, watching in horror as her soul left them forever. Filled with overpowering rage, Steven slammed the wooden leg into their mother's head.

The rest unfolded in front of Riley even faster. Utah grabbed the gun from Megan. Void of forgiving, no second-guessing. Just aim and the slight pull of the trigger, Utah shot Steven, not once but accidentally three times. The first bullet's speed and power forced Utah's finger to recoil, hitting Steven with two more rounds. The gun bounced out of her hand to the floor, kicking Utah back onto her bottom.

Utah scrambled to her feet.

Steven lay on his back. The grungy tan t-shirt turned crimson-red.

Utah ran past Steven and knelt beside her mother. Amy's eyes eerily fixed open, lifeless. Though she had passed, her feet jerked, her body twitched, and then went still. Memories Utah and her sister would take with them for a lifetime. A deadly silence commanded the room.

The twelve-year-old girl took her sister and held her tight.

"Keep watching, Riley."

Utah faded, and Riley saw Steven move.

NOT ALONE

Something woke Riley. She stared into the abyss covered in sweat, waiting for the devil Ringo to reappear.

52

"Pops, I'm heading over to the hall."

"We'll be there shortly," Ben answered as Shay stepped up beside him. "She's a writer, you know?"

"No, I didn't know, pops."

"I'd like to take a look at the newspaper building. Maybe start it back up," Shay said, her face gaining a hint of sparkle. "Something to keep me busy."

Handing Shay the key, Ben smiled, "a newspaper would make folks here happy."

"Be careful," Jack told his father. "Ringo is still unaccounted for."

"Ringo, Shmigo! A circus name for a grown man," Ben muttered.

Ryan chuckled at his father's sarcasm, waved, and followed Jack toward the old town museum. People congregated near the fireplace, making small talk until the buzz heightened when Jack and Ryan walked through the door. The two brothers joined the crowd, gathering inside the main room. Several of the higher-ups, the Mayor in his position less than a year, the police chief having survived the Shift, and several officers greeted the brothers. The town's people showed their respect for both Coltons and their team by merely ending the chatter. They needed leaders, people who wanted to succeed, and resilient enough to fight. It didn't matter where they came from or who they were before the Shift. They were soldiers now.

The town of Prescott had restored power only a few months after the Shift began, and as time passed, over three-quarters of the city's population were dead or missing. They welcomed strangers in, but the rules were black and white, and if you broke them, you were gone.

Jack scanned the room, acknowledging Dan and Blake, who were standing beside Matt. Jack searched for Kid and his dog amongst the many faces in the crowd. All of who wanted to join the fight.

"Okay, Ladies and gentlemen, we have a lot to discuss, so let's get started." Mayor Tom Edwards called out.

"As you may have heard, Jack's team rescued six women and a small boy from those parasites on the outskirts of Seligman. Two of the men who attacked Jack's team at Doc Pam's place in Ash Fork are still on the loose. They've taken a woman hostage." The Mayor took a long pause, took a breath, and then continued. "They killed Pam Kenny and her technician Destiny. We've lost the hospital. Folks, let us not forget the dangers of abandoned homes, buildings, and towns still out there. Don't become complacent to them. They're perfect places for sick and bad people to dwell."

The Mayor paused and then cleared his throat. "Can we please take a moment of silence on their behalf?" The room grew silent as everyone bowed their heads.

"We will miss them," the Mayor spoke softly. Reaching up, he adjusted his glasses. "I'm going to turn the floor over to Jack now. He can give you more details."

Jack stepped to the podium. Speaking to crowds was not his best attribute, but this town knew him, so the talk came easy. "I appreciate you coming down here on a Saturday. I see you weathered the storm, okay," Jack paused. He knew they wanted him to get to the trouble at hand. "We took shelter at Doc Kenny's place only to find out we weren't the only ones there. Does anyone here know of a man who calls himself Ringo?"

The townspeople looked amongst themselves, waiting to see if anyone would answer Jack's question.

"Is he the one who killed Pam Kenny," someone called out?

"Yes. This man also shot a little girl and took an innocent woman hostage. I will be out looking for the woman," he said as a slight chuckle went through the crowd.

"Aren't we all..." a voice chirped in from the group. "Who are we looking for, Jack?"

"Right?" Jack said, rubbing his chin. He'd forgotten to shave, and the three-day shadow itched. "Her name is Riley. Blonde, blue eyes, 5'9, and has a fresh cut on the side of her face. She was on the road before the storm hit. She made it to the hospital, took shelter, and then ran into Ringo. Shortly after, the five-year-old girl who was with Riley caught crossfire. She's in serious condition."

"You need help?" A voice sounded from the crowd.

"We do. The rest of you need to be diligent, aware, and protective. Until we get Ringo, you women, in particular, need to be careful. Last week, people looking for guns attacked our ranch. Several of the attackers got away. People are on the move, and this town is inviting. Be vigilant, but I know when things start going smooth, we become complacent. We've worked hard, but we're seeing a rise in markers and looters." Jack paused. "Some, if not all, of the animals at the hospital are loose, so be alert, watch your little ones?"

"Pam was keeping a few wild cats out there?" A man said. Jack recognized him as one of the town's contractors. "Mexican gray wolves. Do we shoot them? I heard somebody blew up the hospital."

"Take precautions and do what you have to do. Yes, there was an explosion or two. Doc Roberts will be covering until we have another vet who is willing to relocate here."

An excited and concerned buzz started among the people.

"I don't think there are any of us here that want to kill what Pam worked so hard to save. However, she would never want to endanger you."

Pam, with her team, had worked hard to build the hospital in Ash Fork, the ranch in Prescott Valley, and the conservatory further out of town. Pam's philosophy reflected the importance of protecting animals as well as people.

"If you have a tranquilizer gun and you have to use it, call us. Pam has accommodations at her other locations to contain the animals properly. If the tiger doesn't show up before I get back, then I'll personally trap him myself."

A hush went through the room.

"Who got away? Is this Ringo infected?"

Jack waited until it got quiet again. "We're posting a description on the backboard." Jack paused, "he's dangerous. He's armed and knows explosives. Ringo won't hesitate to kill you. Infected or not, he's as dangerous as they come. Terra, do you have anything to add?"

Hesitating, Terra stepped next to Jack. He stayed beside her for support. "It's okay, Terra."

The crowd got quiet at first and then started clapping. Terra thanked them and waited for the room to calm down. "I Thank God Shay ran into Jack, and he and Blake and the boys came to the rescue." Choked up, Terra struggled to regain calmness. "Ringo's not infected. He was a cold-blooded killer before the Shift, and the Shift just made it easier to do what he does best. Kill. He and his men are bad people."

"What makes you think he'll come here?" someone asked.

"His tracks led this way." Jack intervened. Anxious, his mind wandered to Riley, "Ringo and what men he has left are probably holding up somewhere nearby. We have no idea how many men. The plan is to find Ringo before he has a chance to hurt any of you."

"Count me in," Dan said, moving in next to Ryan.

John, and Jeremy Black, ex-marines, stepped up next to Dan and Ryan. John, older than Jack, possessed skills equal to his. John and his son Jeremy renovated their property and turned the space into a training compound. A complete shooting range, dirt track, spacious gym, and a large industrial building for boxing and martial arts were available to the entire town.

NOT ALONE

Trained in the military and tactical maneuvers, Jeremy was a natural sharpshooter and never got the chance to fight for his country until the Shift happened.

Since kindergarten, Scott, Jack's friend, stepped in from behind the crowd, stopping beside John and Jeremy. Scott was all, but when provoked, he could take out a threat when he needed to. As they grew into their adult years, they changed, but their friendship grew.

"Good thing you stepped up. I thought I was going to have come down there and kick your ass." Jack said to Scott under the bussing of the crowd.

"Bring it on, brother," Scott tossed his friend with a slight punch. "Wouldn't miss you chasing after a woman for the world."

"Keep your radios on and with you at all times, folks." Jack reiterated as he moved to where his team gathered. "And tell everyone who didn't come here today."

"Jesus, Jack, I leave for a week, and you all get shot up and shit, mayhem and kidnapping," Scott said, trying to catch up to him. "Heard, this guy is a real psychopath."

Jack stopped mid-stride.

"If he has a lust for exotic animals, think about Red Rock? He could have gone there," suggested Scott.

"The conservatory?"

"It sounds like a place this guy might go."

"You may be right," Jack said, thinking of Pam. "If this guy shows up, he'll take out any extra problems that might stand in his way."

"How's the girl?" Scott asked.

"Nick's been with her," Jack tried to hide his concern. "You make sure Katlynn and the little ones are careful. This guy is immoral."

"You're worried, Jack?"

"Yes."

Kid appeared and moved in their direction.

"I never got to thank you," Jack extended his hand to Kid.

"No need. I'm the one who should be thanking you."

"Kid," Jack turned to Scott, "Scott."

"Nickname?" Scott shook Kid's hand.

"High School. I guess I looked like a kid when the other guys thought they were looking like men. It stuck." Kid smiled.

"Nice to meet you, Kid. Let's go find some bad guys," grinned Scott.

The team, seeing Jack on the move, fell in behind them. Ben met them at the door and tossed the truck keys over to Jack.

"Get out of here before Shay sees you and wants to go along. We'll find a ride home."

NOT ALONE

"Be careful, pops," urged Jack
"I will," he said in a soft tone. "You do the same."

53

Riley drank the water Ringo had given her slowly. The only way to get stronger was through food and hydration. The cool liquid soothed the ache in her throat. She allowed hatred to starve the fear she felt from him as emotion boiled inside her veins. Fresh blood from the bullet wound in his shoulder soaked his shirt. An opened medical pack sat on top of the table. Ringo shoved the bag her way.

"You're going to stitch this up," he said in an agitated tone. "Your bullet. Your problem."

Riley chuckled. He slammed his hand down hard on the table, making her jump. He leaned toward her withdrawing a large serrated knife.

Run.

He read her thoughts and nodded, no.

"There's no place for you to go. I'll gut you. Slow," Ringo said through gritted teeth. "I should do it anyway." Saliva gathered at the corner of his lips, creating a rabid appearance.

Riley believed him.

Leaning back in his chair, he took off his shirt while Riley pulled out a sterile pack containing suturing instruments. Other than the angry bullet wound in his shoulder, Ringo appeared to be in nearly perfect physical condition. By looking at how physically good shape he was in, she knew he'd snap her head like a twig if she tried to run. Riley tore open the autoclaved pack, letting sterile surgical instruments fall into a stainless steel oblong tray, along with needles and thread.

"There's a bottle of peroxide on the counter. Get it," Ringo ordered. "Don't fuck around." His mood foul.

Moving to the counter, Riley grabbed the peroxide.

Riley grabbed the whiskey on the counter, hoping to discover something gnarly enough to cut out Ringo's black heart.

"This is going to hurt," she said, setting the bottle of whiskey on the table. Ringo grabbed her by the arm, yanking her off balance, but he kept her from falling. Grinning, he pulled her close, forcing her to stand between his legs. Sweat beaded up around his brow. This was the end. She'd have to fight if he dared to touch her. Riley closed her eyes and prayed.

"Keep praying to your God but get no ideas," he said in a lowered tone. "Or I'll be the one performing surgery on you."

Riley had no choice. He'd kill her in the ugliest way possible. She needed a knight in shining armor, and she needed one soon.

"I know you'll do a good job," he said, allowing her to move away.

First, make the wound hurt like hell.

She poured the peroxide on the wound, which looked angry as hell. The liquid bubbled up, running out the hole and down Ringo's arm, but he never flinched. Little distance separated them, making her uncomfortable. Riley rotated his arm to look for an exit wound.

I should've used a hollow point.

She found no exit wound. The hole and an angry volcano erupting and oozing with white foam mixed with blood became even more problematic. Riley, forced to dig the lead out of Ringo's arm, took a deep breath. Not wanting to help him in the least bit, Riley hesitated.

"The bullets lodged."

"Not for long," he handed her a pair of long tweezers.

Riley dug in the bag and produced a pair of gloves. Procrastinating what she knew she had to do, she slowly pulled on the gloves.

Riley hesitated.

Ringo glared at her, "you have more to worry about than contaminating yourself with my blood," he growled, but she ignored him. He took a long swig of whiskey. "Nice stitch job on your face."

She said nothing. Ringo appeared unmoved by the pain until she slid the tweezers into the wound. She went deeper. He flinched, Riley jerked back. He grabbed her hand. Not needing to speak, his touch said it all. Sweat trickled from her forehead and along the side of her face. Repositioning his arm, he let his fingers fall to her inner thigh. Uncontrollable fear held her hostage. Riley's fingers trembled.

He slugged down the whiskey, and she hoped the liquor might start to work in her favor. Riley jumped when Ringo spoke. "What did you see the night of the Shift?"

Ringo already attempted to get into her head, analyzing expressions and movements. This time, he said nothing as he waited for her to answer. If Riley refused to say, the results of her silence would be far worse than telling.

"It rained." *What a perfect storm it had been,* Riley thought.

The tweezers tapped metal. The bullet, deeply lodged in the flesh, stuck to the bone. Grabbing a chunk of meat, Riley tried to loosen the tip of the bullet. Ringo remained unmoved as blood oozed from the wound and dripped onto the floor.

Riley's blue gloves turned red.

Sweat ran free from his thick hairline to his forehead.

Ringo's dark hair turned darker.

Pass out, Riley prayed. To help Ringo's pain along, she applied more pressure.

"Riley!" he shouted. "You have one chance left."

Taking hold, Riley clamped onto the bullet and yanked it out. Blood bubbled and erupted from the hole. The round fell on the table and then went to the floor, leaving a snail's trail of blood.

"I knew you could do it," he lowered his voice. "You've killed just like me."

"I've had no choice," she grew annoyed by the analogy between them. "You think you know me. I'm not like you."

"I want the boy." He wiped the blood away, looking at the hole in his arm and then at her. He took another swig from the bottle. "You did good, Riley. Stitch it up and be done."

The thickest needle in the pack had Ringo's name on it. Riley wanted to smile, but before she could begin, he snatched the needle from her. He clenched his fingers around hers, squeezing.

"Not cute, Riley," Ringo said, plucking up a smaller needle. He handed the curved tool to her.

Ringo, obviously a controlled drunk, not a stupid one, sat calmly. After Riley had stitched him up, he checked her work and then stood up to dress. Every abdominal muscle in his lower torso was perfectly defined. There was not an ounce of fat on him.

Riley took a slug off the whiskey, memorizing the room. Plywood covered the windows, and locks held the door, making entry or exit inaccessible. The kitchenette contained a table in the middle of a small kitchen. There were three doors, including where he kept her.

"Not much. Is it?" Ringo looked at her.

Outside, the cry of a cat broke the solitude between them. Riley remained unaffected, but a grin formed on Ringo's lips. He watched her, the circle of fire flickering in his eyes as he reached for the whiskey and took another swallow.

Riley stood and started to move towards the sink, but Ringo stopped her.

"I need to wash."

He pointed at the sink. "There's a bucket of water inside the tub."

Riley took out only what she needed to scrub her fingers clean. She felt him watching, listening, and as hard as she tried to shut off her thoughts, she could not.

There was nothing on the countertops she could as a weapon.

"I wouldn't be so stupid," muttered Ringo.

Outside, an eerie scuttle ensued between what sounded like cats.

"The animals are hungry," Ringo said behind her. "You've worked with wild animals, right?"

"I worked with people and protected animals." The direction of the conversation scared her.

He grinned. "Ever feed a tiger, Riley?"

"I was a field officer, not a zookeeper," Riley said, unable to keep the sarcasm hidden. *Really, you dumb ass? I fed mountain lions every day and played Hide-and-Seek with bears.*

"You better hold on to that fire, Riley. Come on," he said, rising to his feet. He towered over her, making her feel small in comparison.

Riley backed up, but before she could move away, he reached over and placed a rope around her wrists tightly. Already the blood stopped flowing to her fingertips and started to tingle.

"Too tight?" he asked. "Too bad."

Riley tried to pull away from him, but Ringo jerked the rope, drawing her fists to his chest. The whiskey seeped from his breath.

"You behave. You hear."

"I just did you a favor," she said through gritted teeth.

"And I recognize that it was you who shot me in the first place."

Yanking the door open, he pulled Riley out onto a small porch. A stream of freezing air took her breath away. Freedom!

"Shoes!" she said, staring at the layer of snow.

"You don't need any."

Riley knew every minute she lived would be another minute he'd torture her, but it was also time for Jack Colton to find her. Riley stepped out onto a small porch. The sun overhead blinded her, and tears filled her eyes. Her feet almost instantly ached as the chilled air froze the damp sweat on her face. He pulled on the rope, making her tumble down the steps. The snow cushioned her fall.

"Ass...." Riley started, but he stopped her.

"That's not ladylike," he said. "Lesson number one. If you live through this one, you'll get lesson number two." Riley jumped to her feet before Ringo drug her across the snow.

Riley adjusted to the light. In front of her, rows of large enclosures and buildings framed by high fences topped with razor wire. Her throat went dry, and she feared what Ringo's intent might be. Fear turned into panic as Ringo pulled her toward a healthy white tiger who paced impatiently along the fence.

"Please," Riley felt a panic rise inside of her. "Don't."

"Don't what, Riley. I won't feed you to the tiger yet. I only want you to feed him," he said, shoving her toward the tiger's enclosure. Riley slid to a stop several feet from the chain-link fence. "That," he said. "Is a rare, well as you can see, white Siberian Tiger? Bigger than a Bengal and just as lethal as a cougar."

Grasping her by the hair, he shoved her into the fence. Riley used what strength she had left to keep her face from pressing the links. The tiger bolted toward her, so close its whiskers brushed past her clenched fingers. Riley screamed, the cat smelling of meat and blood.

She pulled away, twisting backward, falling to the ground hard. Her left wrist snapped under pressure, sending an electric shock in her arm. She rolled to the side and into a sitting position, bracing her wrist. Riley escaped the cat's paws that were triple the size of her hand and claws that could slice to the bone. The tiger stood, growling, and hissing.

Riley stared into the cat's eyes, but the cat wasn't looking at her. The tiger was looking at Ringo.

"Awe, that didn't go as planned. You hurt your wrist. I'll do it this time," Ringo took a chunk of meat from a metal box and opened a smaller door to the enclosure. The meat slid downward, shot out, and landed inside the pen. The hungry tiger grabbed the meal in his teeth, dragging it off to the side. He went to a prone position with his giant paws in front of him and chewed.

"See! It's not that hard," Ringo said. Careless and rough, he reached toward her, untying the rope from her wrist. She screamed out in agony. "I think you understand. Now, tell me where the boy is."

The cat looked, licking whiskers back. Riley understood. Through her tears, she looked at the row of enclosures. Her fears were adding up as another tiger, and then a panther, and several bears, to name a few, appeared after hearing the dinner bell. Reality overrode hope. Riley only understood how much harder her escape would be. She had become the prey.

Ringo knelt beside her and spoke in her ear. "Where is my boy, Riley? Tell me, and I'll let you live."

Caught between frustration and fury, Riley did something she would regret seconds later even though Ringo earned the spit she blew in his face. Maybe he expected it, and she did not care if the look on his face represented one of admiration or one of anger.

Ringo wiped the spit away.

Riley pulled herself backward. *I stitched you up, you son of a bitch!*

Ringo backhanded Riley across the face. Had he punched her, she would have been no good to him. Bright white stars raced back and forth behind her eyes. Something inside her soul trembled.

The world spun in slow circles. The distance between the ground and Riley's face closed fast. Her cheek met the snow, and everything within her went quiet.

Ringo lifted her, and she feared he'd take her through the gate into the tiger's enclosure. *Make it quick.* A dark fog clouded her head. Utah and

Megan's faces danced in her thoughts, giving her newfound strength. She began to struggle, making him drop her to the ground.

"I don't know those people," Riley screamed out as she climbed to her feet.

Not listening, Ringo shoved her to the entrance of the tiger's opening. Resisting, Riley dug her heels into the snow. If he reached the gate and pushed her in, she would die.

"Jack, Jack Colton," she screamed. "That's all... I know. I swear to God! That is all I know." Riley, still struggling, sensed he knew. "There was no boy with them."

"Jack Colton won't be coming for you," he said, pulling her to her feet and shutting the gate. The tiger watched near the opening. "There were enough explosives to blow that hospital to hell."

"How do you know they didn't get out?" Riley said, keeping her tone even and fighting through the pain in her wrist and now her face.

Ringo let her fall to the ground. "Because I sent my men to make sure they didn't make it."

"Sick bastard," she said, not caring about the repercussion. To think she'd lost Megan and Utah ripped her heart in two.

Ringo taunted her with a chuckle. Then he kicked her in the side, breaking several ribs. If she died, she made a silent vow to haunt him for the rest of his life. Evil radiated from him as he paused to kneel beside her. Riley wanted to kill him.

"I have to go away for a few days, but you'll be safe inside the cabin. Lucky for you, I didn't drink all the whiskey. You're going to need it for the pain." He pulled her to her feet. "Now, let's go get you back to the cabin."

Riley heard him through a thick fog. The words he spoke were broken and jumbled. She didn't care whether he carried her or drug her by the feet as she fell into a darker, less painful world.

54

Scott sat in the passenger seat, waiting. "So, tell me the rest of the story?"

"Which part?"

"The part where she made an impression on you."

"Riley," Jack mumbled, playing dumb. "If I told you, you wouldn't believe me. Hell, I'm having a hard time believing it myself."

"And?"

"Stop worrying about my love life, buddy and focus on the purpose of the mission," Jack said, pulling up to the house. "Let's get what we need and get going. Then you can interrogate her yourself."

"What is the purpose of our mission?"

Jack didn't answer him as Lynn met them inside the house. "What's going on?" She asked.

"Twenty questions," Jack said, giving Lynn a gentle hug. "How're you doing?"

"Good, ribs are healing."

"Good!" Then he hesitated, "How's Megan doing?"

"She's stable." Letting go of Jack, Lynn turned to Scott. "Hey, Scott, good to see you're back."

Scott wrapped his arms around Lynn, also hugging her gentle-like. "Sorry about what happened here."

"Thanks. How's Katlynn?" she asked, changing the subject. "I meant to get out there, but...."

"She's doing well. Baby's kicking her day and night."

"Tell her I said hello," Lynn said, giving them a little wave as she left them to do their business.

The vault, which looked more like a room to display guns, held various weapons from pistols to hand-held rocket launchers. LED lights lit the way, framing the walk-in vault with white light. Rows of semi-automatic firearms, pistols, shotguns, and revolvers lined the walls, and underneath, cases of grenades, rocket launchers, and other various forms of firepower lined the floor. In shadowboxes and admired from afar were several old rifles and revolvers salvaged from different places.

"There's always room for more guns, right Jack?" Scott said. "Every time I come in here, you've got something new."

Jack grinned at Scott, "I'm doing my job by preserving history."

Jack started by gathering autoloaders from their holders, rifles, and grenades.

"You're right in a way. We didn't win wars by fist fighting." Scott picked up a M & P Smith and Wesson.22.

"That one will go with us," Jack pushed the duffle bag closer to Scott. Jack knew the weapon was most recognized in the past as a military and police centerfire semi-automatic rifle, which held twenty-five rounds. Twenty-five rounds he could put into Ringo's chest. He placed a handful of loaded magazines into a separate bag.

Jack grabbed a Weathersby Vanguard .308, followed by a NightHawk Enforcer 45 with a fiber optic front sight. Then a handful of eight-shot magazines and several other semis and fully automatic treasures. To some people, the guns might have resembled an odd mixture of lever-action and automatic loading guns, but to Jack, he had a weapon for every condition. He and Scott grabbed an armful of boxed .45, .22, and .308 boxed rounds. Scott separated them into another bag.

"You can load magazines on the way over," Jack told Scott.

"Gee, thanks." Scott took the bag. "I don't know if this is enough,"

Jack smiled at his friend's sarcasm, tossing him another pack.

"One thing about you, Jack, you lack nothing in toys."

"No one should. At least not the important ones.

"No simple minds in this family. Expensive taste."

"Who said I bought these? Jack grinned. "Who's covering for you in school?"

"Christmas break, Jack. Don't you ever look at the calendar? I noticed you guys don't have a tree up yet."

"Gee, glad someone noticed," Lynn added from behind them, and Jack shot Scott a look.

"Shit!" Jack grimaced. "Thanks for reminding me."

"No problem, buddy. Just trying to help."

"Help my ass. You're always getting me in trouble." Jack set the remaining bags outside the vault.

"Hey, always happy to have your back."

"Good, then you won't mind helping me out," Jack moved out the front door. Scott followed.

They walked the Christmas tree in from the garage. The box, awkward and big, made for a tight squeeze through the front door. Boxes of Christmas decorations stacked the sidewall.

"Hey, sis. I think Santa was here." Jack claimed, guiding the trunk into the tree holder while Scott steadied the fake tree.

Lynn smiled. "Thank you, Jack."

"I have to chalk this one up to Shay and Ben. They pulled it out of the rafters. Have fun. I'm sure the kids and Shay will help you make it all Christmas-like."

"Don't you want to stay and help decorate it?" Scott said, inspecting the tree closer.

"Nope."

"You'll change your tune when you have kids," teased Scott.

"Who said I'm going to have kids? If I had kids, they'd have to attend your history class. That's weird."

Lily and Jonah came scrambling into the living room, sliding to a stop, seeing the tree. Lily screeched out. "Mama, can we make hot cocoa and sing Christmas songs?"

Lynn looked at her brother. "How can that not make you smile, Jack?"

Jack picked Lily up and held her. "What are you going to put on the top, Lily Bean?"

"An angel," she chirped. "Like Utah and Megan." She touched Jack on the cheek with her fingers. "Do you believe in angels, Uncle Jack?"

"Sure, I do. I am looking at one right now." He kissed Lily on the cheek. Jonah stood, staring up at him. The boy's eyes were as wide and shining as Shays. Jack patted him on the head, and he grinned.

Scott chuckled, "I got your number."

"Thank you, Jack. Hurry home." Lynn kissed him on the cheek.

"I have one more stop," Jack said to Scott. "Be right back."

Jack tried to make a short escape, but Scott closed in on him. He followed Jack through the house to Nick's office and then to Megan's room.

Jack gazed at the sleeping girl. She was pale compared to the Colton's, who worked under the sunshine most of the year-round. Long dark eyelashes framed her eyelids. The oxygen mask that covered her mouth looked too big.

Jack moved in close, "I saved her once. I'll save her again and bring her home." The word home rolled off his tongue in such a natural way it scared him.

Jack touched Megan's arm. The warmth of her skin sent a jolt through his heart. She seemed so small, fragile next to him. Soaking in her childlike innocence, Jack then slipped into the hallway toward Scott, meeting up with Ryan as well.

"He'll come here looking for the boy," Jack said to his brother. "I'm going to try to prevent that from happening."

"If he does, we'll be ready," replied Ryan.

55

Dreaming...

"Bingo!" Riley said, holding a brown piece of shimmering sea glass in her hand. Eric, ahead of her, searched through mounds of pebbles seeking out the next treasure. The ocean was turquoise with an underlining glow of green and seafoam zigzagging across rolling waves. The sky appeared darker and closer to the horizon line, crystal blue, and void of any clouds. A thin layer of sea salt tickled her nose, and now and then, a soft spray of mist brushed her face. Warm sand squished, with each step, between her toes, shooting warmth throughout her body.

"Cheater," Eric yelled. His surfer blonde hair fell against his head as if he'd just came out of the ocean from a swim. His skin was kissed brown by the sun's rays.

"Now, how can I cheat, Kid?" Riley yelled back, holding up sea glass between fingers. "See."

"You have helpers." Riley felt hands interlock hers. Megan and Utah were close at her side.

"I haven't found any." Megan giggled, skipping around her.

"Look down. See the rock piles. Skip between, and then when you get to the rocks, stop and look."

Utah ran to the next shadow of rocks, picking something up. She held it so the sun. "Look."

They stepped in closer together, looking down not at a piece of sea glass but rather a fine white feather. "It's beautiful," Riley said.

"Nice," Eric patted Utah on the shoulder. "That's an excellent treasure."

"It's for Riley." Utah handed it to Riley, who took it carefully from her hold. "Take it back with you."

Riley touched Utah's sun-kissed face, wondering if ever she'd seen the ocean before this.

"I love you so very much."

Megan squeezed in and smiled at her. "We love you, Riley," she wrapped her arms around Riley and then Utah. Not far from her, Eric started to fade.

"Utah," Riley started to say.

"You have to go back," Utah's voice faded. "We love you, Riley."

The obscurity of Riley's enclosed cave when she woke took away all hope the dream gave her. Someone as wicked as evil itself held her hostage. She shivered. The movement sent a shot of sharp pain through her ribcage. She tasted blood and prayed that her lung was not punctured. Tiny bolts of lightning bounced inside her skull, creating a stinging pain making her cringe.

Ringo!

Her eyes felt too heavy to open, but she opened them anyway only to find nothing. Then Riley tried to remember what happened.

Ringo!

She heard a faint sound not so far from where she lay and realized she was not in the box under the floor. Tears flowed down her cheeks. Ringo had wounded her bad enough that she couldn't, wouldn't escape.

Outside, two cats fought, releasing explosive and chilling cries that drifted through the walls of the cabin. While the growling and hissing increased, so did Riley's concern over the walls' stability separating them. She needed to get away from this place, wounded or not.

Riley began the painful chore of feeling for wounds or breaks other than her wrist and ribs. There the pain radiated through her from her feet to her head. When she took a deep breath, an unbearable pain shot through her ribcage.

"I have to go away for a few days, but you'll be safe inside the cabin." *Had he left, or was it another trick?*

She lay still staring into the blackness, listening. Other than the animals, she felt alone, as though she were many miles from anyone else. Something inside of her told her that Jack wasn't the kind of man to fall victim to the likes of Ringo. He seemed like the kind of man who wouldn't let anything happen to a child or a person in need.

Jack and his team saved six women and a little boy, she reminded herself. *Megan and Utah are alive. Jack is alive.* Riley's will to survive strengthened.

Outside, animals' cries intensified, distracting Riley from her thoughts. Eerie to the point of chilling, the animal chatter spooked her. She tried to focus on what to do next.

The injuries Ringo inflicted on her might keep a weak person from escaping, but Riley possessed strength in the courage department. He broke ribs to hinder her endurance, which might cause her to fall short of making it very far. The brutality of her wounds mirrored Ringo's idea of a sick insurance policy. If she found a way to escape, she'd have to dig deep to succeed.

First, Riley needed to bind her rib cage for support. The rotted pillow and the blanket she used for warmth might work for supporting her ribs, but her wrist remained the bigger problem. Riley wore a t-shirt underneath the sweater. One or the other might work, but the wool sweater she needed for warmth.

Riley stood in an unbearable amount of pain, stripping down to her bra and then redressing minus the t-shirt. Desperate for something substantial to make a splint for her arm, she started to search the room. Light began to fade, taking the thin rays of the sun, creeping through cracks. The chill inside the room intensified, making her shiver.

"You'll pay for this," she whispered, sliding her fingers to the doorknob. The continuous dull ache in her head clouded her thoughts but not his words. *"I have to go away for a few days, but you'll be safe inside the cabin. Lucky for you, I didn't drink all the whiskey. You're going to need it for the pain."*

The door opened.

Riley slid with caution through the doorway into the dark cabin, not trusting that Ringo left her alone for sure. She leaned against the wall just outside the door, listening. Stillness embraced the darkness, the kind that makes the skin crawl. The remnants of the fire lingered in the air, making her long to be warm.

Tears rolled down her cheeks as her teeth chattered, stinging open cuts. Gun-shy, she waited for any sign that Ringo might still be there, but none came. Sucking up to the pain, she moved to the fireplace where hot cinders under a chunk of wood glowed. Nearby sat a short stack of wood. Not wanting to remain any longer than necessary, Riley knew she needed to warm up and fix her wounds.

The fire took instantly, but the soft glow of the flame did little to console her shattered nerves. However, she had no plans to stay too long. Her feet tingled as the fire began to warm her. Not wanting to leave the warmth now embracing her body, she needed to start rummaging through cabinets and drawers for the rest of her clothes, shoes included. After she lit several lanterns, she found the medical kit she'd used on Ringo in the back of the pantry. One-handed, she grabbed the bag and a can of soup and set them on the countertop.

Before doing much more, she needed to splint the broken wrist that started to ache. Quiet, she accessed the contents in the room. Close to the fireplace was a wooden box that held Ringo's fire-starting materials. After a few seconds, she came across a paper towel roll and then another. The cardboard made a soft tube underneath her wrist. Using sports tape from the medical kit, she formed a soft cushioned splint on her lower arm, securing the joint above and below the break as well.

NOT ALONE

Her ribs were next because every time she moved or breathed, it was torture. Nauseous from hurting, she doubled over, fearing the pain vomiting might bring. She dropped to her knees, dry heaving. Sweat rolled off her face. When the waves stopped, she took a moment to stop the spinning room.

Outside, the sound of a catfight began. The growling and hissing were not coming from the animal's enclosures but somewhere closer. Riley glanced at the door separating her from them. Ringo had a morbid sense of humor. Releasing the big cats was something he would do to ensure her stay with him. Now they also fought for their lives.

"They're going to rip me to shreds," she whispered, praying there was a running vehicle somewhere on the property. "I'm going to need a miracle." The stabbing pain in her ribs reminded her that she needed to find something to compress the broken bones.

"A sheet," she said.

The only bed in the cabin was where Ringo had been sleeping. Not wanting to touch where Ringo had slept, she hesitated as she entered the room. To her surprise, the bed was high and tight, not a wrinkle in the blankets.

"Maybe the devil doesn't sleep," she muttered, taking hold of the top sheet. Not only would the material provide support, but the layers would also add extra warmth once she left the cabin.

Done, she wiped the sweat from her skin with her good hand. Dizzy from the pain, Riley rested and then started looking for her shoes and a weapon. Without something on her feet, she wouldn't make it far, and she was beginning to think her best chance was to wait it out. Confront Ringo before he walked through the door.

Riley felt a surge of excitement as her inner voice kept pushing her forward. She found an old can of RAID, a lighter, and several knives. Escape sat within her reach. Hope returned, the panic started to slip away. Seeing the whiskey bottle, she grabbed it, took a long slug, and then smiled.

"While the cat's away, the mouse must play!"

56

Jack, Kid, and Scott crouched behind a barrier close to the main entrance gate of Pam's refuge in Red Rock. Faded signs that read "Danger" and "Keep out" hung every forty feet warning trespassers to stay away. Security cameras, working or not, faced the main entrance. It had been over forty-eight hours since Ringo disappeared with Riley.

Jack Colton's team was on surveillance, positioned on a slope near the entrance for over four hours, waiting for movement. With a bird's-eye view of the buildings, animals, and their enclosures, they could see anyone coming or going.

Several of Pam's staff cars sat under the carport, though they'd not seen a person. If the caretaker ran into Ringo, he was most likely dead. In Jack's mind, the question lingered was Riley in the cabin with someone guarding her or, better yet, alone? What little they knew of Ringo, the explosives, the ruthless attempt to kill, and his obsession with exotic animals made them take the utmost precaution before making an appearance.

When a grey truck arrived, Jack commanded his team to stand down. With high-powered binoculars, he watched a man, who looked like Ringo's sidekick, get out, unlocked the gate, and then drive through.

"We've got one," Jack informed the others. "Copy. Wait. Someone's in the passenger seat."

When the passenger door opened and a person stumbled out, Jack dropped his glasses down to his chest.

"What the h...?" Jack whispered, watching. Under the bright light of the moon's glow, he recognized Shay. With her hands bound behind her back, she sprinted across the desert floor and away from the truck.

Flinging the door open and nearly falling into the snow, the driver started jogging after Shay. Knee deep in thick snow, unable to see rocks and brush, Shay stumbled. The man behind her dropped to his knees, grabbing her and pulling her backward by a handful of hair. With her hands tied behind her back, Shay scrambled to try to climb to her feet but failed. The man shouted at her. In one step, he trapped her under his boot, pinning her to the ground.

"I've got her," said Kid through the mic.

"Stay put," Jack said. "She knows what she's doing."

Shay was about to be the distraction they needed to get them through the gate. The man started unbuttoning his pants. Jack feared the situation was about to get out of control, worrying about Shay's safety.

Shay rolled onto her back and began to fight. Jack settled back into his position. At some point, Shay must have connected a foot or knee to the man's groin because the man doubled over, and Shay crawled toward the truck.

"Shit!" cursed Jack.

The driver turned so Jack could get a look at his face. The man was Ringo's sidekick Dave. He grabbed Shay and shoved her into the front seat. Jack sprang to his feet before the vehicle's taillights were out of sight.

"Let's roll," Jack tapped his mic.

"They parked," John came back. "Copy."

With Shay playing the problematic hostage, Kid had time to break the locks on the gate, allowing them time to slip through toward the main buildings unnoticed. Lowered night temperatures had frozen disturbed ground into ice, making footing slippery. The moon hung heavy, expelling eerie strands of blue-white light off the blanket of snow. The team, nothing more than mere shadows, moved together, keeping to the shelters. Just ahead, the truck was parked close to the cabin, idling. Inside, Shay sat shadowed under the dim light cast by the dash.

"Want me to go after her?" Kid whispered. Jack hesitated. He was angry Shay had disobeyed his orders to stay put but grateful for the distraction.

"I won't be far behind," nodded Jack. "Watch your back."

57

Kid, wearing a full-face mask and all-black clothing, looked like a shadow. He hugged a nearby tree and watched as Shay struggled inside the cab. Shift growled, seeing and smelling the animals. Just like most things in life, the moment warranted respect, though maybe easier if the animal stood behind a barrier. Save the chocolate stripes, the feline hunter passing in front of him was a chameleon in the snow. In a vast open space but far from home, the tiger moved to the truck's front, tail swishing from side to side. Time should have stood still for experiencing the cat as it lifted its head and smelled the air. Then, sensing something of interest began to stalk, ready to attack. The cat smelled a human.

"Good kitty." Kid heard Shay whisper.

Already in position, Kid pulled the trigger on the tranquilizer gun as the tiger bolted toward Shay. The dart stuck, penetrating deep into the cat's neck, throwing him off balance. The cat's muzzle curled, snapping his head back to bite at the fuzzy end attached to his flesh. The cat stopped, distracted by the invasive sting. With a quick change of mind, the tiger bolted away from the truck, the fluorescent orange tip of the dart bouncing as he trotted off.

Kid waited. The tiger staggered into the enclosure and then dropped to his belly. Kid remained until the cat rested its head on the ground. The slight rise of the giant cat's chest rose and fell in a steady rhythm. Kid hurried to secure the tiger before giving the animal the counter antidote, giving himself ample time to get out of the tiger's space.

Sprinting back to the truck, he found Shay struggling to get the restraints off her wrists. Prepared she might scream, Kid clamped his hand down over her mouth the minute he opened the door.

"Shhhh!".

She nodded, and he pulled her back to him, cutting away the ropes. Shift jumped up into the cab, taking the middle seat. Kid jumped into the driver's seat and put the truck into drive while keeping his foot light on the throttle. Driving toward the car stalls, he moved to an open bay door and parked.

"Riley's here," Shay said as she climbed out. She stood off to the side, watching him cut random wires inside the engine compartment. He gently set the hood down and then tossed Shay a headset. He pulled her back out into the snow-covered refuge.

Between the moonlight and the slight breeze, a mass of shadows danced around them. Shift growled, dropping to her belly. Kid, assuming

Ringo had turned more than one animal loose, presented a bone-chilling problem. Shift growled, rising to her feet, and then faced the building near to where they stood. The ridge on her back lifted as she keyed in on a scent no man could smell.

A second freed tiger strolled in front of them, the rumbling in its belly so deep and throaty the sound caused fine hairs to rise on Kids' neck. The cat moved with such calm confidence, one that no man would ever come close to mastering, pure instinct, wild and raw. Kid pulled the rifle to his cheek, holding the crosshairs of the tranquilizer gun on the hip of the tiger, and pulled the trigger. The dart hit flesh, and the cat sprang forward, spinning around, ready to fight.

Quiet, Kid reached inside his vest, withdrew a pistol, and offered the weapon to Shay. The cat, feeling threatened, positioned itself to attack.

"It looks a little pissed off," Shay's voice quivered.

Balanced like a tight ropewalker, the cat seemed unaffected by the drug. Kid reloaded the tranquilizer gun and aimed the crosshairs on the cat's neck. Kid fired another dart. The tiger, almost jumping the gun, darted to the left. Still, the needle stuck, injecting another round of sedatives into the tiger's bloodstream.

Any second. Kid thought.

"It's not working," mumbled Shay.

Shift posed, ready to obey any instruction Kid might give her. Kid's only intention was to get the tiger secured without anyone getting hurt. Kid raised his hand and pointed at the cat. Shift, bred to hunt lions, sprang forward, almost airborne as she raced across the snow.

The tiger reared back on its haunches, swatting her paw into the air. The ends of her razor-sharp claws glistened under the moonlight. Shift moved from side to side, doing what Kid wanted her to do.

Kid signaled the dog to herd the cat to its enclosure. They needed to get the animal there before the drug rendered her unconscious. Shift remained steadfast, guiding but never touching the cat. Her job was to draw the tiger's attention away from the two people and back into her safe place.

The moment the tiger went down, Kid slipped in behind her, injecting the antidote designed to counteract the tranquilizer.

"That was badass," replied Dan on the radio. "Behind you."

Dan appeared through the predawn light, making little to no noise. He stopped beside them, staring at Kid.

"That was crazy," said Dan in a soft tone. "You want me to take her?" he pointed at Shay.

NOT ALONE

Kid nodded, turning his radio to a separate line. "Both cats are sleeping. I'm on the south wall of the cabin. They're on the backside corner. Mission accomplished."

"Copy," replied Jack.

58

Riley sat in the darkness near the fireplace, finding little comfort in the silence blanketing her. She'd let the fire go out not so long ago, using the coals to keep warm. She held her breath when the distinct hum of a car's engine grew and crunching of snow under tires. Excitement surged through her, followed by fear. A car door slammed.

"My luck just changed, "she whispered, listening to the continued hum of the vehicle's engine. She slid into the room Ringo had kept her, pressing into the closet.

A person with heavy footfalls entered the cabin making weathered floorboards whine under their weight. Riley waited, listening as cupboards opened and closed noisily, followed by a strand of heated cursing. The voice was that of Dave, and he seemed unconcerned for the moment that someone else might be there. Drawers flung open and then slammed shut. Not trying to be neat nor quiet in the least, objects fell to the floor. Riley waited to make her move. She wondered if Dave even knew she was there.

Then the cabin went quiet.

Riley hugged the wall, listening as boots crossed wood flooring, and stopped outside the door.

"Awe kitten, he left the door unlocked. Silly me, I was looking for the key," he said in a soft tone.

The doorknob jiggled under her fingers, and then the door pushed open, and the glow from a lantern shone inward. Riley kept to the shadows, waiting for the perfect moment to strike. Even in the obscurity of the room, she smelled whiskey. Riley smiled, hoping the whiskey would render him sloppy. Riley wanted his weapon, his vehicle, and her freedom. Most of all, she wanted to get to the girls.

"Kitten," he called out.

Riley flipped him off in the dark.

Kitten, my ass!

Dave stumbled inward as Riley stepped out in front of him. She lifted the can of Raid, squeezed her lips tight, closing her eyes as she pressed hard on the nozzle of the can of Raid. A loud hissing produced a broad stream of deadly insect killer that covered Dave's face and then some. A cloud of mist rose. Holding her breath, Riley backed away far enough to get out of the fumes. A scream followed by a choking sound resonated inside the close quarters of the cabin. Running the can dry, Riley tossed the container across the room. Dave's hands flew to his eyes as he sputtered and coughed.

"Doesn't feel so good, does it?" Riley muttered, somewhat gratified and terrified at the same time.

With his eyes squeezed shut, Dave frantically rubbed his knuckles in big circles across his face. While he choked on the chemical fumes, Riley ignited the lighter. He stopped rubbing.

"What are you doing, you crazy...?" he asked, straining to see through reddened eyes.

"The warning on the can said it's flammable." Riley interrupted Dave and pointed at the can, "do you know if that's true?"

"You bitch," he screamed.

Dave stumbled forward, slamming his shoulder into the doorjamb while staggering to keep from falling. He swatted the lighter out of her hand, but Riley swooped down and grabbed it. She ignited it

Dave bolted out of the bedroom, colliding into the kitchen table. Moving blindly, he lunged through the shroud of insecticide toward Riley. Riley pocketed the lighter and grabbed the knife hidden near the sink, plunging the blade deep into Dave's side. Before she could make another move, he grabbed a wad of her hair and pulled.

They struggled, knocking over chairs. No match to Dave's strength, Riley felt for the knife stuck in Dave's side. When she found the handle, she pulled hard, tearing flesh. Dave screamed out, letting go of her hair.

"I'm going to kill you," he sputtered and coughed, grasping the blade. "Ringo can find another bitch. You're all mine." His face began to blister, and his eyes leaked chemical tears.

"That's got to really hurt?" Riley said, grasping her ribs. In pain, exhausted, Riley was also wearing down.

"Looks like you're a little beat up yourself," he muttered.

"I don't have a knife in my side," she replied, backing up.

Dave unbuckled his belt, whipping the leather from pant loops.

Before Riley could escape, Dave made the buckle whip out like a rattlesnake striking prey. The metal caught arm flesh and sliced it open. Dave reached out and pinned her from escape. Crushed between the cabinets and body weight, Riley struggled to get free.

Between the unbearable pain and the stench of bug spray, Riley could not breathe. The fight came down to either dying or fighting. When the belt wrapped around her waist, she reached back into the drawer finding the screwdriver. Pinned but fighting to survive, Riley gripped the tool tight, aimed for the groin, and drove the screwdriver home.

A bloodcurdling scream filled the small cabin and bounced off the inside walls. Dave stepped back, grabbed the handle of the tool, and pulled.

"Son of a bitch," he shouted at the top of his lungs as the metal end came out. A loud cry of anguish followed. Riley leaped to the other side of the room spinning on one foot, turning to face the rage.

"Ouch! Now that's gotta hurt." Riley said with sarcasm.

Dave stood, blood dripping from his hands, cheeks puffed in then out as saliva dribbled down his lip.

"You're dead," Dave said, shaking.

"Not today, Dave. However, you might bleed out, and I am afraid that I will need to borrow your rig."

Riley took a step toward the door. She stopped when she heard the click of a gun.

Dave had a gun all along. Exhausted and unarmed, Riley had nothing more to fight with. Either way, she was a dead woman. The ride to freedom was just beyond the door. So close and yet too far away. Riley turned and faced Dave because the only choice was to advance. She focused on the dangling knife and then on the trigger of his gun. As he pressed, she leaped forward, using the knife as an advantage to slow down the fall and to hurt him so badly, he'd buckle.

She must have connected with something because the bullet intended for her chest ripped through her left thigh instead. An extreme heat followed by pain happened as the bullet hit. Riley dropped to the floor as Dave's wounded laughter blasted her eardrums.

"I'm still gonna have a piece of you, whether your breathing or not," he chuckled.

In her semi-conscious mind, she could not help but think about Lucas, Jack, and Eric. Utah and Megan, who had received loss after loss, may never find another home. Just before her lights dimmed, Riley looked up. A single white feather swirled above her, a blue light trailing as it floated downward, and then everything stopped, the laughter, the cold, and the darkness.

"Come on, Riley. Let's make sand angels on the beach," cried Megan.

Riley dropped to the sand, feeling the warmth surround her. The ocean's sound created an orchestra of waves and water intertwined with the smell of salty seas. Laying back, she moved her arms up and down and then her legs, creating a sand angel. Riley looked at Utah. Then they jumped up and ran toward the water, giggling.

Long strands of glistening sand stretched as far as she could see. Their tanned faces sparkled with the sea's mist. Laughter mixed in with the sound of the surf. When they fell to the ground and looked upward, the sky looked crystal blue except for several clouds that were windswept.

"Look," Riley said, pointing up into the sky. "That looks like an elephant."

NOT ALONE

"I don't see it," giggled Megan because she always did.
"Okay, blur your eyes just a little and then relax them. See."
"I see it. You see it, Utah?"
"I see it." Utah blinked.
"Do you think the sky ends?" asked Megan.
"I don't believe that it does. It just keeps going," Riley said. *"To heaven."*
"He's come back for you, Riley," Utah said, sitting up in the sand.
Riley looked over at her and smiled. *"No one came back for me."*
"He's there. You're just asleep."
"Whose there?" asked Riley.
"Jack. Megan needs you," Utah said softly. *"I need you."*
Riley looked up into the sky, watching a bird soar above them. His wings spread out as he dipped back and forth, looking for a fish to take back to her offspring. With the heart of an eagle and the body of a falcon, the bird plunged downward, bringing a small fish clutched between talons. The bird rose high in the air and then flew out of sight.
"He came back for you." She repeated. *"Go now."*

Blue turned to black as Riley started to argue with Utah. She was trying to open her eyes while words became jumbled and filtered.

"Riley," the voice said. She felt herself lifting upward, but the pain hurt so much, she cried out.

"I'm sorry," Riley heard him say. "I have her."

"Who?" she asked.

"You bitch..." Dave shouted.

"Throw him outside," commanded Jack.

"No problem, Jack," another voice said.

Jack sat Riley on a chair and knelt beside her. Taking her uninjured hand, he placed her pistol into her palm.

"Better?" he asked.

"Be careful of the cats," Riley said, looking down at the pistol. Every part of her body hurt.

Jack chuckled. "Being a cat owner yourself, I wouldn't think you'd be too scared of those big old putty cats," he teased.

She chuckled, "Ouch! Did you get the number of the train that hit me?"

The room spun. Riley swayed, but Jack caught her.

Dave screamed profanities in the background.

She heard a familiar pop and then the sound of a body hitting the floor. Riley looked at the pistol first and then caught Dave's agitated voice. Her fingers pressed around the base of the gun.

"Can I kill him now?" Riley asked in a whisper. Her head felt heavy and bobbed forward.

"John's an ex-marine. His specialty, terrorist interrogations," Jack grinned. "He'll handle it."

"Interrogation, why?" Riley asked.

"We still need to find Ringo?"

"He was here not so long ago. He's a killer, an assassin. He killed his wife and burned his house with his kids inside. Gave him your name accidentally," she said, frowning. Jack took a syringe from his pack and lifted the sleeve of her shirt. "Do you know anything about a little boy? Are you going to kill me now?"

Jack chuckled. "No, I'm giving you something for the pain. You'll be groggy." She felt liquid warm her blood and then a feeling of heaviness without the pain. When Riley looked up, Jack grinned. "You're going to be okay, again."

His voice sounded far away. Riley smiled, "I'm sorry I gave him your name, but he was going to feed me to the tiger."

"Yep, you're feeling no pain," he took her gun.

In and out, she saw a silhouette standing behind Jack, hidden behind a facemask. Riley stared at the man then realized, even hidden, she knew him.

"Hey, Kid. I've been looking for you," said Riley as a single tear rolled onto her cheek. She started to fall, but Jack reached out, and she felt him catch her.

59

Ringo watched the ranch for over an hour. Satisfied, he glanced down at the explosives near his feet. A master at making people disappear, Ringo pretended to be an influential businessman, an investor of sorts. Even his cheating wife thought he was an investor, but the job title eradicator fit him best.

A collector of large sums of money, Ringo rectified many problems for a variety of evil people. What he told Riley held some truth, but he'd left out the main parts. Having spent his life cleaning up other people's messes, he learned the hard way about the person he'd become. Ringo knew how he survived the Shift when others didn't. Evil is as evil does.

Three of his men were waiting close to the Colton ranch entrance. He planned to go in, take the boy, kill a few adversaries, and get out. He and the devil were no different. Jack Colton took his boy and the mother, and they needed replacement. He had the blonde woman. Now, Ringo wanted the boy.

Ringo spotted several of Colton's men patrolling the outside perimeter and an older man, ten days past eighty, carting a shotgun. The codger was more likely to be the dangerous one. He'd evaluated the two Rhodesians as they did their rounds with grandpa, but they were an easy fix.

The dark, once the building blocks for urban legends, but more of a tease to scare those so inclined to believe, now held chilling post-Shift risks most people chose not to take. Not Ringo. He found the night's darkness to be his best friend.

A pack of coyotes yelped to a winning war cry striking high notes, which carried throughout the valley. The clouds hanging in the sky would soon cover the moon, shutting the curtain of light to complete nothingness, the circumstances Ringo felt most comfortable. If he could not get close enough to shoot the dogs with a tranquilizer gun, he carried complimentary laced hotdogs in his coat pocket as plan B. A rock fence led to the barn masking his movements so far. He scaled the brick wall, closing in on the ranch house. When he touched down on Colton's land, he felt something anciently familiar creep up inside of his soul.

Not taking a chance of running into one of the four-legged guards, Ringo chucked them into the yard one by one, waiting until the animals skimmed the perimeter.

Ringo moved to the rear of the barn. Colton's man standing at the back of the house turned away from him. Ringo stepped out into the open, crossing the snow, and pulled up his Colt.38 Super Special Combat Government pistol with a silencer to take a shot at one of Colton's men. Before he could take a shot, the man disappeared.

"Let the games begin," Ringo smiled. He loved a good game of Hide and Seek.

Overhead the clouds shifted, causing the contrast of light to drop several shades, making him invisible. The smell of a cigarette led him to the porch. Ringo raised his gun, but this time Colton's man spun around. The bullet hit his intended target high in the shoulder. A flesh wound at best. The man moved fast, faster than Ringo expected, pulling the trigger on Ringo and then dove through the back door, clicking off two more shots before he disappeared. Ringo readied himself for all hell to break loose, but nothing came.

In the distance, a pack of coyotes yelped in excitement.

"Let's play a little game of chess!" Ringo studied the windows and doors covered with barriers. "Expecting unwanted company," he muttered.

The sound of a horse's hooves moving across the desert floor caused him to turn. For a moment, Ringo thought the reaper wielding his scythe might be coming for him. The punishment for losing the child was reason enough. However, he saw nothing but dancing cactus shadows and oversized boulders under a shroud of thickening clouds.

"Hell has some patience," Ringo said, withdrawing a bundle of explosives from inside his coat, pressing against the side of the house as he removed a toothpick from his jacket pocket. As if bored, he placed the wooden stick between his teeth and took a moment to think. Chewing on the wood and as silent as a snake advancing on its prey, he went to his knees and put the bundled explosives under the front porch.

Finished, Ringo moved to the back door and knocked. "Special delivery!" he yelled, hitting the door harder. "If you give me the boy, no one will die."

Ringo turned. His finger rested on the trigger of his gun. The codger, reappearing without a sound, fired. The bullet landed not a quarter of an inch from Ringo's head, splintering the siding.

Ringo raised his eyebrows, "I'll be damned."

Another shot, but this time, Ringo ducked. The bullet lodged in the bulls-eye where his beating heart would have been.

Moving, Ringo sheltered himself from the older man's bullets. He clicked a few warning shots. The shooting stopped, and silence swallowed the stillness of the night. Even the coyotes stopped crying. The moon, clear of its covering, allowed light to spray down, casting uneven visibility to vulnerable spaces.

Ringo slid to the rear of the house, looking through windows, seeing nothing but metal coverings.

A silent rage festered, "what the fuck?" he whispered, withdrawing the detonator from his pocket. "You want to play? Let's play."

A red laser dot appeared on his chest as he was about to lay his finger on the flashing green light. He dove, dropping the detonator, and still, the bullet caught his left arm right under Riley's hit. The bullet tore into flesh, searing the muscle, breaking stitches above. Blood soaked his shirt as the red beam followed him to the ground. Rolling under the porch, he lost hold of the detonator.

"Shit!" he cursed. The detonator was lying a few feet away. Extending his arm through the steps over him, he reached out.

Thwack. Another bullet lodged in the wood overhead. He yanked his hand back, scraping his knuckles on wood.

"Mother fucker! I'm going to kill all of you."

Ringo righted himself, keeping to the safety of the porch steps. He looked for something he could use to recover the detonator. From where he lay, he saw several pieces of PVC pipe within his reach. Reaching out with his foot, he pulled one closer to him. He had two options, pull the device to him or tap the pipe on the detonator's button.

The red light appeared on the step, and wood exploded into shards of kindling. Impressed, his enemies wanted to play. Ringo fed the pipe through the damaged step.

"You give me no choice."

Pressing into the foundation of the house, Ringo tapped the go button and covered his ears. A giant ball of flame exploded overhead, producing an earth-shaking tremble. The explosion propelled chunks of the house outward, turning particles into deadly projectiles.

Ringo climbed to his feet, waiting to hear screams, but there were no cries for help or fleeing wounded, only the crackling of a house on fire. A large plume of dark smoke began to rise, blocking the radiant glow of the moon. In the shadows, he saw his three men moving toward him, and behind them, a set of headlights coming up fast.

"Jack Colton."

The red spot of death caught up to Ringo once more. He moved before his brain registered where he needed to go. Tiny embers and debris fell like confetti set free from a giant piñata. Bold and fearless, Ringo stepped into the house through the opening created from the blast. Another man shadowed and then disappeared from the damaged room. Slipping behind a corner in the hall, Ringo waited.

"Ryan Colton," a voice whispered to him.

Outside, the sound of a truck sliding to a stop filtered inward. Ringo raised an eyebrow, excited. The leader of the pack had arrived.

Ringo's fingers relaxed around the grip of the gun. The sound of running footsteps broke through the crackling fire. Ringo leaned out to look, but both Ryan and Jack had disappeared.

"Where d'you go?"

Resting his finger on the trigger, he released a round of gunfire where he'd last seen the youngest Colton, getting the party started. The bullets exploded into the drywall.

"Where's the boy?" shouted Ringo.

"What boy?" said a voice shadowed by darkened space for which Ringo could not see.

Ringo laughed. "I'll ask one more time. I want the boy?"

"He is not yours to take."

Ringo said nothing for a moment, straining to see past the curtain of the broken home. He fired a shot, attempting to flush out more than twirling smoke. Shadows and shapes pirouetted in the rhythm of spinning forms.

"Why do you care so much? Who are you?"

"Someone you should have never fucked with!"

Ringo searched for a face to put the voice to but then an inner voice, one in which only he could hear said, *he is the boy's father.*

Ringo craned his head, silent. "Awe, you are the daddy. My boys left you in the desert bleeding like a stuck pig. But not your wife. She was fine."

"You're a dead man."

Kid stepped out of cover, taking confident strides. He advanced on Ringo with no fear whatsoever. A pair of Sig Sauer 45's in his hands. The crackling of wires popping and wood weakening roared overhead. A crossbeam, further from them, crashed to the floor, sending a puff of sparks outward.

Neither man moved nor spoke, watching the other with deadly intent. The fire behind them morphed into a monster, but only because the house and its contents fueled hunger. Images of his children flashed in Ringo's mind. Their still eyes and pale faces were covered in blood in eternal sleep. For the past two years, he'd invested in Jonah, whom he thought to be his.

"You are not from this place," Kid said, regarding Ringo with newfound skepticism.

Ringo's laughter broke the silence between them and echoed inside the remnants of the Colton home. "You haven't seen anything yet!" he shouted above the crackling flames.

60

The speedometer said he was doing sixty-five, but in Jack's mind, he should've been pushing hundred if the truck could have taken the corners without rolling over. Seeing flames coming from the ranch house, he pushed the throttle harder. The gunshots sounded like soft pops until a bullet sunk into the front fender of the Dodge. Jeremy, the team's sharpshooter, sat in the backseat, waited, ready, locked, and loaded. John and Scott leaned back into the seat, giving Jeremy space. Giving the truck full throttle, Jack raced down the drive, sliding sideways to a stop next to Kid's truck. Jack saw Ben cracked the door to the barn and peeked his head out.

"I've been trying to coax that asshole out for a good five minutes. I can't get a good aim on him." Ben said, propping his gun back against the side of the window. "Son of a bitch blew up our house."

"Okay, pops," Jack said.

Jeremy stood nearby and waited for instruction.

"You're scaring me, Jeremy," Scott said, staring at Jeremy, who looked more like a warrior than a kid. Jeremy held an assault rifle extra ammunition hung over his shoulder. "Jesus, you're just a kid."

"Likewise," Jeremy said. "Except neither of us are kids anymore." He stepped to the window.

The older man pointed to one of the shelters. "There." His finger shook. "They're only two of them left and the circus guy who's in the house."

"Circus guy?" Jeremy pulled his rifle up, positioning himself.

"Pops is referring to Ringo." Jack asked, "Can you get him?"

"No problem," Jeremy grinned. "Circus, huh. Bet he doesn't care too kindly for that."

"I'll draw him out for you." Jack patted Jeremy on the back.

"That asshole blew up the house," Ben repeated, shaking his fist. "Lily!"

"It's okay, pops. Lily is safe. Ready, Jeremy?"

"Ready," Jeremy pushed into his gun and waited.

Jack set his headset in place and then slid outside. Stepping under the eerie glow of hungry flames, he heard the first shot and then a "thunk" as the bullet slapped into the barn. Jeremy needed only one shot. Now, he had the position of the shooter. Seconds ticked by until Jeremy fired, taking out the man hidden behind the sun shelter.

NOT ALONE

Jack hurried toward the house. The smell of burning wires, plastic, and wood made a toxic aroma burning his nostrils. Crossing over the first step, he heard Eric's voice.

"Kid, location?"

"Take cover!"

The force of the explosion propelled Jack backward, not giving him a chance to retreat. Jack, on his knees, covered his head as pieces of the ranch home rained downward from the sky. He rolled to his side, searching for his lost headset.

A giant balloon of smoke billowed upward, stealing both oxygen and moonlight. Jack lay on the ground, trying to catch his breath. His ears ringing and his nose burning, he climbed to his feet and stumbled forward, swooping up the earpiece and setting the ear set back into place. Static sounds crackled in the speaker until Kid's voice filtered through.

"Jack, Jack, do you copy?"

"Copy," Jack replied.

"I got one, but it wasn't Ringo," Kid informed Jack.

"Could we be so lucky that he blew himself up?"

"Not likely."

"My families in the safe room," Jack moved across the burning debris. The front door transferred into a stack of kindling and a large hole. Kid and Shift appeared on the other side.

"Ringo was there one minute and then gone the next."

"Seems that's his M.O.," Jack led Kid over pieces of glass and debris. "Keep your eyes open, team."

The dog, already in front of the false door, waited. Chunks of material, big and small, blocked any possible entry.

"Anyone see Sadie and Tank?"

Kid started moving debris blocking the security panel and hidden door, "Tranquilized, alive and resting in the barn."

Ryan appeared. He looked at Jack and said, "let's get them out."

Jack, Kid, and Ryan were silent as they moved broken sections of the house away from the area where the entry door was to the safe room. The air grew hot as the fire behind them grew.

"Did anyone turn off the gas?" asked Kid, looking at his shoulder.

"Everything's shut off, and we've got several people hosing down the tank to keep it cool."

Once the panel concealing the door worked free, Jack stepped over the remaining rubble. The keypad that controlled the opening and closing of the main entry rested behind a small door.

"Where's the override switch?" asked Kid, pointing to the torn wires overhead.

Ben stepped across rubble and mumbled, "what a mess."

"I need to get to the side. Over there," Jack pointed. "It's near the floor."

Jack and Kid moved fast, hoisting large pieces of debris away from the wall.

"What's the status on Ringo?" Jack asked into his mic.

"He's gone," answered Scott.

"Where's Riley?" asked Kid.

"She's safe at Pam's house," Jack felt his temper rise because the night seemed to be slipping out of his control. He looked down at the debris, thinking of his family trapped in the safe room.

"We got to get them out, son," his father pleaded.

"I know, pops. I know. I'm working on it."

"Son of a bitch blew our house up," Ben yelled out again.

"We'll build a new one, pops. Okay." Jack looked back at the old man only to see despair and anger on his father's face, forcing composure.

"It'll be better, pop's," Jack reassured him.

"Desert One, pick up in progress. Copy?"

"Affirmative. Copy," Jack replied to Scott.

With Scott and Jeremy on their way to pick up Shay and Riley, he could focus on the task before him. He fished for the wires that controlled the override, refocused, calming the anxiety boiling inside him.

Jack, having moved more debris, stepped in closer to the door. "Bring them back here. We'll figure out the rest later."

"Copy that."

The air inside the house grew increasingly toxic. The fire, greedy for fuel, searched to destroy. Crossbeams moaned, and wood crackled and popped. Outside Jack knew a handful of men armed with garden hoses fought to keep the fire from jumping to the bunkhouse.

"Where's the snow now?" Jack coughed. He waved Eric over to help him. "Get the boys over this way with the hoses."

Kid nodded and sent a request over the radio.

John appeared within seconds, pushing his way through an opening in the kitchen wall, showering water onto the hissing serpent of fire that was causing the oxygen's noxious odor. The hot beast hissed, refusing to die down. Water pooled on the hardwood floor, mixing fine silt from debris into what looked like pancake batter. A section of the wall, soggy with water, crumbled. The house, battered and weakened, would soon fold.

Covered in sweat and dirt, Jack and Ryan were getting closer to the switch. They stripped down to their t-shirts, moving through sludge and rubbish.

"I got it," said Jack, hitting the override button and clicking the release on the door. The steel barrier opened but not all the way.

NOT ALONE

"Everybody's okay, Jack," Blake said through the opening.

"Okay. We'll get you guys out," he promised, pulling on the door. "I need you to push."

Wrapping his fingers around the edge, Jack pulled hard, but the steel door outweighed him ten to one. Twisted by the explosion and under pressure from weakening support beams, the door would not budge. The smoke from the living room started to roll through the kitchen, pulled by the outside air.

Another wall fell, this time somewhere deep within the house.

"The roof isn't going to hold much longer, Jack," shouted Ryan.

Compromised by fire and water, the roof began to sag under the weight of structure damage. Grabbing a pipe, Jack stuck it into the opening. Seeing Jack's intent, Kid stepped in behind, and together, they used the pipe as a lever. The door moaned and then opened.

"One more time Kid." They put all of their weight into the pipe. The door creaked, caught, and opened.

"Follow Kid," Jack instructed his family as they came into view.

61

The warm, soft blanket covering her eased the return of fading hope. Maybe she was dreaming. However, the memory of Kid and Jack drifted behind her closed eyes with the sweetest of warmth.

Safe with friends and family, she surrendered to comfort until she tried to turn, and the pain in her side, leg, and head exploded into a throbbing sensation, causing her to catch and hold her breath.

"You have three broken ribs, a broken wrist, and stitches in your cheek again, and one hell of a shiner, probably a slight concussion." The voice softened. "Nick took the bullet out of your leg. There's no real damage, but I bet it hurts like hell."

She opened her eyes, but they felt heavy. She knew the voice to be one of her heroes, Jack Colton.

"I feel like a truck hit me," she moaned.

"It wasn't a truck more like a parasite named Ringo, and he banged you up pretty good," Jack said in a low tone. He stood, lowering the blinds.

"No, leave them open, please," Riley wrinkled her nose smelling smoke. Maybe she missed having a campfire last night. Riley took in a shallow breath figuring a deep one would hurt like hell.

"Sun will be setting soon."

"Megan?"

"She's unconscious but stable. Nick thinks you can bring her out of it." He sat next to her.

Riley looked down at the cast on her wrist and squinting to read the writing on it.

"Your wrist is broken in two places. Nick used baling wire to put it back together."

"No way."

"Just kidding. Both breaks were clean." He was quiet for a minute.

"I feel like a zombie, and if I never go to a zoo again, it wouldn't break my heart."

Jack grinned.

She melted into the safety of the bed, allowing every inch of her body to hug the comfort. She felt safe enough to fall back asleep, waking a few hours later as she remembered one of her dreams. She lifted her uninjured hand, finding a white feather resting in her palm.

"Thank you for coming back to get me," Riley said, knowing he was still there.

"It'll cost you," he teased. "You hungry?

"Starving."

"Welcome to Prescott. A group of women in town cooked last night for us. Some of the best apple pie I think I've ever eaten, but please don't tell my sister that." Riley heard a slight clatter of utensils. "You like ice cream?"

"More than…, anything?"

He chuckled.

"How long have I been out?" she asked. "Where are we?"

"You've been out for a few days. You're at my ranch or what used to be a ranch outside Prescott."

"A few days? Used to be?" Only awake a few minutes, she already felt confused.

"Ringo showed up looking for Jonah. He left a fire in his wake."

"I thought maybe you had a campfire last night."

"You can smell it, huh?"

"Slightly. I'm sorry."

Jack set a tray down on the nightstand. Riley saw him for the second time through sleepy eyes, and she thought him to be more handsome than the first time. Not realizing his hair was on the longer side, curly and salted with gray. Pulled back, it appeared shorter than it was. His eyes were a mix of green and blue with a hint of gold. If looks were intimidating, then Jack Colton was a dangerous man, maybe even lethal. Seriousness showed in his eyes, determined and sexy. He was sporting a two-day shadow, and beyond the smoke, he smelled of something spicy and pleasant.

"If he blew up your house, where are we?"

"The barn."

Great! I look like a train wreck, and you look like you just stepped off a movie set, she said to herself.

"Nicest barn I've ever seen."

"Everyone else is in the bunkhouse."

"I am sorry about your house."

"Why? You didn't do it," he smiled. "Change is good. Sometimes."

"The little boy Ringo spoke of, Jonah. Is he here?"

Jack shook his head. He leaned in closer to her. A blanket of warmth crept over her face. She could smell him again, and damn, he smelled heavenly.

"Ready to sit up. It's going to hurt."

Riley glanced down at the flannel pajamas she wore and then looked at him.

"I didn't look," he smiled. Riley flushed, and he chuckled. "Lynn dressed you."

"Lynn?"

"You'll meet her later. She's the better half of the family. The glue that holds us all together."

He reached out, stabilizing her. With shallow breaths, she sat up in the bed. Her rib cage wrapped in something soft gave her support. The left side of her face felt swollen. She could not only feel the ache, but she could also see the side of her face when she looked down. Riley reached up with her hand to touch it, but instead, she clunked herself with the cast.

"Ouch!" she frowned. "This isn't my best moment, is it?"

"Depends who is looking at you," he answered, setting the tray on her lap.

Riley looked at the slice of pizza smothered with olives, onions, and Greek feta cheese. Despite the soreness in her jaw caused by Ringo, she took a bite, chewing slowly. A missed yet familiar explosion fell onto her taste buds like an army of mouthwatering flavor soldiers. How long had it been since she tasted something so savory? She chewed slow, closing her eyes and ignoring the pain.

"Mmmm. I'm dreaming, right? I mean pizza? Who gets pizza these days?"

"You do. Thanks to Margret's Pizza. We're remodeling a building in town for her to open her Pizzeria. Meanwhile, she keeps my boys fed." He sat back in his chair and watched her eat. Riley pictured him on a billboard wearing a pair of Ray-Bans and sitting on an old classic Harley-Davidson motorcycle.

"You traveled a long way?" he shifted in the chair, keeping his eyes on her the entire time.

"California. However, Eric was supposed to meet me in Oregon at his cabin. I went there first, hoping to find him." The stitches pulled, and a tingling sensation tingled across her cheek. "He left a note telling me to come to Arizona. That was a long time ago."

"The roads, pretty treacherous from there to here?"

"Yes. I thought everyone was dead until the girls found me."

"You have some pretty good scars," he pointed out, lowering his voice.

"You saw my scars?"

"Maybe a few."

The apple pie and ice cream were next. He waited, watching her, and she enjoyed every bite. Fighting off the fluttering of her heart and cotton in her brain, she took another scoop while thinking about the scars mapping her body.

"I was a game officer in Sacramento."

"Dangerous line of work, but that's not where the scars came from, is it?"

"No. I ran into some bad guys the night of the Shift. The night I was trying to leave."

Jack lifted his gun as the door handle clicked.

Eric slipped through, trying to be quiet. He frowned most likely upon seeing the injuries on her face, the bruises, the stitches, and the casted arm.

"I'm going to kill him!"

Eric had a way of looking reckless one minute and then a powerful, well-defined military instrument the next. His blonde hair shorter than ever and having gained a wrinkle or two, where the forehead creases when one is worried, seemed to be slight changes since she'd saw him last. His eyes mirrored hers. A brilliant blue showered in a transparent contrast of gray. Jack Colton and Eric were like day and night, both ex-military and both fighters of the future.

"How you feeling?" asked Eric. "Cuz, you sure look like hell."

"Thanks for that. Because you always come out of train wrecks looking like a million dollars."

"It's a curse," he replied, looking over at Jack. "I came from my place, and things are pretty quiet."

"Now we hurry up and wait. You all done with that?"

She nodded. Jack took the tray and dropped a pill into her hand. "Doctor's orders."

"Thanks," she already felt sleepy.

"I missed you," Eric leaned down and kissed her forehead.

"Ditto!"

"Let's talk, Kid. Let her sleep."

She nodded. Unafraid because both of them would be there when she woke up.

62

"He's a walking dead man," Eric followed Jack into the living room, shutting the door behind him.

"We are lucky we found her when we did. Ringo would've killed her."

"I never got to thank you for finding her the first time," replied Eric.

"Wish I'd gotten there sooner. This entire chain of events is nothing short of ironic."

"He wants Jonah, and now he wants Riley. The irony in it all gets thicker all the time."

Jack sat down in the chair, pressing his fingers to his forehead. "He wants people he can't have, and he can't have either. He's sitting quietly somewhere right now, making a new plan. The next go-around will be uglier."

"You get any sleep yet?"

"Yeah. Why do I look like hell too?"

"Yes." Eric sat down on the couch across from Jack. "Let him come to us. If he doesn't show, you and I will go looking for him."

"I know he won't stop until he gets what he wants. I refuse to have to keep looking over my shoulder, knowing he is alive." Jack said, irritated. "Thanks to the Shift, I wasn't able to take him out the first time."

"I don't think he'll be gone. Ringo thinks like a hunter. He's scouting the land, planning his next hunt." Eric leaned back, closing his eyes. "Riley's special, and he knows it."

"What if he succeeds? Are you willing to risk Riley or Jonah's life?" Jack asked. "What were the odds of him being the one who ran you off the road and taking Shay?"

"Ironic, I know?" They took turns rubbing their foreheads, a sure sign of growing frustration. "I don't think we have any other alternative."

A moment of silence fell between them, and though having first met years ago, the immediate connection keeping them together was the very thing they both loved. Eric sat forward and started to say something before a soft knock stopped him.

"It's Shay, Jack," Shay spoke from the other side.

Eric looked at Jack and stood.

"I think she's here for you, Kid," Jack said.

Eric opened the door.

At first, Shay stood in silence, her face paled.

"I knew it," she whispered, taking a step forward.

Eric stood still. "Shay."

She stepped closer to him, "Oh my God, Eric. I thought you were dead." Her expression turned soft as tears rolled down her face.

"I never stopped looking for you, Shay."

Shay stepped closer to him, putting her arms around him. She laid her head against his chest as if listening to the beat of his heart. "I would've let you know sooner, but..." Eric stopped.

"I should go," Jack interrupted.

"Stay." Shay pleaded, lifting her head. "Please. Stay. You saved my life and Jonah's. You both did."

Jack nodded, "Okay."

Eric's face softened, "Jonah?"

"He looks like you."

Jack cleared his throat. "I'll let you two alone," Jack patted Shay and Eric on the shoulder. "This is what I call an ironic but happy ending."

63

Christmas knocked on the Colton ranch door bringing cold temperatures smothered with sunshine. After having an excellent breakfast delivered by Jack's sister Lynn, whom Riley adored, was the kind of woman who dressed in jeans and a long-sleeved button-up shirt but had the class of a lady in an evening gown. Some much-needed makeup covered the remaining discoloration of her bruises, and the stack of clothing Lynn gave her suited her style in many ways. A pair of rough-out cowboy boots sat at the end of the bed, a bonus.

Smiling, she heard neighs coming from the breezeway and hurried. She felt safe, comfortable, and now back to the things she loved and knew. Pulling on the boots, careful not to overextend her rib cage, she stood and looked in the mirror. It had been five weeks since Ringo took her hostage. The swelling in her left eye was nearly gone, and the bruises faded from black purple to a shade of light green, a vast improvement. Nick removed the stitches in her cheek and leg a few weeks back, but the scars remained visible. Reaching into the makeup bag, feeling silly and clumsy, having not applied makeup for a long time, she set to work covering what she could. Layering makeup around her eye to cover discoloration, Riley finished brushing mascara on lashes and lip balm on dry lips. Reaching back, she unwound the band tying her hair in a braid, unraveled the strands, letting blonde hair fall free around her shoulders.

Gazing at her reflection, Riley realized the person left to die in the parking lot the night of the Shift might not be the same woman standing in front of the mirror now. The scars, almost invisible under the makeup, were laced in gold because she'd survived. She took one last look in the mirror, the face painting worked, and though there was nothing to hide the hurt done to her soul, she was healing one day at a time.

A soft whistle came from behind her as she stepped out of the barn doors into daylight. She blushed, turned, and then smiled at Jack. The sun showered a warm blast, not able to tame the chilly air. Jack, seeing her squint, handed her a pair of sunglasses.

"Lynn thought you might need these."

"Is there nothing she doesn't think of?"

Jack nodded. "Rarely."

Riley looked over at the pile of burned debris. "The house?"

"Building a new one. Won't take long. Especially since I don't need to pull any permits," Jack grinned.

NOT ALONE

Riley returned the smile, and then her expression grew serious. "Where can I find Megan?"

Jack gestured for her to follow him.

"In there," he said, stopping at a building large enough to be a ranch house. "Doors open."

Riley took the steps slow and then looked back at Jack, who nodded at her. When she entered, she saw Utah and grinned as big as she'd ever smiled.

Utah jumped from her chair and wrapped her arms around Riley.

"It's time for her to wake up," Riley whispered to Utah, holding out a white feather. "Maybe this will work for her. What do you think?"

You need to keep that one. Megan has one." Utah turned, leading Riley to the bed where Megan slept. She slid the feather back into Riley's hand.

Riley bent down, kissing Megan's cheek.

"Megan. Wake up, sweetie." Riley leaned in close to her ear. "Please wake up. I so want to hear you laugh."

Utah stroked Megan's hair. "She's been sleeping a while."

"Harry Potter." Riley picked up the book. "This has got to work."

She read for some time until she realized Utah had drifted to sleep. Then Riley leaned back and closed her eyes, falling into a world where answers turned to nightmares.

The black cocktail dress should've made her feel sexy, but instead, the constriction of the material irritated her. Mark appeared confident in a dark gray suit, hiding his candor ways as his hand rested on the table, and a cold, self-assured smile played on his lips.

Suits and dresses filled the room. The soft chatter of conversations combined with the smells of good food played with Riley's senses, but inside, she felt empty. Riley tried to look interested, gliding her fingertips over the wine glass and stared at the delicate fluid trapped inside.

"I am this wine, trapped. We are two worlds apart, Mark and I," she thought to herself.

Three attractive women, two tables down, laughed at something unheard. The most beautiful of the three was the blonde-haired woman, dressed to attract men. With plump lips, she'd painted red, and a dipped neckline revealing expert enhancements glanced their way, Mark was like a puppy waiting to go to mama. The pout, intended for whoever would look, took notice. Mark noticed the flirting stung Riley, making her uncomfortable without feeling any sorrow. She wanted the dinner to be over quickly so she could go home.

"How's your salad?" Mark asked.

"Good," but she tasted nothing.

Small talk is cheap and goes fast.

"More wine?" Mark asked her.

"Please," Riley spoke, robotic-like, and she thinks, "give me the entire bottle."

The waitress, a beautiful red-haired woman, brought their food to the table. Her nametag reads Sam. She and Riley smiled at each other as she sits Mark's plate down, giving him little attention. However, Sam turned to Riley, who recognized Sam as someone Riley should know.

Shifting her gaze across the room, the waitress, with her eyes, urged Riley to look away from Mark. As Riley did, she saw Lucas dressed in a sleek pale gray suit with a black silk tie. Riley took an instant breath of relief. Lucas no longer looked like the cowboy she met in the saloon. His hair appeared darker, longer. His face clean-shaven, exposing every ounce of his striking good looks.

Lucas glanced over at her and raised his glass. Riley grinned, feeling more than comfort.

"Finish your dinner, Riley," commanded Mark.

Riley wore his anger tonight, some disguised under makeup and some unfixable.

"This is an expensive meal. Don't waste it."

Mark reached over, putting his fingers around her wrist. For those watching, the move looked like a moment of tenderness. He touched her only to satisfy himself and to inflict pain. His fingers dug into her wrist. She winced under pressure.

"Do we have a problem, Riley?"

"Let her go," Lucas appeared, speaking with the tone of a gentleman but one with serious intent.

"I'm sorry. Do I know you?" Mark asked. His chin jutted forward. His jaws clamped together.

"No, but you're about to if you don't let go of her wrist," Lucas demanded. Lucas's voice sent bolts of electricity through Riley.

"Get the fuck away from my table," Mark hissed. He yanked Riley's arm, digging his fingers into her flesh even deeper.

"Let go of me, Mark," Riley kept her voice even, but the demand made her shiver. The skin under his fingers burned under pressure.

As Lucas stepped forward, Mark released his hold on her wrist. Riley went gracefully to her feet, pushing the chair off to the side.

"Listen to her," Lucas demanded.

"She's my wife, asshole. So back off!" shouted Mark.

The restaurant grew silent. Lucas reached up and moved her hair to the side. Riley knew he could see the bruising of handprints painted on the sides of her neck. She looked at Lucas, and his eyes softened for a *heartbeat. He let her curls fall, covering the brutal marks made by her husband. Lucas's fingers brushed Riley's skin. An electric shock bolted through her.*

"Get your hands off her." Mark stood and then stepped forward. "You know him, Riley," he screamed. "You little whore!"

Lucas moved with lightning speed. His right fist smashing into Mark's left jaw, sending him backward...

"Riley," a soft voice called her away from Lucas.

Riley blinked, "Jack."

64

Life continued with a series of challenges because good things happen, and bad things follow. They knew Ringo would return. None of them had forgotten about him, but as time went by and people took the calm as a time to heal, they may have relaxed too much.

Christmas Eve brought sunny skies and a hint that a new year loomed around the corner. With new and old scars, Riley learned that the wounds now healed were a part of her. The cast, decorated with graffiti by everyone, would soon be coming off, and though her ribs stayed tender, those were on the mend as well.

Megan, however, slept. They all took turns watching over her, reading to her, and even singing to her. If Nick had to leave the ranch, he tended to Megan first. Utah remained vigilant, staying at her little sister's side.

Eric's proposal to Shay didn't surprise anyone, but with the news came a newfound excitement and apprehension.

One sunny cold afternoon Riley, still staying in the barn apartment, heard a knock on the door. Max jumped on the chair, purring, a give-away Jack was on the other side.

"Sucker," Riley grabbed Max's tail in a playful gesture.

Max met Jack with a swat of his paw, and Jack returned the gesture with a scratch behind the cat's ears.

"Traitor," Riley eyed the cat.

Jack grinned, slipping a pink bag onto the couch, which Max tried to jump in.

She swatted him away. "No!" she scolded. "What's this?"

"I thought we could ride to Scott and Kate's party together?" he said. Resilient and handsome, Jack Colton seemed nervous.

She forgot about the Christmas party. A panic rose in her stomach. Not ready to face a group of people, Riley started to decline. Jack's closest friends would be there.

"I don't..." she started.

"You're going, Riley," not taking no for an answer. "Sherry is already here for Megan. It'll be good for you."

"Really," Riley sighed. The last time she socialized, her husband had almost killed her because she wore the wrong dress. "I thought I was pretty okay."

"You are..., okay," he said in a softer tone looking at her. "Everyone would miss you."

"I don't have any gifts," she said, digging for any excuse she could find.

"They don't need presents. You're going."

"I can't," Riley said, looking down at the faded jeans and t-shirt. About to say something about the scars, clothing, and cast, Jack wasn't about to give her a chance to back out.

"Four then," he tapped his fingers on the bag.

Riley nodded in a cold panic. "What's in the bag?"

"Lynn thought you might like it."

Riley parted the bag seeing red. "Where did she get this?"

"I told you, Lynn is very resourceful," he murmured. "She's a lot like our mom."

Surprised, Riley grinned at Jack.

"Come on, I want to show you something," he pushed her boots toward her.

Riley pulled them on and followed him outside. Every time she stepped out the door and gazed at the sky, she felt a breathtaking sense of peace. The horses frolicking in the pasture made being outside even better. For the past few weeks, she took to cleaning stalls and grooming the horses. She would have gone to Eric's, but Jack wanted her to stay, he'd insisted. She wanted nothing free. Instead, she agreed to work for her rent.

They stood quietly in front of the barn. Then Jack grinned. "Have you ever seen a Friesian?"

"In books. I've drawn a few of them. Beautiful horses. Why?"

"You draw?" He pulled his hat down further on his face.

"A little. Are you expecting someone?" Riley asked, seeing Jack look down the road. He looked at his watch and then at her.

A slight cloud of dust rose in the distance. Riley shielded her eyes from the sun, watching a truck and trailer approach.

"I bought a mare and a stallion from a man in Flagstaff. He rescues horses."

A silver truck towing a midsize trailer pulled up to the barn. A tall, lean man with thinning hair and gaunt features got out, stretched his legs, and then yawned.

"These guys will eat you out of house and home."

The cowboy's skin looked tanned by the sun and kissed with age. Riley followed him and Jack as they stepped to the back of the trailer.

"How you been, Andy?" Jack asked, reaching out to shake the man's hand.

"Oh, you know, day by day and not getting a day younger," he replied. "You have yourself a nice set here."

"I appreciate the delivery. Things have been a little crazy around here."

"You know me Jack, always down for a short time away from the misses. She had my thermos and lunch packed the night before," he laughed and then sputtered out a slight cough. "What happened to the house?"

"We had a little trouble. Hey, Andy, this is Riley Collins," Jack said. "Riley, this is Andy McCain. Seventy-five percent of the horses on this property came from Andy's place."

Riley stepped forward and shook his hand. "Nice to meet you, Andy."

"About time you got yourself a pretty little lady." Andy teased. "This must be your Christmas present."

"No, I..." she started.

"Yes," interrupted Jack. "You said the mare has a big heart and an adventuress character, so I thought they'd be a perfect match."

Riley moved beside Jack. Standing on tiptoes, she tried to see one of the giants. Andy opened the door, patting a black apple-shaped rump and stepping aside, giving the horse room back down. Once the giant was out of the trailer, he stood his long thick black mane and tail billowing like a silk cloak in the breeze. Head held high, the horse's eyes glistened, and nose lifted, smelling the other horses. The black coat shone so brilliant with shades of violet and blue. The mare stepped down and stood near the stallion. Her long mane and tail thick, and her coat velvet black. Large brown eyes peeked through a long wavy forelock. Broad and tall the stallion, she commanded as much respect and admiration.

"Like I told Jack, some markers shot the mare, but she's recovered and doing fine. Lucky for us, those guys didn't kill her." He rubbed the mare's forehead. She lowered her head, wanting more. "She's lucky to be alive."

Jack looked over at Riley, "Sounds like someone I'm getting to know."

"What's her name?" asked Riley asked as she stepped in close to the mare and slid her fingers from the withers down the velvet coat.

"You name her," Andy said. "Every man and woman should name their horse. Well, I got to get going," Andy said, taking a long sip out of his thermos cup. "I got one to pick up over in Prescott Valley and another in Chino Valley. There are many abandoned horses out there needing rescuing."

"I was hoping you'd stay and go home tomorrow," Jack took the lead ropes from Andy and handed her the mares. Riley could not say anything.

"You don't have a house, Jack. Anyway, I got a feeling the one in Prescott Valley might be a little rough around the edges. Loading may take more time than I planned." He climbed up into the truck and looked back at her. "There's a little surprise that goes along with that package," he chuckled, shutting his door and starting the truck. "Nice to meet you, Miss Riley," he hollered as he pulled away.

NOT ALONE

Riley stood there, looking at Jack, who had a way of making her fears fade. This moment of happiness allowed her to set trouble on the backburner for another day. Had the Shift not happened, would she be standing next to Jack Colton right now? Any relationship scared the hell out of her, but she wanted this one.

While the horses settled into their stalls, she and Jack stood in the breezeway watching. Jack smiled even after telling him several times that she could not accept such a gift. Saying nothing, Jack walked her back to the apartment where a little red dress waited for her. Riley could not say no.

Jack knocked at the door at 3:50 p.m., ten minutes early. When Riley opened the door, she found him leaning against the porch wearing a relaxed look on his face and as attractive as a rogue paramilitary man could be. Jack stood dressed to kill in a tuxedo. She tried to be calm, but he left her speechless. He stood there, silent, and stared at her. She looked down at the red silk dress.

"What's wrong?"

He stood before her, tall, handsome, and witty. "Nothing is wrong. I don't know what you did with Riley. Is she here?"

"No?" she grinned, jokingly closing the door.

Riley grinned, teasing aside, and let him in. Jack Colton smelled as good as he looked. Refined and polished, he stared at her.

A flash of Lucas entered her thoughts, and she saw the likeness between them. Devilishly handsome and looking outlaw, he drew her in and held her attention. Jack had been careful to contain his emotions so far, but hers were quietly on fire. He stepped closer, and she trembled, stepping back.

"You look so beautiful. You need an entire closet of dresses like those." He moved, but this time she remained. "Good thing I'm armed."

Riley smiled. "If you can't find yours, you can borrow mine."

"Where is yours?" he asked. "There's not a curve I can't see."

Riley smiled. With Lynn's help, she got the dress on, fixed her hair, hid most of the scars by makeup, and found a clever hiding place for her gun.

He looked at the decorated bags of goodies. Reaching into one, he brought out a jar and read its label. "Oregon Jam?" He looked at her and raised his eyebrows. "Funny, I've heard about this place."

"I was lucky that day. Looters overlooked those," Riley said. "I stole them, you know. I took the truck. I gained the girls that day too. They stole me."

"Thieves," he teased. "A brilliant and charming thief." He set the jam down and moved closer to her. She could smell a soft hint of whiskey.

Their gazes locked. Riley felt a warm rush of heat as Jack slid his fingers over her dress.

"We're going to be late," Riley blushed.

Jack mumbled something and reached out to touch the scar on her face. He stroked her cheek, and she leaned into his touch. Jack stood so close to her that she thought he might kiss her. The anticipation forced butterflies to take flight inside her stomach, large monarch butterflies pulsing into a sensation of distraction.

"Scott knows I am always late," he replied, stepping back. Somehow, he'd sensed her vulnerability, although her body said otherwise.

"We'll finish this later."

Already, she looked forward to later. A methodical man, even when it came to his emotions. The act would have been disappointing if he took her to bed, too fast, hurried, and with no time to repeat.

While Riley caught her breath, Jack picked up the presents, leading her to the door, stopping long enough to pat Max on the head.

"I'll take good care of your mama," Jack said.

Thanks to Scott and Katlynn's festive decorating and the fragrances of food floating from every corner of the house, the party exemplified a traditional Christmas not lost. Classical holiday music, great food, good wine, and much storytelling carried through dinner. Riley thought about Megan and Utah, and as Jack saw her ponder, he came to her side. If he stood apart from her, he watched from afar. Riley knew this because she watched him. The conversations reflected certain lightness, and by the late evening, as the kids fell asleep, the grown-ups gathered in the game room where hunters dare not trespass.

65

As the weeks passed and December turned into January and January into February, Riley fully recovered while Megan remained in a coma. Riley worried that Megan was still unconscious, but Nick encouraged them not to give up.

Utah remained steadfast. She told Riley every day, Megan would wake up. Keeping the faith in her sister's recovery, Utah seemed unbreakable. Considering the girl had some supernatural mind-reading ability, Riley believed Utah. However, the girl, distant to others, loved the horses, Sadie and Tank, who followed her everywhere.

One day after watching a movie with Utah and Megan, Riley fell asleep in the chair. There remained a piece of the puzzle that Riley still didn't know about the girls. When Riley fell asleep, Utah decided the time had come to show her what happened to her and Megan?

Utah pulled Riley back to the girl's apartment where they had last left off. *Steven charged Amy. Rage prickled the air, madness so violent it would destroy a mother and her children. Amy never saw the fatal blow, but Utah and Megan did. Plagued with insanity, Steven slammed the wooden leg into Amy's head. A horrific sound echoed inside the small apartment. Bone fractured, and blood splattered as she fell. The girls watched as the last sparkle of life left their mother's eyes, clinging to each other in horror as her soul vanished from them forever.*

The rest of their story unfolded too quickly. Utah grabbed the gun from Megan. Unfaltering, no second-guessing, Utah aimed and then pulled the trigger. Utah shot Steven not once but three times. The power from the shot pushed Utah backward, and the gun exploded two more times and then fell to the floor. Utah scrambled to her feet. Steven lay on his back. Crimson liquid, the color of a red rose, consumed the grungy tan t-shirt and the worn-out carpet underneath.

Running past Steven, Utah knelt beside her mother. Death fixed Amy's eyes open into a lifeless gaze. Utah lingered there as if willing her mother to breathe. Death came to be the last thing she saw from Amy.

The window to Amy's soul gave way to no secrets, not from Utah anyway because she'd been through all of them with her mother. Amy's feet jerked and then went still. A deadly silence infected the room.

Utah took her sister and held her tight. Then she moved, knowing what she had to do. Utah pulled Megan to the door, but her little sister sobbed, trying to tear away from Utah's hold as they passed by their mother.

"She's gone, Megan. We have to go," Utah cried.

"Mama," sobbed Megan.

"We have to go." Utah pulled on her hand.

In the dark and pulsing into the night air, sirens wailed in chaos. Megan tried to put her hands over her ears, but Utah pulled on her. The sirens screamed as the emergency vehicles flew past the apartment complex and faded. No help would come for them. Utah and Megan stood outside, awarded an escape they so deserved.

Nearly free, a loud unwanted voice caused Utah to pause. Riley's heart skipped a beat. Utah turned, letting go of Megan's warmth. The door creaked open.

"Happy fucking birthday, Utah!" Steven gurgled, hugging the doorframe. He stood unsteady and bleeding, but the bastard wasn't dead.

Megan screamed, grabbing hold of Utah. The sound of the gun exploded behind them, but not before Utah shoved Megan away from the door.

"Run, Megan," screamed Utah. "Run."

Now, Riley saw through Utah's eyes. Riley felt the bullet explode into Utah's back, shattering vertebras, bone and ripping apart flesh. The impact shoved her several feet forward. Together and the same, she and Utah went down. Riley felt the burning sensation in her back. Sharp stinging pulses shot through her body. The pavement ripped into her flesh as if the coating were a blanket laced with shards of glass. The pain quickly grew unbearable. Suddenly, Riley felt no pain.

A brilliant blue light exploded around her, and her body drifted as if floating on water. As shadows cast out giant arms of angels, Riley saw Megan running away, and then she disappeared.

Utah released her. Riley and Utah stood together as Utah glanced back at her fallen body.

"Megan," she screamed, running to where she lay. No answer came. Blood covered the new shirt her mother had bought for her birthday.

"Oh, mama," she cried, stroking her curly hair fanned out in front of her and her face pressed to the pavement.

Riley felt the layer of sweat covering her brow and the tears falling down her cheeks.

"Riley. You okay?" asked Nick.

"Sorry," she said, looking up at Nick. "What's going on?"

"There's a slight change in Megan."

Riley jumped up.

Utah stood next to Megan, their hands interlocked, but Utah's skin had turned ghostly pale.

"Utah," Riley whispered.

NOT ALONE

"She's showing signs of waking up," Nick said, pulling Riley's attention to Megan. "Talk to her."

Riley took Megan's hand, feeling a slight pressure of response. Riley slid down and sat down on the bed. Utah sat on the other side.

"Megan, wake up, honey," Riley said, feeling the girl's hand twitch again. Riley gave a slight squeeze to let her know they were there and glanced at Utah. Her face grew milky white. "Utah," interjected Riley. "Are you okay?"

"I had to be sure, Riley. I had to be sure you would never leave her," Utah's voice became almost hollow.

Riley felt a surge of panic, "Utah, what's going on?"

"You already know, Riley. I wish I could stay," she said. "I would've loved to have been your daughter too. I love you, Riley."

Then Riley knew. Utah had shown her, and all made sense to her.

"Utah," she murmured. "I can't do this without you."

"You already have Riley. Mama needs me now. She asked me to tell you to take good care of her baby. We've chosen right." Riley felt a deep ache in her heart, knowing all along Utah was special.

Nick stepped forward, wearing a look of confusion. He stared at Utah as if seeing her for the first time.

"Who are you?"

"Utah, Megan's sister. Thank you, Nick, for saving my sister." Utah spoke, her voice angelic. "Thank you for saving so many."

Nick stared at Utah, "Who are you?"

"Utah. I'm Megan's sister. I can reaffirm what you might question."

"Utah, what Steven did to you was horrible," Riley said softly.

Utah faced Riley.

Tears fell from Riley's eyes. "I'm so sorry, Utah. I love you both so much." Riley placed her white feather on Megan's chest. Utah reached out with her fading hand and extended her palm. There, too, sat a white feather.

"I love you too," she replied. "I will always be with you both. Believe me."

Riley blinked through the tears, and as Utah faded, Riley knew the journey they started together ended. Utah saw Megan and Riley through a turbulent journey starting the night Riley slept in the cranberry farmer's building. Their undying commitment to complete the trip to Prescott, Arizona, together should have been the end. Utah knew she could not stay. However, she'd remained until Riley was well and Megan awoke.

No more than a child, an older sister sheltered her younger sister from the cold, deceptive evil and hunger for days, even months, until they found Riley. As Megan woke, Utah's blue light started to drift away, and the two single white feathers began to fade.

The time past felt like an eternity since Megan, with big baby blue eyes framed by long eyelashes fluttering like butterflies, looked at Riley. Megan's eyes opened, and she smiled at Riley. Then pointing upward, she waved at Utah.

"Don't worry, Riley. She's always going to be with us."

66

By mid-March, the new ranch house neared completion. Lynn put her personal touch on it by way of flowers reminding Riley of the house on the hill where she stayed alone for too long. The memory remained a well-polished treasure of good and evil, a place of healing and loss. On occasion, she worried about Mark, not in the sense of his well-being, but instead, scared that if he were alive, he'd find her someday. To her advantage, there was no more internet, no instant way to research someone's address, and no social media.

Megan healed fast. Her recovery even astounded Nick. Riley often set an extra plate for Utah out of habit, and though she mourned the loss of the girl's presence, Utah would always be with her. Some of the phenomena on their journey to Arizona now made sense to Riley as she reflected back. Riley and Megan possessed the ability to see Utah, but having met Lucas and Slade made her uneasy. The unanswered question on how remained unsolved.

The day Megan woke, Nick saw Utah. He tried to tell the others, and they listened. Riley knew Jack heard her talk to Utah, saying her name on several occasions. He never questioned Riley, probably chalking it up to the stress, too many confrontations with crazy people, and bullets.

I would've thought I was crazy, too, her inner voice told her.

They would have had to see Utah in order to believe. The others believed Megan created an imaginary friend, Utah, not unusual for children under stress.

As for Ringo, no one had seen him hide, or hair and the unknowing kept Riley and the others on edge.

As time passed, the Colton ranch saw the coming of spring. One warm day in March, a slight breeze stirred, the cloudless sky a cerulean blue. Riley ran a little behind the horse's exercise schedule. The day was bustling with activity, and when she saw Jack on the way to the barn, she paused. Sweaty and working up on the roof with the men he hired.

"Good morning!" she called out, moving on toward the barn.

"Nice day for a ride," Jack walked up behind her making her jump.

"You scared me," she exclaimed, taking a deep breath. "I just saw you on the roof."

Lynn walked out of the tack room, wearing a modest grin. Tethered in the breezeway was Lynn's horse Baily and Jack's horse Sam. Riley felt a setup coming.

Jack leaned against the closest stall, chewing on a piece of straw. How many men could look so sexy, wearing a worn t-shirt and dusty jeans? A weathered cowboy hat sat low over his face, almost hiding the two-day shadow on his chin. He lowered his sunglasses on his nose enough for her to see his eyes. So there he stood, looking at her, all badass and cowboy-like.

Now there's your cowboy!

"He put me up to it," Lynn handed Jack the reins. "I saddled Baily for you."

Riley chuckled. "Thanks. You should go with us."

"I can't. Busy," Lynn grinned.

"What about the other horses?"

"I got it," Lynn said, winking. "I think my brother likes you a lot."

"My sister forgets how good my hearing is." Jack stood, watching them.

Riley led Baily out the double doors, Jack followed.

"Okay, you have my full attention." Riley climbed on the mare.

They rode a short way from the ranch, Jack leading Riley across a sloping valley framed by a ridgeline seen only at a distance. They rode next to each other in silence, listening to the sound of the horse's hooves on the sand and rock. The tranquility of riding didn't take long to ease her nerves.

"I didn't know you could ride so well, but I been watching you," he commented.

"I was six when I rode my first pony."

"Eric ride too?"

"Motorcycles. He rode when mom wouldn't let me go by myself." The sun warmed her face, and the warmth felt good.

"You're parents, they're...,"

"Dead. All that's left is Eric and me."

"You know a lot about us, but we know little about you."

Riley felt her heart quicken, and then she calmed herself. Riley had nothing to be ashamed of other than picking a loser as her husband. The only skeletons in her closet bore the name Mark.

"You're right. You can ask me anything, but you might not like all of it."

"What's your favorite color?"

Riley grinned, "That's not what you want to ask me."

"You're married?" he asked, getting the most important question out of the way.

"Yes. Eric told you?"

"Where is he?"

NOT ALONE

"I don't know. It sounds horrible, but I hope he's dead. I was leaving him when the Shift happened."

"Why?"

"He deceived me, hurt me, cheated on me, and lied to me," Riley gazed up toward the sky. "Eric wanted me to leave him a long time ago. I was waiting for a deputy's position in Prescott, but then the Shift happened."

"He told me, but I wanted to hear your side of it from you, I guess."

Riley told him about Mark in a short version because there wasn't much to say about the man. They told each other their stories while keeping the conversation light. They laughed and joked. Jack grew quiet as she told him about the night the Shift happened and the events that followed, leading up to her arrival here. She told him about how the girls became stowaways and some of their adventures.

They stopped by a narrow creek dividing the meadow into two portions, letting the horses drink and rest. The surrounding land consisted of high desert and open skies, but greener plant life and flowers flourished where the stream ran. On the horizon, snowy peaks lined with taller trees and steep rocks completed God's handy work into something picture-perfect.

"How come I feel like I know you?" she asked.

Jack said nothing, leaning back on his elbows, blending into the tall grass. He rested his hat on his knee. She did the same, but she let the grass fold in around her body, picking an occasional flower while melting into the warmth of the sun as the pedals tickled her skin. The sky looked down on them, and they upon the endless blue space, watching the parade of clouds float by.

A mass of cotton formed overhead, resembling an angel. Trying to remember those last days before the Shift, Riley followed the silhouette until the cluster pulled apart and turned into something else.

She waited for him as he moved closer to her. Patient. Still saying nothing, he began unbuttoning her shirt. With deliberate slowness, he allowed her time to withdraw. Instead, she pulled him to her, and they kissed with an unseen hypnotic pull. Warmth spread through her body, developing into a slow ache. The heat between them formed an indestructible union, and while lingering fear escaped her, a new concern began.

They could not get close enough with such tenderness and care, ignoring grass and sand, sunlight, and water. Jack pulled back just far enough to finish unbuttoning her flannel shirt. He slid the material off her shoulders, exposing the black lace bra he'd seen before. Lingering fingertips traced her shoulder, sliding up to her neck, pulling her slowly, kissing her so tenderly, she felt intoxicated.

Now with her body on fire, Jack reached back, peeling away the last of her clothes. Neither of them wanted to hurry. There was no stopping what they both felt. Riley pulled on his shirt as he touched her. Her body screamed with urgency the more he teased her.

Their bodies intertwined in gentle play. Riley and Jack both grew impatient for what had been building for so long. Ecstasy teetered on madness as their lovemaking grew to a long-awaited unleashing of lust and foreplay. Under the attack of erotic play, Riley released all of herself to Jack, who followed her. Skin exposed, covered in sweat, Riley rested her head on Jack's chest, over his racing heart. Something told Riley this man would forever be her protector, and she Jacks if ever the time rose.

67

Trouble always sent out a warning. Riley tried to ignore what they all knew was coming. She was no good at waiting when trouble was knocking on the door. They all expected Ringo to make a show, and that made for a restless group of people. Riley sensed the storm of fury and hatred coming, and the knowledge made her feel edgy.

She just finished working out the last horse when she heard a truck approaching quickly.

"Eric," she said in a soft tone.

Jack stepped through the front door out onto the unfinished porch to watch the approaching truck. Ryan parked, meeting Jack, where the two moved into the unfinished house, leaving her to try to catch up to them.

Ringo's face popped into her memory, and for the first time in several weeks of forgetting, she wanted him gone. Lynn stepped in from the kitchen at the same time Riley entered but at opposite ends.

"What's going on?" asked Riley.

Lynn shrugged her shoulders, "let's go find out."

Eric's words commanded Jack and Ryan's attention, but the conversation grew quiet when she and Lynn entered the room.

"Hi, sis," he hugged her. "You're looking good."

"Thanks. I feel good," Riley felt a surge of concern for the tone of the conversation. She and Lynn stopped. "What's wrong?"

Silence fell.

"What's wrong?" repeated Riley.

"Amy was found dead yesterday," Eric murmured.

The room turned quiet again.

"Who...?" Lynn stopped and looked at Jack. "Ringo?"

Riley felt her heart drop. A slow-burning sensation crept into her cheeks, not just angry but fearful.

"He left a calling card," Eric handed a note to Jack.

"Let the games begin," Jack read aloud. "Games?"

"Childs play," Ryan murmured.

"He'll kill us one at a time," insisted Riley.

"Amy's car was found in the alley of the Desert Sportsman," Eric said, lowering his voice. "In a dumpster."

"Oh my God," Lynn's face paled.

Riley stopped pacing, and her face grew even warmer. "He's been here the entire time. Watching. Waiting."

Jack said nothing, but the look on his face expressed enough.

"He's on a mission, but this time, it's different."

"Blake and Matt are with Shay, Jonah, and Terra. I have Sherry over at Scott's place. I sent John and Jeremy to pick up the twins."

"Anyone see him?" asked Ryan.

Eric nodded, "no."

"Good thinking on the women and children's behalf," Jack's tone remained calm.

"What about the wedding," Riley asked Eric.

"Shay wants to go through with it," he said.

"You know that's the perfect storm," Jack said in a low tone. "It's bringing us all together in one place."

"I know, but it might be a perfect chance to draw him out and end it." Eric paused, but Riley doubted Eric liked the idea himself.

"That's not a wedding you want," Jack suggested. "I don't think it's wise to use you two as bait and especially on your wedding day. Talk some sense into your brother Riley."

"Jack's right," Riley agreed. "What if he brings twenty men with him? It'd be a giant bloodbath instead of a wedding. Is that what you want to remember? If any of us even make it?"

"We want to be married. We can't make up for lost time, but we sure as hell can make good of the time we have now."

"Wait," Riley pleaded. "Or have a quiet ceremony. I think Jack's right. It's bringing everyone together."

"What if we can't end it? How long will we have to wait?" Eric asked, his eyes meeting Riley's. She knew he wanted her support. "Think of it this way. There's going to be more manpower and more gun power at our wedding than anywhere else. He'd be crazy to mess with us there."

"I don't want to lose you or Shay or anyone. You're all I have left." Riley said.

"Damn it, Eric, listen to your sister," Jack said in a soft tone.

"We've waited long enough." He looked at Jack. "We have a few weeks before the wedding." Eric paused, and then he grinned, but with a twist to express his hatred for Ringo, "anyone up for a little hunting?"

"Tell no one until the day of the wedding. Not knowing might be enough to throw him off." Jack paused, waiting for Eric to think about it. "I have a bullet with his name on it, and it's getting dusty."

"That's funny. I have a bullet with Ringo's name on it too." Eric raised his eyebrows, but then his expression softened. "Okay, we'll have a shotgun wedding. Happy?"

"Sort of," Riley replied.

"I'm sorry. I know you understand." Eric kissed her on the forehead. "You know Shay has a room ready for you."

"I know," she said, hugging him.

Ben strolled into the room with his shotgun slung over his shoulder.

"That horse's ass Ringo is going to make a mistake, and it'll only take one shot to end it," Ben said. "So everyone stop looking so gloomy. We have a new house to finish and a wedding to attend." The old man looked around, grunting, "looks real, nice, Jack."

"Thanks, pop."

"Hey, I heard old Randall has the phones working in town," Ben said with excitement.

Lynn chuckled. "Great!"

"Got to go," Eric patted Jack on the shoulder. "They'll be a service for Amy the day after tomorrow. Eleven at the Prescott Memorial."

"Thanks, Eric," Riley said. "Be safe. I love you."

"I love you too, Sis," he called out as he left. She said nothing until the sound of his truck faded.

"Trouble's coming," she whispered. "More than likely, Ringo already knows about the wedding."

She and Jack stood in the living room, the same place that Ringo had stood demanding possession of Jonah before the explosion. She turned to face Jack and their gazes locked.

68

A day before the wedding, the Colton family moved into their new home. When the workers left, the ranch turned quiet. She counted three patients coming and going that morning from Nick's new office and a pizza delivery from Margret's Pizza. Therefore, when the fourth car pulled up and two people stepped out, one appearing wounded, she assumed the man to be another patient.

The afternoon had barely come and gone, and the horses seemed restless as they often were before dinner. Sun Dancer, her Friesian mare, had birthed a healthy colt and anxiously stomped her hooves against the sawdust floor. At the same time, Pistol, oblivious to everything, but playtime, stood near his mother, nipping and pushing. Riley, distracted by Piston, who proceeded to show off, soaked up his playful mood until she heard a loud pop, and then a car starting and peeling out of the drive.

Recognizing the sound of gunfire, Riley whirled away from mare and foal and rushed through the breezeway of stalls past Ben, who moved toward Nick's office as well. Not entering but instead holding close to the wall near the door, she motioned Ben to hang back. Quiet-like, she entered, keeping her footfalls soft and gun to the front of her.

A dark-haired man lay sprawled out on the floor. Blood pooled under him and then forked left and right through the grout like narrow rivers. Riley's eyes flew to where Nick sat buckled over against the counter. Blood covered his hands and shirt, and a layer of sweat speckled his brow.

"Nick," Riley fell to her knees. "Where are you hit?"

"My shoulder. Son of a bitch came in here like he needed help."

Ryan pressed through the door with his pistol drawn. Riley jumped at his footfalls, reacted, pulling her gun on Ryan. They quickly lowered their guns, turning their attention on Nick.

"There were two!" Riley pointed at the dead man bleeding out on the floor. "One got away."

"You got this?" Ryan asked Riley.

Riley nodded. Ryan rushed past her out the door.

"Breathe slow, Nick. I need you to try to relax."

Ben looked at Riley and Nick and then the dead man. "I thought you were supposed to heal the patients, not kill them."

"Get Lynn," Riley instructed, but she was already charging through the door. Her hair and t-shirt were wet from a shower cut short. Standing behind her, Megan and Lily burrowed near her like warned baby quail.

"Nick!" she shouted.

"Help me get him up on the table," Riley urged, but Lynn stood still, a horrified look on her face. "Lynn," Riley yelled out.

"Take the girls, Dad," Lynn motioned her father to take the kids out of the room.

Lynn and Riley hoisted Nick up. He reached down and tore away his shirt and jacket. "Did it go through?" Nick asked. They looked underneath him as he leaned forward.

"It went clean through," Riley answered, pressing her hand into his shoulder to stop the bleeding.

"Press hard," Nick said, wounded and still playing the doctor.

Riley knelt next to the man on the floor, feeling for a pulse. She shook her head no and grabbed up towels and a bottle of antiseptic, tossing them to Lynn.

"What the hell?" Nick clenched his teeth. "I didn't see that one coming."

"It was a setup," Riley worked to slow the bleeding, her t-shirt soaking up Nick's blood. "You're lucky to be alive."

"It's time to get some tactical training from Jack and the boys," Nick proposed.

"Why? Good shooting," Riley teased Nick. "You got a taste of the fight now."

"Good, now you can play doctor. There's a surgical pack in that cupboard," Nick pointed. He rotated his shoulder. "I think the bullet missed the bone. Nothing's broken."

"I'm getting pretty good at fishing for bullets and stitching things up," Riley said, remembering the excellent job she did on Ringo, "son of a bitch."

"Not you. Ringo."

Riley reached in, grabbing several sealed packages.

"So, you've done this before?" Lynn asked.

"Ringo made me stitch him up. Then he tried to feed me to the tigers," Riley said, holding up the packages. "I dug a bullet, my bullet, out of that assholes arm." When it came to Ringo's name, all restrictions were off in the cursing category.

Lynn pulled the towel off. "Better you do this, then." She stepped over to a locked cabinet, gathered a few supplies, and then handed Nick a vial and needle. "Suppose you want to do this yourself?"

He nodded, poking the needle into the vial, withdrawing fluid, and then gave himself a shot near the wound in the flesh. "Okay, stitch the flesh front and back."

The sound of Jack's truck pulling up close to the office door caused them to turn. As he stepped in, he glanced at the dead guy on the floor.

"Your brother-in-law's been initiated into the fight club," Lynn informed Jack.

"You okay, Nick?" Jack asked.

"I'm good. You?" asked Nick, his sense of humor intact. "He called in yesterday, made an appointment, showed up today, and pulled out a gun. I should've known when I didn't recognize the name."

"Did he say anything else?" asked Jack.

"He said Ringo wants what's his." Nick gritted his teeth as Riley stuck the needle near the wound.

"You'd better do a good job. Nick's a perfectionist," Jack said, teasing Riley.

"Great. No pressure," Riley said, sitting on the doctor's stool up and personal with Nick's shoulder. Lynn grinned, cleaning the blood away. "Find something for pain?"

Nick pointed. Jack grabbed the vial and a syringe.

"Lynn? Just look for a good..." Nick started to say, but Lynn stopped him.

"I've done this before, Nick."

"Did you get the right stuff?" Nick asked Lynn, who gave him a look only a wife could give a husband, and then held up the vial for him to read.

Ryan stepped through the door, shaking his head, "nothing."

"Who's been helping you all these years? Geeze." Lynn turned back to her husband.

"No arguing, you two," Riley said, pulling another stitch through. Nick's shirt darkened with sweat.

"Anytime would be good, honey. Press slow."

"Another word, and you get to do it," teased Lynn.

Nick smiled at her.

"That should keep you quiet for a little while," Lynn said with a smile. "Anybody got questions for him. He'll be painfully honest now."

"Almost done," replied Riley. "Grab some bandages, and I'll finish him up. Maybe a clean set of clothes. For me too."

Lynn came back with clean clothes as Riley put in the last stitch. "I think I'll step out while you do this part." Riley washed her hands and stepped out.

Free of blood-soaking clothes, Riley gazed at the one constant thing, the sun making a steady descent on the horizon. The temperature dropped a few degrees sending a slight chill across her skin. The desert breeze cooled her flushed face. Warm because Jack Colton sat so near to her. His long legs draped over the edge of the porch, dangling. A darkly wrapped cigar sat between his teeth. The smoke curled and then looped around, finding a ghostly trail toward her, mild and rich.

"He's coming," Jack said.

"I know," she said in a low tone, and as much as she tried, she couldn't dismiss a feeling of the impending danger coming their way. "There's so much space out here. He could be anywhere."

"He's a narcissist. A limelighter. He'll show," he said, looking over at her. "If it's not Ringo, it'll be someone else and someone after him."

"I know. How do you know so much about psychology?"

"I took some classes," he grinned.

Jack lifted his arm, and she slid under it. "This is a beautiful place."

They sat there for a moment, saying nothing. Shadows elongated, and the radiance of the sky turned slightly red. Riley glanced over at the barn, hearing one of the horses stir. She saw the tiger slinking alongside the bunkhouse toward the barn. Riley jumped to her feet, almost taking Jack's arm off. She stumbled, making a clattering sound on the porch. The tiger turned, emerald eyes set on her.

"Jack."

"Move slowly and go into the house," he ordered, snubbing out the cigar.

"The girls."

"Get inside."

She stepped through the door backward.

"What's wrong?" Lynn asked, standing up.

"Tiger," Riley muttered. "Where're the girls? Where's Ryan?"

"The girls are upstairs," Lynn, needing assurance disappeared up the stairs. Ryan rushed into the room, brushing past her and out the door. Tank and Sadie rose from their new beds, following Ryan.

"I wouldn't go out there," Riley watched him go. The dogs began barking.

"Ringo," she whispered.

Lynn moved toward the vault. Riley followed her, entering the steel-sided chamber accessed only by a keypad. The door opened, and the room lit up. They grabbed the tranquilizer gun from a locked container and a handful of tranquilizer darts.

"Cat took off. We locked the horses in their stalls and left the dogs in the barn to watch over them." Jack said from behind.

Riley handed him the tranquilizer gun. "I'm heading back to the barn."

"I think you should stay in the house tonight," suggested Jack.

"The horses," Riley smiled at him. "Good try, but no."

"Megan can stay," Lynn added, "they're upstairs playing. I checked."

"Okay," Riley nodded in agreeance.

"If you don't stay here, then I am going to sleep over there," said Jack, gathering several more guns.

"No," Riley returned. "I'll be okay. Anyway, I will have the dogs with me."

"Too bad. It's my place."

"Do you always get your way?"

"Always," Lynn said in a sisterly tone. "Even when we were little."

"I really don't want to hurt Elmo," Jack said.

"Elmo, can't we rename him. Something like "Shadow" or "Warrick," frowned Riley. "no wonder that cat is so pissed off. Speaking of cats, I need to check on Max."

"Elmo isn't embarrassed by his name," Jack changed the subject back on Elmo.

"I'm embarrassed for him," Lynn replied. "Who names a tiger after a sesame street character?"

"I like Elmo," Ryan butted in.

"You can call him whatever you want. I'm calling him Warrick." Riley grinned, feeling satisfied for giving the tiger a new name.

"What does that even mean?" asked Jack. "Bet you don't know."

"A strong leader who defends. English," Riley answered. "I went to school too. Anyway, the cat is getting a bad rap because of Ringo. The tiger didn't eat me, and I got a distinct feeling; he didn't like Ringo in the slightest."

"At least we know where Ringo's been," Ryan suggested. "We made sure all the loose animals on Pam's property were contained, so he's been back to the conservatory. He's using them as a distraction and a warning."

"It didn't work," Jack replied. "That means he probably killed the caretaker again?"

Ryan nodded. "I'll take a look. Blake can go with me. He's been itching to get out of the house."

"I'm ready when you are," Jack said to Riley.

Riley sighed, crossing her arms, "Hope you fit on that couch."

Lynn chuckled.

69

Riley admired the evening sky that turned into a montage of cool purples and oranges enveloping Prescott in a bouquet of color for Eric and Shay's. Several of Eric and Shay's guests stood outside the Inn, making small talk and stealing a smoke before the ceremony began. A soft, warm wind stirred the spring air, a gentle reminder that summer drew near.

Riley spotted Jack, who was busy placing men at all the entrances. Jack had security at a maximum level, covering Eric and Shay's big day to the best of his ability. Ringo killed Amy, meaning he was hiding out somewhere close, and that meant being vigilant. Jack had spared no manpower to secure the venue, but in times of chaos, the risk was high.

The interior of the prized chosen historical Inn was beautiful. Because of the much-needed security, the ballroom turned out to be the best selection because of the room's size. Riley loved the inn, which was safeguarded from the townspeople's trespassers by teamwork. The red brick building was the perfect venue for Eric and Shay's wedding.

Jack, looking devilishly handsome, sat down next to her in time for Shays entry. Riley let a few tears fall in those moments of exchanged vows but only because she knew how much both Shay and Eric had endured. The actual ceremony ended quickly, and as the pastor pronounced Eric and Shay man and wife, the guests cheered and bellowed out a few whistles. Jonah climbed up into Eric's arms, hugging his father as Shay held tight to Eric. In those moments, Riley knew Eric would never allow anyone to hurt his family ever again.

Afterward, Riley found a quiet space where she could sip on a glass of champagne and survey the room, searching for anything or anyone out of the ordinary. Trust was not her best trait. Most of these people were still strangers to her. The men in their tuxedos and women in their best dresses delightfully entertained Riley as they danced across the floor. Here and now, it was as if nothing outside the walls were amiss.

"I'd tell you that you are the most beautiful woman in the room, but that wouldn't be fair to the bride," Jack said.

Riley grinned, turning to face him. Maybe the smile she wore a bit mischievous, but by the look on his face, he liked it.

"Thank you, Jack. You look rather handsome yourself," she returned the compliment, but in the short time she knew Jack, he had yet to look bad regardless of what he wore, and she guessed even on his worst day, he still looked good.

"The wedding was beautiful," Jack said. "I smell a room full of gunpowder." Jack grinned. "Where are you hiding yours, Miss Riley?"

She blushed, "wouldn't you like to know?"

Kate saved her by pulling her away, leaving Jack to think about where her gun might be. Dressing for a post-apocalyptic wedding meant getting creative about keeping your gun close when not in full military gear. Especially when you know an attack is imminent. Thanks to her wardrobe assistant Lynn, she'd pulled it off.

Over the next few hours, champagne and drinks flowed, and people's spirits heightened. Laughter intertwined with the humming of music and conversation.

"Riley, have you seen Shay?" Eric asked anxiously.

"She was talking to Dan. Why is everything okay?"

"I can't find her. She said she left something for me on her desk at the paper. When I turned around, she was gone".

"You don't think she would have left the Inn?"

"I hope not," Eric answered.

"Let me check the little girl's room first before we get too concerned. You guys find Dan. I'm sure she's here somewhere," insisted Riley, suddenly and secretively sensing the presence of evil.

Riley checked all the rooms. No Shay.

She hurried back toward Ryan and Eric. No Shay, and the joy in the air morphed into a skin-prickling tension. She found Jack talking with Dan.

"Have you seen Shay?" Riley asked urgently.

"She was here ten minutes ago," Jack replied.

"Eric said she told him she left his present at the Newspaper office."

Scott hurried toward them as they moved outside to the front of the inn, "I don't mean to spoil the party, but there was an incident at the hospital."

Jack said nothing, waiting for Scott's news.

"Sherry was found dead," he murmured.

Jack furrowed his eyebrows, undoubtedly upset while staying in control. "Ringo's here."

"I gotta find Shay. She has to be at the office," Eric said. "You'd better let the others know what's going on." Eric looked around, shaking his head. "My truck is gone? Shift's with her."

"Let's go," Jack already had his keys in his hand. Riley stepped in to follow, but he stopped her. "Nope."

"I'm going."

"I wish you wouldn't," Jack said sternly.

"You're going to need me if anything happened to Shay," she whispered. "It'll be okay. I'll stay behind you."

NOT ALONE

"Promise," he asked.

"I promise."

They left the reception in an unorthodox hurry as Jack drove fast toward the Prescott Times. Jack wasn't all the way parked when Eric jumped out of the truck. A soft glow of light penetrated through the thin cream Venetian blinds, showering out onto the sidewalk. Jack got out, and Riley followed.

Not a soul wandered the streets, not even a rat. A gust of night air thrust an empty can forward, pushing the tin and forcing a tumble action down the vacant pavement in a series of acrobatic rolls. Above them, the newspaper's sign swung and creaked. Still, they listened as an eerie silence fell over the city and as something far more sinister than the sounds of the night called. Then a dog's muffled cry sliced through the screen of silence.

"Shift," Eric said, leading the way around the back of the building. Shift rose to her haunches and scratched at the truck's window, letting out a strand of distressed howls.

Eric reached up, let the dog out, stepping back as she raced through the cracked back door and disappeared.

"Careful, Eric," Jack warned, but Eric disappeared inside the building.

Riley started forward, but Jack caught her, holding her back.

Eric's cries resonated out into the street, desperate and despairing.

"Jack," cried Riley.

Eric called out Shay's name several times, his words declaring more anguish each time.

Jack pushed through the first door and then the second, not allowing Riley through. Holding onto Jack's coat with her casted hand, she clenched material tight between her fingers.

In her hand, Riley's pistol quivered. Jack took a deep breath and then slowly stepped aside.

Eric knelt beside Shay. Blood covered his hands and white shirt. Still kneeling, Eric bundled Shay in his arms, his fingers stroking her hair and around her face. Her dress no longer beige but smeared with blood. Riley lost her breath in shock. Her body trembled.

Not far from Shay lay one of Ringo's men. Someone had cut his chest open. Where the man's heart used to be, a black hole gaped open. The entire room looked like a horror flick gone bad. Blood splattered the floors and walls.

Riley fought back nausea as her heart ached, the symptoms and emotions of losing someone you love. Riley felt an instant emptiness, a death kissed cold and by immediate loneliness. Jack stood behind Riley, who stood behind Eric, helpless. Shay's wedding dress no longer a symbol of love and devotion. Instead, if violence and destruction. Eric pressed Shay into him.

Riley, dizzy with grief, caught sight of the present bound in gold ribbon sitting on the desk. An envelope propped up against it with Eric's name and a blood handprint too big to be Shay's.

Riley blinked, her head swimming in disbelief and confusion, but for the better of her brother, she found the strength to act. She pushed past Jack and went to Eric, putting her hand on his shoulder. Having lost Shay once, now he'd lost her twice. Riley lifted the package and envelope in her hands, setting them in Jack's arm. She leaned down toward Eric and whispered one word.

"Jonah."

Eric stopped trembling, understanding.

No one hurried Eric from Shay's side. After all, nothing could save her from the death that had already taken her, the healthy, vibrant woman who survived after being feared dead lay silent.

Riley's gut ached, and she knew Ringo was watching. Being Eric's twin, Riley felt his struggle of what to do next. Remain beside his wife or go after Ringo? Riley also felt her brother's rage.

Eric took a deep breath, reached out. Laying his fingers on Shay's eyelids, he closed them. He then took off his jacket and placed the folded material under her head.

Riley stood up.

Eric glanced down at the pistol in his hand. He gazed at Shay a long moment and then at Jack and Riley. A hint of defeat hid under Eric's sorrowful expression, fading after one breath, two breaths, and then gone entirely. Eric's eyes cleared. They stood in the violent scene, unmoving as unspoken words buried in Eric's soul screamed silent. Except for Riley, she heard them. Ringo's crimes warranted punishment.

Riley would not want to be in Ringo's shoes because her brother would go after him. The hunted was about to turn hunter, and the prey was about to be executed.

Eric paused, standing beside Riley. His face down. He didn't look at her or speak to her. No words justified such a vehement act. Riley acknowledged in silence the acceptance of what Eric must do, and then her brother stepped out the door, gone.

"Maybe I shouldn't have let him go," Riley said, turning, but Jack stopped her.

"He needs you to do this for him," Jack said, holding her in place. "Do you hear what I'm saying to you, Riley?" he asked.

"Yes," Riley responded, but numbness crawled through her along with fear of losing her brother.

NOT ALONE

Jack rubbed his forehead, looking at Shay. "Riley. Jonah is going to need you." Jack held Riley's shoulders gently, and she caught herself from falling apart. She took a much-needed breath to allow oxygen into her throbbing brain.

"I will watch over him. I promise, Riley." Jack's words brought her back to the present.

Riley shook her head.

Jack left her side, looking around the office, searching. He picked up several of the phones on the desks, but she guessed they were dead. He tried each of them. "Where's a working phone when you need one?"

The sound of footfalls approaching caused Jack and Riley to both turn weapons drawn and aimed. Ryan, Scott, and Blake stepped through the door, locked and loaded. Jack and Riley lowered their guns.

"We just saw Eric and Shift running down the street," Blake said but stopped when he saw the entirety of the scene. "What the hell happened?"

"Oh my God," Scott gazed down at Shay. "Shay!"

"Jack needs to go. Can you guys help me with Shay?" Riley said, sounding choked up, or perhaps her tone sounded trite in contrast to the blood spilled on the floor, on Shay's dress.

Jack glanced at his brother.

Ryan nodded.

Jack sprinted out of the building.

Ryan stepped in next to Riley, putting his hand on her arm. Together they knelt next to Shay.

70

Eric caught sight of Ringo and ran. He tried to shove the visions of Shay and all the blood to the back of his mind, but he could not. Blood on her dress, on his hands, and forever ingrained in his memory branded by an evildoer like Ringo. The anger raging inside him made him tremble, not with fear but with eagerness. Shay had only been dead two hours when he saw the giant strolling through the alley between Fifth and North Ridge Avenue. Ringo's broad shoulders and lengthy stature, cloaked in black, almost looked invisible. Slinking through dark alleys and narrow streets, Ringo drifted in one house and out of another. He guessed the man, if a man at all, was bloodthirsty and hunting for more victims. Eric watched Ringo, prominent in stature, did not move like an ox but rather graceful and with stealth-like strides.

"If you're not a man, what are you?" Eric thought as he followed him, keeping his distance.

They moved through dark alleys, even jumped over razor-wired fencing like height was nothing. Somehow, Ringo slipped between gates with little space for even Eric to pass. Unknowing Eric was closing on him, Ringo wove in and out of the city's streets unconstrained. Eric knew how to be invisible, using the night as a shield and the moon as his guide. With great patience that would drive any sane person insane, Eric waited for one chance to introduce himself, unaccompanied, to Ringo as his reaper.

As the wind picked up and the shadows of the night pirouetted around Eric, he became one with the darkness. Being far more methodical than Ringo, Eric also proved to be more dangerous and calculating than his enemy. The only advantage Ringo had over Eric was size and the lack of morals.

Animosity would carry Eric past any disadvantages. He would use hatred to inflict whatever means of violence necessary while never losing control.

Eric, deep in the shadows, watched Ringo, formulating in his mind plans for the hunter, which, to some, might seem far too radical to comprehend. The tranquilizer gun lay over his shoulder. A dart loaded into the chamber and the safety off.

He watched Ringo step back into an alley, pausing to reach into his shirt pocket and withdraw a cigarette. The glow of the flame from the lighter cast a shallow light on his face. The smoke drifted into the wind and blew in Eric's direction. A few puffs later, Ringo tossed the cigarette, suspicious, glanced around as if smelling a threat. Then he slipped back into the folds of the night where shadows turned to imagined apparitions.

Eric moved in the direction where Ringo had stood. Pausing, he stared at the cigarette. While smoke lingered in the air, he closed his eyes and listened until he heard movement. The emptiness in Shay's lifeless eyes flashed in his mind bringing a surge of anguish. Another sound.

Eric caught sight of Ringo, who stopped on occasion to listen. Then he headed for a black Denali parked behind the old River Tavern. Eric brought the rifle up to his cheek, placing the crosshairs on Ringo's back. The rules of the hunt, if there were any, were about to change. Just as he pulled the trigger, the light inside the vehicle came on. The dart hit Ringo in the back with a thud.

Ringo spun around, surprised to see Eric standing calmly, and then his expression changed. Ringo was worried.

"What the fuck?" an older man in the driver's seat shouted.

Eric stepped from the shadows of the alley out into the night breeze. Adrenaline surged through him, overriding the visions of Shay's death.

"Pop, Pop."

The silencer on the tip of his pistol impeded the sound of the shot. The man's words faltered as the first shot hit him in the chest, and the second ended his life. Eric moved forward, his pistol aimed at the two crumpled bodies lying in the alley in front of him. He knelt beside the man he'd shot and felt for a pulse. Blood pooled on the pavement.

The air turned electric. Eric stood looking down at Ringo. Eric wasn't surprised when Ringo reached out and grabbed Eric by the leg. Hell, he was glad. Quick to recover, Eric slammed the gun down on Ringo's skull. The blow knocked Ringo out only for a second. Eric jumped back.

"Come on, pretty boy. A tranquilizer gun? Really?" Ringo growled, rolling to his side. Ringo looked at Eric. "Let's get this over with so I can retrieve the biggest prize of all."

"You can't have Jonah, and you never will."

Eric already had the second dart between his fingertips. Ringo climbed unsteadily on his feet. Somewhere in the predawn obscurity, a gust of wind found its way through the deserted alley. The wind caught Ringo's coat, making him appear taller.

"I don't want the boy. I want your twin sister." Ringo snarled. "If we are going to play, then let's play fair," he laughed at Eric.

Eric had a pistol in one hand and a dart in the other, weapons to sedate the snake attacking him. Ringo hurled all his weight toward Eric. The knife reflected off the streetlight from above. The tranquilizer in his bloodstream affected Ringo's speed and balance, but the big man fought it well. Ringo swung the knife, but Eric kicked the blade out of Ringo's hand.

Eric hit him with the second dart, but not before Ringo landed a hard fist to the side of Eric's head. Ringo went in one direction and Eric the other, but this time Ringo lay still on the cement.

"Son of a bitch," Eric said through clenched teeth. About to reach for Ringo's shoulders, he heard footsteps and spun around.

"Kid," Jack stepped out of the shadows. Eric lowered his gun. He turned back toward Ringo. "What's the plan?"

"You might not want to be a part of this one, Jack," Eric moved toward Ringo.

"Looks like you need some help, and I'm pretty sure I've been a part of this from the start." Jack reached down, grabbing Ringo by the feet. Eric took his arms. They carried him to the Denali, heaving him into the rear of the vehicle.

"Okay, but don't say I didn't warn you," Eric answered.

"Ties?" Jack asked.

"Nah! He has enough tranquilizers in him to knock out a horse," Eric shoved his bag into the driver's seat.

Jack glanced over at the dead man. "I hate it when people leave trash in the streets. When does trash pickup come around?"

They picked the deadweight up and swung him into a dumpster in the alley. A mouse darted out from underneath, dove, and then disappeared.

"We have thirty minutes, maybe." Eric climbed into the Denali.

Jack went silent. There were no words.

Eric put the keys in the ignition and then paused. "Where's Riley?"

"With Blake and Ryan. She's safe."

"She won't like what I'm about to do," Eric said, starting the engine.

"So, don't tell her."

"Agreed?" Eric looked out the window.

"Agreed."

They entered an extreme quietness moving further away from town and into the desert. Eric veered onto Highway 66 and headed toward the conservatory. Eric's inner voice tossed around possible solutions, but there were none other than the one he planned. Shay kept entering his mind. The years they lost, taking Riley hostage, the blood, their son, and the fact he'd never get to tell her how much he loved her ever again gave him no other choice.

Jack rummaged through the glove box producing a Sig 40, a wad of cash, and a bag full of jewelry. Setting them aside, Jack grabbed Ringo's bag from the back seat and emptied it onto his lap. He withdrew several sealed baggies of a white powder, drug paraphernalia, and a few tools covered in blood.

"Jesus," Jack said.

With that said, Jack rolled down his window. He took out a pocketknife and made a deep cut into the plastic bags. Then he emptied them into the open air. A white stream of drugs trailed the Denali as Jack unloaded all the bags. Eric sped up.

"That'll piss him off," Eric remarked.

"Yeah! It was my pleasure," Jack replied, letting the fresh air into the Denali. He checked his watch. It was three in the morning. Before long, the sun would begin its ascent up into the western sky. Numbness set in. Only last night, Shay and Eric had plans of being together forever. Jack knew what he would do if he were in Eric's shoes.

71

Predawn neared as the white Siberian Tiger paced back and forth in her cage. Giant paws thudded on the desert floor. Well, past feeding time, the tiger grew hungry. The big cat licked her lips, her tongue rolling over her pink nose as she pulled strands of whiskers back with her tongue. Her blue eyes never left Jack. As the cat spoke, she slunk backward, pulling her lips up into a snarl. Intentionally, she exposed her bloodstained teeth, which were part of the well-oiled 485-pound meat-grinding machine. Jack backed up, giving the tiger room. On the other side and in the middle of the cat's territory sat Ringo with feet and hands bound. Eric stood a few feet from him.

Jack saw the irony in the act, and sadly, he could not find any reason to argue. Jack called to the tiger and then tossed a chunk of meat through the feeding gate. The mass rolled down onto the ground and stopped in front of the cat. He wished Eric would hurry because Ringo was beginning to wake. Jack washed the meat off his hands under a nearby faucet and then picked up his rifle.

The tiger turned and looked at Ringo, who, for now, was unaware of his coming fate.

"He tried to feed me to the tiger." Riley's voice entered Jack's thoughts. What Ringo had done to her and Shay, Amy, Sherry kept Jack from stopping Eric now?

Eric moved around the tiger's enclosure from side to side, the five-gallon bucket in his hand heavy with meat. He let small amounts of the blood and chopped-up pieces fall to the ground to tease the cat's senses.

The tiger's space consisted of an enclosed yard with a solid, twelve-foot chain-link fence, landscaped with trees and boulders for a natural look. Tangled razor wire trimmed the barrier's top, assuring neither man nor cat could get out. Eric finished laying down the appetizers while making sure the cat's enclosure stayed secure.

Jack looked down at his watch. Riley should still be resting. He hoped Nick had given her something to assure she'd sleep longer and not come looking for them. The minute those blue eyes opened, she'd be worried.

Jack tossed the stick he'd been whittling on and checked on Eric. He was still wearing his white button-up shirt soaked with Shay's blood. From where Jack sat, he saw the strong resemblance of Riley. Jack knew guys like Eric, deadly as the big cat and twice as clever as the devil. Ringo would come to realize, even if too late, he'd messed with the wrong man.

NOT ALONE

All of a sudden, the devil woke up, and Ringo's evil laughter pierced the early morning air. The sound sent a prickling chill across Jack's skin. The insanity in Ringo's voice echoed off the boulders. The big cat lifted her head to face his cries, her ears moving forward and then backward, listening.

"What happened to the honeymoon?" Ringo roared.

With his white button-up shirt now splattered with more blood and pulled from his tuxedo trousers, Eric set the bucket down and then cold-cocked Ringo hard with a right hook. The impact forced Ringo to his side, spitting a mouthful of blood onto the ground, adding to the blood painted in the cat's territory. Calm and collected, Eric picked up the bucket and let the remaining blood spill onto Ringo. The devil faced Eric and laughed.

Jack moved to the gate, pressing his fingers through the links, watching as Eric took a set of wire cutters and made a small cut in Ringo's restraints. Ringo jerked hard, trying to throw Eric off-balance putting more pressure on the restraints. Ringo screamed at both men, knocking the tool out of Eric's hands.

Jack stepped in about to rush forward, but Eric swooped down and recovered what he'd lost. Ringo laughed again, but this time, a realization bled through him. Ringo needed more than a solid pull to break his restraints free. Eric stepped back as Ringo rolled onto his back.

"She thought I was you when I walked through the door," Ringo called without remorse. "She looked so lovely. I took another go at her to remember her by."

Jack's stomach churned at Ringo's words. He needed to get Eric out of there in one-piece unharmed.

Eric went silent just as Ringo lunged at him, but Eric had left Ringo's legs bound for that reason. Eric withdrew his pistol, and for a minute, Jack thought he'd end the man's life then. Seconds ticked away.

"Get out of there, Eric," Jack spoke in a calm tone.

Jack opened the gate.

Eric worked quickly, allowing no room for mistakes. Ringo's blood held the drugs Eric injected him with, but they too were wearing off. Ringo climbed to his knees, fighting the cord as he lunged at Eric one more time. Quickly, the devil worked to loosen the restraints.

Eric stepped away, but not before placing a small knife halfway between Ringo and the gate. Ringo gazed at the tiger behind the barrier and crawled toward the blade. Sweat broke out on his brow as he grabbed hold of the knife, cutting away at the rope in hurried swipes, cutting his flesh in doing so. Frantic, he started sawing on the leg restraints. As the exit gate shut behind Eric, Ringo sprang to his feet, facing the fence line.

Stumbling several times before reaching the fence, Ringo slid to a stop and wrapped his fingers around the metal links pressing his face forward. He smiled at Jack, watching as the only exit locked.

"Cut your way out of that one, you son of a bitch," Jack mumbled.

"Here's Ringo," Ringo yelled, his eyes wide, bloodshot, and rimmed with blue fire. With nostrils flared open, jaw trembling saliva flew from his mouth. He took hold of the fence and shook the metal with great force.

The tiger let out a long low growl, irritated. Ringo's rage-filled eyes shifted to the left. Blackness consumed his smile as he white-knuckled the chain-link fence. Jack saw the red embers spark in the man's eyes.

"I can still smell her," Ringo said, lifting his nose into the air. He rolled his tongue across his bloodied lips. "Here, kitty, kitty," he said. "Some of the best kitty I've ever had."

"You son of a bitch," Jack said, but this time Eric held Jack back.

"He wants to get to you."

"It's just a shame I didn't get to taste Riley," he sang out. "She would've made a good mother to my son."

Jack and Eric looked over at the tiger waiting in the cage. Once released, the big cat would gain access to the enclosure where Ringo stood. The cat talked in her language, pausing long enough to let out a long low hiss. She revealed her feline weapons, teeth, and claws to grind and tear flesh and bone. The sound and the sight grew frightening, but it suited Ringo, the hunter, the killer, and the rapist.

"Bring her on, boys." Ringo drawled as saliva foamed between his lips. "I'll see you on the other side."

"Open the gate," Eric said to Jack staring into Ringo's eyes. "Open the gate." Eric's voice sounded both eerie and calm.

Jack hesitated. Once he opened the gate, there'd be no turning back.

"No, Jack, wait."

Jack thought for an instant that Eric had changed his mind. So did Ringo. His laugh cut through the air like razors, slicing, cutting to destroy.

"I knew you didn't have it in you pussy, boy!" Ringo taunted. His expression so distorted it bordered over the edge of evil insanity.

"You're wrong, you piece of shit," Eric said. Jack stepped aside, letting Eric take control. "I'll open the gate."

Jack let go of the lever. The cat growled again, rolling her lips back into an angry snarl. The two of them stared at one another as if coming to some understanding. Then the big cat turned to where her release would come from and waited to enter her enclosure. Eric smiled at Ringo and pulled the lever.

NOT ALONE

Before the gate opened a quarter of the way up, the cat clawed to get out. She rushed the gate in an agitated state, and Ringo froze. The tiger darted out, circling the enclosure several times. Jack and Eric stood back in hushed awe as the cat moved around the boundary of her yard. Then she dropped her nose to the ground stopping several times to smell the blood. Her chocolate stripes, moving with her sleek body.

"This hunt is over." Eric's voice trailed off to a whisper.

Ringo snorted, turning to face the cat as she waited for Ringo to move. She crouched down low on the ground to begin her attack. For the first time in a long time, the great cat had live prey.

"I'll be back. I promise you!" yelled Ringo.

Jack turned away first, climbing into the Denali parked near the tiger's den.

Eric followed close behind.

Jack started the engine, cranking up the radio and air-conditioning before looking away.

The first signs of dawn appeared on the horizon as the sun rose above the jagged hilltops. Rock-formed mountains became painted silhouettes in the Arizona sky. The airtight cab drowned all outside noise as Eric drove down the long drive of the conservatory. Neither Eric nor Jack felt the need for visual closure, so both men looked straight ahead.

They caught the sixty-six in silence, heading toward Prescott Valley. They were ten miles from the ranch when Eric finally spoke.

"You don't think he could have....." Eric started to say, but Jack interrupted.

"No."

"I don't know, Jack. He doesn't seem human to me."

"He couldn't have gotten out." Then a slight hint of doubt crept through him, making his blood feel icy. "I'll have John handle it. That way, we'll be sure."

Eric nodded. "I'm gonna need a little break. But I'll be back."

"I'll take good care of your Riley, Eric. Jonah too."

72

The descending Arizona sun shimmered on the lake, deepening the blue-purple colors in the sky. As dusk approached, the explosion of colors turned to yellow and orange.

Riley loved the lake cabin, the one surprise Jack wanted to show her. Timber and high desert framed the place, creating a peaceful surrounding. She focused on the sound of hooves crossing over sand comforted the sadness deep within her soul. The past few weeks had been quiet, and unlike before, she welcomed the tranquility. For now, there was nothing to fear but fear itself, and if she had to put names on them, she could. However, Jack and Eric assured everyone that Ringo would never return, ever.

Riley knew little to no details of what happened the night Ringo murdered Shay or where Eric and Jack went. They came back to the ranch later that morning, and five days later, they attended Shay's, along with Amy and Sherry's, celebration of life. Jack told Riley he'd keep her safe, but then he didn't know her ex-husband. Mark popped into her mind now and again. Though her worries over Ringo were gone, she feared the unknowing.

Eric went away a day after he put Shay to rest on the hill near the ranch. He left Riley a note, leaving without saying goodbye. Riley would not have let him go otherwise, and Eric knew it. Eric told no one where he went. He said he had something he needed to do. He asked if they would look after Jonah until he returned. That was six months ago.

On occasion, Riley had reoccurring dreams of Mark, a man with a dragon tattoo. Jack had woken her from every horrible dream, holding her until she fell back asleep. The visions scared her and, at the same time, empowered her. Since Utah left, Riley gained the ability to see things before they happened. Little things predicted to the last detail.

Since the night of the Shift, everything changed, and they continued to evolve. Riley felt something coming and sensed they were all still in danger. Unable to find anything definitive about her thoughts, she tucked them away for another day. She and Jack lived day by day, taking precautions and waiting for destiny to guide them to the next mission.

The sound of the pony brought Riley back to the present. She let the ambiance embrace her as she glanced over at Jack, Jonah sitting on his shoulders watching Megan ride the pony in the corral. Jonah was Safe. All was well today.

"Look, Riley, I can make her gallop." Megan nudged the pony, and she responded to Megan's request, breaking into a lope.

She and Jack clapped, and Jonah joined in. Megan smiled, patting the pony's chestnut coat with her fingers.

"She rides like you," Jack said, stepping in next to Riley.

Megan pulled the pony in, and Jack took the reins.

"So, what do you think? You like her?" Jack asked Megan.

Megan smiled as big as Riley had ever seen her smile. A tiny squeal escaped her, something she's outgrowing but slips out occasionally.

"Oh, yes. I promise to take good care of her."

"Good then, I'll let Andy know she's got a home," he said, turning Megan loose again.

Jack wrapped his arms around Riley's legs as they dangled. Jonah patted Jack's head as though he were a horse. "I read your story."

"Oh," Riley said nervously.

He looked up at her.

"It was good. Really good," Jack looked at Riley, who smiled, sliding down into the pen with him.

"Really?" she asked excitedly.

"Yep," he grinned, kissing her on the forehead, letting his lips linger there for a few seconds.

Jonah leaned forward and patted Riley on the head too. "Good," he said.

Riley chuckled, taking the little boy's hand.

The sky was beginning to darken as she looked over at the lake, mesmerized by the sparkles bouncing off the surface of the water. For a moment, she thought about Oregon. All those months she'd spent alone.

A slight breeze passed over the tops of the trees, making a swooshing sound. Riley looked at Jack. She tried not to think how this might end.

"I love this place," Riley said. "Megan does too. And Jonah." Max jumped up on the rail, licking his paw. "Max too."

The ringing of a phone broke the calm. Jack winked at Riley, answering the call.

"Yep." He held the phone, saying nothing for a long strand of silence. "Okay, we'll be there." He set the phone back in his pocket, giving Riley a look.

"What?" she asked.

"An old friend from Long Beach. He wants our help." He leaned over and kissed her again. "You don't have to go."

"But I will," she responded. She called Megan in, who frowned but obeyed. "When?" Riley asked, opening the gate to the round pen. Megan slid down off the pony.

NOT ALONE

"Tomorrow." Jack tugged on Megan's ponytail playfully.

"Then we better make the best of tonight," Riley said in a teasing tone. Jack smiled at her, and she felt a hot rush.

In the distance, the cry of a Mexican Gray Wolf sounded into the late summer evening air. Riley always looked for the white Siberian Tiger. Some townspeople believe it wanders the high desert, searching for something or someone unseen.

The story told by the refuge caretaker Harry goes as follows; "I was just about to feed Saber, our female Bengal tiger when something stung me from behind. The next thing I knew, it was morning, and old Martin, he's my relief, was shaking me out of my skin. Hell, I have no clue what happened. I was lucky that big cat didn't eat me for not feeding her. How she got out, I don't know the answer to that. I always check to make sure the gates are locked when I go down, so you figure the mystery out."

Harry wasn't the only one talking about the tiger. Some locals swore they heard a cat in the early mornings as the skies cast a montage of shadow and darkness. They claimed an animal stalked the hills near the refuge, upsetting the animals and keepers from their sleep.

Jack hired several men to search, but she eludes everyone, running outside the refuge, escaping each time. Most townsfolk believe the rogue tiger escaped from either Pam's place or the hospital. Still, many have doubts about the cat and the stories.

Riley turned to follow Jack and Megan. "Wait up, you two," she said in a cheerful tone.

Suddenly, the hairs on her neck rose. Riley stopped. The voice was not her own but one familiar to her.

"Wake up, Riley," Lucas whispered. "They're coming for you."

ABOUT THE AUTHOR

Kolleen Bookey brings her characters into a life minus the luxuries people have grown familiar with, challenging their capacities and needs to survive in a lawless society. She built a realm where the less fortunate have second chances and fight to become heroes as they fix a broken world.

Moved by her hero and villain, Kolleen keeps the good and the bad in conflict while driving her characters forward with a passion all of their own.

Kolleen has written over ten complete novels, two published. She received her Associate's Degrees in Psychology and Administration of Justice and found her education best used for writing. Growing up in Northern California, she spent her summers breaking trails in Shasta County, drawing and writing about horses, and dreaming of someday becoming a writer.

Please visit Kolleen at kolleenbookblog.com and kolleenbookey.com to learn more about her background.

Be sure to read the rest of The Fighter Series:

In the Shadow of the Tiger, The Shift, and The Hunted.

Made in the USA
Las Vegas, NV
03 September 2022

54638604R10164